TALON

COMBAT TRACKING TEAM

RONIE KENDIG

BARBOUR
PUBLISHING

OTHER BOOKS BY
RONIE KENDIG

Trinity: Military War Dog (A Breed Apart #1)
Nightshade (Discarded Heroes #1)
Digitalis (Discarded Heroes #2)
Wolfsbane (Discarded Heroes #3)
Firethorn (Discarded Heroes #4)

Scripture quotations are taken from the HOLY BIBLE, NEW INTERNATIONAL VERSION®. NIV®. Copyright © 1973, 1978, 1984, 2011 by Biblica, Inc.™ Used by permission. All rights reserved worldwide.

Additional scripture taken from the King James Version of the Bible.

This book is a work of fiction. Names, characters, places, and incidents are either products of the author's imagination or used fictitiously. Any similarity to actual people, organizations, and/or events is purely coincidental.

For more information about Ronie Kendig, please access the author's website at the following Internet address: www.roniekendig.com

Cover design: Müllerhaus Publishing Arts, Inc., www.Mullerhaus.net

Published by Barbour Publishing, Inc., P.O. Box 719, Uhrichsville, OH 44683, www.barbourbooks.com

Our mission is to publish and distribute inspirational products offering exceptional value and biblical encouragement to the masses.

 Member of the
Evangelical Christian
Publishers Association

Printed in the United States of America.

DEDICATION

To all military working dog handlers and their amazing K-9 counterparts.
Dedicated especially to Vietnam-era handlers
who were forced to leave behind their best friends.

ACKNOWLEDGMENTS

Special thanks to military handlers, who prefer to remain anonymous, for their help and direction.

Thanks to Elgin Shaw, a former Air Force handler and reader, who has encouraged me and shared his story of MWD Max in *Trinity: Military War Dog*.

Thanks to my agent, Steve Laube, who remains steadfast and constant in an ever-changing industry. For *not* pushing me off the ledge but holding me back when I wanted to jump.

A million thanks to Julee Schwarzburg—editor extraordinaire!

Thanks to the Barbour team, relentless in their efforts to make our books successful: Rebecca Germany, Mary Burns, Shalyn Sattler, Elizabeth Shrider, Laura Young, Linda Hang, and Ashley Schrock.

Rel Mollet of RelzReviewz—tireless supporter of fiction but also one of the truest and most genuine people I have ever met.

Special thanks to Heather Lammers for helping me connect with MWD handlers.

Special thanks to MWD handlers/trainers 1st LT Brian Sandoval, SSG Jeff Worley, and SGT Andrew Kowtko for sharing a glimpse of the MWD world with readers. You are all heroes!

LITERARY LICENSE

In writing about unique settings, specific locations, and invariably the people residing there, a certain level of risk is involved, including the possibility of dishonoring the very people an author intends to honor. With that in mind, I have taken some literary license in *Talon: Combat Tracking Team,* including renaming some bases within the U.S. military establishment and creating sites/entitles. I have done this so the book and/or my writing will not negatively reflect on any military personnel or location. With the quickly changing landscape of a combat theater, this seemed imperative and prudent.

Glossary of Terms/Acronyms

ACUs—Army Combat Uniforms

AK-47—Russian made assault rifle

CLU—Containerized Living Units

CTT dog—Combat Tracking Team dog

DIA—Defense Intelligence Agency

FOB—Forward Operating Base

Glock—A semiautomatic handgun

HUMINT—Human Intelligence

IED—Improvised Explosive Device

JAG—Judge Advocate General

Klicks—Military jargon for kilometers

Lat-long—Latitude and longitude

M4, M4A1, M16A4—Military assault rifles

M203—A grenade launcher

MIA—Missing In Action

MP—Military Police

MRAP—Mine Resistant Ambush-Protected vehicle

MWD—Military War Dog

ODA452—Operational Detachment A (Special Forces A-Team)

RPG—Rocket-Propelled Grenade

SCI—"Sensitive Compartmented Information" security level

SOCOM—Special Operations Command

SureFire—A tactical flashlight

TBI—Traumatic Brain Injury

UAV—Unmanned Aerial Vehicle

Prologue

Kariz-e Sefid, Afghanistan
Two Years Ago

Flames roared into the sky. A concussive boom punched the oxygen from the air. Eating an IED, the lead Cougar MRAP in the convoy flipped up. As if dancing atop the raging inferno. Shrapnel hurtled from the blast.

"Buffalo! Buffalo!" Sergeant Lee Dawson shouted into the mic, hoping to hear from the first vehicle.

"Anything?" Gunnery Sergeant Austin Courtland coiled his hand around the lead of his Combat Tracking Team dog. Talon stood braced, alert. His bark reverberated through the steel hull in warning.

Lee slanted a glance at the "observer" who'd come along. "Report!" Peering through the cloud of black smoke and debris, he searched the chaos to make sure the others were still alive.

A breeze stirred the flames just in time to see an RPG streaking toward the front end of their MRAP.

"Get out, get out, get out!" Courtland and Talon launched toward the back door.

"Oh cr—"

BOOM!

The MRAP bucked against the blast but held. Whiplash had nothing on the ramming sensation pounding into his chest now. Fire burst through the engine.

Fear of being cooked alive or choking to death on smoke shoved

9

Lee from the Cougar MRAP. Coughing and with a hand over his mouth, he choked out, "This way!"

Sand and dirt blasted up, peppering his face. Tiny grains and dust particles swirled under the blazing Afghan sun as he took cover, shouldering his way around the side of the mine-resistant ambush-protected vehicle and out of their attacker's line of fire. Plumes of heat warbled along the hull.

"Find me some terrorists," Court shouted over the roar of the fire, then keyed his mic. "Base, this is Echo One. Ambushed and taking fire!"

Peering down the sights of his M16A4 gave Lee nothing but dirt. . .crumbled building with dirt. . .and more dirt. "I got nothin'."

"Same," came a shout from behind as Truitt "True" Anderson slid up behind him, a nasty cut across his cheekbone. "Where the *heck* did that RPG come from?" The muzzle of his M4 swept Lee's periphery.

Lee kept his sights aligned, adrenaline pumping through his system faster than the blood. "Court," he yelled over the gunfire that crackled in the blistering afternoon, "what d'you have?"

"Nothing!"

Staying behind the disabled vehicle, Lee searched the road. Only two buildings north. Several south. Focused ahead, he studied the structures. He scanned the roofs. Since the RPG's trajectory had been downward, whoever fired it held an elevated position. The roof of one didn't look strong enough to hold someone, and the other had more holes than coverage. He whipped back to the first, waiting. *C'mon! Show your coward head so I can—*

"Quirk, report!" Court shouted to the Buffalo team again.

Only crackling and the shouts of the other teams dragging the lead team to safety met the command. Mind locked on the white plastered structure with the right half of the front wall missing told him that's where the attack had originated.

"Use the drone?" Lee shouted, not lifting his gaze from the scope.

"It's down!"

Lee wanted to curse. Everything had gone wrong. With the drone down, they'd have to do this the old-fashioned, bloody way. *Mano a mano.* Hand to hand.

Dark flashed in his reticle. "Court, two o'clock."

"Let's clear it out."

Sweat raced along the side of Lee's face and spine as he inched around the MRAP. His boot thumped against something. He glanced down—and flinched at the limp body of his buddy. On a knee, weapon still aimed at the building, he gripped the vest of Quirk, the young corporal.

Wide, unseeing eyes etched with the shock of the moment. Pressing his hand against the chest wound, Lee plunged into assessment mode, ignoring the warm wetness that squished through his fingers. The gaping hole— "Sniper!" *Sweet Lord, help us.* They were ambushed. Sniper. RPG. What prayer did they have left?

"Corpsman!" Lee gripped the man's vest straps. "Quirk, hey. Don't do this, man. No quitting."

Another Marine sprinted toward them, allowing Lee to refocus on breaking this ambush site. Breaking the sick cowards who hid and played lethal games of tag with U.S. troops.

He met the steely gaze of his fire-team members—minus one. Another trio of Marines joined them as their cover team. As he lifted the weapon and trained it on the building, he nodded to Court and True, then darted across the fifteen-foot space that separated the partially disabled convoy from the hideouts.

Halfway across, Court dove to the left.

Tat-tat-tat!

The report rang in Lee's ears as he threw himself against the plaster and cement wall.

"Base, this is Echo One, we need that air support—five minutes ago!" Court nodded to Lee before keying his mic again. "Going in."

Stacked—True behind with his M4 trained on the point of entry— Lee waited for the signal.

A tap on his shoulder.

Lee fired a short burst against the door handle. Balanced on his left leg, he slammed his booted heel against the door. *Crack!* It whipped open.

Court stepped around him and tossed a hand grenade into the room. "Frag out!" He jerked back behind Lee, who spined the exterior wall.

Clink. . .clink. . .BOOM!

Lee threw himself into motion. Over the threshold, he registered the southernmost wall missing. He swung left. Dust puffed as he rushed the darkened corner. Light streamed in, taunting the smoke and debris rustled by the grenade. Two steps in, one foot from the wall. His weapon grazed the smoke-drenched interior and cleared a path to the left. He heard Court step in and do the same to the opposite corner. Lee hustled toward the left corner, tracking back and forth, adrenaline on high.

To avoid fratricide Lee called, "Next man in," and hurried along the wall, pieing the room to divide up the coverage.

The swish of tactical pants preceded True as he entered. Effectively covering both corners and the door, the three-man team moved forward. To Lee's left a door boasted a spray of bullet holes. Half a window frame drooped against the wide-open maw in the rear.

"Clear," Court called.

A shadow killed the light.

Lee swung hard right. Movement skittered just beyond the hole in the wall. *Scritch-scritch-scritch—*

"Stairs!" He hustled forward, staring down the muzzle of his weapon.

Behind him, he heard the others cluster. To his right, the wall was missing. To the left, cement and darkness—and that's where the mystery guest had gone. They were blind, so they'd have to use extreme caution. He took up a dominant position. Experience told him Court was behind him and True pulled up the rear.

Eyes trained on the corner in case someone rounded it, Lee knelt and focused on the smooth movement of the team. They'd done this dozens of times. Still, one careless mistake and they were dead.

Court's boots crunched against the dirt floor as he pied out to the right as far as possible. Then slowly advanced to increase his angle of fire farther into the dead space.

"Ready," Lee grunted.

"Move!"

They both angled into the open, True tailing. In the blazing afternoon sun, Lee cleared left—stairs! Just as he'd thought. Open, cement steps. No railing. Just a path up to the roof. He climbed two steps, knowing Court would be one step down and to the side. Lee turned to cover overhead, mentally noting his partner oriented to the front, to cover him from getting shot in the back.

Tracing the edge of the upper level with the tip of his muzzle flash hider, Lee backstepped carefully up the stairs, sweeping. Covering. Pieing. Though adrenaline and a need to kill the puke who'd taken out the MRAP and killed Quirk sped through his body, Lee wouldn't take another step without fully clearing the area. As he approached the roof, he bent lower with each level until he crouched, the roof skimming his head.

Lee drew in his fears and harnessed them into taking out some cowards. Glanced to the side—to Court. Then True. Both nodded their readiness. He blew a breath from puffed cheeks. Gave a curt nod.

Court went first.

Lee and True followed, weapons ready. They hurried over the lip of the roof, scanning...chairs, blankets, a Styrofoam cooler...a small room jutted up from the middle.

Tension high, stomach knotted, Lee hurried toward it. Scissor-stepping, he swallowed hard, expecting an enemy combatant to leap out at any second. He and Court cleared the L-shaped corner with ease. Nobody. He was almost disappointed.

"Where are they?" True growled through gritted teeth.

Lee glanced around. Looked over the front of the building and shouted to the team, "Where'd they go?"

Raised arms and shrugs replied.

He kicked the knee-high wall. Cursed. Swiped the beads of sweat from his face and eyes. Another fire team streamed onto the roof. Confusion squeezed his brain. How could he have gotten away? They'd chased him up here. Lee saw him!

"Looks secure," one corporal said as he stalked across the terrace-like roof.

They needed to clear the other building. "Court," he said, looking around. He frowned. Where'd his partner go? Had he already headed for the other building? Lee started for the stairs.

"Let's see what some terrorists were eating and drinking while they waited to kill some Marines."

An ominous fear washed across Lee's shoulders. "No!" He spun—

Fire exploded. The concussion whipped his feet out from under him. Over his head. Lee felt himself sailing through the air, searing heat licking his backside. Then falling...falling...black.

One

Markoski Residence
Baltimore, Maryland

*T*o *live a lie is to remain alive.*

Military documents recorded his name as Dane Markoski. That he's the son of an American missionary and Russian father—Vasily and Eliana Markoski. That he joined the military at eighteen, immediately upon high school graduation. That he soared through the ranks and his distinguished career, replete with badges of valor and courage under fire that revealed his natural ability and ambition toward becoming a career Army officer. A man's man. A hero.

None of it true.

Barefoot, wearing only gray sweatpants, Cardinal—his handle, his only form of tangible identity for the last ten years—gripped the rope he'd anchored into to the steel support of his second-story loft bedroom and pulled himself off the ground. Hand over hand, he climbed, legs spider-posed and held out to maximize the workout to his abs and thighs.

When he reached the top, he gripped the ledge-like floor and performed twenty pull-ups. The reps burning, they taught him discipline. Reminded him that he was weak, that opportunity existed with every breath to become better—or weaker. The Gentle Art of Submission—Jiu-Jitsu—helped him harness the poison that threatened his life every day: anger.

Cardinal lowered himself and took the rope. Angling back, he moved hand over hand, backward along the hemp that traced the length of his condo, his body parallel to the floor. Breathing hard, arms and abs on fire, he continued the workout he'd started hours earlier.

A fit body equaled a fit mind, the masters had always said.

So had his father. And it was the one thing the general had said that Cardinal heeded. . .willingly.

Behind him the bank of cantilevering windows sat open, allowing a balmy breeze from the Potomac that did nothing to cool or calm him. The news delivered last night served to be the harbinger of death. The final straw that would break the camel's back—his.

Unless Cardinal found a way to turn this around.

He must. Everything—*everything*—depended on it. Hours training his body and mind to focus and he had nothing. Straightened on the ground, he pressed his palms together and drew in a measuring breath, then slowly blew it out through puffed cheeks.

There, where the sun hit the window, stood a ghost of himself. More apropos than one would expect. What was left of him? Still had the black hair and blue eyes, but what lay beneath those eyes. . .who was it? Was *he* good enough to justify the listing of the commendation medals on his records? At thirty-three, he'd hoped to have more of a legacy than secrecy and anonymity.

Breath evening out, he stared. Willed that person in the glass to find the solution. Solve this disaster. He had a new enemy: time. Beyond the balcony, across the road and stretch of greenery, he spotted a woman jogging with her dog.

A tone flicked through the condo.

Cardinal pulled himself straight and plodded out of the gym, between the sofa and armchairs, to the Spartan kitchen, where he plucked his cell phone from the granite. He registered the number and hesitated. Then pressed the phone to his ear as he watched the woman make her way down the sidewalk. "Yes?"

"Code in."

Cardinal punched a button and the windows slid shut. "Cairo-One-Four-Two-Nine-Nine."

"What do you have?"

They were already breathing down his neck? "It's been six hours."

"I didn't ask what time it was." A long pause strangled the line. "You

15

don't have a single thing, do you?"

"What do you have?"

"This is not good. The longer we sit on our—"

He would not be made into the weakling here. "Do you have something useful to say, or is this just a social call?"

Wait. . .*dog*. His gaze snapped to the sidewalk, now occupied by a young mother pushing a stroller.

"I am *socially* telling you time is running out. If *he* finds out—"

"The only way he would find out is if I am betrayed. And the only people who can betray me are on this phone call. Since we both know the consequences for betrayal, I'll take it he doesn't know." Cardinal folded up his anger and tucked it under a cloak of civility.

"No need to get all James Bond on me, Cardinal."

"Bond is British and highly overrated." What. . .what did that file say? His mind rifled through the documents he'd studied and landed on one phrase: *military working dog*. "I have an idea."

"I knew you had it in you." The man's voice boomed with amusement. "What do you need?"

"I'll be there in twenty. Have a team ready."

Cleaned up and garbed in standard military issue, Cardinal drove down South Washington Boulevard to the geometric five-acre, five-ring structure that was a nightmare to navigate for the uninitiated. He pulled up to the guard hut, showed his ID, and signed in.

"Thank you, Lieutenant Markoski. He's expecting you."

Cardinal drove through and parked. Inside, he made his way to the second floor. A door opened. General Lance Burnett emerged. "General."

"You're ten minutes late," Burnett said, without looking up from the file in hand. He continued down the drab gray hall, and Cardinal fell into step with him. "We got a lead."

Cardinal's heart skipped a beat, but he waited for the general to continue.

"There was activity on his account, but he must've smelled us snooping because the activity ended before we could get a lock."

"What type of activity?"

"Accessing bank accounts, e-mail, etcetera."

"Isn't that obvious? He knows better than that. I trained him."

"Apparently not well enough." Burnett slapped the file closed and smacked it against his leg as he flipped the handle on a door and leaned against it.

"Where?"

"Didn't you just hear we couldn't get a lock?"

"Yes."

The general grinned. "Republic of Djibouti."

Cardinal slowed as they entered a conference room where six men in Naval uniforms waited with another team of six—analysts and experts. "Djibouti. . ." He hadn't seen that coming. "What's he doing there?"

"Hanged if I know."

"It's over 90 percent Islamic." A really bad place to hide when you were obviously white and American. Cardinal nodded to the sailors and took a seat near the head of the table.

The general dropped the file in front of him, roughed a hand over his face, and sighed. "Okay, let's get on with this. Markoski, these men have been briefed on what's happened. Tell us your brilliant idea."

Amadore's Fight Club
Austin, Texas

"Watch your stance!"

Exhilaration swept through Aspen Courtland as she responded to her trainer's shout and realigned her feet, shoulder-width apart. She threw a jab and followed through with a right. Sweat dripped into her eye, stinging. Today. . .the anniversary. . .

Mario, her opponent, threw a hard right then tried a left jab.

Block! The thud against her gloves carried through her upper body. She flipped her mind into the ring again as the impact from his strike rattled down her arm.

Aspen countered and angled to the side. The move could frustrate him by preventing a return hit.

It'd been eight months since the news. But it hurt as if it'd happened today.

Breathing through her nose, jaw relaxed, she engaged a series of redundant punches, all numbing her mind. She couldn't let them get away with this. They had to. . .do something.

An uppercut.

Shielding, Aspen blocked Mario. Hands and shoulder forward. What if. . .what if she went in after him? The thought fueled her boxing. In quick succession she fired off several strikes. Going in there—yeah, real smart. Right into the heart of the Middle East, where Americans were served up with every meal.

A jab. A cross. Angling away.

Mario swung at her.

She blocked. So, she couldn't go alone. She'd need a team.

Again—right. Real smart. How would she get a team into the Middle East to track an invisible trail? She slammed a hard right. Connected with Mario's jaw.

"Nice—face!"

Too late. The counterpunch nailed her cheek. She stumbled backward, stunned.

"Take a break, Mario."

Aspen straightened and turned. "No, I'm good." Batting her gloves together, she drew in a ragged breath, hating the look on Amadore's face as he bent through the ropes and entered the ring. "I'm serious." Another tap of her gloves. "Let's do this."

"No, let's not."

Irritation squirreled through her intestines. "Why? I'm—"

"Fighting with fury." Gentle brown eyes held hers. "Not with focus."

He was right. She knew he was. But she had something to work off, and boxing provided the perfect outlet. "I'm good." Glancing around him, she found Mario still in the ring. "Ready?"

"No." Amadore pointed to Mario. "You do this, you never come in my club again. You hear me?"

Mario grinned and held up both gloves in surrender as he backed away then slipped through the ropes.

As her breathing evened out, she tamped down the anger that spiked. "I'm okay, Amadore."

"No." He cupped the back of her head and tugged her close. "What is wrong with my angel today? You are like a big storm off the coast when you come through that door. What gives?"

Aspen swallowed. Peeked into his eyes. . .and caved. He'd been a part of her life since she was a baby—her mother's father. "It's his birthday." She stuffed her gloves against each other. "He would've been twenty-eight."

The peppering of silver along the sides of his face only made the barrel-chested, former pro boxer look more handsome and distinguished. Even now as the repercussion of her words hit him. "Ah yes. I remember."

Her gaze skirted the boxing ring and fell on the Lab curled up under a bench in the corner, his soulful eyes watching her. "Presumed dead." Her nostrils flared and her eyes stung. "Eight months," she said through ground teeth. "He was only missing eight months and they declared him dead." She fought the trembling in her lower lip. "I thought for sure, he would. . .that we would. . .find him."

"Oh my girl." His other arm came up as if to hug her, but Aspen ducked from his touch.

"No worries." Sucking up the dregs of her crumbling composure, she flashed him a thin-lipped smile. "They might have written him off. But I haven't. I'll deal with it."

"I am not sure your way of dealing with things is the right way."

She folded herself through the ropes. On the floor, she looked back up at him and shrugged. "Whatever works, right?"

"Aspen, wait." He was with her in a second. Nudging her to the side, he urged her toward a bench. "Sit."

With a huff, she plopped onto the wood. Using her teeth, she ripped the band and tugged off the gloves as he sat next to her.

"I worry about you."

She frowned.

"No. I see that look in your eye, and I know—this thing? It will end bad."

"It already ended." At least according to the U.S. Marine Corps. Unwinding the wraps from her hands, she tried to shove back the squall of emotion. "Ya know, what I can't figure out. . ." Her chest rose and fell as the words from the letters and e-mails from the military filled her mind. "Why. . .*why* would they declare him dead when there's no body, no proof he died?"

Sorrow pinched the middle-aged Italian's hard features.

"A little blood." She breathed heavily through her nose. "A dog tag with no evidence of a fight or scratches, and a dog with minor injuries." Her gaze automatically slid to the Lab, who pulled himself out from under the bench and lumbered her way, head down. She smoothed a hand over his head as he sat between her feet. "It doesn't make sense."

"I understand, my angel, but. . ."

"There's no more 'but,' Amadore. Uncle Sam sealed the note." She climbed to her feet, the weight of the letter she'd opened today pushing against her.

He touched her arm. "Be careful."

She scowled.

"This thing you are planning, I see it in your eyes," he said as he rose and stood over her. "Be careful. Your father would kill me if I let something happen to you. Know what I mean?"

Her heart skipped a beat. How did he know? She opened her mouth to deny it, to deny she would go after Austin.

His laugh cut her off. "No, Angel. I know you better than you know yourself. There is a plan in that beautiful head of yours." The smile remained in place. "Which is why I stopped your session with Mario. That head wasn't in the ring. It was at home, still mourning his birthday."

Aspen tucked her chin. "He's all I've got left, *Nonno*." She drew up her shoulders. "I'm not going to let the Marines relegate my brother to the grave without a fight."

 **TWO**

Pentagon, Arlington County, Virginia
Two Days Later

Say it again."

Cardinal drew in a breath, tempering his frustration. "This isn't my first rodeo, to borrow your phrase, sir."

"Good. Then this should be better than expected." Undaunted, General Lance Burnett, the deputy director of Defense Counter-intelligence and HUMINT Center, popped the top of his umpteenth Dr Pepper of the morning and slurped from the can. With a satisfied sigh, he set it down. "Begin."

Flexing his jaw, Cardinal gave a curt nod. Practice never hurt. Wasted time, but never hurt. "We'll maintain my identity as Markoski. The interview—"

"Sir," Lieutenant Smith announced from the door. "We got Larabie on line 3."

Amusement twinkled in Burnett's eyes. "Let's hope you're as ready as you say."

Cardinal resisted the urge to smirk. "Let the games begin." He strode to the phone, lifted the handset, and pressed 3. "This is Dane Markoski."

"Ah, Mr. Markoski," her voice sailed through the receivers—his and the general's. Cardinal kept his gaze on the old man. "This is Brittain Larabie. You'd e-mailed me about—"

"Please. Can we keep the details"—he added hesitation and concern

21

to his voice to make this work. He'd never had a problem manipulating the media who manipulated the world. Great satisfaction could be gained from maneuvers like this— "Are you able to meet, Miss Larabie?"

"Um. . .yes. Yes I can. I will have a cameraman with me. You understand, for my own safety, I won't meet strangers alone."

"Alone, or not at all. I'm not trying to murder you, Miss Larabie. I want to tell the truth. I want to do what's right." That sounded all patriotic and gallant.

"Of course. What time and where?"

"Are you familiar with Reston ice-skating pavilion?"

"That's in Virginia."

"Correct."

"That's a bit out of my way, Mr. Markusky."

"Markoski." Why couldn't Americans get that right? No doubt they'd butcher his real last name. "And if it's an inconvenience, I can call—"

"No, it's fine. When shall we meet?"

"The sooner the better. Tomorrow night?" Silence plagued the line, and Cardinal tried to ignore the general waving his hand in a circle. "I'm out of time, Miss Larabie."

"That's fine. I had a dinner date, but I can reschedule."

"Eight o'clock." Cardinal hung up and turned to the general. "Everything is in my medical and military history files?"

"You're not the only good operative I have, Cardinal." General Burnett had never asked for Cardinal's true identity. But the old man probably had it locked in that steel vault he called a brain. All the same, Cardinal felt safer with the moniker than with his real name floating around in paperwork and cyberspace.

Burnett motioned to his lieutenant, who slid a file across the table. "Larabie is best friends with Courtland's twin, Aspen."

Why did people name their kids after cities? Cardinal retrieved the file and lifted it. "Odd. What, are they dating?" He glanced down.

"I sincerely doubt that."

Dread poured through Cardinal's stomach, freezing like an iceberg as he met the blue eyes of a curly haired beauty. He darted his gaze to the general. "A woman?" His pulse thunked against the possibility then spun into chaos. "Austin's twin is a woman? How did I *not* know that?"

The lieutenant shifted, shooting a nervous glance to the general. Burnett grinned. "Maybe you're not as good as you thought."

Cardinal flung the documents back. "Forget it. Deal's off. I'm not doing this." He stormed toward the door. "We'll find another way."

"Cardinal, you are U.S. Government property. You will do as ordered."

"I won't." Rage flung him back around. "I won't work this woman. Or *any* woman. Not ever. That was Cardinal Rule #1 when you came to me." Breaths came in deep gulps. "I'll find another way to get Courtland back." Anger gave way to desperation. He raked a hand through his hair. "Figure something out."

Silence hung rank and thick in the room. Burnett nodded to the others in the room. "If you'll excuse us." He waited for the room to clear then sat on the edge of the conference table. "Cardinal, I respect what you're saying, but it's impractical. Your protégé vanished two months ago in a remote village in northeast Africa—right out from under your nose. You and I both know that is trouble. *If* he is still alive, every second matters. We can't afford to waste another minute, let alone two more months *figuring* something out when you have a working plan right here in front of you."

Cardinal, in a half shake of his head, dragged his gaze downward. "I can't."

Images of innocent brown eyes. . .her laughter. . .seeing her worked over, time and again. *And then the angel flew. . .*

"You knew this." His pulse thumped against his temple as he worked to restrain his temper. "*No. Women.*" Right then, an absolute certainty rushed over him. He stabbed a finger at Burnett. "You." How had he not seen this earlier? Was he too eager to get Courtland back that he hadn't considered all the possibilities? "You knew—you hid from me that Aspen was a woman."

Burnett let out a long sigh. "Son, we've been trying since Austin vanished to find a way to track him and get him back safely. When you came up with this absolutely ingenious plan to use his dog. . .I had no choice."

"We *always* have a choice."

Shoulders slumped, Burnett crumpled his Dr Pepper can. "No, no we don't. And right now, neither do you."

Lips tight, Cardinal glared at him. "I'm not doing this."

"Do this or you're through." He folded his arms over his chest. "Something's haunting you, and I need you to bury that—for now—and do your job."

"You forget," Cardinal spat out, "I came to *you*! I offered *you* my services."

"Yes, but now you're owned. By us." Burnett pushed up and moved to the other end of the table. "I consider myself a nice man who works hard at his job. But that's just it—I have a job. I'm tasked with protecting my country and its citizens. And that means I have to do things I don't like."

Throw that political bull at him, but it wouldn't work. "This isn't my country." Tremors rippled through his arms and legs. What choice did he have? Burnett held more dirt on him, could bury him at the bottom of the sea for ten lifetimes. Or expose his whereabouts to a certain Russian general.

I'm trapped. As always.

Had to get out of there. Disappear. He would not do this. Could not. "I don't owe this country anything. I don't owe *anyone* anything." The words were cruel. And wrong. It was the anger talking. The demons he'd inherited.

"Maybe not, but you *are* a citizen of it. We granted that, remember? And you signed on the line for this job. We own you, Cardinal." Burnett's eyes narrowed. "And that missing boy is your responsibility." He smacked a hand on the table. "Now man up and do what needs to be done!"

Cardinal stormed out of the office, down the hall, the stairs, to the parking garage. In his car, he left the grounds and headed west. Though Reston was only thirty minutes away, traffic dictated the three-hour drive. Familiar with the area, he made his way to a nearby park and planted himself on a bench. He'd promised himself he'd never do this. Never become the epitome of filth and slime that had defined Cardinal's life for twenty years.

Elbows on his knees, he stared at the ground covered in a fresh blanket of wildflowers. Cold seeped into his bones despite the summer heat, but it was nothing like the chill settling over this mission. Over his objective—getting Aspen. Courtland to cooperate and think it was her idea.

"I promised," he muttered past his hands, fingers laced and held in front of his lips.

But. . .Austin.

Cardinal had hand-selected the young man for the field. He'd trained him, guided him, become friends with him. The government intentionally withheld information about Austin's family so Cardinal would not have any impetus or inclination to alter his decision or recruitment.

Nearby a horn honked and snapped him out of his somber thoughts. A quick check of his watch shoved him to his feet. He headed past the hotel, down the sidewalk, and straight toward the pavilion.

The sister—she would want to help, right? This plan he'd concocted depended on the twin's reaction. But he'd thought he was dealing with a guy. Not a woman. A twin was a twin, right? The connection should be there. She should see the imperative nature of using the dog. At least, he hoped she did because he'd take the dog—that'd be so much easier. But they couldn't afford the time or risk to yank the dog and force him to settle in with a new handler.

The dog was the key. And getting to the dog, the key was the sister. Aspen.

He turned into an alley and thrust his fist in the air. "God, why must You torment me? You know what is in me. You know the blood that beats in my heart." Fists over his eyes, he ground his teeth. "Do not. . .do not let me lose myself."

Was it possible. . .was it at all possible to complete this mission without becoming his father?

A Breed Apart Ranch
Texas Hill Country

Soulful brown eyes held hers, eagerness and willingness to go the long, hard mile for her pouring out of them. His eyebrows bounced with meaning.

"Hey, handsome."

He scooted closer, his happy impatience melting her heart. She didn't deserve his loyalty. His passionate attention. But he gave it all the same.

Cupping his face, Aspen smiled down at him. "You are amazing."
He smiled.

Or near enough for a Labrador retriever. Talon swiped his tongue
along her face, his backside wagging so hard she thought he might wipe
out. She rubbed his ears and planted a kiss between his eyes. "Thank
you, boy."

"How's it going?"

Aspen straightened and turned toward the voice of Heath Daniels,
lead trainer at A Breed Apart. His Belgian Malinois bounded into
the training area with zest and zeal Aspen was convinced Talon once
possessed. She eyed her blond guy. "We're making progress."

Heath, arms folded over his chest and hands tucked beneath his
armpits, smiled at her. "You got him over the hurdles."

Beaming beneath the hidden praise in his words, Aspen grinned
back. "Six months ago, I would've thought this was possible." And
six months ago, she'd had an uphill battle getting her grandparents
to allow Talon to take up residence with her at their sprawling estate.
Nana wasn't entirely pleased about having a dog, whose fur sprinkled
her marble and gilded décor with yellow hairs. Or Granddad, who had
objected to Talon living *in* a house his own father had built at the height
of his wealth and power in the roaring twenties. But in time, knowing
Talon had been best friends with Austin, they'd relented.

"You're giving him his respect back but also helping him remember
he's a dog—the best life." Heath touched her shoulder. "Your brother
would be proud if he were here to see this."

Aspen ducked her chin, fighting the stinging in her eyes. "That's
just the bear of it, isn't it? If Austin were here, I wouldn't be." The
rawness at the back of her throat made it hard to swallow.

"Hey," Heath said, his tone softer. "Don't go there, okay? You can
stay true to his memory without feeling guilty about everything. You're
doing right by him with the way you're watching out for his partner and
best friend." He gave a curt nod. "Understand?"

Surprised at his words, Aspen bobbed her head. "Yeah, I guess
so." She clicked Talon's lead on and ruffled his coat, finding as much
pleasure in the move as it seemed the six-year-old guy did. "I just don't
want Talon to forget Austin."

"Oh, I don't think that will ever happen. Even if it takes years."

"It *has* taken years. Two, to be exact."

"Yeah, but in a dog's mind, I think that equates to two days. They don't forget smells, and he's got Austin's burned into his head. I'd bet my life on it."

A country song sailed through the air. Aspen started and grabbed the phone from her jacket pocket. "I'd better get this. Hope you have a good session with Trinity."

"We will."

Aspen led Talon from the training ground and headed toward her SUV as she pressed the TALK button on her phone. "Hi, Britt. What's up?"

"Girl, we need to talk."

"Okay, go ahead."

"No. I've got something you need to see."

Aspen slowed at the urgent excitement in her best friend's voice. "Okay. . ."

"Can you come over?"

"I had some errands—"

"Girl. Listen." Noise crackled over the line, as if Brittain had put her hand over the phone. "Okay, I can't say too much here, but I think. . . I *think*. . .I interviewed a man last night, a soldier. You have to see this."

"You're not sure you interviewed a soldier?" Aspen loaded Talon in the back of the SUV in his crate then climbed behind the steering wheel.

"Don't mess with my head. Come to my house. It has to be now. You know I wouldn't ask if I didn't think it was important, and this goes to the moon and back on importance."

"Wow, how cryptic." Nerves jangled, Aspen turned over the engine.

"I know. But I have to be. And when I get to the studio, I've got to turn this in to the manager to approve. But trust me, you'll want to see this before it goes live. Aspen, this guy was at Kariz-e Sefid."

Aspen's heart climbed into her throat. "I'm on my way." How she got from the ranch to Brittain's condo, she didn't know because her mind was all awhirl and tumbling from the mention of the Afghan city that stole her brother. Was it possible. . .just maybe. . .that she'd been right? Was he alive somewhere? Maybe held hostage by some radical group?

Talon lumbered toward the door with Aspen. She hesitated, ready to say something positive to the canine who'd been there, who'd seen what happened to Austin but could not speak. "I wish you could—"

The door jerked open.

Brittain's fro spiked out in odd places rather than the perfectly coiffed hairstyle she managed to tame the curls into for her broadcasts. "Girl!" Wide, mahogany eyes held hers. "You are *not* going to believe this."

She reached into the hall and grabbed Aspen's jacket shoulder and pulled. "C'mon. I don't have much time." Halfway across the living room by the time Aspen lured Talon into the apartment, Brittain chattered a hundred miles an hour. "You are not going to believe this man." She threw a look over her shoulder. "But this man? Is *fine*. With a capital *F*."

"What man? How did you meet him?" Aspen shed her coat and trailed her friend to the dining table that cozied up to a bay window in the sunroom.

"That's just it—he e-mailed me. Said he had a story he had to get off his chest. He couldn't live with himself and keep the secret."

Aspen put her hand over her stomach, wishing she hadn't eaten that Angus burger. "What secret?"

Brittain came behind her, set her long, dark fingers on Aspen's shoulders, then guided her to the office and into a plush chair. "See for yourself." She lifted a remote and pressed a button.

Perched on the edge of the chair, Aspen clasped her sweaty palms in her lap. Talon's cold nose nudged her hand. She smiled down at him.

"Could you please state your name for the camera?"

"Are you recording?"

"Yes, is that a problem?"

Pale blue eyes hit the camera head-on. The man shifted. *"No. No, I guess not. My name is Dane Markoski."*

"You contacted me and said you had to clear your conscience."

"Yes, ma'am. I did—do." He sat up straighter. Broad shoulders. Thick chest. The guy was no stranger to fitness.

"Please, go ahead."

"O—okay. I was in the Army. . ." His story went on for several minutes, noting his unit and what they were doing. *"We went to Kariz-e Sefid, and things just felt bad, ya know? We rolled in and things were crazy quiet. Then out of nowhere, we heard the shriek of an RPG rip past our MRAP.*

This was just supposed to be a routine patrol, so. . ." He shrugged. *"Sometimes that happens. And it puts lives on the line, but we don't stop fighting, ya know?"*

"So I've heard," Brittain said. *"Now, you said there was an attack? What happened?"*

"Well, the vehicles were targeted, so we went for cover, tried to find the source of the weapons' fire. A SOCOM team headed to the roof of a building."

"SOCOM?"

"Special Operations Command. A team of Green Berets were there. They said they'd seen something. But. . .that's when things got strange. . ." He looked up to the right and seemed lost in the memory.

"Please, go on."

He blinked as if startled. *"Sorry. I just. . ."* His eyes darted around, as if searching for something. *"The building exploded, and it threw me into the dirt. As we all came up out of that mess, smoke and dust was everywhere. You almost couldn't see."*

"Almost?" Brittain leaned forward. *"But you did see, is that right, Mr. Markusky."*

"Markoski. And. . ." He gave a one-shoulder shrug. *"Yeah, I saw something. Or I think I saw something."* He scratched his head.

"What do you think you saw?"

"Well, that's just it. It's not what I saw then, but. . ."

"But what?"

Three

Pentagon, Arlington County, Virginia

*W*ell, *the Army seemed really eager to write off one of the men, and then something I saw later. . .one of the men I'd swear was on top of that roof, who should have died. . .I saw him in northeast Africa. I was there helping with a relief team. . . . I thought I saw him there."*

"Who?"

"I'm not sure we should say that because"—he glanced directly at the camera—*"you know."*

Leaning back against the black lacquer conference table, Cardinal stared at the wall-mounted screen. Arms crossed, he ran a hand over his jaw as he thought through the answers he'd given. Had he been too obvious? Or perhaps not obvious enough about the implication.

No, if he'd been too direct, Aspen would've detected something. He'd pored over her records since that meeting. She served in the Air Force as an admin for the judge advocate. Meant she had a good brain.

Knuckles against his mouth, he didn't understand. The plan was perfect. Even Burnett had said so. Why hadn't she made contact?

"Hey, you okay?"

Cardinal glanced over his shoulder to the woman who owned that voice. Lieutenant Brie Hastings. "Yeah, sure." He didn't need to be alone with this girl. She'd made her interest in him known all too well.

"That your new mark?"

Cardinal cursed himself for letting his research notes play on the wall. He *X*-ed out of the video on the laptop, noting it vanishing from the wall, then slapped the computer shut. He tucked it under his arm and started for the door.

"You know." Brie turned as he walked around her. "The female population isn't as scary as you think. You ought to give us a try."

Cardinal stalked into the hall and continued toward Burnett's office, praying the general had some news.

"Cardinal!"

The urgent, hissed call pulled him around. Lieutenant Smith jogged toward him, his face wrought until he spotted Hastings, slowed with a stupid grin, shot her a "hey," then refocused on Cardinal as he waved a paper.

Cardinal pointed to the paper in the lieutenant's hand. "Is that—?"

"E-mail just came through."

Snatching the printed communication, Cardinal felt the first surge of relief in a long time.

> *SGT Markoski—I want to thank you, personally, for honoring Austin's memory with honesty and integrity. They've relegated my brother to six feet under without a body to place there. Our country has long worked hard to bring home the fallen, so I don't understand how they can forget about my brother so easily. Thank you for remembering him.*
>
> *It would be nice to talk and trade stories and memories. Austin & I spent a lot of time at Amadore's Fight Club. I'm still there, every Tuesday & Thursday evening, as he and my father taught me to fight to defend myself and to fight for what's right. Semper Fidelis.—A. Courtland.*

Cardinal read the e-mail again.

"Not quite the response you expected, huh?" Smith said.

"No, it's not." Cardinal patted his shoulder. "It's better." He started for Burnett's office.

"Better?"

"Get me on the next flight to Austin." Cardinal folded the paper and rounded the corner.

"Huh? But why? She just said—"

"I'll need a team prepped for Djibouti. We'll need to alert Kuhn we're headed his way." Cardinal carded himself through to the offices of General Burnett and a couple of other four-stars.

From the admin's desk, Cardinal looked through the glass pane and held up a hand to Burnett, who waved him in as he talked on the phone.

He leaned in and held up the paper. "She contacted. We're a go."

Holding up one finger, Burnett spoke quietly into his phone. So quietly Cardinal couldn't hear him. But he could read his lips. *Let me take care of it. I know. . .no, he's not a loose cannon. I can—yes, sir.*

"Problem, sir?"

With a disgusted sigh, the general shook his head. "Always a problem."

Cardinal thumped the e-mail with a finger. "She made contact. I'm on my way up to the Lone Star state."

"Actually, you're not."

Heat spilled down Cardinal's spine as Burnett hung up. He said nothing. Just waited. It always worked better.

"That was General Payne."

A royal *pain* in the backside. Also Chief of Staff of the Army. Burnett's boss's boss. Cardinal knew where this was going. They never approved of the general using him for operations. They questioned his loyalty. Questioned his motives.

Well, one they had no need to question. The other was his business alone.

"Approval for the Djibouti mission has been rejected."

"On what grounds?"

"Nigeria."

Cardinal smothered his reaction. "Unbelievable." He jerked his head down. Looked to the side. Closed his eyes. Then glanced at Burnett. "We have her and that dog. I put eyes on the target. He's down there. We have to go down there and get him out. If we don't—"

Burnett held up a hand. "I know. And so does Payne. They're sending a team—"

"They send anyone who smells like American military down there, the hounds of hell are going to rip out their hearts. Then you'll lose him for good."

Blue eyes held his. "Son, this is not my first rodeo and you're not Cardinal, god of the spy sea."

The terse words pulled Cardinal off balance. The general had never snarled at him like that. Which meant one of two things: Burnett agreed with Payne, or Burnett was ticked off, too.

Either way, his mission just got tanked. Austin's life had been put in dire straits.

There was no battle to fight here. Payne tied Burnett's hands. Which cut off Cardinal's limbs. And possibly severed the heart of a family—the Courtland's.

Not that they'd ever know their son had been abandoned by their country.

Aspen already knows that. She just didn't have the right definition to MIA: Presumed Dead. To her, it meant they couldn't find a body. Cardinal knew the truth—the U.S. buried the body with its complacency and bureaucracy. He respected laws and procedures.

They defined civilizations, prevented collapses.

They also crippled civilizations. Initiated collapses.

He'd seen it too many times. Cardinal gave a nod of surrender. Gritted his teeth, then turned for the door.

"Cardinal."

He opened the door and dragged his attention back to where it did not want to go.

"Don't."

A smile almost made it to his face.

"I mean it." Burnett leaned forward, rested his arms on his desk. "That very propensity to go rogue is why you got benched. Let them handle this."

"Of course."

"I mean it. I'd hate to see you fly off without his stamp of approval," Burnett said. "Then get down there and need help. They'd be all over my hide." A smile twinkled behind the terse words. "I'd have to send my very best after you to drag your sorry hide back here."

Cardinal stared at the general. The man who'd taken him under his wing, guided him, honed his skills, taught him things, learned things from Cardinal. . .and always, always saw things the same way Cardinal did.

"Understood."

Amadore's Fight Club
Austin, Texas

"Good gravy, girl."

Aspen eyed her friend as they headed into Amadore's, assaulted at once with the thick odor of sweat and BO wafting toward them. "What?"

"You only e-mailed him two days ago. What do you expect? He was in DC, for crying out loud. For him to drop everything and come up here?"

Bristling at her best friend's wisdom, Aspen strode back to the women's locker room, which wasn't more than a converted broom closet with a shower well. "He's military. He'll get it. If he was with Austin, then he was a Green Beret."

"Girl, I don't know. I couldn't find record of that."

"You're an investigative reporter, Britt, not the FBI. Records like his would be blacked out or concealed." It was a stretch, but hey, it made her feel better.

Brittain Larabie tossed her bag onto the bench. "What if he doesn't come?"

Aspen turned to her friend. "We went over all of that with the others before I e-mailed him at your condo."

"Yeah," Brittain said, with a roll of her head. "And if I remember, not everyone thought it was a good idea to bring this guy into the plan. In fact, Timbrel said you were digging a grave. And Darci says this man's psych profile showed a lethal dedication to his career. She's not convinced he's right. I was with this guy an hour and he never smiled. I mean—creepy! And—"

"Enough!" Aspen thrust her hands into her hair and tied it back with black elastic as she met Brittain's gaze in the mirror. "We *need* him—he was there with Austin the day of the attack." Yanking the zipper on her bag, she felt the tension tangling her mind and thoughts. "He knows what happened. Maybe I'll have enough to file an appeal or something with the judge advocate. General Gray and his wife still invite me to their Christmas parties. They like me. Maybe he'll listen."

"Yeah, and maybe the Easter Bunny will deliver a gold egg."

Aspen glared at her friend. "I don't need your negativity—"

"It's not neg—"

"I know. It's the facts. *Negative* facts, I'd point out."

Britt let her shoulders sag in an exaggerated way. "What about Austin's fire buddy? He said he doesn't remember this guy."

Aspen rolled her eyes. "Will was a player whose loyalties were with himself." She sighed. "As much as I don't want to put my last hope in this Mar-whatever guy, I will take him over Will any day." When she'd hit SEND on that letter, a thread of hope stitched up her broken, angry heart. She plunged her hand into the bag and drew out her wrist wraps.

Warm hands cupped her shoulders, drawing Aspen's gaze from the yellow wraps she secured around her palm and wrist. Compassion oozed from the milk chocolate eyes.

"No." Aspen stepped back. "Don't do that." She snatched the gloves from the bench and strode into the gym, acutely aware how much her best friend wanted to apply the brakes to this before they got started. But Aspen couldn't—*wouldn't*—let Austin's name end up on some memorial wall. He wasn't dead. She could feel it.

Or. . .could she?

It'd only been in the wee hours of the morning as she wept over his disappearance that she wondered if their twin connection was still alive. Was he still alive?

Batting the gloves into a better fit, she crossed the open floor, passed the free weights, the ellipticals, and treadmills. At the speed bag, she warmed up. When a slow burn radiated through her muscles, she started for the ring.

Mario straightened as she passed, stilling the kickboxing bag he'd just struck. He grinned. "Hey, beautiful. Ready for more?"

Slipping in her mouth guard, she arched an eyebrow at him.

He whooped.

As she reached for the ropes to step in, Amadore, ghostlike man that he was, appeared out of nowhere. "You with us today, Angel?"

With more conviction than she felt, she nodded.

He pointed to Mario. "You hurt her, you answer to me."

Smiling, she nudged his shoulder then bent through the ropes. She strode toward the center and met her opponent. All six feet of the man towered over her five-foot-five frame. Muscles rippled beneath his dark skin as those eyes—Timbrel called them lady-killers—sparkled back at her. In the center, she bumped gloves with Mario, their official start signal.

He threw the first punch, launching them into a rigorous workout. Though they were well matched, he always seemed determined to bring her down. She enjoyed the challenge. Much like this new venture of hers—finding her brother. Bringing him back. Darci insisted Aspen had gone one too many rounds in the ring and incurred TBI, traumatic brain injury, to attempt this. But like Aspen, Darci's mind and heart raced at the thought of doing something everyone else said they couldn't.

Would the guy come? Though she wasn't a former intelligence operative like Darci or a borderline Mensa like Khaterah, Aspen had been gifted with an insatiable thirst for truth and justice. But without this guy, without Dane Whatshisname—who named their kid after a dog, anyway?—she could hang up this plan. He had been there. He knew her brother. Knew the location. The terrain. And he still had connections with the military. Desperately needed connections to get them in and out of Afghanistan. Besides, going in with a team of men alone. . .well, even Aspen wasn't that stupid.

Black slammed into her face with a resounding thud.

Aspen spun away, stumbling.

Mario cursed.

"Hey," Amadore's shout sailed through the cavernous, split-level gym. "What'd you do?"

"Nothin'," Mario said.

Aspen sniffled, smelling and tasting the metallic glint of blood. She wiped the warmth from her upper lip and sneered at Mario. "You'll pay," she mumbled around her guard.

Mario grinned, but even beneath that she saw uncertainty as he darted a gaze to Amadore, who loomed over the front counter, his face aflame. "I warned you, Mario. You hurt her—"

Aspen threw a right cross at the distracted man.

His hand flew up and blocked. He angled to the side and countered.

Her mind had left the ring, and that'd cost her some blood. She wouldn't make the mistake again. And now, she had to pay back this player. Besides, she was tired of Amadore protecting her. The men here needed to know she could hold her own. If she'd proven that in Iraq, she could do it at Amadore's Fight Club, too.

Tracking him around the ring, she deflected several aggressive—and stupid—moves. Mario was running on his victory. He'd die on it, too.

He raised his knee—she shifted, turned slightly, and rammed her elbow down on the meaty part.

Mario flinched and dropped his guard.

Aspen threw a hard right. And connected.

His head snapped back, but he was already in motion. A left jab. Right. Light glinted off the glass-front door—the glare flared across Mario's face. Then Aspen's. Both looked toward the front, ready to holler at whoever had forgotten to pull the curtain to prevent such a distraction.

"Hey," Mario shouted. "The bwind." His mouth guard made him sound like he had rocks in his mouth.

"Sorry, sorry"—Luke, the new hire, rushed and secured the curtain. The streaming sunlight wreathed a tall, muscular figure before the light vanished. Aspen blinked, and when her gaze hit the reception desk in the open-area gym, she froze.

Four

Amadore's Fight Club
Austin, Texas

Can I help you?"

Distrust and disgust stared back from a face that said trouble was best left outside. If Cardinal were the guessing kind, he'd peg this guy as the Amadore whose name stretched across the painted-black window gracing the storefront. Built like a barrel, with hands as big as two ball-peen hammers, the guy had hair that had once been jet black and curly. The proverbial Italian Stallion. And by that no-mess greeting, the stallion had things to protect.

Musty and dim, the fight club had all the glamour and odor one would expect. Light dribbled through the spots where the window paint had flecked off the large panes lining the front of the old warehouse. Dust danced on the light beams, as if locked in their own boxing match.

Cardinal brought his gaze back to the guy who waved off a scrawny kid. "Looking for someone."

"We ain't a date joint," the burly guy said.

Amusing. "Good, I'm looking for a guy."

A shrug of the massive, well-muscled shoulders. "Don't ask, don't tell." The man almost grinned. "We don't judge." He slowly looked Cardinal up and down. "Well, most of the time."

Cardinal cocked his head and met the man's entirely too pleased eyes. "Look, someone asked me to meet him here. A—"

Thwump!

38

The burly guy jerked his attention to the ring where two fighters, wearing headgear and other protective gear, were heavy into a match.

Thwump!

"Hey!" The burly guy stalked to the other end of the counter. "Mario! What'd I tell you? I'm warning you, punk!"

The guy in the ring held up his gloves in a show of submission.

"Angel, eyes up. Focus!" Scowling, the burly guy backstepped, still watching the match in the ring at the center of the gym.

Cardinal could understand why.

"Up, watch—that's right!"

A woman—had the big guy called her Angel?—bounced around the mat, going toe-to-toe with a bully of a guy. And holding her own. He'd half expected her to be laid-out flat after the way that guy swung.

A hard right. She deflected and threw her own.

"Whoa," the scrawny kid mumbled from the other side of the counter.

"She's good," Cardinal said.

The man's head snapped toward him. "What?" he barked. "What'd you say about my angel?"

"She's a solid fighter. Good form. A little slow on the return, but—"

"Hey, Angel," the man yelled, still glowering at Cardinal. "This punk says you're too slow on the return."

Cardinal laughed. "Hey, it was just—"

She waved her gloved hands. "Bring it!"

He glanced at the ring. Brown, wet ringlets sprung from a pulled-back ponytail, framing the face and doe-like eyes—well, doe in shape. The fury spewing from them made her seem more like the siren who'd coaxed Odysseus from his voyage—mission.

"No, no, I'm here to meet someone."

The burly man laughed, long and loud. "Mister," he said with a menacing gleam, "meet my angel." Finally, he looked away. "Mario, give the guy some gloves."

"No, seriously." Cardinal wanted to punch the scrawny kid who stood laughing at him. "I meant no harm."

"He's just chicken," the kid taunted.

Laughter bounced through the fight club, and only then did Cardinal realize he had an audience. A large one. He wanted to curse.

He rounded on the guy when he started making clucking noises.

The kid's smile vanished, and he backed away. "I'm going. . .to. . ." The guy pivoted and ran.

When Cardinal turned around, something flew at him, thumped against his chest, then dropped to the floor. He glanced down to find gloves and wraps at his feet. Though he retrieved them, he had no intention of fighting, especially not a woman.

He held the equipment out to the man behind the counter. "I'm not here to fight. I'm here to meet someone by the name of Courtland." He looked to the ring, expecting the woman to perk up when he said her name. She didn't. "You know where I can find Aspen Courtland?"

Something dark flickered through the man's eyes. "Yes."

"Where?"

He pointed to the ring.

"Now who looks slow?" came a taunting voice—a female voice. She stood at the side, red gloves hooked over the top ropes. The white tank accentuated her curves—and her toned arms and trim waist. Dark spots—blood?—splattered her shoulder. He'd seen the number she did on that other guy. Though young, short, and athletic, she had a fight the size of Alaska—and as cold—in those cobalt eyes.

The burly guy lifted the gloves. "One round. If you fight fair and remain standing, I'll introduce you to Courtland."

This wasn't the first time he had to buy loyalty from locals. Probably wouldn't be the last. Slowly, he reached for the gloves. "I'll hold you to that." He hesitated, looked at the woman again, then back to the big guy. "Two minutes?"

"As I said, one round. I'm a man of my word."

"So am I."

The man slapped his shoulder. "You can change back there. Luke will get you suited up."

Within minutes, Cardinal had a pair of shorts, shoes, and a tank on. His newfound friend, Luke, led him back into the gym.

"Hey," Cardinal said to the man who'd been in the ring with the girl, "any tips? I don't want to hurt her."

Mario laughed. "Yeah, go easy on her. She's not as strong as she looks."

Why did that sound a lot like "you're stupid enough to believe me"?

Cardinal slowed. "Then what does that make you since she beat the snot"—he motioned to the guy's red nose—"out of you?"

More laughter. Mario bumped his fists against the gloves, a sign of camaraderie. "Don't hold back."

Surprise leapt through Cardinal.

"Angel won't."

Angel. It felt like a sick, cruel joke. The name invoked a haunting memory.

Applause and cheers broke out around the gym, pulling Cardinal back to the present, back to the ring. Surprisingly, most of the others gathered round. Angel waited in the ring, conferring with two other women, who indicated to him as he stepped through the ropes.

The burly guy stood at the center of the ring. He held out his hands. Angel approached, and only as she came closer did he realize she was small. . .and beautiful—er, young. Way young. Was she even out of high school?

"Fight fair. Two-minute bell."

★ ★ Five ★ ★

Amadore's Fight Club

Generate momentum off the right toe. Keep balance. Take balance away from the other guy. The tall, muscle-bound man rivaled anyone she'd ever matched. In the first thirty seconds of their sparring, she realized he knew boxing. A lot about boxing.

Fair enough. No holds barred.

Aspen backed up, forcing him to come to her. He moved fluidly, which amazed her that a man his size could do it smoothly. Acutely aware of the throng gathered on the bleachers surrounding the ring, she tried to keep her focus. Shake off the words Timbrel had muttered as the guy climbed into the ring: *"A hottie like that—let him win so he'll feel bad and take you out."*

The glove came up, glanced off her chin. She rolled out of it and followed through with a right hook, which he deftly avoided. The jabs and punches came quicker. Apparently, he'd gotten over fighting a girl—the trepidation clear on his face as he lumbered onto the mat was gone. Agitation wound around her stomach. She'd seen that look on every airman who'd been paired with her in the field. They quickly figured out there were bigger sissies back in their bunks. But she hated the assumptions, hated the looks and jeers. This guy had held that presumption for all of ten seconds before unloading.

Hands up, she protected herself against a jab. Though he stood as tall—no, taller—than Mario, the bulk on this guy added some leverage she hadn't expected.

Keep your feet moving. A left, right. She swung hard.

He deflected.

Harder.

A quick strike snapped her head back. Stunned, she backstepped. He eased into the space. She slammed a solid left, which he protected, then she rammed a right. Caught his side. He grunted but swung upward. The momentum carried through, popping her head back. Aspen gasped as her feet left the mat.

Ding!

She landed on her back. *Oof!* Air whooshed from her lungs.

The guy leaned over her. "You okay?"

"Get away from her!" Amadore's shout pervaded the club. "What'd you do, punk?"

Aspen peeled herself off the mat, indignation creeping through her shoulders. She stretched her jaw and neck, amazed. He'd flattened her! Mario hadn't managed that in a long time. Sitting, arms over her knees, she waited to catch her breath.

"Angel, you okay?" Amadore hooked her elbow and helped her to her feet. He twisted around. "You, get out of my club!"

"What a minute."

"Out!"

Dane Whatshisname drew back, glancing between them. "You said you'd—"

Chest puffing, Amadore tightened his lips and biceps. Coiled, ready to strike like the cobra tattooed on his arm. "I said if you survived a round."

Dane glowered. "I did."

"No, you knocked her out. The bell hadn't sounded."

Grit out, she sighed. "He didn't knock me out, Amadore." She patted his side. "I'm okay. Just. . ." She shot Brittain and Timbrel a glance then looked toward the two men hovering near the far corner of the ring. Picking her pride up off the mat took everything she had. At the corner, she offered her glove to the winner. "Good fight."

Confusion and concern crowded his handsome features as he stood on the floor, looking up at her. "You're a good boxer."

Holy cannoli! Was the heat in her face from blushing? No way. "Thanks." She swiped a sweaty curl from her face, hoping she covered the red tint no doubt filling her cheeks. Whipping off the gloves, she smiled. Extended a wrapped hand. "Aspen Courtland."

"Dane Markoski. And for the record, you look nothing like your brother."

"I know. He got my mom's side—full Italian. I got our father's, Irish." She wrinkled her nose. "So, Mr. Mar. . ."

"Markoski. It's not really hard to pronounce."

She shrugged. "I need to shower and change. Meet out front after?"

"Works for me." He turned and walked toward the men's locker room.

Aspen didn't trust herself to talk anymore. Not here, not in front of everyone. And not after ending up flat on her back. She showered and changed, anticipation of talking to Mystery Man pushing her a little faster than usual. Disappointment dogged her steps as she waved bye to Nonno and made her way out the front door, where her friends waited on the wrought-iron bench.

"Something's not right about that guy." Timbrel Hogan, another handler with A Breed Apart, crossed her arms over her chest and stared at the gym doors.

"Is any guy right in your book?" A smile glowed against Brittain's mocha-colored skin.

Timbrel smirked. "A rare few."

Aspen tossed her gym bag in the back of her SUV. "I agree— something feels off. But if he was there with Austin and he knows what happened, then I need to explore this possibility."

"Just don't explore him."

"Timmy," Aspen chided, "I don't care about *him*. Answers about my brother are what I'm after."

Timbrel's eyes narrowed. "But I know you, Aspen—you're soft where it comes to romance. And that guy—he's trouble. He knows how to work people. I can just. . .tell."

Touching her puffy cheekbone, Aspen cringed. "He definitely worked me over." She meant it as a joke to lighten the conversation, but Timbrel seized on it.

"Exactly what I'm talking about. What kind of man would hit a woman?"

Brittain laughed. "Girl, get off your hate wagon about men. Aspen challenged him in a boxing ring. She got what she asked for." Her tall, African American friend brushed Aspen's curl from her face. "All kidding aside, Timmy's right: be careful. We don't know nothin' about this man. And it is strange that he shows up after all this time."

"I know. I know." She touched her fingers to her temple. They were right. It wouldn't be the first time she'd been swayed by blue eyes and smooth talking. Unlike Timbrel who didn't trust at all, Aspen trusted far too easily. She called it optimism. Her friends naivete.

Was it her fault she wanted to believe people were good?

"Why don't I go with you to the ranch?"

Hmm, maybe it wasn't a bad idea. With Timbrel's negative outlook coupled with her own positive outlook, maybe they'd find a safe middle ground.

"Hey, won't Daniels be there?" Brittain nudged her arm. "You said he was good people, that he had a strong ability to read situations."

"She's right. Prince Charming has very good radar."

"Whoa." The wind gust rifled its fingers through Brittain's caramel curls that puffed up in a halo around her face. "Did Timbrel Hogan just pay a man a compliment?"

"It's a fact, not a compliment." Timbrel bristled, but they all knew Daniels had pried a little sister out of Hogan during their mission in Afghanistan last year. The two behaved like siblings and had a mutual respect for each other.

"Here he comes."

Aspen looked over her shoulder.

Showered, changed, and looking quite handsome in a dark blue button down and jeans. . . A breeze tussled his hair and threw it into his face. Cut short along the sides and back of his head, his black hair glittered wet and shiny in the afternoon sun. Longer strands on the top whipped along his forehead and temples as he strode toward them.

"Mmm," Brittain muttered. "Yep, one *fine* man."

"Okay. That's it. I'm going," Timbrel said.

Aspen started to glance at her friend, but Talon let out a low growl. "Out, Talon," she said as she looked over her shoulder.

Dan spoke up. "So, where to?"

"A ranch that's a half-hour drive out of the city."

"Should I ride with you?" he asked.

"Absolutely not." Timbrel pointed to his car. "Easier for you to leave after she throws your butt out."

Blue eyes, surrounded by olive skin and framed by black hair, held Aspen's. "You do remember you invited me out." He towered over her but not in a threatening way. In the six-inches-taller way. In a way that left her unbalanced and far too aware of a strange current that bounced between them. And the way his jaw was dusted with stubble. "Or did I misconstrue the note you sent via the studio?"

Had he leaned closer?

She took a step back.

"I'm sorry," he said as he looked at the three of them. "I feel like I'm intruding or something." He fixed on Aspen. "You said you wanted to talk to me about your brother. But if I'm making you uncomfortable, or if I crossed some line, then I'll leave."

"No." Aspen cleared her throat, praying that didn't sound as desperate as it felt. "You're right—I asked you to come." She started to touch his arm, a move to reassure him, but she thought better of it. "It's no problem. Timbrel just doesn't like men."

He studied the petite brunette for several long minutes.

Timbrel crossed her arms again, squaring off with him. "What?"

"Nothing." He didn't smile, but his eyes did—weird. "I just. . .if that's your preference, great."

"Preference?" Timbrel's eyebrow arched.

Brittain laughed. "She's not gay. She just. . .hates men, Mr. Markusky."

"Markoski." Confusion whirled through eyes that matched the sky behind him. "Then who do you date?"

"My dog," Timbrel said through clenched teeth as she stomped toward her little import.

His shoulders weren't tensed. Eyes held no barbed-wire accusations, only. . .amusement.

Aspen twisted toward him, her Asics crunching dirt and rock. "You did that on purpose, suggesting that."

"Sorry. I just don't appreciate people questioning my character when they don't know me."

"Don't apologize, Soldier Boy. Anyone who can tie Timbrel's tongue has my vote." Brittain turned, locked gazes with Aspen, and started humming the song "Getting to Know You."

Aspen flashed her friend a warning. Not the most suitable song. There was no king here. And if she recalled, the school teacher ended up falling in love with the king.

So not happening.

Trailing the white luxury SUV left Cardinal with more questions than answers. Things didn't seem to be getting off on the right foot. Or any foot. Aspen was guarded, even more so with her posse of girlfriends. *How do I get under her radar?* What would it take to convince her to trust him?

The truth.

No way. That would risk everything—*everything!* His job and carcass would be on the line. Burnett would fry him. Then stick him in that smoker he raved about.

As they crept out of the Austin city limits and dug farther into the countryside, he evaluated what he'd perceived of Aspen Courtland. The woman had grit, but she also had an...*innocence* about her. Ironic considering she'd been an airman. A pretty tough one from the records he'd seen. And the way she'd gone up against the Brass regarding her brother's status—the very reason Burnett wanted her kept ignorant because this could get ugly fast—and the way she'd taken control of the situation.

At least, she thought she had. He'd anticipated that about her. It'd worked. Exactly as planned. He banged his hand against the wheel.

"You are weak!"

Teeth grinding, he pulled himself straighter in the car. What was that? Dropping out of reality and drowning in the past would get him killed. Create mistakes. The way things were, he couldn't afford a single mistake. He'd keep a line of demarcation between their two worlds. The line in the sand would be reinforced with powerful barriers.

The SUV slowed, snapping Cardinal back to the present. To the country road. He applied the brake as the Lexus turned into a gated drive. The trellised ironwork stretched over his sedan with the words A BREED APART.

The dog!

He eased his car along the tree-lined road. *Head on a swivel. Eyes and ears out.* The old military lingo to watch his surroundings served as a good reminder. Ahead fifty yards, a brown home rose in quiet beauty. Glass and lines marked it with elegance, yet simplicity. Two men stood on a wraparound porch. Waiting.

Aspen's white SUV aimed toward a fenced-in area away from the house. Already her door opened by the time he pulled up alongside. He slid the gear into PARK, eyes on the rearview mirror. Well-muscled, sporting a Glock holstered to his thigh, a former Army grunt, if he ever saw one, approached.

Cardinal stretched his jaw and snagged the bandana from the glove compartment. He climbed out, sizing up the competition who gave Aspen a warm familiar hug.

"How's he doing?" she asked.

"Fine. Trin's got him on his toes."

Aspen laughed.

The man shifted and extended a hand. "Heath Daniels." Though the words were friendly, his posture was not. The man had territory issues.

Take it slow. "Dane Markoski."

Aspen motioned to him. "Dane was on the news—you might have seen him."

Daniels nodded. "Mr. Markoski."

"Oh, and this is Jibril Khouri." Aspen turned, brushing a blond curl from her face. "He owns the ranch."

Cardinal shook the man's hand. "The land is beautiful."

"I couldn't agree more." Khouri's gaze lingered longer than it should have. He was right to be cautious. They all were.

Behind the fenced area came the barking of dogs. Heart rammed into his throat, he looked toward the broad gate marked TRAINING YARD. "Training?"

"Yes," Khouri said as he motioned and started walking. "The ranch is a training facility for working dogs."

"Hey." Cardinal glanced to the side where Aspen walked with them. "Austin's dog—whatever happened to him after. . . ?"

Aspen's expression fell, but she crammed a smile into place.

Cardinal felt like a jerk for asking the question he knew must twist that dagger in her heart, but he shoved aside the feeling.

"He's here." Aspen opened the gate. "I adopted him after Austin went missing."

"I. . .I thought dogs were—" He cut off his words but knew she'd understand where he was going.

"A new law protects the dogs. They're currently classified as equipment, so I had to pay to bring him home once they wrote him off, but it was worth it." Aspen stepped into the training yard and strode toward the center.

A yellow Lab lumbered toward her, ball in mouth.

"Two months ago," Daniels said, "Talon wouldn't lift his head to even look at her."

"Seriously?" Cardinal watched the handler and dog. "What was his problem?"

"PTSD." Daniels's gaze locked on to him. "So, you were with him in Al-Najaf."

Cardinal feigned distraction with the dog. Maybe the woman. She had confidence yet a brokenness that felt familiar. He met Daniels head-on. "Oh. No, Kariz-e Sefid. That's where I worked with Court." Had he noticed Khouri limping? "That patrol, the bombs—it wiped out my career. Put me flat on my back for two months."

"With what?" Relentless, Daniels tucked his arms under his armpits, gauging, monitoring. There was a reason he'd been a Green Beret.

"Broken back. TBI. PTSD."

"You have no noticeable scars."

"It's the invisible ones that get you." Cardinal needed to extract himself from this interrogation. "Excuse me."

Had Daniels figured things out? He'd never been unraveled that fast. And he doubted it'd happened already here, but there was no time like now to put distance between him and the man who'd dig deep enough to find some holes.

Another dog bounded toward them. Lowered her front and tipped up her tail, snarling at him. Cardinal reached out a hand to try to show her he was her friend.

She snapped.

"Trinity, out!" Daniels looked at him and shrugged. "She's protective. So am I."

Something wet nudged his hand. He glanced down to find the Lab sniffing his hand. And prayed hard his plan worked.

To his relief, Talon sat at his feet and stared down the obstacle course. Wide-eyed, Aspen gawked. "He knows you."

"You sound surprised." Technically, the dog *should* know him if he'd worked with Courtland, so this was a good test marker to also gain Aspen's trust.

A pretty blush seeped into her milky-white complexion.

"You didn't believe me." He tried to sound surprised.

"Sorry." More red. Matched her pink lips. "I've just been fighting to get him back, so it was a little strange that I'd never heard your name till you showed up on the news."

"But you're willing to believe me because of him." He pointed to the dog.

Aspen ruffled the Lab's head. "Talon knows people. Better than I do." She clipped a lead on his collar. "If he accepts you, then I will."

"You didn't before?"

Her lips quirked, and she shrugged. "Your name wasn't in the official report."

Cardinal held her gaze, infusing it with reassurance as he spoke words that could unravel. . .if they weren't the truth. "That's because I don't exist."

Watching

St. Petersburg, Russia
Age: 14 Years, 3 Months

The world sped by in a whirl of greens as the train spirited Nikol Tselekova toward Brno. Though he sat with his eyes closed, his mind was alert and rampantly going over every detail. Yes, his bed was made. No wrinkles or ripples. Windows spotless. Footlocker unfettered for inspection. Bedposts aligned with the grain of the wood floors that ran toward the towering window. Yes, all had been in place. He'd made sure. Stood there at the door to his room for ten minutes, inspecting. Obsessing.

He tugged the backpack on his lap closer, tighter. It was worth it. To deliver the gift. To see her face. If only but for a second. It would be enough to hold him over till he could attempt another excursion.

The train slowed as it entered the city. Nikol glanced at his watch, mapping his time and journey. Still well within parameters. Fifteen minutes later, the train pulled to a stop in the heart of the Moravian capital city.

He hoofed it through the streets, avoiding cars and cyclists and pedestrians alike. Invigorated with each step, he headed west, out of the city, up the country road to the missionary's home. As he trudged up the road, he moved out of plain sight. Drifted farther into the trees lining the road. If he was right—

Laughter sailed from a yard. He tucked himself among the trees. Watched. A group of children played among a cluster of small homes. He searched their faces, anticipation thick. On one hand, he wanted to see her—out in the sun, laughing, playing the way she should. She deserved that. And so much more.

51

Reassured she was not there, Nikol moved forward. A young boy threw a ball toward his friend.

"Dobrý den!" Nikol greeted them.

The boy hesitated, then waved. It was not good that the child recognized him. That would be bad. Especially if the colonel discovered the secret. It would be a path straight back to Nikol.

Sitting on the bench, his back to the main road, Nikol smiled at the boy and lowered the pack to his lap. "Petr, jak se mate?"

The boy shrugged. "I'm good."

"Would you do me a favor?" Nikol extracted the white box from his backpack.

Petr sighed. "For Kalyna? Again?"

Nikol nodded. He would have to find another way to deliver the gifts. It was too known. The boy was as comfortable with Nikol as he was with his friends. Perhaps he should just send them via the post.

But then, he would not get to see her open them. And that. . .that was what kept his heart alive.

"If you like her, you should tell her."

The words brought a smile to his face, but Nikol merely nodded. With the eight-year age difference, it was not so simple as liking the girl.

Fisting his hands on his brown corduroy pants, Petr huffed. "What do I get?"

"Smart boy." Nikol produced a bar of chocolate and a green banknote. "First, you must tell me—" He broke off when he noticed the boy's gaze drift to the edge of the field. Following the gaze, Nikol tensed.

A girl stood there.

Watching.

A Breed Apart Ranch
Texas Hill Country

What do you mean you don't exist?"

Sunlight peeked through the cedar trees whose branches waved in the unusual summer breeze. Aspen hated the nerves that skittered through her veins. As she waited for his answer, noting that Heath and Jibril now stood a little taller.

The almost-there smile flickered for a second before it vanished, and Dane lowered his gaze. "I was being facetious." He shrugged those broad shoulders. "Have no idea why I wasn't mentioned in the reports. I was there." He motioned to Talon. "He even recognizes me."

Instinctively, Aspen's hand went to the Lab's broad skull. The big lug leaned against her leg panting, oblivious to the tension that had just coated the afternoon.

"Seriously." Dane held up his hands. "If you aren't comfortable with me being here, I can leave."

"No." The word shot out before Aspen could process her response—or the why. The urgency that tightened a fist on her didn't let go. This guy was the first possible good news she'd had in a very long time. "No, I want to hear your story." Something sparked in his blue eyes that unsettled her. "Then, I'll decide for myself if you need to leave."

"Fair enough."

"Why don't we take this up to the house?" Heath said.

"Yes, yes." Jibril started up the hill that led to the house. "I have tea and lemonade."

"You or Khat?" Heath taunted him.

Laughing, Jibril stepped onto the wraparound porch. "It is my house, not my sister's, yes?"

Though Heath and Jibril continued with their banter, Aspen drew into herself. Dane might have the answers. Or he might not. And what good would it do to hear his story for herself? Even if he did see Austin in Africa somewhere, it wasn't proof.

Seated in the cluster of deep-cushioned sofas that overlooked the pool and outdoor area, Aspen motioned Talon to her side. He lumbered to her and flattened himself against the cold tile floor.

Dane folded himself onto a chair next to her. Somehow, the low ceilings and short sofas amplified the guy's height. While he stood several inches taller than her, he wasn't a giant. Though his presence carried powerfully in the room.

"Let me get some refreshments," Jibril said. "Don't wait for me."

Hands folded, elbows resting on her thighs, Aspen steeled herself. "So, Brittain shared the interview with me."

He sat on the edge, forearms on his knees, and nodded.

"So, you were there when the bomb went off."

"I was."

"Tell me what you remember."

"I told Ms. Larabie everything I know."

"I know." Aspen drew in a breath and looked at Heath, whose presence gave her the gumption to push. Not that she was weak. But something about this guy unsettled her. Left her feeling nervous. "But I want to hear it for myself."

"Okay." As he launched into his story, into being down on the ground when the bomb went off, getting knocked unconscious and coming to, it all rang true.

"And in Africa?" Prompting him felt artificial. As if he wasn't willing to tell her what he saw. But he couldn't come this far then drop her off a cliff. Aspen inched closer. "You saw him there?"

He darted a look at her then to Heath before sloughing his hands together.

She touched his arm. "Please. Tell me what you saw."

"That's just it—I can't guarantee what I saw was real." He snorted. "I mean, I saw *someone*, but. . ."

"It could've been anyone." Heath towered over both of them.

Dane's blue gaze rose to Heath's. "Yeah." He skirted her a glance. "I just. . .I don't want to get your hopes up, ya know?"

"I appreciate that." She smiled, noticing for the first time how much depth rested in his face. "But you wouldn't have gone on national television if you didn't think there was a chance it was my brother you saw, not just *anyone*."

Ice clinked against glass as Jibril returned with a tray of drinks. He set them on the coffee table cuddled in the center of the sofas. "Here we go." The ABA owner slowed as he set the tray down. As always, he didn't miss a thing. "Is something wrong?"

"Hot Shot here is getting cold feet."

The challenge soared through the air, and Aspen could tell it hit center mass. Dane rose. Aspen with him. "Hey," she said, catching his forearm as she glared at Heath, "no baiting."

"You know, this was a bad idea."

"Why?" Heath held his ground. "Am I right?"

Dane swallowed. "I don't have cold feet." He started for the door.

"Then what's the problem?"

"I'm not doing this." Dane shook his head and stomped toward the foyer.

"Wait!" Aspen speared Heath with her fiercest glare as she rushed around the U-shaped sofa. "Dane, please."

Sunlight shot through the open door.

She hurried onto the porch. "I want to talk. I need to know everything."

"Why?" He spun toward her. "There's nothing that can be done. The government won't go after him. They won't even listen to me, though they've shoveled threats at me by the ton."

"What threats?"

He snapped back into composure and lowered his chin. "Never mind."

"No. I won't never mind. You have information about my brother and I want it."

"Why?" His brow furrowed, but those blue eyes shone through.

"What are you going to do, Aspen? Go after him?"

Indignation rippled through her and yanked her courage to the front. "If I have to."

"Be realistic. I've been there on a mission. Have you been there? Do you realize the temperature?"

"This is Texas. I'm familiar with hot weather."

He let out a half laugh, half snort as his eyes closed, and he lowered his head again. "I meant the political temperature."

"Oh."

"They aren't friendly to Americans. It's predominantly Muslim. There's an American base there, but that doesn't mean anything except more trouble. If your brother was there, finding him is one thing. Getting him out of there is another."

"Why? What are you saying?"

"I'm saying if he's there, if he went missing—there are myriad possibilities. He could've been snatched. He could've been brainwashed or have amnesia. He could be—" Dane chomped his mouth closed, and his gaze flung to the trees.

Aspen didn't need him to tell her his thoughts. Because hers went there, too. "He could be a traitor." Her next breath felt like it weighed as much as an MRAP. "That's what you were going to say, wasn't it?"

"It doesn't matter. This whole conversation doesn't matter."

"Why? Are you saying my brother doesn't matter?"

"I'm saying we have no way to find him."

She squared her shoulders. "Are you saying you'll go with me?"

He blinked and shook his head. "Aren't you listening to me?"

"I have a team."

"Who?"

"Talon—"

"The dog?" The incredulity in his voice scraped over her spine.

"Yes." She practically hissed the answer. "Talon knows Austin. Better than anyone. He never forgets a scent, even the one of a purported coward."

Dane cocked his head, understanding her accusation. "You said he had PTSD."

"He's getting better."

He ran a hand through his hair. The longer strands swung into his face. "*Getting* better doesn't do us much good in hostile territory."

"Let her worry about that."

They both spun toward the door. Propped against the jamb, Heath had his arms folded again. The proverbial big brother look plastered on his face. No wonder Darci loved that man. Would Aspen ever find a man so protective and gentle, yet every bit the warrior?

"She can worry about anything she wants," Dane said, an edge to his voice. "But taking a damaged dog into who-knows-what—"

"Please." Aspen's heart jammed into her throat as she caressed Talon's head. "Don't call him that."

"I meant no harm."

"I know." Nobody ever did. But it hurt more than anyone could imagine and more than she could possibly explain. "You said you know the last place Austin was seen—"

"*Possibly* seen."

Aspen held up both hands. "Right. But if there's a chance, then that scent is one Talon can pick up. He's our best chance of figuring out if who you saw was Austin." Tentatively, she touched that trembling thread of hope. *Austin. . .* "If we can get a team together—"

"I can put one together."

Point of no return. He'd said the words. Started the opening dialogue of commitment to this mission. With her.

He wanted to curse himself. Cut his eyes out so he couldn't see the hopeful longing in her icy-blue eyes. Eyes so pale they looked cold, yet nothing but warmth flowed from this woman. Angel. The fight club guy had called her that. Now Cardinal understood why. The fire lingering beneath that cool, sultry surface could singe the unsuspecting.

But he wasn't unsuspecting. This was his doing. She'd walked right into his trap. Grinding his teeth, he stood there, waiting as she stared up at him. Expecting. Hoping.

"You can?" A voice soft and pleading like that should be illegal.

Soft, pleading voices had never affected Cardinal. Most often, as now, the woman had no idea how they'd played into his carefully laid plans. But her voice. . .that hope. . .the common thread of knowing Austin.

That's what was different this time. They both knew Austin. That's why it pulled at him. Barreled over his conscience.

"How can you put together a team?" Suspicion oozed out of the former Green Beret. Daniels was bred to mistrust those he didn't know. The Army and multiple tours of combat did that.

"I got a call after my interview with Ms. Larabie." Cardinal avoided the woman's gaze, watching as the Lab and the other dog, Trinity, loped around the porch. "There is a team ready and willing to help." He gave a light, halfhearted shrug. "A high-ranking DIA officer offered it to me."

"DIA?" Daniels perked up.

Act hesitant. Didn't want to give himself away. "Uh, yeah. You know them?"

A wall of granite would've been easier to read than Daniels's face. "Go on."

"Right, okay. Well, he told me they're with me if I decide to do something." Cardinal checked out Talon, now on his belly. "Just not sure about this, especially about the dog."

"Talon should go." Aspen stepped closer to Cardinal.

Pure. Pure trust. Pure beauty. Pure innocence. Pure Aspen. Angel.

And then the angel flew. A cold breeze swept over him. Cardinal hauled his thoughts into line and flogged them. "Are you sure? What if he shuts down or goes nuts on us?"

"He was Austin's partner." Fiery determination sparked in her eyes. "If Talon caught his scent. . .I think there'd be no stopping him."

"But what if there is?"

"We take Trinity." Daniels joined them and leaned back against the railing that stretched the perimeter of the house. "She's Talon's new woman. She keeps him motivated." He smirked. "He'll find his way. If Austin is out there, she'll help Talon find him."

Not good—having the former Green Beret and his MWD on hand would increase the chances of things falling apart, of Cardinal's identity and dealings being compromised. He'd have to find reasons to exclude the man that wouldn't appear artificial. Arrange something. . .

No, he wouldn't put this man in danger. Getting married in two weeks, Daniels should be able to walk down the aisle on his own two feet.

"Give me forty-eight hours." Cardinal had to take control of this before they stepped in. "I'll be in touch."

Aspen nudged into his way. "If something comes up, how can I reach you?"

Cardinal hesitated, ignoring his steel barriers that demanded he spout off some gruff answer like he'd call her. He tugged his wallet out, plucked a card, and passed it to her. "Forty-eight hours."

She scanned the information, tapped it against her hand, then bobbed her head. "I'll be waiting."

The way she said that, why did he find himself reading into those words?

He gave a curt nod to her and the others then climbed into the rental. As he aimed the sedan down the dusty road to the gate, he kept his gaze forward, though in his periphery he could tell Aspen watched. For that reason, he restrained the disgust spiraling through his veins. The urge to punch the dash. The fire that lit across his shoulders.

It worked. Perfectly.

She'd played right into his hands. Easiest deck he ever dealt. It could not have been scripted more precisely. He read her right. Read the men in her life right. Every ploy had been dead on. She responded as if he had puppeted her. He'd known—*known*—what was in her because of the hunger, the deep, burning ache for resolve where her brother was concerned. Resolution.

He could relate. There were answers in his life he wanted, questions eliminated. Loved ones located.

But that man no longer existed. Cardinal. That was his name. His identity. Bestowed on him by Burnett because of their first meeting at the church.

That's exactly what he needed right now. A church. Confession. To purge this evil he had allowed to seep into his soul. Cultivated by manipulating Aspen Courtland.

She trusted him. Those blue eyes. . .so much like—

Cardinal drove his fist into the dash. Pain and fire spiked through his knuckles and darted up his arm, nerves tingling. Teeth clamped, he accelerated. The faceplate of the stereo system cracked. Warmth sped down his arm, dripped onto the gearshift. He snatched his phone and coded in.

"Go ahead, Cardinal."

"I need Burnett."

"He's unavailable."

"Well, you tell him I'm through. I'm not doing this. I'm gone."

Seven

Somewhere in Somalia

Plaster exploded.

Neil Crane threw himself backward with a curse. Pulse hammering, he scrabbled over the dirt, dust, and Sheetrock. Light speared through the hole created by the bullet. As he checked his six, three more beams of light fractured the haven of darkness.

AK-47 cradled in his arms, he sprinted through the darkened hall. "Go, go!" he shouted as he ran. Ahead, he saw her burst from behind another wall. In a dead run, she broke into the searing brightness of another brutally hot day.

He caught up with her. Catching the drag strap of her vest, he prayed for just one more mercy. They'd lived every day of the last three months on nothing but mercy. That fed his conviction that they were doing the right thing. That they had a purpose beyond sucking up oxygen.

"There." He pointed to an alley to the right. "Go!"

As he sprinted with her at his side into the narrow space between two buildings, he heard the shouts of their pursuers behind them. Thudding boots and creaking-groaning vehicles. More shouts. Rock and dirt burst up. From the side, wood splintered.

She tripped. Went down.

He dragged her back into motion.

"There," she gasped, her breath sucked in by the grueling pace.

He searched, uncertain what she referred to. "Wha—?"

With a grunt, she threw herself toward a wall.

A split second of panic snatched the air from his lungs. Was she hit? Then he saw it.

She rolled forward and dropped out of sight.

In a dive, he prayed this worked as he dropped into the darkness. Into the stench.

A Breed Apart Ranch
Texas Hill Country

The trail banked right and down. The cedar leaves provided little protection against the brutal summer heat. Aspen jogged around the bend, sweat dripping down her spine, her neck and temples. The swallow seemed to stick in her throat, the air so dry and dusty. With the lead wrapped around her waist and clipped to Talon, she glanced down at the animal she'd come to think of as a part of herself. Maybe that's the way it'd been with Austin. Living day in and day out with a dog, becoming one, moving as one. She'd never dreamed she'd be able to run with a dog lead coiled around her waist.

His tongue hung out, pink and wagging.

Down the path, she made her way back to the house. At the bottom of the trail, she slowed, walked a few circles with her hands on her hips. She tugged a water bottle from the pouch that hung from the nylon cord. Squirting some in her mouth, she closed her eyes. Swished the liquid that quickly went from cool to warm on her tongue. She swallowed then aimed some at Talon. He lapped it up, tail wagging.

The grief that had been hers for the last five days—well, longer, but amplified over the last several days—tightened around her chest. She smoothed Talon's yellow fur. "Sorry, old boy."

At six, Talon didn't act or look his age, but there was something "ancient" about the war dog. He'd seen more combat than she had as an assistant in the JAG office. The brown eyes, rich and deep, saw a lot.

"I'm sorry he didn't come back, Talon."

The Lab ducked when she said his name. Her heart cinched at the brokenness that engulfed her life. Losing Austin, seeing his once-strong, indomitable dog now cowering.

Remembering what the trainers and Heath had said, she rubbed him behind his ears. The T-touch soothed him almost instantly. She eased up and planted a kiss beside his ear. "I really thought. . ." Emotion in her throat was raw. "He seemed like someone who. . ."

Who would what? Care about Austin as much as you? Champion your cause?

Aspen plopped onto the ground, hugging her bent knees as she wrapped an arm around the bulky build of the Lab. She stared off over the land that sloped down into a valley. "I thought we'd get some answers." Her lower lip trembled, but she let out a shaky laugh. "Even fantasized we'd get Austin back."

Talon twisted around to look at her as if he understood. As if to say he wasn't giving up so she shouldn't either.

Aspen buried her face in his shoulder and gave him a squeeze. "Somehow, we'll get answers."

Oh God, why. . . ? She felt teased, taunted by God. She'd prayed, believed. She'd never stretched her faith as far as she had over the last year, refusing to believe rumors of Austin's death. Just when she'd surrendered and released the idea of finding him, here came this guy who seemed to have the answers.

No, not just answers, but the guts to do something about what he believed—that he'd seen Austin somewhere in Africa. She'd become convinced once again that there was a chance to find out the truth. To resolve this once and for all. For the last two years since the incident, she'd put her life on hold.

Then Markoski vanishes. Just like Austin.

Talon came up off his haunches, his gaze to the north.

Aspen glanced in that direction. A second later, Trinity bounded around the corner, trailed by Heath. Aspen stood and brushed off her backside.

"Hey." Heath came up, his expression tight. "Wanna come up to the house?" The terse way he said that drew her up short.

"Something wrong?"

He hesitated then glanced back. "Just come on up."

Back up at the house, she found Timbrel Hogan there with her infamous Hound of Hell, Beowulf. Beside her at the glass table sat Khaterah, Jibril's beautiful veterinarian sister, who talked with Jibril.

A tray of finger sandwiches sat on the table.

Still catching her breath, Aspen dropped into a chair. "What's going on?"

"Well," Timbrel said, "we got tired of waiting for your troublemaker to show back up."

"*My* troublemaker?"

"Yeah." Timbrel adjusted the ball cap that shaded her brown eyes. "You know, Mister SexyKillerBlueEyes."

Aspen laughed. "So because he has 'killer blue eyes,' he's trouble?"

"One hundred percent." Timbrel reached for a sandwich and tossed it to Beowulf.

"Hey!" Khat objected.

Timbrel ignored her. "That and the way he took you down. I wouldn't trust a guy who'd do that."

Bristling at the way Timbrel was practically telling her what to think about Dane, Aspen shrugged. "I like that he didn't pamper me."

"Pamper is one thing. Pummel is another."

"Hogan." Heath planted his hands on the table as he looked at everyone. "I made some calls today."

Silence dropped like a missile, flattening moods and conversations.

"And?" Jibril sipped his tea.

"I would've turned this over to Darci, but she's out of the country right now. So I put in a call to General Burnett."

Aspen eased forward. "Wait…" Her mind ricocheted over this setup and who he referred to. "You mean the general from Afghanistan—Darci's boss?"

"Former. He's a family friend of hers, so I have his home number."

"Why—I mean, why'd you call him?" Aspen tried to swallow past the lump in her throat. What wasn't he telling her? "What did you find out?"

"Nothing. Burnett, of course, said he couldn't tell me anything if he did find something on the guy, but he said he'd look into it."

Aspen let out a shaky breath. "Oh." She glanced around the table. "I thought you were going to tell me something bad."

"If this guy shows back up, I want to know he's legit. Nobody's going anywhere with him unless he's been fully vetted."

"Wouldn't that be Khat's job?" Timbrel snickered.

Heath stretched his jaw, clearly working to temper his frustration. "Look, something about this isn't sitting right. He went on national television, then came here and talked a good number, then vanishes. I want this guy or his head."

Aspen sat a little straighter. "I really appreciate your protective nature, Heath." Her courage rose to the surface. "But this isn't really your decision. If he turns up again, going with him, searching for my brother is *my* decision."

"Whoa, chickie." Timbrel plucked off her hat, brown hair tumbling free. "It's your decision, but we're a team. A family, ya know? You're not alone, and this decision is a big one."

"She is right," Khat said. "You don't have to do this alone."

"But you aren't going to go, Khaterah, if this happens." Aspen turned to Heath. "Neither are you—wedding in just over a week, remember?"

Timbrel propped her feet on the table and slumped back. "Well, you don't have an excuse to shove me off the cliff of friendship, so don't even try. If this thing happens, I'm stuck like glue to you."

"Why?" The question wasn't meant to be confrontational, but Aspen had never seen Timbrel show that much interest in their affairs. "Why do you care so much?"

"Because." Timbrel narrowed her brown eyes. "I'm not letting him get the best of you."

"Get the best of me?" She tried to keep her words from pitching, but with the heat creeping into her face, it was a lost cause. "I am former Air Force—with the JAG. I am twenty-eight years old and perfectly capable of taking care of myself."

"Oh, don't I know it," Timbrel said. "But two girls who can kick butt are better than one. And if this guy shows me it's necessary, I will take him down. Blue eyes or not."

Austin, Texas

"You grounded me!"

"You went dark. I had no guarantees you weren't dead or under coercion." A laugh erupted. "I still don't."

"I gave you the nonduress code."

"Mm. So you did."

Cardinal bit down on the curse that lingered at the back of his throat. This wasn't about Burnett thinking he'd been captured. This was about the general exerting his *influence*. About the general putting Cardinal's wings to the flame. Or trying to clip them and force him to be his own personal carrier pigeon.

He turned and strode to the window overlooking downtown Austin. Hand on the cold pane of glass, he steadied himself—memories, virulent and agitated, coiled around his mind. Shoved him back. Away from the glass. Away from the drop. Away from the memory.

He fisted a hand, ready to drive it through anything painful. Being forced to do something was one thing. Being trapped was another. He'd been shut down once before. Ten years ago. But it'd been too late by then. Cardinal had already escaped.

"You know I can get around this." He'd become good at going off-grid when he needed to. Burnett knew it, too.

"You're right, I do." Creaking seeped through the line as the general let out a soft groan of relief. "Which makes me wonder why you haven't."

Cardinal looked away. From what, he didn't know. The city held no threat. The phone neither.

"What are you running from?"

The truth. The past. The angel.

"I think you know deep inside, you're supposed to help this girl. I think the fact that you had a hand in her brother's disappearance makes you feel like you owe her something."

My life.

"But. . ." A slurping sound tickled the earpiece. Burnett burped. " 'Scuse me." A breathy grunt emitted as he caught his breath. "There's more to this. You're antsy. Jittery. Do I need to know something?"

Cardinal killed the line. Thudded his forehead against the wall. He turned back to the hotel room and sighed. He slumped on the bed and stared back out over the city. Then the sky. Clear blue sky with a few streaks of clouds. But mostly sun. Lots of sun. Texas heat that had surely fried his brain. Then why did it feel cold and cruel, like winter?

When he'd left Aspen at the ranch, he'd done nothing but drive— that is, after he'd disabled the GPS. No need for unnecessary monitoring by good ol' Uncle Sam. Down to the Gulf. Back up. All day spent trying to unwind his mind and body. His muscles ached.

His heart ached more.

At a moment like this in the movies, the hero would tug out a photograph, stare at it longingly, stuff it back in his pocket, then move on forcefully.

He didn't have a photograph. Refused to allow himself mementos. Anything that could connect him to the past. Anything that could be held against him or used to cripple him. Nobody knew about those things. Nobody would have that much power over him. Ever.

Besides, she'd fallen off the map five years ago.

Bent forward, he laced his fingers and rested his forehead on his knuckles. Going forward with this mission. . .it felt like the complete undoing of everything he'd worked for. But that would mean abandoning the one man he'd mentored. Trained.

Cardinal had failed him. And sitting here not tracking him down wasted time.

But doing this, with Aspen—

"God. . ." The prayer died on his tongue. Cardinal closed his eyes, focused. Yearned for some indication, some sign of what to do.

In the distance, a sound resonated through Austin.

Pulled to his feet at the somber sound of bells, Cardinal grabbed his room key and tucked it into his pocket with the phone. Out on the street, he headed toward the capitol. Light peeked at him between the buildings. Then the shadows lengthened. On Lavaca Street, he hesitated before the prestigious First Methodist Church building. Striking with its columns and pale plaster, it certainly bespoke the austere setting. Pretty. Beautiful even, but. . .no church bells.

Cardinal continued down the street and banked left onto 11th. As he walked the length of the lawn that stretched before the great building of the Lone Star state's seat of power, he admired the structure. The lines, the dome, the architecture. So dominating. Spoke of power. Prestige.

Power corrupts.

He'd seen the fruit of that as a boy. In his father. His father's friends. Even missionaries in country. Everyone wanted power. Those once thought to be nice, kind people had climbed the backs of friends to get to the top.

Cardinal strolled to the corner and looked up and down San Jacinto Boulevard. He crossed the street then glanced right. Block letters adorning a white limestone building drew him down San Jacinto. The darkness in his soul shifted as he crossed onto 10th and strolled along the white stone building to the front steps.

He peered up. Smiled. Bell tower.

As if some force gripped him by the shirt, compelling him into the sanctuary, Cardinal climbed the steps. Inside, he paused. Breath stolen, he waited for the warmth to flood him. He couldn't explain it. Just. . . *knew* things were different inside a church.

The great stained supports that arced over the cathedral reminded him of a ship's bow. The apse bore striking columns that looked like marble, stretching up into the cobalt ceiling, dotted with gold stars. And there in the center hung a stained-glass depiction of Mary. No doubt the one they'd named the cathedral after. And below it, on His cross hung her Son.

Jesus.

Cardinal slipped between two pews. Hand on the row in front, he eased himself onto the gold cushion, his gaze fastened to the altar. The stained-glass windows that gleamed overhead and along the walls bathed him in a warm embrace and a strange glowing wonder.

Here. Here he could focus. Could sort out the insanity that had threatened him.

He sat, thought, silently talked—to whom, he didn't know. . . He lowered his head, shutting out the chaos. The forces vying for his allegiance. His obedience.

As he had every time before, he whispered, "God, if you're there. . . help me." Desperate. Sloppy. But it was all he had. If he said more, he'd berate himself for talking to someone invisible. Intangible. Unprovable. A god for the weak minded.

That's what his father had said of his mother's faith. One of the many *kinder* things he'd said of her and her Christianity.

The comforting rays of sunlight through the stained glass that lined both walls faded and gave way to low-lit sconces. Though his inner self had quieted, he had no answers. For anything. So he stayed. Stared at the likeness of the crucified Christ.

"He was a madman who claimed to be God! Of course they killed him!"

68

Mary hovering over her son, ethereal and gentle with blue eyes and the Anglo appearance. He'd always smirked at that.

"She was a whore! She got pregnant and lied to cover it up."

Cardinal hung his head with a dangerous thought lodged in his mind. *No, Father. That was what you did to my mother.*

Crack! A scream knifed his soul. He clenched his eyes. Blood. She'd bled so much. . .

A noise. . .repetitive. . .

Cardinal peered up at the altar, attention trained on the *click-click* on the stone floor. What. . .it sounded like. . .dog's nails. Here? In a church?

A shape took form at the end of the pew. A feminine form. He turned his head, coming to his feet. Something swirled in his gut as he looked into pure blue eyes. Hair a halo of white. Just like Saint Mary in the stained glass. Or an angel. The thought pinged through him. Amadore had called her that, and here she stood in this church just like one.

She smiled then looked down the aisle toward the altar. Taking it all in.

His heart beat a little heavier. And faster. He wanted to ask how she'd found him. Here, of all places. He shouldn't ask. It showed weakness. Showed he hadn't been smart enough with his moves. "How did you find me?"

"Heath knows a general who tracked you down. Heath is engaged to a good friend of the general—actually, one of his former employees."

He looked down and shook his head. Burnett. The general had sold him out?

"He said you liked churches." Again, she glanced at the altar. "Cathedrals, in particular."

It wasn't forgivable that the general ratted him out, no matter how vague the tip he'd given. The video camera in his head played out a scene where he stormed out of St. Mary's, shouting into his phone about being sold out. Of him walking away from this.

But that's why Burnett sent her here. Gave her enough information to find him—so she could corner him. So those blue eyes would peel back the years of hardness. To whittle down what little he had left of his identity. To break him.

Force him to face what he didn't want to face: That despite his fears, despite his rigid determination not to, Cardinal knew he had to take this gig. He had to help Aspen find her brother.

Since he already knew the answer, maybe the reason he'd come to church was to toss it back in God's face.

Cardinal focused on the structure of reverence and solace, not on the tumult roiling through him. "It's a lost art, churches like this." His gaze traipsed the bowlike supports, the stained-glass panels standing like sentries around them. . .and collided with those blue eyes.

"It's a good place to be." Her voice was soft, almost a whisper, as if talking might offend the heavenlies.

And yet her words felt like just the beginning. He wanted to know what followed. "When. . . ?"

Aspen shrugged and shook her head. "Always." Perspiration made her face glow. The blush in her cheeks wasn't because of him, so he knew she'd been walking for a while. Searching churches. Searching for *him*. Why did that do strange things to his mind, the thought of her looking for him? Desperation had him culling the possibilities.

Back on track, Cardinal. He pointed to the Lab hunkering at her side. "He probably shouldn't be in here."

"He's a working dog, so technically they can't throw him out. Besides, I wouldn't have found you if it weren't for Talon." She beamed. "About two blocks over he got a hit. Nose to the ground, he was hauling in scents and moving." She giggled. "It was amazing. I haven't seen him do that. . .well, ever!"

Startled, he looked at the dog and tried to school his expression.

"I mean, I know you probably saw him doing it with Austin day in and out, but this was a first for me. Exhilarating." She lifted a red Kong ball from her pocket. "I owe him some playtime now."

"Then maybe he's ready." Oh man, he couldn't believe he was doing this. It was wrong. He'd slip down that slippery slope and there'd be nothing to anchor him. Cardinal started toward the back of the church, the thoughts pushing him out the door.

Aspen's lips parted, her mouth hanging slightly open. Expectancy seemed to hold her captive. "For?"

"A little adventure." He wanted to return the smile that twinkled in her eyes, but he didn't dare. "Eastern Africa." He owed this to his protégé. Owed it to Aspen.

She fell into step with him, Talon trotting alongside. "Then, you'll go?"

Understanding what it meant that she'd come looking for him, that she'd tracked him. . .that if she found out what happened in Djibouti, she'd never speak to him again, Cardinal knew he had to win her now or she'd be lost forever.

And if that happened, Austin Courtland was as good as dead.

UNDISCIPLINED

Brno, Czech Republic
Age: 14 Years, 3 Months

Nikol punched to his feet. Patting Petr's shoulder, Nikol stuffed the money into his hand. "I must go."

The girl took a tentative step forward, her hand raised. "*Okamžik, prosím.*"

He didn't have one moment, not even for her. Nikol's feet grew leaden at the soft voice. Move, he had to move or he would be caught. Heat and weight pressed against his chest, but he strode to the trees, toward anonymity.

A man stormed from a home—no, not *a* home. *The* home. The one she lived in.

"Who are you?" She rushed across the small yard. "Why do you bring the gifts?"

Hands stuffed in his pockets, Nikol tucked his head and hurried, his gaze on the trees.

"Please," she pleaded.

She couldn't know. Absolutely forbidden. Leaves crunched beneath his feet.

"Thank you." The shouted gratefulness carried past the crunch of the leaves beneath his feet and the rustle of branches overhead and wrapped around his heart.

A sob punched from his chest, but he choked it back. He stumbled. As the branches slapped his shoulders, he heard voices—adult voices. Closer. Nikol broke into a run. A branch lashed his face, stinging. As he ran, he felt warmth sliding down his cheek. He cursed.

Only as his foot hit the curb of the street where the bus would retrieve

72

him, did Nikol slow. In the devouring chaos of thousands fighting their way through life and crowding the streets, Nikol allowed himself to look back. Clear. No flushed faces or panting men.

At a corner shop he bought water and guzzled it. He had been careless. And for that, he might never be able to make the trip again. Disgusted and discouraged, he made his way to the metro line. Running his hand through his hair, he groaned. Rubbed his face—and cringed. He spun and used the window to eye the cut on his face. Red, swollen around the edges. The colonel would demand to know what had happened.

Nikol needed an excuse. The bus ride back would give him nearly three hours to sort it out, contemplate the fact he might never see Kalyna again. An ache squeezed his chest—the same one that marked her height. His mind flipped back to the yard. To seeing the girl. Cropped just below her chin, white-blond hair wreathed her angelic face like a glowing halo. She had the voice and blue eyes of an angel, too. A voice so soft and sweet. . .

What was it his father had said of his mother? That she had bewitched him with her voice and looks. That loving her had made him weak. Undisciplined.

★ ★   **Eight**   ★ ★

In Flight to Djibouti, Africa

Nothing but pale blue atmosphere embraced the plane as it climbed to cruising altitude. Clouds, rare and miniscule in the vast landscape of the horizon, peeked through the portal-shaped windows. Sunlight glinted against the plane's wingtip. Cradled in the seat, Aspen stared out at the sky that held beauty and wonder. It was so incredible. So amazing. The way the universe had been constructed. The way if the planets had been aligned one degree to either side, they would not have the view of the galaxies they had now. Amazing.

And somewhere beneath it all was Austin.

She couldn't let go of the hope that he was still alive. And it fueled her faith that Dane seemed to believe it as well. Otherwise, he wouldn't have agreed to this venture.

Hmm, maybe she shouldn't confuse his willingness to seek out the truth with her optimistic beliefs. She wasn't sure why he'd walked out. If she dwelt on his vanishing act, all sorts of doubts would plague her. The point was he came. And clearly, that decision upset him. He wasn't the same person she'd met at the ranch that day. Something was different about him. Something. . .closed off. But finding him in St. Mary's. . .

The man had a core strength of steel. Even his eyes mirrored it. But the cathedral, peaceful and reverent with the comforting sconce lights and candles, had revealed a vulnerability. It'd been one of the most surreal experiences she'd had, like seeing a reflection of a person in flickering candlelight.

74

"How did you find me?" His words had been husky. Charmed with the accent of the shadow of stubble and. . .

Something. She wasn't sure what, but it ensnared her mind since that night a week ago. The way he stood there, tension—but also surprise—radiating from his well-muscled shoulders and neck.

Who was he? Dane seemed like so much more than a grunt who'd worked the war zone with Austin. Why would General Burnett know the most likely place to find Dane? Where did he go when he left the ranch? Did he stay in Austin? Or was there a reason—or a someone—that drew him away?

Aspen tilted her head back, stuffed her fingers through the tangled rat's nest of curls, and groaned. *Why do you care?*

Because standing there beside him, wrapped in the serenity of that austere structure, she'd had this insane idea that there was a divine connection teaming them up. Okay, yes—definitely a crazy thought. Probably borne out of her finding him in a church. What was that about? Did he believe in God? Did he hold fast to his faith the way she did? At least, the way she *tried* to hold on to it.

Aspen glanced down at her hands and rubbed them together. Faith. Intangible in a lot of ways, but it felt so soluble, like water, in her hands when she grappled with it in relation to Austin.

A soft whoosh drew her attention to her right.

Timbrel slipped into the seat and groaned. "I hate flying." She adjusted her ball cap, then her jeans, then the boots, wiggled her shoulders as if burrowing into the seat like a dog turning circles in a field to flatten the vegetation. "If I could fly on a Lear with leather seats, champagne, and—" She held up a hand in a *stop* gesture. "Just give me a bottle of sleeping pills." She paused again. "No, just dope me up and knock me out."

Aspen couldn't help but laugh. "You were Navy. Didn't you have to jump out of planes in basic?"

"Jumps are one thing. Crammed in a mostly empty and entirely boring passenger jet, is another." She shifted in the seat to face Aspen. "So, spill."

Aspen raised her eyebrows. "About what?"

"About him, Mr. SexyKillerBlueEyes." A greedy gleam darted through her brown eyes.

Aspen sucked in a quick breath. "Quiet." She peeked between their seats to make sure Dane hadn't heard. Relief swept through her at the way he sat in the seat, head back, eyes closed, and mouth open a little. Sleeping like a baby. "You know as much as I do."

"So not true." Timbrel leaned in. "What dirt did you dig up to force him to come?"

"Dirt?" Aspen shook off the confusion. "I didn't dig up any dirt. We found him at the cathedral like Burnett said and. . ." Why would Timmy think they'd dug up dirt on Dane? "He came."

"And what?"

"And nothing." She shrugged. "He asked how I found him, and I told him. The next thing I know, we're"—she motioned around the cabin—"on our way."

"You're kidding, right?" Timbrel stared at her. Disbelief as distinct as her beauty. Whipping off the hat, Timbrel scowled and pushed herself straighter in the seat. "Please tell me there was more."

Aspen darted another look to Dane then back to Timbrel. "What do you mean? What else am I supposed to know or tell?"

Unease slithered through Aspen's stomach. What had she missed? How many times had Austin told her she was too naive? Though she'd vehemently argued it wasn't naivete but willingness to believe the best of people.

"He walks out, goes silent for ten days, then you find him in a *church*"—Timbrel rolled her eyes—"and suddenly he's back in the game? I don't think so."

Aspen eased back into her seat. "Just because you don't grace the doors of a church with your presence, doesn't mean it's not a legitimate way to seek guidance."

"It's not that." Timbrel wagged the hat as she spoke. "It's the whole thing—who is this guy? Seriously? He was with your brother? Then why wasn't he in the report? Why did he wait two years to give us the goods? To step up to the plate?"

"Timmy, I don't know. But he knows too much *not* to have been there. And now, he's here. He's willing to do something. He got us access to the military base—the same one that all but threatened to take legal action against me for"—she hooked her fingers for air quotes—"harassment. A team is waiting for us." Her anger over the insinuations strangled her excitement. "Nobody has been able or willing to help me get this far. I'm not going to look a gift horse in the mouth."

"I wouldn't look into that man's mouth—or eyes—for anything." Timbrel dropped back against the seat with a grunt. "And I don't like the way he looks at you."

"Don't." Aspen squared off, her heart thumping a little harder than it should. "Don't do this, Timmy."

"Do what? Look out for you when you won't do it for yourself?"

"No, don't rain on my parade. Again." Aspen drew in a steadying breath. "This is my one chance to get answers about my brother. He vanished. Nobody else died that day, nobody else got mangled or ended up with missing limbs. Yet my brother's entire body is blown to pieces—and so many, they can't even verify with DNA?"

Timmy averted her gaze.

Cuing Aspen into the awareness of having lost her temper. She slumped against the seat. Pushed her hair from her face and held it on the crown of her head. She let out a breath. Calmed, she let the tension out of her limbs and released her hair. "Please. Let me have this one chance. I'm not being naive. I'm not being gullible. I'm being reactive to a suspicion. Give me room to be an adult. To cement this once and for all."

"What if this guy isn't on the up-and-up?"

"If he wasn't, I don't think Burnett would've sent us after him." Aspen's pulse settled into a regular rhythm, but the anger hadn't quite settled. "Just give me this chance. I need it. Or I'll never forgive myself or anyone who tries to stop me from following through on this lead."

The petite brunette didn't say anything. She stuffed her booted feet against the back of the seat in front of her. "Look, I gotta protect what's mine, right?"

"Yours?" Aspen nearly choked. "What's yours?" Was she implying Austin—?

"Family." Timbrel's chocolate gaze bounced to hers then away ten times faster. "I've never had family. Not *real* family. My mom—" Red splotched her face, and she dropped her feet. "Well, anyway. I think of you like a sister. And"—she shrugged—"I'm just saying...be...careful." She stood and stalked away.

Aspen peeked up over the seat to see Timmy stalking to the rear of the plane. Family? Timbrel saw her as family? What little Aspen knew of the girl's story—that was as bare as the interior of this 747—wasn't pretty. Not anywhere close. Timbrel rarely spoke of family or her mother. So, to find out she thought of Aspen like a sister. . .

Guilt clutched her by the throat. She shouldn't have chewed Timmy out. Or lost her cool. Not when her friend meant well. And to be honest, Aspen hadn't really had much in the way of family herself since Austin went MIA. Their dad died when she and Austin were young, and her mom succumbed to cancer while Aspen was in boot camp and Austin on his first deployment. Having entered a year after her twin, she trailed him into military service. . .and was still trailing him.

As she eased back into the chair, her gaze collided with steel blue eyes.

Somewhere in Somalia

"*Now* what are we going to do?"

"Walk."

Mouth open, blue eyes wide, she didn't move. "Walk? Are you insane? There's nothing but desert out there."

Neil Crane did his best to stay calm. He didn't have energy to burn on getting angry. Or into a fight. . .again. "And back there are enough countries and ticked-off people to kill us for a thousand years." He stomped down the road, irritation and exhaustion clawing him apart.

"We don't have food or water."

He kept walking. *Thank you for stating the obvious.* He wouldn't give voice to his thoughts because she'd go off the deep end. Again. She'd been borderline hysterical since they'd escaped the last ambush. Fear drove her. That was good, it kept her alive. But it also kept her on his nerves.

Had things been different, he wouldn't have even brought anyone, let alone this woman. But circumstances had tied them at the hip for the last several weeks.

"What if they find us again?"

"I'm counting on it."

"What?" She hustled up a step to catch up with him. "What do you mean?"

78

"Somehow they constantly know where we are and what we're doing." He didn't get it. How were they being tracked? Going to the mines would be the last place they'd expect him. But he'd gone with some seriously high-tech gadgetry to try to get proof that had pushed him into this underworld. *Come out with the evidence, show it to the world, get my life back.*

That's the way it should've worked.

But the exact opposite happened. They were ambushed, lost their equipment while escaping, and he'd taken a bullet—in the arm. No big deal, he'd already tended it.

What had he done wrong? Mentally, Neil went over his notes, over the plays, over their moves. Just as he'd been taught, and he'd been trained by the best. It just didn't make sense.

As the night deepened, so did the silence and void between them. He'd thought he was in love with her. He'd never forget meeting her at the embassy gala. Man, she looked good in that red silk number. And she knew it. Lina Bissette, admin to a French envoy's assistant. Diplomatic relations swiftly turned to romantic relations between them.

Then things went south.

Neil wouldn't let this trip define their relationship, if they still had one by the time they got back. If she didn't stop blaming him and whining and complaining, he might kill her before then. Nah, he wouldn't kill her. It made sense, her fear and panic making her emotional.

Her hand slipped into his as they trudged down the dusty road. Resignation allowed him to tighten his fingers around hers. It wasn't her fault. Nor his. Getting out of Djibouti had been crucial to staying alive.

"Sorry," she muttered.

Neil pulled her head closer and kissed the top of her dusty, dirty hair. "We'll make it. Just trust me."

Trekking through the barren savanna that was Djibouti fried his brain. But onward he went, hand in hand with the woman who had stuck with him for the last four months. They'd been chased from a mine, hunted across the Sudan, and now walked for four days—well, nights were cooler so that's when they made their way across the land that had no natural resource. Thus the extreme poverty that landed Djibouti on the list as a third-world nation.

Get back to the hotel, dig out his secret stash of money and passports, then vanish again. That was his game plan.

"Do you think they'll stop looking for us?"

"Eventually," Neil responded, his mouth dried, his lips cracked. "As long as we don't blow the cover on their operation." The thing was, Neil had no intention of keeping quiet. He intended to rip this thing wide open, once he found the right vein and the right conduit under which to do it. "But I want to stop it."

"Do you have enough to do that?" She hustled a step to catch up with him. "You asked me to go with you—"

"No." Neil stopped and turned to her. "I told you I was leaving. And I said there were a lot of people coming after me—I told you it wasn't safe to stay with me. You could've stayed, made it to your embassy, and worked to prove your identity." She could've, but it would've been a long shot.

"Yeah, but you and I both know someone in that French embassy was involved, too. My passport suddenly invalidated? My name not showing up?" She shuddered then stopped short. Looked at him. "Did you want me to stay behind?"

"Lina, you're the best thing that has happened to me in years." Neil grunted. "Stupidest thing I ever did, leaving. Anyway, come on. We're about fifteen klicks outside Djibouti city."

"Listen." She tugged his hand and stopped him. "I don't think it's so smart to go back to the city. There are too many Americans there, and many who would recognize you."

"Exactly." He felt a smile for the first time. "It's the one place where I fit in, where I don't stand out. We just go in and act like nothing is wrong. Slip into the hotel room, get some food and rest, then. . ." What, he didn't know. He had information that could bring down a lot of people, and most of them didn't want him alive to breathe word of it.

"Then what?"

Squeezing her hand lightly was all the answer he could muster as they plodded down the side of the dirt road that led back to the city that had sent his life into a tailspin. An hour and a lot of blisters later, Neil led her to the bay of the Red Sea.

"Okay, let's dunk."

Lina gaped at him. "Dunk?"

"Trust me." He couldn't help the smile at the way her face almost froze in that expression. He'd seen a lot of that over the last few weeks as they navigated the perils of holding a secret nobody wanted leaked. Neil slid into the water and let the cool liquid rush over him. It felt good, after so many hours of walking dusty, dirty, rubble-laden roads.

He emerged from the water, dripping. Pushing the water out of his face, he grinned. "Ready?"

"For *what*?"

"C'mon." He took her hand and led her up the street to the Djibouti Palace Kempinski.

The bellman's white eyes shone with surprise as he raked them over with a disapproving glare. "May I help you?"

Neil gave a dismissive wave of his hand. "Sorry. We took a bit of a late-night swim. When I left my wallet on shore, someone stole it."

"Very bad luck, sir!" The man opened the door and ushered him to the counter, but his expression warned Neil that he didn't believe them. "Your name, sir?"

"Neil Crane."

The girl behind the counter typed his name into a computer. "Ah yes. Welcome back, Mr. Crane. We were concerned. It has been several days."

"Sorry. We were visiting a missionary in the area and decided to return for some privacy and a bit of luxury." He winked at Lina, who stood beside him playing the coy girlfriend. "Could I get a new room key?"

"Of course, sir." She placed the plastic card on the counter then handed him a piece of paper and circled some names. "Here are the names for the American embassy so you can report your stolen wallet. Your passport—"

"In the room safe, thank God."

"Very good. Thank you, sir. Have a good evening."

"Thank you." At the elevator, with Lina plastered to his side, he smiled at her. Kissed her for the benefit of those watching. Once inside the car, he dropped back against the wall.

"How long do you think we have?"

He eyed her. "Thirty minutes."

Nine

Camp Lemonnier, Combined Joint Task Force—Horn of Africa
Republic of Djibouti, Africa

Wheels touching down saved him from the void of her acceptance. At least, that's the way it felt—a void that he could vanish in. She accepted him, trusted him. . . . Innocence bathed her fresh confident face. Not naïveté as some might presume. She wasn't naive. He could see it in her mannerisms, in her dealings with others. But she *did* believe people were good.

A fatal mistake. Not that he would intentionally hurt her, but who was he kidding? Manipulating her, playing this game—how could she *not* be hurt? All the same, he had a job to do.

Backpack in hand, Cardinal hustled down the metal stairs and disembarked the plane, leaving behind Aspen Courtland and the baggage of guilt that came with her.

Four men emerged from a building and crossed the tarmac, warbling with heat waves. Compliments, no doubt, of both the heat and the plane's engines. The screaming whine of the jets slowed as the plane shut down.

A tall man with dark hair strode toward him, dressed in his desert camo and a pair of ballistic Oakleys. "Lieutenant Markoski?"

"Yeah."

"Captain Watters of ODA452." He shook Cardinal's hand. "Welcome to Djibouti." He angled a shoulder and pointed to the soldiers. "My team will escort you and the others."

Cardinal gave a curt nod then glanced up the flight of stairs where Aspen appeared with a leashed Talon. Due to anxiety, he'd been crated and sedated during the flight. His strong body hovered at the hatch. Panting in the oppressive heat, he looked down the flight of steps. Then his soulful gaze struck Cardinal and the military unit. Immediately the yellow Lab turned. Tail between his legs, he scurried back inside the cabin.

"Talon." Aspen's gaze darted to Cardinal before she hurried back in after the dog.

"That could be a problem," Watters said as quiet descended on the tarmac.

"Let her worry about that." But the captain had a point. A very sharp one that could poke a hole in Cardinal's plans. He climbed back up the steps. Inside the cabin and bathed in the remnant of cooled air, he found Timbrel slouched against a seat.

"What's going on?"

"Talon doesn't like it." Hogan slid her ball cap back on. "And neither do I."

Cardinal shouldered his way past her. "Well, only one of you is vital to this mission."

At the back of the plane, Aspen squatted at the wire crate that once again housed the Lab. Head down, Talon's brown eyes bounced between Cardinal and Aspen.

"He's shut down on me." Aspen straightened, arms folded. "He hasn't done this in months." She hunched her shoulders. "I don't get it."

"Yeah, but he does." Poor guy. If he already smelled danger and shut down, did they have any hope? "He knows this is trouble." Cardinal crouched at the crate. "Did your brother ever come to Djibouti with Talon?"

"Not that I know of. But then Austin's missions were usually SCI or above."

Cardinal nodded as he reached into the crate and rubbed his fingers along the top of the Lab's head. "Want me to carry him down?"

"No." She sighed. "I've seen him bare his teeth on those who force him into something he doesn't want to do."

Cardinal straightened and glanced at her over his shoulder. "Has he bared his teeth with you?"

She slowly shook her head. "No, but in a normal training session, I would give him a bit of space then reattempt the situation."

"But this isn't a normal training session."

"Exactly." She turned to him. "Look. I want to be honest with you—I'm not sure Talon is up to this. Maybe I got a little ahead of myself." Long fingers traced her brow.

"But we need him." He tucked his chin, feeling the tension tightening the muscles in his shoulders. "You know how to handle him, right?" He waited till she agreed. "And you brought him to find me, which he did."

"Yes," she said, her voice pitching. "But this. . .this base, the noise, the chaos—it's shutting him down. It's out of his comfort zone." Aspen gnawed the inside of her lower lip. "I think if we can get him out there, out of this plane and walk him, let him know there's no danger out there, he'd be okay."

"But there is danger."

She blinked. "Right."

"Can you carry him down?"

"He's seventy-five pounds of muscle and heartache."

"And you carried a sixty-pound rucksack in boot camp."

"That's different."

"Yeah, only in that you strapped the ruck to your back because some burly sergeant shouted at you." He raised his eyebrows and looked around the interior. "Here, it's your choice. You're bailing."

"Excuse me?"

He wanted to grin at the fire that leapt into her blue eyes, and it fed the fire in her gut. And then a fire lit through him realizing he was working her, a maneuver so easy and effective, it almost never failed. "Fear. I see it in your face. You have doubts about this mission. You want to get your brother back, but you're second-guessing yourself. Dump the doubts and the excuses."

"How dare you! That's my brother—"

"Then do something. Find that strength that got you through boot camp, that got you into JAG, and show this dog who's in control." Cardinal's chest heaved. *Easy there. Take it easy.* "Put on that confidence you wear so well and carry him down. Show him you mean business. Show him this isn't therapy. He needs to know you're not afraid. *I* need to know you're in the game to the end. I have a lot to lose if you aren't in the game all the way."

Aspen swallowed and wet her lips. She hesitated before brushing those long, loose curls from her face. Without looking at him, she squeezed past him. Then stopped and looked back. "This is about Austin, about finding out who did this to him. Don't ever. . .*ever* think it's about you."

A war erupted in his chest—pride over her gutting it up battled the disappointment that stung briefly that she wasn't willing to be honest with him. He saw her fear. Read it in her body language. In her hesitancy with Talon.

He stepped back as she squatted and reached into the crate. Talon darted her a nervous look as she hooked her arms around the broad part of his chest and beneath his hindquarters. She hauled him out then pushed to her full height.

Cardinal raised an eyebrow at the sight of her arching her back to balance the large canine overwhelming her upper body.

"What?" She grunted as she angled around him.

"That's a lot of dog—and drool."

Anger still colored her cheeks with a pink tinge. "It's nothing compared to Timbrel's hound."

"He's not a hound," Timbrel called from the front. "He's a bull-mastiff. I weigh his love in gallons of drool."

"That's disgusting," Cardinal said with a chuckle.

"Only to the uninitiated."

"Then, *please*, don't initiate me." He paced Aspen as she navigated down the steps, his heart in his throat at the steep incline and her struggling to see around the dog to place her feet.

At the bottom, she set Talon down. Ears back, head tucked, Talon started lowering himself, but Aspen broke into a jog. "Yes! Let's go." She cast a look in Cardinal's direction as she trotted away. "Where to?"

A woman with stamina, determination, and siren-like blue eyes. . .

He wouldn't come out of this mission unscathed. Neither would she.

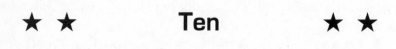

★ ★   Ten   ★ ★

If a guy talked to me like that, he'd be next week's leftovers." Timbrel shoved open the door and held it for Aspen, who led Talon into the conference room. With the heat, the confined space smothered her with claustrophobia. The long table and chairs didn't help. Considering the chipped paint, the scuffed cement floor, and the chairs that looked like they were *literally* on their last leg, she got a swift picture of the state of affairs here in Djibouti. She couldn't imagine this room with another dozen or so bodies stuffed inside.

But that was just it—there *should* have been a dozen others. "Guess we're early."

"Or they're late." Timmy hopped up on the table and dangled her legs. "Okay, so seriously—don't let this guy railroad you."

Aspen tugged the red ball from her leg pocket and showed it to Talon. Tail wagging, he panted his excitement. She rolled the ball across the floor since there wasn't room for a good throw. He turned, hesitated as if saying, "Now why did you do that?" then lumbered after it.

"Look, I get it—you're a good girl, you try to be nice." Timbrel hiked a leg up and hugged it. "But that guy? Don't give him an inch or he'll take the whole freakin' world from you."

Aspen reined in her frustration. "Timmy, relax. I'm not letting him take anything." She pointed to the ground, indicating Talon should drop the ball at her side as he returned with the slobber-covered toy.

He deposited it at her feet then settled on the floor. She sat on the ground, her legs stretched out and ankles crossed. Talon reclined against her, his side pressed against her thigh.

"I know you believe that," Timbrel said. "But I've seen you drop your guard before."

"And you don't?" Aspen shouldn't have said it, shouldn't have let her frustration get the best of her.

Tension radiated through the gorgeous brunette's face and shoulders. "Don't change the subject. This guy is trouble if you let him be."

"I'm not letting him *be* anything."

"Then why have you been all morose since we got off that plane?"

Aspen smoothed her hand over Talon's dense fur. Remembering the way Dane had spoken to her renewed her belief that he'd crossed a line. "You're right. He was wrong in the way he spoke to me." She didn't know him. He didn't know her. She took direct talk from her friends, but from a guy she barely knew?

Wariness shadowed Timbrel's features. "But?"

"But. . .he was right." She cocked her head, looking at the complete surrender of Talon's anxiety as he rested with her.

"How can you say that?" Timbrel planted her hands on her hips. In black tactical pants and black tank, she looked like she'd stepped right out of an action flick. "The dude totally dissed you."

"No, he put it straight. He got to the point. I needed to hear it."

"What are you saying?"

Admitting she was afraid, that she wasn't sure she could find Austin. . . What an absolutely basic, foundational problem. "What am I doing here?"

"Hey!" Timbrel's gruff, loud word snapped through the sterile room. She hopped off the table and stomped toward them.

Talon lifted his head, and though it was quiet, Aspen felt a rumble in his chest. She placed a hand on his side to reassure him. Timmy read his body language, the way he sat up a bit and eyed her, and slowed.

"Don't." Timbrel crouched on the other side, away from Talon, looking directly at Aspen. "Don't you dare do that."

Tears stung Aspen's eyes. "I'm not a warrior. I'm not a special operations soldier. I haven't even seen combat like you and the others."

"You're Austin's sister, and you have the most to lose if you don't find him." Timbrel's expression flared with fury. "*That* will get you where you need to be. Don't let that jerk get in your head, Aspen."

"He's not a jerk." Why on earth was she defending him?

"You don't get a vote on that right now." She leaned in. "You're the strongest woman I know. We're here to find Austin, and we're not going home without a mountain of proof either way. Don't let Mr. SexyKillerBlueEyes wiggle into that innate soft spot you have. Give him the fight of his life, and make him think twice about playing you again. Got it?"

"Got it." The voice boomed from the door.

Timbrel swiveled around and up as she faced off with him. "No manners either. You could've knocked."

Dane towered over them both by a head and shrugged. "Why? It's a public room."

"Courtesy," Timbrel said as she strode back to the table and crossed her arms. "Doubt you know anything about that."

"Probably not, since I'm a jerk who wiggles into soft spots." The smirk of a smile—did the man *ever* really smile?—squirreled through Aspen's hastily erected barriers, the ones Timbrel said she should have up. Was he taking the jibe she'd dished out in stride, or was he annoyed? Probably both.

"See?" Timbrel turned to Aspen. "The man confesses to it. Maybe *that* is why he was sitting in a church after ditching you—*confession*."

Heat flooded Aspen's face, and she widened her eyes at Timbrel, ordering her to cease and desist. The humiliation was enough knowing Dane had heard their conversation. She didn't need it worse.

But Timbrel had no effect on Dane. "Watters is on his way with the team and the plans."

"Where did this team come from?"

"Burnett."

Aspen hesitated. "Why. . .why would he do that?" How did everything suddenly become so easy and attainable? "I tried for the last year to get them to listen to me, and they told me to move on, get over it." Her pulse raced. Maybe they knew something. Maybe they—

"It's my fault." Dane looked sheepish. "By going public on the news, I made them dig deep and take a serious look."

His charm, his easy mannerisms pushed her back a mental step, forcing her to remember Timmy's warning. "How long has it been since you saw him, again?"

"Two months." A glint registered in his stormy eyes. Recognition. Awareness that she was questioning him, his story.

That awareness folded back on her and wrapped around her own doubts. "Do you think he's still here?"

He lowered his head as he propped himself against the table. "Probably not. If he's alive and hasn't contacted someone he knows, then that means he's either in trouble or causing it."

Aspen jerked. "Causing it?" Even as her words rang in her ears the indignation ripped through her chest. "What on earth does that mean?"

"Exactly what you think it means."

"Listen, Blue Eyes," Timbrel said, coming alive, "you don't get to talk to her like that."

"Yeah?" Dane crossed his arms over his chest as amusement and irritation surfed his rugged face. "So, you think Aspen would prefer I sugarcoat it, feign ignorance and stupidity to make her feel better?"

"Slick snot!" Timbrel let out a disbelieving laugh. "And everyone thinks *I'm* abrupt. This guy is downright mean."

"Not mean. Downright blunt. Being coy, playing roulette with truth isn't going to bring Austin home or get answers." He locked gazes with Aspen, and she felt as if he'd hooked into her soul, drenching her with resolute strength. "I'm not going to play with your emotions by shoveling platitudes down your pretty neck. And I won't give you false hope or play nice." His face hardened. "I *don't* play nice. I play to win. Can you handle that?"

Aspen swallowed, shaken by the ferocity and virility of his words.

"Because if not, then we need to part ways. Now."

Part ways? With the single hope of finding her brother or the truth about his disappearance? "I wouldn't want it any other way. I might be nice or a good girl, as Timbrel says, but I don't quit." She hated when people felt the need to protect her instead of fighting *with* her. "I don't want to be pampered." She gulped the adrenaline then gave him a curt nod. "Thank you for knowing the difference."

Silence dropped as he stared at her for what felt like minutes.

The door swung open, and a flood of uniforms entered.

"Whoa! Thank You, God!" One of the men with a sandy blond beard and Oakleys clapped a hand over his chest. "Be still my beating heart!"

Timbrel groaned. "Not you again."

"Candyman at your service." He grinned and tugged off the shades.

"Baby, I was right."

Aspen watched as Timbrel moved a foot back, taking a defensive posture. Yet she didn't move. Didn't punch. Or strike out, not even with words. Hesitation silenced Timbrel as she gave the guy a sidelong glance. "About what?"

"Told you a face like yours would inspire a man to stay alive." He held out his hands. "And hooah! A year later, here we are, and I'm still alive."

Timbrel's eyes narrowed. "I can fix that."

"Down boy," a guy with a dark brown beard intercepted with a grin. "I'm Captain Watters. First op will include medical escort to Peltier Hospital."

Aspen frowned. "Why are we doing that?"

Watters turned to her. "The Djiboutians need our help." He grinned. "And for cover—we can look around, ask questions without attracting attention."

"Without attracting attention?" Dane snorted.

Aspen wasn't following. "What?"

Dane met Watters's gaze. "She has white hair, fair skin, and is pretty. You don't expect her to draw attention?"

Peltier General Hospital
Djibouti, Africa

Loaded into a Cougar MRAP with Talon sitting beside her, staring out the window, Aspen smoothed a hand over his yellow coat. Such a handsome, noble-looking dog. So willing to go the extra mile, to lumber on even though he probably wanted to just go back home and trot around the safe environment of the ranch. She could relate. The mission had already set her on edge, upturned her expectations.

Crammed between Timbrel and Dane, Aspen considered the others. Watterboy, as the others had called him, and Candyman—the man who'd earned the moniker handing out candy bars to Afghan children to win hearts and minds and who'd taunted Timbrel from the moment he encountered her on their first mission—drove the second Cougar creeping toward Peltier General Hospital, where the medical team in the first vehicle would aide with surgeries and the like.

Timbrel groaned beside her as the front right tire hit another crater and jolted them into each other. "If I get bruises. . ." *Thud. Bang.* "You do know the point is *not* to hit the holes, right?"

"Sorry," Candyman shouted back. "Did I miss one?"

Sweat sliding down her temple, Timbrel glowered at the Special Forces soldier driving. "Next one, and I'll throw *your* head into the window."

Aspen elbowed Timmy, feeling the sweat and grime that came with being in an African country during one of their hottest months. Even though they'd just left the base and would spend the day in the city looking around, she already yearned for a cool shower when they got back.

One of Talon's drool bombs landed on Timbrel's tactical pants. She half groaned, half laughed. "If I didn't love dogs so much. . ."

Dane leaned forward, his arm stretched across the back of the seat, affording a little more room. "So, you prefer a drooling beast over a man?"

A caustic look slid into Timbrel's features. "Is there a difference?"

The front end jolted, then the deafening noise and jarring beating the Cougar stopped.

"Blacktop!" Candyman announced as he patted the dash. "Knew you could do it, baby."

"Thank God," Timbrel muttered. "Now, can someone teach him how to drive?"

Candyman shot a wink over his shoulder. "She's crazy about me, can't you tell?"

Aspen resisted the urge to laugh. The two had been dogging each other since they reunited. If she didn't know better, she'd think there was some serious romantic tension beneath all those jibes and cutting remarks. Well, not for Timbrel. But she worried Candyman might be getting some ideas about her.

Though only eighteen miles stretched between Camp Lemonnier and Djibouti proper, the atrocious road conditions slowed them. Now on the paved roads, they might make up a bit of time, but what was two minutes when it felt like the heat would bake flesh off your body?

As they turned onto Avenue Marechal, Aspen eyed the street of white buildings shadowed by trees and littered with women robed in black and their heads covered with vibrant, beautiful scarves. The town looked as if it had been designed in the seventies then never touched afterward. Still... "It's pretty."

"This side, yes." Dane sat on the edge of the seat, forearms on his legs. "Go farther north or west, and you'll find a stark difference."

"Why?"

"French embassy." Dane pointed to the building on the corner. "Farther down, a right onto Lyautey, and the American embassy is on the left."

Ah. Of course. Couldn't let some dignitaries or politicians live in poverty.

"Is that your way of saying we need to know where they are?" Timbrel's words held accusation.

"Ignorance is a swift road to death." Dane braced himself as they turned into a drive. The gate's overhead ornamentation reminded her of the outline of a stepped pyramid. The vehicles pulled forward.

Concern rippled through Aspen. "Why are we here?"

Hand on the door, Dane hesitated. "To deliver the doctors."

Her stomach twisted at the buildings around them. This? This was the hospital? She stepped into the unrelenting and balmy heat and stared at the buildings. Perhaps an inner-city clinic might look so dilapidated, but the main hospital for the city?

Talon sat by her feet on the dirt, panting. Aspen looked from one building to another, the familiar arches and the stark white, the smattering of pebbles that almost formed a road through the compound. . . She couldn't fathom seeking medical help in a facility like this. She fed Talon some water then ruffled his fur. Red lettering over the doors—in French, leftover from the French influence and control of the country—identified the buildings. *ORL MAXILLO FACIALE.*

"See?" One of the doctors pointed down the drive a bit. "New facilities. Slowly, they are making progress."

"U.S. has donated a lot."

"Including hands-on help." Aspen nodded as they followed the medical team into the multistoried building.

Over the next half hour, they toured the grounds. No marble tile or slate linoleum that lent a sterile feel to the hospital. Cement served its purpose, and where more sterility was demanded, tile covered 80 percent. Her heart misfired as she saw the building marked *PÉDIATRIE*. Around the entrance of blue-painted wrought iron stood several Muslim women, covered head to toe. Some held the hands of children.

Oh, Father, no. Aspen's stomach tightened. She could endure and tolerate a lot of things, but seeing children in pain or hurting... A touch at the small of her back startled her.

"You okay?"

She peered up into the steadfast gaze of Dane. And felt foolish. "Yeah. Sure." She shot a look at the pediatric unit. A cold, wet nose nudged her hand, pulling her attention toward Talon. As quick as she looked down, he trotted ahead, aiming straight for the children's building. Blue trimmed the windows, curiously drawing her attention to the window AC units that had discolored to a dirty tan. Shrubs poked up from a hard-packed dirt flower bed. Not exactly the lush green lawns found at most American hospitals, but it added a bit of green to the stark landscape.

"This is unbelievable," Timbrel whispered.

"Djibouti struggles," said one of the doctors who led them onward. "Two out of three children will face life-threatening medical problems due to poverty." He grinned and pointed to Talon. "I bet the kids will love to see him."

"He's not a pet," Timbrel warned.

The doctor hesitated. "Will he be okay?"

Aspen smiled. "I'm sure he'll be fine." In fact, she'd taken Talon to parks to help him adjust to sounds, to learn that not every loud noise was a threat. He still had a long way to go, but the handsome guy had come far.

Inside, the doctors quickly made their way to a multibed open area where children lay in hospital gowns, bandages here and there, IV lines snaking in and out. Brightly colored cartoon characters were painted on some walls, their perspectives a bit distorted and odd against the aging wood, peeling trim, and dirty tile. Aspen cringed. This would never fly in America.

As they made their way over to the bed of a little boy, who sat up in the bed, his leg propped on a pillow, Aspen steeled herself. Why was it always so hard to see children suffer? Because they were helpless?

Because it exposed her own vulnerability?

Dr. Gutierrez nodded to Talon. "Hassan would like to pet your dog."

Gathering her courage, Aspen kept the lead loose so Talon wouldn't feed off her tension if she'd kept it tight. "Tell him to hold out his hand, palm up."

Gutierrez relayed the instructions, and the boy extended his hand. Small, brown, marked with scars.

Without any instruction, Talon nosed the boy's hand then swiped his tongue over it, eliciting a peal of laughter from the boy. Pride ballooned through Aspen's chest. It reminded her of what Austin's partner—and superior—had done for her when he'd first joined her family.

Talon sniffed the air. What, had he detected the strong antiseptic odor? He shifted back and glanced to the hall, bathed in shadows.

Trained on the hall, Talon barked. Then quickly sat. Aspen's heart climbed into her throat. She couldn't see anything down there, but Talon was rigid as a board.

The boy jerked visibly. Let out a scream.

Talon bolted.

$\mathbf{H}$e didn't see that coming. Aspen blurred past him. Cardinal glanced to the rest of the team, already swarming toward them. They broke into a sprint down the hall. She whipped to the right, out of sight. Pushing himself, he fell into the training that was first nature as breathing: memorizing his path, monitoring his surroundings, listening ahead and behind, formulating a plan, then a backup.

Boots and shouts erupted from behind. Another turn. A flight of stairs presented themselves at a cross section. He peered up then right and left. Behind him.

Watterboy pointed to Cardinal's left. "You go right, we'll cover this."

Cardinal lunged down the hall. Empty. He glanced back. The others were already backtracking. Hogan's face bore the fury of fear. "Where is she?"

Thud!

To his right, light burst from another hall.

"Talon," came Aspen's faint call.

She'd gotten farther away than he thought. He hopped back a step and spun around. They were on top of him. He felt the friction of someone else's elbow near his own. That ticked him off. Aspen was his responsibility. His priority to get her back home safely. No way would he be the cause of her death, too.

He burst out into an alley marked with aged buildings, dirt, a few dehydrated shrubs, dirt, a chain-link fence to the right, more dirt, and sun. Lots of sun. It felt like they'd stepped into a sauna. Sweat streaked down his back.

One of the men cursed.

"Aspen!" Timbrel shouted.

"What do we do?"

"I didn't think Talon could move that fast," Timbrel said. "He's been nothing but lumbering and moping since I met him."

"What spooked him?" Watterboy asked.

"No idea." Cardinal stalked south of the pediatric building. There were any of a half-dozen routes they could've taken.

Hands cupped over her mouth, Timbrel shouted, "Aspen!"

Another curse.

"Hey," Candyman said, "watch the language. There's a lady present."

"You wouldn't know one if you saw one." Timbrel called out to her friend again.

Candyman grinned. "She's in love with me."

For that, he was punched by two of his teammates as they fanned out, tense and alert, checking corners, alleys, buildings. Cardinal felt the heat—the 110 degrees and the scalding his conscience gave him for losing his target.

He turned, thinking he'd heard a dog bark. Head cocked to the side, he listened...

Hands stabbed at him.

Deflecting the move was instinctual. But he hauled those instincts in as he registered Hogan shouting something. "...fault. You better find her." She'd drop him in a heartbeat. That is, if he let her.

"Shouting at me won't help us find her." Cardinal ripped out his phone. Punched in a number. Then a code. "I need eyes." Teeth grinding, he stalked toward the gate, checking in, around, under, and over anything possible.

"Aspen, where are you?" Hogan's shout reverberated through the hospital compound. Curious eyes peeked out of windows. Others stepped outside, watching as if they were some freak street sideshow.

"Here."

The ever-so-faint word threw him around. He sprinted down the dirt road. South. Straight south. That's the direction it'd come from. Aspen. He wasn't one to panic. But this was close.

"Here."

Just as her voice reached him, he saw paw prints in the dusty dirt.

"Over the fence," she called.

Unbelievable. The dog had to have hopped up on that crate and leapt over the fence. It was several feet. But if he never stopped. . .incredible. Cardinal vaulted over it without a second thought. He touched the tarred alley that led back to Avenue Marechal.

Another dozen thumps and he knew the team had made it. He reached the corner, his breathing just above normal. Staying in shape benefited his career. Scratch that. It benefited staying alive.

Across the unenforced intersection, past a cluster of trees, a street led to what looked like a field. He shifted around and looked down the road. . .alley. Nothing.

A flicker to the left snagged his attention.

Aspen around the corner, already on Lyautey, waved before she started running again.

"Got her," he threw over his shoulder. He stepped into the street. The wail of a horn nudged him back. Another car practically kissed the bumper of the first, but Cardinal launched himself over it to get to the other side. He aimed left—then skidded to a stop.

A rippling movement.

There, down that alley that led to an open area.

Talon!

Cardinal plunged down the alley. Pumping as hard as his legs would carry him. Blanketed in the shade of the buildings and the small trees lining the road, he pressed on. Thudding boots trailed him, followed by shouts and streams of communication one of the men had with Command.

He burst into the sunlight again and slowed. Where had she gone? He searched the circular area that looked as if it'd been cleared for building something. He breathed a little heavier, ignored the sweat sliding down his chest. His neck. His back—for cryin' out loud! He was drenched.

Aspen trotted toward them, gulping air. Red splotches glowed against her white-blond curls now a sweat-stained brown. Hands on her hips, she shook her head. "I don't know what's gotten into him."

"He's tracking," Timbrel said.

"Tracking *what*? There wasn't. . .anything in that children's"—she swallowed—"ward," Aspen said with a gasp, still out of breath from the run. "And where did he go?" She threw her hands up and walked out into the middle. "Talon, come." She took a draught from the CamelBak strapped to her spine. She lifted a whistle, placed it between her lips, and blew.

Nothing.

"That thing even work?" Cardinal asked just to open the conversation. He knew it was one of those that emitted a high-frequency signal.

Worry lined her fair features. "He can hear it. Up to two miles."

A string of old buildings lined the property on the northern side. To the south and southwest more recent buildings or those that had been updated. Like the Sheraton and casino cradled at the corner.

"Command ordered us back to base."

Aspen spun toward Watterboy. "I'm not leaving without him. You shouldn't either—he's a soldier, just like you." Her shoulders dropped, and Cardinal could almost read her thoughts, *or he used to be*. She scanned the area. "Just give me five more minutes." Brows knitted, she looked ready to cry.

And in some weird way, that twisted Cardinal's heart. "What can I do?" It was a stupid question. Even as it rang in his ears, he berated himself—*what can I do?* Find the dog! But it wasn't that he asked because he'd had a brain fart.

No, the reason behind that question was far more dangerous. Because with those words, he knew beyond a shadow of any doubt or intention, he would break a Cardinal rule: Never be at the mercy of another.

"Find him." Aspen felt like she'd just placed her heart, her very life, in the hands of a man who had the power to be her undoing. He knew too much. Like the words to say to convince her to do anything. The words to twist her soul into knots until it took hours—as it had last night—of quiet meditation on God's Word to untangle it.

She chided herself, being on this mission to find her brother, but her thoughts constantly straying to this man. Blue eyes. Broad shoulders. Trim waist. Powerful chest and arms. But an even more powerful presence. *Commanding*. He had that effect on most everyone. She was certain of that because of Timbrel's reaction. Like when water hit a hot frying pan. There's that initial explosion then the sizzling till evaporation.

Aspen chuckled to herself. *So, which of those two would evaporate?*

"What's that?" Dane asked, curving his spine a bit to bend toward her.

"Nothing." See? There. He'd done it again. Picked up on a cue she hadn't even realized she'd given off.

"Then you didn't hear me?"

Her heart slipped a gear. "What?"

Dane stretched his long, tanned arm toward the row of crumbling buildings with bent, broken, missing windows. One no longer had a roof. "A couple of those are on brick supports."

"Yeah?"

"He might've crawled under there."

The thought seized her. "That's what he does when he's scared—gets under something."

"Come on."

"What's going on?" Timbrel came up behind them.

"We're going to search the buildings." Aspen nodded toward the structures. "They're on bricks, so—"

"He might be hiding."

Nodding, Aspen fell into step with Dane. A move that felt as natural and comforting as if they'd held hands. *Whoa, chief.* She had to shake these thoughts. Stay focused on finding Austin. "He's been worse since we landed here."

Dane squatted next to a small building then skirted around the foundation curling away from the rest of the house. He tugged it back.

Growling burst out.

Dane grinned. "I think we found him."

"Talon!" Dropping to her knees, she felt a giddy bubble work its way up her throat. She touched Dane's arm. "Thank you." Palms pressed to the dirt, she peered under the building. Were it any other animal, had she not spent the last year coaching Talon through therapy and teaching him how to be a dog again, the hollow gold eyes glowing in the dark would scare the heebies out of her.

She resisted the urge to baby-talk him. Heath had challenged her on that the day dog and handler had met. Keeping her voice calm and controlled would help Talon's mental state. Knowing he could smell her fear, she stowed it. "Talon, come."

A high-pitched whimper.

Aspen dug his ball out of her pant pocket. "Here, boy."

Gravel and dirt shifted in the darkened area.

Repeating the command went against all the training she'd accrued. But she wanted to coax him out. This was different, though, wasn't it? He was in a dangerous place, with the heat and she wasn't sure what else. She did, however, feel like they were exposed and vulnerable.

"Command's ordering us back to the hospital. Temps are skyrocketing."

"Here." Candyman removed his SureFire and crouched beside them. He aimed it beneath the house. Light shattered darkness. "Here, boy." He looked at Aspen. "Want me to go in and get him?"

"No." Aspen lay on her belly. "If you go in, you block his only exit. He'll feel trapped."

Dark blond beard and green eyes considered her. "So, what you're saying is he'll bite my face off."

"That'd be an improvement," Timbrel heckled.

Candyman rolled onto his side and looked up at her, a hand over his heart. "I'm mortally wounded."

"Does that mean I get your weapon and CamelBak when you finally die?"

"Just give me room." Aspen nudged him out of the way. "Talon, come."

He belly-crawled a couple of inches then dropped his head to the ground with another whimper.

Aspen sought Dane's eyes. "This might take awhile." Like. . .forever.

He gave a slight nod then stood. "Why don't y'all get the vehicles and pick us up. Maybe with the tac gear and the heat, he's. . ." Why did that sound whacked?

"What? Having a flashback?"

Timbrel snapped her gaze to one of the men crowding around. "Yes, and if you could smell as well as him, you'd know how much you and your attitude stink."

"Hey," Dane said, cutting in, "just give Aspen some room to work with the dog. If we stress him, this whole gig will be one big fail." He rested a hand on Watterboy's shoulder. "Try explaining that to Burnett without a case of Dr Pepper and protective gear."

Watterboy considered Aspen. "Think you can get him out of there?"

"Yes." Which was another question, but doubts couldn't be part of this equation.

"You've got ten, fifteen max." He pushed back through the group. "Move out."

"I'm not leaving them." Timbrel squared off.

Watterboy stopped, and even with the shades his frustration was obvious.

"I'll stand guard," Candyman said.

"Done." Watterboy and the others headed out.

"I don't need your protection." Timbrel folded her arms.

"Baby, this wasn't about you." He tugged out a packet of jerky and squatted. "Think this will help?"

Appreciation swam through Aspen. "It's worth a try." She took the jerky and ripped it open.

Dane monitored Talon. "He lifted his head."

She tugged off a piece and tossed it to Talon. He wolfed it down. The next piece didn't quite make it to him. He scooted forward to reach it, chewing the dried meat.

"It's working," Dane muttered.

Excitement spiraled as Talon inched toward them.

She pulled the straw of the CamelBak free, took a mouthful, then squirted some water from the bite valve. Talon lapped and lapped. Aspen lazily tossed the last few pieces of meat, forcing him into the open.

"Almost—"

Thwack!

Gunfire!

Twelve

Fire streaked down Cardinal's arm as he threw himself into Aspen. Adrenaline muted the pain. Drove him. Used his momentum to hold Aspen in his arms and roll. Straight into the building. Heat licked the top of his head. He ground his teeth. "Under, under!"

Aspen folded herself under the building.

As they scurried beneath the crumbling structure into cover, he heard Timbrel and Candyman scrambling. This wasn't the smartest place to hide. But he'd hidden in worse.

"Base, taking fire, taking fire," Candyman shouted.

With about eighteen inches of space, they had no room to maneuver save a belly crawl. Flush against Aspen, he shifted. Or tried. Aspen hadn't moved, and he knew why—Talon's low growl.

"Who's shooting?" Cardinal shouted.

"No line of sight." Candyman sounded ticked. "Why's the dog growling?"

"Seeing your mug is enough to scare even the most-seasoned combat veteran like Talon," Timbrel said, a smile in her voice.

"Ha. Funny."

Though Cardinal couldn't see where Candyman and Hogan were, they were obviously close enough to hear Talon's rejection of this situation.

"He feels trapped," Aspen interjected.

Cardinal drew himself around, shifting and trying to get in a better position. The floorboards of the building scraped his arm. Might as well have poured lemon juice on the slice in his bicep.

As he did, he spied Aspen stretching her hand toward Talon. Cardinal tensed and waited for the dog to snap. Instead, the sound of sniffing blended with the thumps and cracks of bullets hitting the house.

Who on earth was pummeling them? Cardinal pulled himself along the belly of the building, ignoring the warmth slithering down his arm. . .then his underarm. . .and along his oblique muscle. Hand over hand, he used loose boards, exposed pipes, whatever, to drag himself around.

"What are you doing?" Aspen asked.

"Getting out." Cardinal finally had a decent view to the exterior but could not locate Candyman or Hogan. To the left, a thin beam of light fractured then reappeared. The two were holed up at the southeastern corner.

"Backup en route," Candyman shouted.

As if to confirm his words, in the distance screeching tires prevailed against the crack of weapons' fire. As Cardinal dragged himself between earth and wood to reach the north face of the building. Something glinted in the dirt. A rock? Token? The fact that something lay beneath this rubble of a building and was still shiny. . . His fingers curled around it, and he continued on. At the other side, a mere four meters or so, he shoved his feet against the splintering boards. It gave out, light fracturing the darkness.

He glanced over his shoulder.

Light streaked along Aspen—and his heart slowed. Blue eyes locked on him. Aspen had an arm hooked around Talon. "He's trembling."

"Can you get him out this way?"

"I. . .I think so. I have to, don't I?"

It wasn't really a question. And she was already scooting along.

"C'mon, boy." Her voice remained calm and authoritative. "Talon, go. Seek."

And as if another dog took over the Lab's body, scritching told of his movement. The sound of sand and dirt dislodged by his nails and soft pads joined with the affirmation he no doubt needed from Aspen. Something swelled inside Cardinal at the dog and handler. Or maybe it was just the handler. The no-surrender policy she lived out.

Even if it was the handler, what mattered was their movement. They weren't sitting ducks. . .dogs. Whatever.

Cardinal pushed against the skirting. It budged but not enough to release them from the suffocating, narrow void that felt very much like the underworld. Mentally, he ratcheted down the thoughts of the amount of space—or more precisely, the *lack* thereof—and trained his efforts on busting out. He swung his legs around and angled—

Whack!

He jerked back and cringed—he'd hit heads with Aspen.

"Sorry," she said.

He worked on setting himself, flat on his back, at a perpendicular angle to the skirting on the north side. "I probably did more damage with my hard head."

"I'll probably have a shiner," she admitted with a laugh that was anything but convincing.

On his back, Cardinal glanced to the side.

She was. . . Right. There. Wide eyes. Full lips. Prim nose. Innocence. Everything about her radiated a vibrancy that defied the shadowy underground they crawled through.

"What?"

Cardinal flinched. "Nothing." *Cad, you just gave her a black eye.* "Sorry. 'Bout the eye." Gripping the pipes, he shoved his mind back into line and his feet into the skirting.

Light erupted.

A breathy laugh skated along his ear and down his neck, flooding him with a preternatural warmth that had nothing to do with the Djibouti heat. *Get out. Before it's too late.*

"Let's go." He scrambled out into the open and stayed low, eyeing the road that stretched east and west in front of them. Empty. He wagged his fingers toward Aspen. "C'mon."

"Talon, go."

Soon soulful brown eyes twinkled in the sunlight.

"Good boy." Cardinal held out his hand, palm up, so Talon could reassess him.

Dirty blond curls rustled as Aspen broke free. Cardinal helped her up.

She drew in a long, greedy breath of air and exhaled it quickly. "I hate tight spaces." She smiled at him—and the red welt on her cheekbone glared back.

Noise from behind yanked him around. He reached for the weapon holstered at his back but stilled the instinct. Candyman and Hogan hustled toward them. "Team's coming."

A blur of tan burst around the corner. Dust plumed out, providing ample cover around the steel-reinforced vehicle. A door flew open. Watterboy jumped to the rear and leaned against the Cougar, watching. "Go, go," he shouted, waving them into the MRAP.

Bullets pinged the hull.

Candyman bolted to the corner and knelt, weapon pressed to his shoulder as he provided suppressive fire.

Cardinal reached back to Aspen, who stood to his five. Pain rippled down his side. He cringed but stuffed it. "Go on," he said with a nod.

She gripped Talon's collar and rushed into the safety of the Cougar, followed close behind by Hogan. Cardinal trailed them into the vehicle, landing hard on a boot, then shifting out of its way as he hauled himself onto a seat. Arm pinned to his side, he tried to quench the fire licking through his shoulder.

Loaded with Candyman and Watterboy, they were in motion.

"What happened?" Watterboy demanded, his face smeared with dirt and anger.

Cardinal glanced at Aspen with Talon sitting between her feet, stroking his ears. She didn't return his gaze, but he could tell she was aware of his attention. "Took fire. Don't know who or why."

Watterboy shook his head. "We're going to get our butts handed to us back at Lemonnier."

"Lemonnier?" Removing his helmet, Candyman snickered. "Captain, I'm worried about Burnett."

Heat spread through Cardinal's back and side.

"How's that shoulder graze?" Candyman asked. "Probably should have one of the docs check that out back at the base."

With a slow bob of his head, Cardinal knew he wouldn't. Medical attention meant medical records. A trail.

Never leave a trail.

Twenty minutes later, they unloaded at the base.

"Hey, that dog going to be a problem?" Watterboy asked, his tone providing the answer he expected. "Do we need to pull this mission?"

"No, I. . .he hasn't done that—"

"He hit on something." Cardinal stepped between them, a hand on

Aspen's shoulder as he guided her out of the conversation. "It means he's back in action." The mere motion of his arm at that angle made his side warm again. Wet trickled down his side.

His eyes closed for a fraction of a second.

Whirring air conditioners and chatter embraced them as they stepped into a building. He didn't know which one till he heard the clanking of utensils and trays: mess hall.

Aspen paused. Her hand came to his side. "Thank—"

Groaning, he arched his back, pulling out of her grip. Hot and cold washed through him. What was this? He'd been riddled before without feeling like this.

Blue eyes widened as she pulled her hand away, stained red. "You're bleeding!"

The weak smile he mustered wouldn't convince her. "A graze."

"Of an artery!"

"No, but thank you for your concern." He inclined his head and stepped away from her.

"Let me help you."

"I'm fine." Cardinal forced his body to comply, to walk out of the building, to head back to the bunks they'd been assigned for the next few weeks. *Let me help you.* She would help him. Straight into the grave. He'd made mistakes out there. Tripped up over a pair of ocean-blue eyes. Swam in them.

The bunkroom sat empty. He dropped on the striped mattress and dragged out his first-aid kit. Stuffed it into his toiletry bag. In the showers, he flipped the shower knob to cold.

Heated water blasted from the head.

Cardinal slumped. Of course. The water purifier only pumped hot water. To kill anything in the water. Maybe it'd kill the bad bacteria forming around his wound. Under the saunalike spray, he washed the wound, dug out the bullet, and sewed it up. Used the searing pain to remind him—not to fail. Not to. . .

She'd been so alarmed seeing his blood on her hand. Not just an apathetic "you're bleeding," but a—

Cursing himself, Cardinal spun the handle and cut the water. He had to gut this up. Get over it. Get the mission done. Get back to Virginia. Maybe. . .maybe he'd even go. . .home.

"Are you stupid?" She batted her long, black hair from her face. "*Shooting* at them?"

"They're getting too close. They need to go back, leave."

"Leave?" she shrieked. "They aren't going to leave. They're going to come looking for us."

"They won't."

"How can you know that?"

"Because, they're too invested in protecting the dog." It was a theory. One with as many holes as a strainer. "She won't put that dog in the way, not if she thinks he might get shot."

"She was protecting him."

He nodded, remembering how she'd pushed beneath the house to shield the dog with her body. Then the big guy had joined them.

Neil's bullet wound, though stitched, had become red and irritated so he'd gone to Peltier for antibiotics. He couldn't afford to see a doctor and expose himself. But he knew his way around the building. What were the odds the Americans would be there at the same time? And the Lab. . .

Neil wasn't trying to kill them. Just get them off his back. It'd been too close.

Everything had been too close.

In fact, everything had gone wrong. Two days ago at the Palace Kempinski, he'd taken a two-minute shower, dressed, and was stuffing a pack full of the items he'd hidden in the room when he heard squealing tires. He ordered Lina out of the shower as he checked the window. A dozen cars barreled toward the hotel.

They'd made it out the doors with barely seconds to spare. He hotwired a car, and they vanished down the street, where they abandoned the car ten minutes later. They'd been at the hotel less than fifteen minutes when he heard shouts and gunfire.

"Let's leave, get as far away—"

"No." Neil tightened his jaw. "They stole my life from me. I'm not leaving till I get it back."

Camp Lemonnier, Combined Joint Task Force—Horn of Africa
Republic of Djibouti, Africa

Slumping onto the thin mattress bed, Aspen stroked Talon's fur as he slept on the gray-striped mattress. The words Dane had shot at Watterboy still rang in her ears. Is that what happened with Talon? Had he hit on something? Or was he running scared? What happened had made no sense. They'd been there, he was fine, engaged the little boy, then everything went nutso.

It just didn't make sense.

It's why she came back to the bunkroom, why she'd found that lame excuse about washing off Talon. She wanted to talk to Dane. He had good sense.

Did he really think they'd find Austin? Why did she keep asking that question? Was it her doubt? If she truly believed they'd find him alive, these questions wouldn't haunt her. Right?

She felt the presence more than heard it.

Aspen pushed to her feet, heart catapulted into her throat as she found Dane standing on the other side of the steel bed. Hands at her side, she gulped the adrenaline burst—saw the angry red wound on his side.

"What are you doing here?" He snatched a shirt from his bag and stuffed his hands through the sleeves.

"I. . ." She ran her fingers along the ridges of Talon's lead. "What you said earlier to Watterboy, about Talon getting a hit on something and being back in action. . ."

"Yeah?" Dane ran his hands through his hair, but the strands around his crown dropped back into his face. Beautiful olive skin. A dusting of stubble that made him appear rugged. Those eyes that somehow managed to funnel strength and courage to her heart like an IV.

"I. . ." She sighed. "I'm not sure that's what happened."

"Then what did?"

She looked down at the seventy-five-pound dog, his oh-so-steady brown eyes, and the smile that tugged into his face when he panted. He had panicked. As he'd done before at the ranch. At home. In any new situation. He'd settle for a bit, but once he went into that "vigilance" mode, it was like trying to lasso a mountain.

She'd hoped. . .hoped so dearly that he'd be able to do this. But was it fair to put such high expectations on a dog? A dog with more hurt than courage.

The truth hurt. She braved Dane's gaze again. "I think he got scared and ran off to hide." She shrugged. "I mean, look where we were finally able to corner him."

He held up a hand to her as he retrieved his boots with the other, perched on the edge of the bed next to Talon. "Let's examine your theory." He threaded his socks over his feet—big, flat feet. Nana's old wives' tale about men with flat feet having a bad temper flitted through Aspen's mind. Though she'd seen him determined and perhaps a bit intense, she couldn't imagine him with a bad temper. It just didn't fit.

He let down one foot, booted but not tied, and lifted the other boot from the mattress. "Tell me what you remember—every minute detail."

Rubbing her forehead, Aspen let her gaze skip along the spidery cracks on the floor. "I was talking to the little boy. . ."

"And Talon was cool with that."

"Yeah." She remembered being proud of him. "He sniffed then licked the boy's hand. It was a good connection."

"Tail?"

"Huh?"

"Was Talon's tail up?"

She returned to that memory. "Yeah. . .tail and head. Ears were attentive but not drawn back."

"Right." Boots on, he started tightening the laces. "Go on."

She liked this, the going over details to pick out what happened. She used to do this sort of thing with Austin since their childhood, being latchkey kids—if you could call it that with a maid, a nanny, and a groundsman while Mr. and Mrs. Courtland were busy making millions at the family empire, Courtland Properties. Days gone of an era that she'd once thought gave her happiness. Her childhood hadn't been typical. But she'd come out fairly normal. What kind of upbringing had Dane had? He was so grounded, it had to be a decent one.

Back to the present, Aspen. "Okay, so Talon was fine one minute then barked the next."

"And the kid screamed because it startled him."

"Right, then Talon took off." Scared and looking for a place to hide. Hope deflated in her chest, pulling her courage with it. "So, see?" She was tired. Tired of working her heart out for Talon and believing beyond belief that Austin was alive. Tired of the doubts. Tired of the listing nature of her life. Tired of. . .everything. Even of being tired. She felt the tears burning, the prickling in her sinuses. And hated them.

In a rush, Dane stood over her, hands gently on her shoulders. "Don't go there, Angel." His voice was soft, gentle, like her favorite down comforter. "Don't give up on him."

"He's *not* better, Dane." Her voice cracked. Suddenly aware that her hand was on his side, heat flared through her and she removed it, wiping her fingers along her face to make the removal seem innocuous. "I keep thinking he's getting better, but he's not. How are we going to find out if Austin is here, if he's alive, if Talon can't keep it together?"

"Slow down there," he said, craning his neck to look into her eyes. "Think about it. When Talon barked, what was he looking at?"

"The boy."

Dane started to shake his head then slowed then gave a firmer shake. "Think—"

She drew in a hard breath as the memory spilled over her. Aspen widened her eyes as she drew in a breath. "You're right." A bubble of laughter trickled up her throat. "He was looking down the hall." Her heart beat a little faster. "I think he saw something or someone."

"Which means he had a hit."

"He didn't break behavior." Relief warmed her belly. She laughed. "Thank you!" She tiptoed up, threw her arms around his neck, and hugged him. "You're right."

Awareness lit through her as his arms encircled her waist and tightened. Aspen stilled, the realization sudden that she'd thrown herself into his arms. Then it coupled with the intense exhilaration that blossomed.

But. . .would he take it wrong? Would he. . . ?

Slowly, she eased back to the ground, her hand resting on his shoulder then onto his bicep. He must think her stupid. Or—loose.

She flicked her gaze to his.

And froze.

His fingers swept her cheek. The spot where they'd banged heads earlier. And trickles of electricity shot through her face and neck at his touch. "I was afraid it'd bruise."

Unable to keep her gaze from his for any decent amount of time, Aspen tried to maintain a smile, but everything in her felt ablaze. "I. . . I'm not as soft as I look."

Dane's eyes lowered to her lips.

Oh. . . Her breathing shallowed as his head dipped toward hers.

"No!"

Startled, Aspen drew up short.

Dane swallowed and turned toward the bed, reaching for something.

"No," Timbrel repeated as she stomped toward them. "You stay away from her!"

Indignation squirmed through Aspen. "Timbrel!"

"You don't know this guy, Aspen." Timbrel wore a mask of outrage and protectiveness, but something else was there. "I warned you—told you I didn't like how he was looking at you. Can't you see it? He's working you."

Dane swung around. And what Aspen saw in his face pushed her back a step. The rugged face, the gentility, the quiet powerful presence— gone. In their place, a terrifying fury.

SAFE

Back in St. Petersburg, Nikol disembarked the bus. As soon as his foot hit the cement, he stopped. *My backpack.* Breath jammed into his throat, he stared out at the bustling city. How would he explain that to the colonel? Fear swirled through his body, deadening him to the din around him. Was there anything in it that would identify him?

No, of course not. Another thing he had been trained to protect—his identity. Besides his national identity card, he carried nothing with his name or residence on it. The colonel vowed he had sworn enemies who would do anything to get to him.

Believing that was believing in Mikuláš.

A grimy window blurred his reflection—but also reminded him of the cut. *Need to remedy that.* But how? Rounding another corner, he made eye contact with a police officer then veered left and headed down an alley. Skirting a three-story building, he heard the heavy footfalls behind him.

Nikol continued on. Left, then right, he searched. Farther into the darker sections of the city. Should not be too much farther—

"Hey, you lost?"

Perfect.

Nikol turned. "What is it to you?"

The brawny kid came toward him. "This is my territory, that's what."

"As if you could stop me." Showing his back to the guy should be enough.

A gust of wind and a foul smell warned him of the attack. He let it come.

112

The guy grabbed his jacket, swung him around. In the fraction of a second it took to see the fist coming, Nikol angled his face so the guy would hit his cheek. *Crack.*

Pain shot through his head. His neck whipped back. Stupid kid missed—busted his lip instead.

Nikol drove a hard right at his opponent.

The kid stumbled but came at him again. Nailed him straight on.

Fire streaked through his face and jaw. About time. Nikol threw a flat-handed slice right into the guy's throat. The kid dropped to his knees, clutching his throat.

"Stop!" The police officer raced toward them, aiming a weapon. "Step back."

Hands up, Nikol shuffled away from the thug.

In the minutes it took another police officer to show up, Nikol closed himself off. Mentally compartmentalized. He had accomplished his mission, covered his mistakes.

"You belong to Colonel Tselekova."

Hands behind his head, Nikol merely stared at the officer through a knotted brow.

They laughed as the fatter officer stuffed Nikol's national identity card into his pocket. "He'll get enough punishment at home."

"But you saw—"

"Do *you* want to explain to Tselekova why he had to come down and pick him up?"

"I'll return him to the colonel," the younger officer said.

Silently, Nikol thanked God for the reprieve. Taking him into custody would have made it worse. Having documentation, having to experience the humiliation of retrieving him from a jail, the colonel's fury would be heard throughout the city. It had happened once, and though Nikol had been willing to endure it again this time, he had always done everything in his power to avoid another lesson.

"I ask not for a lighter burden, but for broader shoulders." His mother had said that a thousand times and then would clasp his shoulders and say, *"You will have broad shoulders."*

Nine hundred heartbeats passed before he stood at the door to the apartment, under the control of the officer who announced their presence with two hollow yet booming thuds on the door. Though Nikol tasted the blood from his lip, he cared not.

The door swung open.

Cold dumped into Nikol's stomach as the colonel towered over them both, darkening the doorway. Darkening life. Fury smudged a scowl into the steely features.

"Thank you, Lieutenant Kislik."

Chest puffed, the police officer relinquished control; gave a curt nod, then stomped off.

The colonel moved back without a word. Stood straight and stiff, demanding with his silence that Nikol enter.

Pushing every ounce of contrition into his face and posture, Nikol trudged inside. He paused as the door closed. There would be no dialogue—no excuse was good enough to bring shame on Colonel Tselekova. Or to arouse his anger. The offense didn't matter. A beating would commence. Always had.

Nikol did not care. He had accomplished his mission, and the colonel was none the wiser. Remembering the face of an angel, he turned.

Swift movement tensed him. The butt of a Tokarev collided with his temple.

The blunt force thrust him backward. He hit the wall. Blood sped down his face. As his vision ghosted, he had one thought: *At least Kalyna is safe.*

Thirteen

Camp Lemonnier, Combined Joint Task Force—Horn of Africa
Republic of Djibouti, Africa

Tame the fury.

Gaze locked on Aspen, on the widening of her eyes, the tension radiating through her frame, Cardinal hauled in the hurricane-strength storm that erupted at three words: *"He's working you."*

"I know your type." Red-faced, fists balled, and in a fighter stance, Timbrel stood between Aspen and him. "I know how you work on soft-hearted women—"

"Timbrel—" Aspen moved to the side, closer to Dane.

"No!" Timbrel whirled toward Aspen, who'd moved closer. "No, I'm not going to let this go. I won't let him hurt you. You're too good of a woman."

"And a strong woman capable of making her own decisions," Cardinal said, his heart pounding at her accusations, at the way she portrayed him to Aspen. "Give her some credit."

"Oh, I do, Slick Snot. But not you—and don't think you can put a wedge between me and her with your smooth talk and rugged good looks. Because it's so not happening." Her eyes narrowed. "Step off where she's concerned, or I promise I won't be so nice next time I see you moving in for the kill."

"Hey."

Cardinal wouldn't dare remove his gaze from this little nymph staring him down. But as he looked at her, he saw the truth. "I am sorry you've been hurt—"

115

"No! You don't get to get in my head. And don't even try to get on my good side." Her lip curled. "I don't have one. And if I did, it'd be booby-trapped to take your head off."

"Hey!" Candyman moved into Cardinal's periphery. "Are you people deaf?"

"Back off." With a shove against Cardinal's chest, Timbrel turned. When Candyman grinned at her, she glowered. "Did you have a reason to be here besides. . . ?"

Interest piqued, Cardinal watched Hogan and the Green Beret. A silent conversation seemed to carry on between the two.

Finally, Timbrel raised her arms. "What?"

Candyman nodded. "Sat chat with the good general." He shot a piercing look Cardinal's way. Then it softened. "Looks like we got a lead." He turned to Hogan. "Can I talk to you?"

"Isn't that what you're doing?" Though there was an edge to her words, it wasn't as caustic as before.

"Outside." The soldier's face betrayed nothing as he stood a step back, eyes linked with hers, and waited for her to move. With one more disapproving glare at Cardinal, he trailed Hogan out of the bunkhouse.

Aspen shifted to face him. "I'm sorry about that." She took Talon's lead. "She means well."

"I know. There's a lot of hurt beneath that explosion she just unloaded on me." He understood more than anyone could believe. But he'd been trained to conceal his anger.

As they started for the door, she hesitated. "Is it true?"

His world slowed into a painful rhythm. Cardinal wouldn't insult her by playing dumb, but he also would *not* lie to her any more than he had to and only where absolutely necessary for the interest of this mission and the safety of his asset.

"Are you playing me?"

"Don't we all do it?" He pointed to the bunk Talon had occupied a second ago. "Isn't that why you happened to be in here with Talon, so we could be alone and talk?"

"That's a pretty jaded perspective."

"It's realistic and logical. Just because we arrange situations to suit our interests does not mean it's bad."

Disappointment lurked in her eyes, but she said nothing. She knew as well as he did that he'd called her hand. But it'd hurt her. And that stabbed his conscience. Hand on the door, he stopped. Shifted toward her, noting that Talon sat.

"Thank you for playing me so we could be alone and talk." The words were meant to tease her, to reassure her—through a roundabout lie that creased his attempts to be honest and direct with her—not open a chasm of hope that lingered in her eyes and tempted him to fall in and never regret. But that's what happened. Especially when she flashed him a coy smile and slipped out into the sunshine, light ringing her white-blond curls in a halo.

Angel.

And you're the Angel of Death, Cardinal. Trust implicit, she had no idea who she was falling for. And falling she was. What made it worse, what made him want to cut out his heart with his own knife was that he wanted her to fall. He wanted the kiss Hogan had stolen. He wanted Aspen to believe in him. He wanted. . .her.

The thought slowed him. Sickened him.

Fists balled, he stowed those feelings. Those misguided hopes. And reminded himself of the venom that ran in his veins.

Pentagon, Arlington County, Virginia

Lance Burnett popped the top of his Dr Pepper, took a slurp. As he let out a slow belch, he spotted Lieutenants Hastings and Smith hustling his way. Hastings held a laptop and papers, while Smith juggled what looked like maps and a phone pressed between his shoulder and ear.

They burst into his office.

"What in Sam Hill is going on?"

Smith turned the blinds and shut the door as Hastings delivered the laptop, her expression hurried. "Cardinal got a lead."

"And why are we hiding?"

"Because, apparently, so did General Payne—on Cardinal." Hastings set down the laptop and pointed to the embedded window. "He's going to call in, but we only have thirty seconds before Payne's team leeches."

Lance gulped his sugary addiction then sat forward. As the Dr

Pepper splashed down his throat, he watched the screen activate with an incoming message. He accepted.

"Sir," Cardinal said, his brevity dictating he knew the call would be traced. "Local feelers report a missionary couple named Justin and Camille Santos sheltered a man matching our asset's description."

Lance grunted. Missionary. Often a cover story for spies.

"Got it," Smith said as he scribbled, his feet already carrying him out to research the names.

"On our last trip into Peltier," Cardinal said, his voice staticky in the connection, "we came under fire."

"An attack?"

Cardinal's gaze was direct and confident. "We're on the right trail." He glanced to the side.

"Agreed. How's the dog and handler doing?"

A flicker on the normally rock-solid face. "They're fine."

Lance frowned. "Good. We need them."

Hesitation lurked through the grainy feed. Then, "Agreed. I'm going dark for a while."

Dark?

"I'll code-in within fourteen days. Cardinal out."

The connection zapped. Lance stared at the screen. What was that about? Cardinal hesitant? Was it because of the girl, the dog, both? Mother of God, if something went wrong and Payne—

"What'd you see?" he asked Hastings, who sub-monitored the video feed and analyzed as the transmission progressed yet recorded nothing.

"A shadowy figure"—she angled the laptop toward him and showed him a reflection in the glass—"is just outside the room. A woman."

"The handler."

"Yes, sir." Hastings straightened, her lips pulled tight.

"Why's he going dark?"

"Most plausible scenarios—"

"No." He hadn't meant to speak that question out loud. Lance didn't need ideas. Cardinal felt it was necessary. Lance would give him the requested two weeks. "What else did you notice?"

"There were others, but they stood too far away for the reflection to be clear." Hastings swallowed. "And Cardinal wasn't himself."

Lance laughed and slumped back in his chair. "Himself?" He

muttered a curse and shook his head. "Hastings, if you know what 'himself' means when it comes to that man, then you're a better soldier than any one of the twenty analysts who examined, interrogated, and psychoanalyzed him."

Her face tightened. "I know a man when he's distracted by a woman."

Laughing even harder, Lance reached for his soda. "If you believe that, you *definitely* have no idea about our Mr. Cardinal." He waved her toward the door. "And don't let your feelings for Cardinal cloud your judgment next time."

She widened her eyes.

"Oh, give me the benefit of the doubt, L-T. You don't think I know what's going on under my own nose? With my own dadgum team?" He shooed her with his hand. "Go on. Do the research on"—he glanced at the transcript that autoprinted from the call—"the Santos couple."

"Sir, I—"

"Dismissed," he growled. At the click of the door, he dropped back against his squeaky chair and pinched the bridge of his nose.

Another rotten nightmare. Embroiled in international chaos.

Hastings was right. Something was off about Cardinal. On his computer Lance coded in, bypassed several security protocols, each one more advanced than the next, till he came to the file he wanted. Time for light reading. About a man he'd met in a cathedral in New York City eleven years ago. A man who'd refused to cooperate. Who refused to become a liar and a stealer of lives.

In espionage terms, in terms of recruitment, he'd been ideal—young, burned by idealism, a burning rage that drove him. Controlled him. Those types of people believed they controlled the anger. It was that illusion of control that men like Burnett turned on their ear to capitalize for the benefit of the United States.

Took a year to lure the guy in. But Cardinal had proven to be a brilliant asset. The kind movies and books were written about. That was exactly why Payne and Morris had vehemently objected to him. If that man went rogue, he could bring down everything. If he wasn't truly turning against his own country to spy for America...the damage would be unfathomable.

With the man's fiery conviction and determination to topple one of the most powerful Russians, Lance never worried that Cardinal would betray his trust.

Until now.

But maybe. . .just maybe Lance had a wild card. One that would ensure the loyalty and control of this asset.

Fourteen

N ertz!" Aspen declared as she slapped down the last card.

She and Timbrel high-fived.

Candyman banged a fist on the table. "I liked it better when you two were mad at each other."

Timbrel laughed. "We're best friends. Mad doesn't last for long. Besides, she knows I am just looking out for her."

"But," Aspen inserted, "Timbrel agreed to take it down a notch. Let me handle my own affairs."

Candyman and his teammate Rocket hooted.

Aspen rolled her eyes as she gathered up the cards she and Timbrel had played. "Oh grow up."

"Where is that old man anyway?" Candyman took a swig of his Coke.

"What old man?" Aspen shuffled the deck.

"Markoski."

"He's not old."

Candyman grinned.

"You're incorrigible."

Timbrel took the deck. "Don't *encourage* him."

Aspen laughed but silently wondered where Dane was. He'd vanished since their near-kiss and the fallout. She had counted every minute. At least, it felt like she had. She wanted to see him again. Liked being with him.

Shouts carried down the hall outside the rec room.

"Someone's ticked," Rocket said as he worked the cards like a pro. Sliding them in a snakelike pattern from hand to hand. Then shuffled them in rapid-fire succession.

A loud noise thudded through the building.

"What was that?" Rocket turned, his magic with the cards stopped.

Crack! A crash rumbled across the floor. *Thud!* A primal shout roared through the stale, not-so-air-conditioned air.

Candyman jumped to his feet with Rocket on his tail.

"I'm not going to miss the action," Timbrel said as she hopped to her feet.

Aspen called to Talon and joined the others in the hall.

Papers, chairs, and desks littered the entrance to a small conference room. Blinds hung askew.

"What the heck happened?" Candyman asked to whoever was in the room.

"...on my life, I will hunt you down...no, *no!* This is wrong. I'll kill you. So help me God—you knew this would—*no!" Crack!*

Aspen peered around Timbrel and saw Dane standing at the window, his hand freeing itself of the gypsum board wall it'd punched through. He faced away from them, a phone dangling from his left hand. He flung aside the device and planted his hands on his hips. He breathed—hard. She shouldered her way into the upturned conference room and stepped over a trail of papers. "Dane?"

He hung his head.

"What. . . ?" A certificate caught her eyes. Her heart stuttered as she reached for it, recognizing her own name. "What is this?" She couldn't breathe. This wasn't...wasn't possible. "Dane? Is this...a joke?"

He spun around, face a ball of rage. Stormed past her. Without answering her, he yelled to the others, "Out! Now!"

"I'm not leaving her with you, not like this." Timbrel's objection didn't contain half the ferocity Dane's had.

"If you value your pretty little head, you'll leave now."

Aspen jerked toward them, met Timbrel's bulging eyes. She gave a curt nod, trying to reassure her friend things were fine. But the paper in her hand proved things were anything but. Dane herded the others out of the room. Shut the door. Despite the damage to the blinds, he tried to close them, to no avail. He slapped the glass.

She flinched. Dropped her gaze back to the paper. Numb. That was the only word. "I don't understand..."

"Don't try." His voice was hard as he righted the table. From the floor, he retrieved the paper trail. Tossed it on the table. "I need you to understand something."

She snapped the paper at him. "Start with this."

He took it from her. "In a minute." He looked down, closed his eyes, and roughed his hand—with cracked, bleeding knuckles—over his face as he let out a hard sigh. "When they asked me to do this, I..." His chest heaved. Raw power rolled off him. "This isn't how I work," he said with a growl. "I do it alone. I don't need anyone. I don't want or care about anyone else."

"Next time," she said, staving off the stinging reproach, "slap me. It'll hurt less." She tried to stalk past him, her fear, her panic strangling sane thought.

Dane hooked her arm. "Please..." His shoulders sagged. "Burnett knows I'm the best chance of finding out if your brother's alive."

She braved his steely gaze. And saw the teeming agony.

"And you're the best chance of tracking him because of Talon."

"What?"

"I refused to work this case. Yesterday, I contacted him, said I was off the case. That I refused to go any further."

"Why?"

"So, he forced me. Forced my hand."

Why wasn't he answering her questions? "If you don't want to help find my brother, then I don't want your help."

"Don't put words in my mouth."

Confusion clotted her patience. "Then *what* are you trying to say? What's the point of this?" She tapped the document in his hand.

"A marriage certificate."

Aspen laughed. There was no way it was real. She hadn't signed anything. Yet even as the thought crossed her mind, she remembered her name. No— "It has my signature."

"And mine." He held it up as if to prove it. "Original seal. Recorded in Virginia."

Panic and ice churned through her chest. "Why?"

"We're going in undercover. You're Austin's sister, seeking closure. I'm your husband, watching out for you."

"That's stupid!"

He shook his head and walked to the window. "You have no idea."

Aspen, fingers trembling, rifled through the other documents. "Birth certificates, passports"—she flipped through the pages, her breathing shallowing out—"Oh my word. They're stamped."

Dane slumped against the far wall. "Apparently, we honeymooned in Greece."

"I've never been to Greece!" The shriek in her voice scraped down her spine. "How can they do this? Get him on the phone. I'm not standing for this."

Dane smirked. Retrieved his phone, dialed, pressed more numbers, then handed her the phone.

Surprised, she took the device.

"I knew you'd call back." A man's voice boomed.

"Yes, this is Aspen Courtland—"

Burnett cursed. "Put that son of a—"

"General, I want you to stop this game."

"I'm sorry. It's done. Get the mission done and you get your life back." The line went dead. She stared at the silver phone. "He hung up on me. Told me to do it and I could have my life back."

Dane's shoulders fell. "I hoped he'd be better than that." He righted a chair and dropped into it. Fingers steepled, he pressed the tips to his forehead and closed his eyes.

Incredulous, she tossed the papers from the table at his feet. "They're fake! Anyone will know."

Grief tugged at his features as he pushed back in the chair and slumped. "They're authentic. One-hundred percent real. Legal. Legitimate."

"I don't care. Make them undo it."

Dane looked down and leaned forward. He threaded his fingers, a heaviness on his brow as he studied the floor.

"You can't possibly be thinking—" She yelped. Spun around. Lunged for the door. "Forget it. I'm leaving."

Hands caught her shoulders. Spun her.

Aspen's fist flew on its own.

Crack! Pain plowed through his skull and neck. Instantly, he felt the gush of warmth. Felt his nostrils closing up. He cursed.

Aspen clapped her hands over her mouth, eyes wide.

He stumbled back to the chair and pinched the bridge of his nose. It felt like someone was driving nails through his eyes. Clenching his hand into a fist, he squeezed his eyes and breathed through his mouth as he waited for the bleeding to stop.

Hell had to be a better existence than this.

He'd shouted obscenities through the phone at Burnett that would've made his mother blush. The general had not yielded.

"Just. . .get the mission done. Use this to cover your trail."

"I don't need this to get my job done. Undo it. Now."

"No can do." Burnett snickered.

"No can do? Or you won't?"

"What would I have to gain by tying your sorry carcass to that sweet girl? This isn't about anything but getting my asset back before someone else gets to him, if they haven't already."

"I'm sorry."

Surprise stabbed through him. Her words were soft. And close.

He opened his eyes—already the swelling was puffing around his eyes. Aspen stood in front of him, holding what looked like a towel with ice.

He accepted the peace offering. "That's an awesome right hook. I should've remembered." Their first meeting—the fight club.

"My grandfather taught me that when I was five."

Cardinal slowed. "Amadore. . ."

She shrugged. "My grandfather on my mother's side." She squatted. "Please. . .*please* tell me this can be undone."

"Burnett promised as soon as we get Austin—if he's alive— everything will go back to normal."

"You're sure?"

"His words. I can't predict the future." And he certainly didn't trust Burnett as far as he belched.

"I can't believe they can get away with this." She crossed her arms. "Can't we do anything?"

"What?" He pointed to the passports. "If you try to go anywhere with your other passport you'll get arrested. We have two tickets into Djibouti from Virginia—of course, we won't be coming from there, but flight records will probably show that. Most likely, they'll take us to

Egypt or somewhere and put us on the second leg." He sighed. "Look. I know this is asinine, but it will work."

"But why can't we just do it from here, the way things are?"

"Whoever has Austin, if they smell military, we'll get more of the same from Tuesday."

"I thought that was random."

Cardinal gave a snort. "You are smarter than that. They knew who we were. We aren't going to get anywhere with these military grunts breathing down our necks."

She drew a chair over and sat in front of him. "I'm really sorry about your nose."

"Not my first."

"Maybe, but I never wanted to hurt you."

"You know what they say about payback." He'd never forget her horrified expression when she saw the papers. It came pretty close to what he felt as he opened the overnighted box.

"Dane. . ." She worried the edge of her lip. "That certificate is in paper only."

Did she really think he was a cad? He raised a hand. "Give me a little more respect than that. In case you didn't notice"—he waved his hand around the room—"I didn't take the news very well either. I don't want this. I'm not the marrying kind of guy."

Her eyebrows winged up.

He shook his head and it felt like he was under water. "Look, let's just get this done and get out of here."

"But why real certificates? Why not fake it?"

"Technically, they're faked. You didn't sign it. I didn't sign it. But there our signatures are." He'd be mouth breathing for a few days, and the thunder roaring through his head would stop in a few hours. . . maybe. "But they're *not* fake because of who we're dealing with and how convincing we need to be."

"And who is that?"

"We don't know for sure, except that it's pretty high up the ladder."

"How would you know that?"

"Because Burnett sent *me*." He let the full meaning settle in as he applied the ice pack to his nose, cringing at the added weight and pain.

"And who are you, Dane?"

He met her eyes. "Your husband."

Aspen folded her hands and looked down.

He regarded her. Playing her husband was something he feared. And he didn't fear that she'd fail at playing his wife—the word curled around some inner piece of him and made it hard to breathe—or that anyone would doubt they had feelings for each other, because that too was true. He could play the role like an ace. And that near kiss—well, he'd memorized the expectation that hung in her beautiful face as she waited for his lips to touch hers.

No, there'd be no problem pretending. What scared him was how much he'd enjoy it.

I am becoming him.

Aspen reached for the express box and lifted it. Something clunked in it.

Cardinal groaned.

She dumped the item out. A box. Small black box. She flipped it open. Two rings—one a plain, gold band. Another a stunner of a rock poised over a silver band. He cringed—no, not silver. Platinum.

Aspen's eyes widened. "Is this real?"

He smirked. "Are you proposing?"

Pink fanned her cheeks.

"You're beautiful." Only when her eyes flicked to his did he realize he'd said that. *Whoa. Hold up!* "When you're proposing."

She stared at the rings, her eyes tearing.

"Aspen." He reached forward and covered the box with his hand. "I wish we could stop this right now. Call Burnett and—"

"He won't listen." She shook her head. "Just like all the times I called them and told them to find Austin, that he wasn't dead. They ignored me." She shrugged. "You already tried, that's why you were shouting and cursing earlier. And he hung up on me, remember? He won't listen."

"If we both swear out of this, if we walk, they can't do anything."

"But they can." She swallowed—hard. "I can see the fear, the fury in your eyes."

He drew back, startled that she'd seen that. Nobody had seen that. "I'm right aren't I?"

He felt naked. Exposed. This wasn't good that she could see into him like this. He'd worked too many years protecting himself, erecting barriers.

127

"What did they threaten you with, Dane?"

He ducked even more.

"I think I deserve to know."

"It doesn't matter." He stood, struggling not to cringe. Again, he stomped around the room. There had to be another way. He couldn't tether himself to a woman. Relationships didn't work. Not for him. Not now. Not ever.

"Look, I'll just get out of here, vanish." That might work. "Tell Burnett it's my fault. He'll let you off."

"Wait." Aspen joined him. "If we don't do this, I don't find Austin. Right?"

"Is it worth going through this?"

She frowned then drew straight. "Yes." She nodded again. "I want the truth about my brother—and now more than ever, it seems like a doozie of a truth."

"Even if it means marrying me?" It was meant to be funny. But it wasn't. He wanted to punch the wall again.

He didn't trust himself to speak. It was the foulest betrayal Burnett had pulled on him yet. And he'd strangle the man if he could get within arm's reach. Burnett knew. . .somehow, he knew what angle to pull with Cardinal. His one weak spot.

Not this fake marriage. Not the putting on of rings.

But his heart.

Get out! Get out, now!

Cardinal gulped back what he felt. The fear. The panic. His anger wasn't about himself—he could walk out of here and never worry about what Burnett or anyone else would do to him. But Aspen. . .this would destroy her. Not finding out about Austin—

Somehow, Burnett had figured out what was happening in Cardinal. Even before Cardinal knew—he was falling for Aspen Courtland. And he'd do anything for her. Including staying.

Aspen lifted the black box, opened it, and plucked the plain band. She lifted his hand, slid the ring on, and looked up at him. "With this ring, I thee wed." Her laugh fell flat. "Boy, that felt weird. But that's all we have to do, right? Put on the rings and off we go."

Into the deepest, darkest pit of hell.

FORBIDDEN

Nevsky Prospekt, St. Petersburg, Russia
Age: Nearly 10 Years

Hunger tore at him as his shoes beat a steady rhythm on the shoveled sidewalks. Icy wind pinched his face and neck, but he swiped a sleeve along his nose and pressed on. Plumes of icy breath danced before him in the March morning as he completed his fifth circuit. Lungs aching, limbs frozen, he savored the warmth of the sun clawing its way over the frozen city and willed it not to hide from him any longer.

"Nikol."

Startled at his name, he looked around.

Mr. Kaczmarek waved from his shop's front stoop on the other side of the street. "Hurry, boy."

Even though he knew the colonel could not see him from here, Nikol looked over his shoulder and slowed. Buildings protected him, but time did not. "I cannot stop, sir."

The Polish baker smiled and stepped farther out, arm extended. Even from here, Nikol could see the warmth rising off the pastry. "You can finish it before you get home, yes?"

Nikol grinned, crossed the street, and accepted the treat. "Thank you, sir."

Yes, he could finish it before he returned to his building. In fact, before he left this street or the possibility existed that the colonel would see him. He took a large chomp out of it. Cinnamon and butter swirled through his palate. Then a cold dread replaced the delicious flavor. Out of sight of Mr. Kaczmarek, he flung the pastry as far over a small home as he could throw it. . .kept jogging, sweating, panting. He bent and scooped up a fistful of snow. Stuffed it in his mouth. Quickly it liquefied.

He swished. Then spit it out.

The spittle landed on a fresh blanket of undisturbed snow. And there he saw the telltale brown grains. He repeated the process. On his seventh circuit, nearly five miles, he slowed and paced in front of the building, cooling and slowing his breathing. Back inside he turned on the pot for coffee, quickly showered, then dressed. He stuffed an apple in his satchel, made breakfast. From the cabinet, he took down one white plate and a clear glass. He turned toward the table and stilled.

Two chairs? Why were there two chairs at the table? The colonel never allowed him to eat with him. *"You must learn to depend on nobody, to see nobody's company. To be self-sufficient like me."*

"Why are you standing there like an idiot?"

The booming voice jolted him. Good for him that he did not drop the plate or glass. "Sorry, sir," Nikol said as he set the table as he had done every morning, noon, and night—and without looking at the colonel and proving he was the aforementioned idiot. How had he not noticed the sun that had escaped from the only window on that side of the apartment—the one that was in the colonel's bedroom?

"Set two." With that, the colonel stomped down the hall to the bathroom.

The light beams flickered and danced, drawing his attention to the room. Someone was in there. Nikol dropped his gaze. It wouldn't be the first time the colonel had brought home a woman to have his way with her.

Still, it ignited Nikol's fury. The colonel had tossed his mother out like a prostitute, shouted profanities at her. Beat her. Shamed her. Berated Nikol for crying for her. Then beat him, too. He had not seen her in three years. He dreamed of her but never told the colonel.

"Nikol," came the soft, feminine whisper.

With wide eyes he looked to the bedroom. Wrapping herself in a robe, the beautiful form took shape, wrapped in a halo of light. "Mama!"

She waved him into the room.

He stood there, mute. Terrified. And shook his head. "I'm forbidden," he whispered.

She darted a look down the hall, then hurried across the small dining area to him and drew him into her arms. "Oh, my sweet boy!"

In his mind, he clung to her. Cried against her soft chest. Savored her love that he could sense. She pulled back, cupped his face, and wept. "You have become such a young man."

"I am nearly ten."

More tears.

"Please." He darted a nervous glance toward the hall. "Do not cry. It will make him angry."

She brushed away her tears then nodded. "I am so proud of you, Nikol."

Then the panic started. The thoughts of what the colonel had done to her last time. "Why are you here?" His heart thundered. "You should go. Hurry. Now, before he comes out." Frantic, he tugged on her arm, drawing her toward the door.

"No, Nikol, it is well. He. . .we made a deal." Her smile was small and did not make her eyes sparkle the way he remembered. "It is okay. It is worth it to see you."

"No! You must go."

"Nikol, be calm, my son. He only has the power we give him." She held him again, then knelt in front of him so he stood over her. "Besides, he said if I. . .if I"—her gaze darted to the bedroom and her voice trembled, but she smiled up at him—"if I *came*, I could see you."

"See but not speak to." The venomous voice melded with the words as the colonel appeared, dressed only in a pair of pajama bottoms. "I will not let you poison him, make him weak!"

His hand came down hard on his mother's face. Her head. Curled on the floor, she cried, "You promised! I did what you wanted. You said I could see him."

"Shut up, you whore!" His fist nailed her nose. Blood spurted over her cream-colored robe.

Something in Nikol died that day.

Fifteen

The plane hit cruising altitude, and Aspen settled back, her mind and finger still weighted with the ring she bore. Timbrel had vowed bodily harm against Dane if he made one wrong move. Warned them as soon as they were back in Djibouti they would have eyes on them, and she'd find a sniper to take him out.

Though Aspen warred with the thoughts that she'd somehow violated her belief in the sanctity of marriage, she knew this was a logical path to finding Austin. They wouldn't do anything immoral. Candyman *and* Watterboy threatened intense personal pain if Dane crossed lines. And Rocket alluded to something he'd seen the two do to terrorists who'd kidnapped another special-ops comrade.

It'd taken her the six hours from the time they'd left the others, boarded a military jet, and then made their "connecting" flight back to Djibouti to relax.

Which she couldn't say for Dane.

He hadn't spoken a word.

"I don't remember you two," the Middle Eastern man next to them said as he pointed to Dane's face. "I would have remembered that mess. I'm a plastic surgeon."

Dane smiled, the swelling still obvious. "Like my trophy?" He grinned wider. "Got this when a guy tried to hit on my wife."

The doctor tsked. "Are women worth such a price? How did you get to sit up here? It was full."

Dane thumbed toward the back. "We were in business class. They had an opening—something wrong with someone's papers—and since my wife wasn't feeling well, we upgraded for the last leg."

The passenger leaned forward and peered at her. "Ah, she does look pale. Between your black eyes and her sickness, it's a wonder you are traveling." He grinned. "First class is better, no?"

"Much. It's nice and quiet." With that, Dane closed his eyes.

Aspen wanted to laugh, but she was supposed to be sick. She looked out the window and placed her hand on her stomach, which caused the heavy wedding ring to thump softly against her fingers. *Weird. So very weird.*

"I don't want this. I'm not the marrying kind of guy."

The words had startled her and crushed her at the same time. She had been interested in Dane, was willing to explore things. They seemed to have faith in common. And he was handsome. He seemed to like her, too. But apparently not.

Her mind whirred at what lay before them. Convincing the missionary they were a couple. That would be interesting, considering they'd never even held hands, kissed, or—well, anything.

But she kept coming back to one thought: Dane had tried to leave the mission.

Had she done something wrong?

Or was it because of the near kiss?

She snorted. That's what she got for reading romance novels with arranged marriages. The romantic notions of falling in love with the unlikely man had her going places she'd better not. Dane had wanted to kiss her, then tried to get removed from the mission. And he wasn't the marrying the kind. He'd said so himself.

That made him the last man on earth she'd ever marry.

Hmm, except that you are *married to him.*

Aspen Markoski.

She shuddered. That didn't sound right together at all. Not the way Sam Herringshaw's name had sounded with hers in fifth grade. Oh good grief. She was doing it again.

Timbrel was right—she was a hopeless romantic. Even though this was the most insane thing she'd ever done.

Was it so wrong that she was willing to do anything to get her brother back? Faking a marriage wasn't a sin. Okay, it was lying, so maybe it was. Pushing the damning thoughts from her mind, she focused on finding Austin. Bringing him back home. Reuniting him with Talon. Life would be normal.

Maybe not normal, but a new normal. He'd go into law the way he'd talked about after their parents' deaths. To bring justice. That's what he wanted. She'd been so proud of him. Talon would live out his days happy, and she. . .

What? What would she do? She'd never really had any goals. And working with A Breed Apart had infused her with a sense of purpose. With Austin taking Talon back, what would she do? Would ABA cut her off?

Life without the saucy Timbrel? Heath—oh heavens, what would he say about this?

Forget Heath. What would her nana say? Oh that would be a sight—and sound!

The plane began its descent and delivered them into the tiny international airport. Even as they disembarked onto the tarmac, she searched for the crate carrying Talon. He was lowered from a pressurized cabin, and she saw him lift his head.

Warmth wrapped around her hand. She stilled and found herself staring up into Dane's blue eyes. He leaned in, pressing a kiss to the sensitive spot beneath her ear. Heat flared through her chest at the intimate gesture. "Your two o'clock. About a klick out."

Shuddering as he straightened from his whispered words, she let her gaze traipse that direction. A vehicle sat idling. ODA452 and Timbrel?

"Let's get our bags."

Tripping mentally to keep up with Dane's natural strides, she chided herself for the visceral reaction to his kiss, which still felt like someone held a torch to her jaw. But he led her into the terminal. She waited with Talon while he grabbed their bags. Whatever was packed in there, she didn't know. She'd only brought a rucksack to Lemonnier.

As they gathered their things, she spotted a man holding a sign that read MARKOSKI. She stilled.

"Ready, babe?" Hearing those words out of Dane's mouth. . .the same mouth that kissed her. . .

God, help me. I can't do this. I really can't.

Dane was with her in a second. His arm around her waist.

She pressed her hands against his abs. "Don't." Their eyes met as she stiffened. "Let's. . . .let's just get to Santos's home."

"Relax." He glanced over her shoulder. "Ah!" He waved. "Here we are." He released her and lifted their luggage.

Drawing on the remnants of her courage, she pushed the dolly with Talon in his crate toward the man.

"You are Mr. Mar—"

"Markoski." Dane lowered a bag and offered his hand. Then he angled back. "This is my wife, Aspen."

The man raised his hands. "Ah, so much like your brother."

Aspen hauled in a breath. "Austin, you saw him?"

Santos's face softened. "Not in a while, dear girl. I am so sorry to say." He waved them toward his beat-up Jeep-looking vehicle. "Let's talk at the house."

At the two-story home, Dane carried the bags up the steps to the upper level, where a beautiful master suite spread out before them. It must have taken up half the second story. Aspen stood by the window, Talon whimpering in his crate.

"Come on downstairs after you have refreshed. We will have lemonade." Santos backed out and closed the doors.

Dane set down the luggage as Talon was freed from his crate and watched Angel. Aspen.

Curse, curse, curse Burnett. That kiss on her neck had been a huge mistake. He'd tried to make things appear natural, but she'd reacted so...thoroughly. So had he. It'd taken every microscopic ounce of control he had not to pull her into his arms and kiss her the way he'd wanted to two days ago. Instead, he'd forced his fingers to release her, his feet to move away, and his voice to remain cold and unattached.

The way he should be. Cardinal rules—enforce them or become mastered. Now, he couldn't clear his mind of that or her smell. Light and floral. When he'd noticed her panic at the airport and tried to intercept, she'd gone stone cold.

Talon whimpered and paced then sat down. Whimpered again. Paced.

"Think he can still smell Austin's scent? Santos said he hadn't been here in a while."

He ripped out a piece of paper and scribbled two words on it—*listening devices*—then moved behind her. He stuffed the note in her hand. Then he held up a pen and clicked it once. "We can talk when it's depressed but only for a few seconds."

Her eyes widened as he came closer. She twisted to face him. "You think someone is listening?"

"Never underestimate the enemy. Listen, take Talon and have him check the rooms. I'll keep Santos busy." *Click.* "Fair enough, Angel. But tonight. . ." He laughed and hated himself for the flirting he'd added to the tone for the sake of anyone listening in on them. And hated the fear in her beautiful eyes. Hated that this whole thing would make her wary of his every move. He went to his suitcase and unzipped it. He stared at the clothes. Jeans. Cotton shirts. Underwear. Burnett had been prepared. This wasn't something he'd done on the spur. He'd been planning this.

With a soft thud, her suitcase landed on the bed. She unzipped it and lifted the flap. A soft gasp preceded her gaze ramming into his. Her face brightened to a deep red.

He couldn't help the laugh trickling through his throat. He well imagined what they'd provided for her, especially to make it appear that they were truly newlyweds should anyone rifle through their things while the bags were unattended.

"There's a screen, if you'd like to freshen up." He pointed to the antique hinged panels that stood guard in the corner and raised his eyebrows, indicating that was her out to staying here with Talon.

She hesitated then looked to the screen. "Perfect."

"I'll see you downstairs then in a few." He slipped out and closed the door.

As he stood in the hall, he took in the layout. Two rooms, one to the right, one left. Both sparsely decorated. Bathroom downstairs, most likely. This wasn't the Sheraton, but it would provide shelter and get them answers. . .hopefully.

Cardinal moved down the shadowy stairs and slowed when he heard voices. He angled to look around the corner.

Santos stood talking with another man. Tones were low, hurried.

He strode into the open. "Room's great. Thanks, Mr. Santos."

Santos spun. The door came out of his grip.

Cardinal met the brown eyes of a man who stood about six feet with dark brown hair. "Afternoon." He greeted the man.

"Afternoon."

Could be from anywhere with that British accent.

"Ah," Santos said with a shaky smile, but Cardinal pretended not to notice. "Mr. Markoski, this is Joshua, one of the missionaries who works in another village. He stopped by to warn me of a new flu strain hitting the villages there."

"Sad."

Joshua stared at him. Hard. "Indeed." He gave Santos a smile. "If it weren't for his mad medical skills, we would be hurting a lot worse than we are."

"It is fortunate timing." Santos looked toward the stairs. "Is your wife well?"

"Yes. She wanted to freshen up. A terribly long trip, and a bit daunting, too."

Santos turned to Joshua. "They are looking for her brother."

"Say." Cardinal stepped into the sunlight that crossed the threshold of the open door. "You haven't seen an American, black hair, brown eyes?"

"I've seen a lot of men fitting that description in Djibouti," Joshua said with a laugh.

"Of course." He sighed long and hard. Swiped a hand along his jaw, noting the stubble that had grown to a five o'clock shadow. "My wife has her hopes pinned on this trip." He shook his head. "If Aspen can't find Austin, I just don't know how she'll keep going."

Though there was no change in body language, a look in the guy's face flashed in and out like a bolt of lightning. So fast, so sharp, Cardinal almost didn't see it.

Voices carried up the dark stairwell as Aspen led Talon from the room. She went to the right, to the one with pink walls. The bed cuddled the corner with a pink floral rug at the side and a chest at the foot. A dresser with an oval mirror sat near the small window. Talon walked in and returned to her side.

Nothing.

"Yeah, I'm not crazy about the color either." She turned around and hurried past the stairs, listening to the voices...and stopped. She backed up. Laughter, the voices lowered. That was weird.

Talon trotted ahead, sniffing like mad. She followed him and froze.

Cold dread spiraled through Aspen as Talon let out a high-pitched whimper. He paced back and forth in the yellow room, whimpering. Sniffing. Licking. Paws on the edge of the bed, he leaned up and sniffed the pillow. Barked.

The sound felt like a gunshot through her gut. "Talon?" Her heart raced. But Aspen couldn't move. Her eyes traced the setup of the room. The headboard and footboard were at the wrong ends.

Tentatively, she entered the room, feeling the tug on the lead as Talon sniffed and whimpered and yelped over and over. At the wall where the footboard sat, she reached toward a spot in the middle, just a few inches above the board. Slightly darkened spots. *It can't be...*

She should get Dane up here. But she couldn't talk just yet. Couldn't bring herself to give credence to what was happening. She turned to the dresser. Glanced at the bed. Then the dresser. Less than an arm's length apart.

It's just a coincidence.

Right. The bed. The wall. The dresser. And—

Talon. The Lab nosed her hip then sat down, peering up at her expectantly. "*I did good, now show me where he is.*"

She took in the room once more. Empty mostly save the dingy curtains, the rug...

"*I like to feel the cold floor when I climb out of bed. It wakes me up.*"

Talon paced more. Whimpered. Dropped onto the rug.

Oh man—the rug. Curled up in the corner. Shoved aside.

Certainty rang through her. Austin had been there. So recently the beds hadn't been rearranged. She walked the room, memorizing, imagining—

Why? Why would he be here and not contact her? It didn't make sense.

With a whimper, Talon rose and started wearing a path in the floor as he tread from one wall to the next. Sniffed the rug. Pace...pace... sniffed the bed. Whimpered.

This wasn't a jail or a prison or a jungle where he'd been taken hostage. Santos had a phone, electricity. If Austin was here, he could come and go as he pleased.

"Talon, come."

He complied. For a minute. Then took up his trek again. Whimper-pace-pace-sniff-whimper.

"Talon, stop."

Why? Why would Austin do this? Leave Talon, leave his friends. . . She shoved her fingers into her curls and fought back the confusion, the tears.

Dust had accumulated on the dresser, save in one rectangular spot. She noted a thin line a few inches from the larger one. A picture frame. What picture had been moved, and recently?

Talon's whimpers grew louder. He dug into the carpet. Settled on it.

What picture had been there? Why was it gone now?

Talon barked, sniffed, then sat back down. Mission accomplished. Whatever he thought he found was here.

She turned 360 degrees, searching, begging for a reasonable explanation. Nothing came to her. Nothing sated the panic swimming mean circles around her mind.

Talon whimpered yet again. "Talon, please. . ." His cries pulled on her heart. He was distressed. And that was distressing her. More of that high-pitched noise.

"Talon!" She ducked and covered her face, hating that she'd snapped at him. The sweet, loyal boy who had a heart bigger than Texas.

Whimpering continued without ceasing.

Her head hurt. Her *heart* hurt.

She wrapped her arms around his chest, hearing Heath tell her not to baby Talon. *Go away, Daniels.* "It's okay, boy." She squeezed him tighter. "Please." Tears stung her eyes, his cries an eerie reflection of what she felt. She buried her face in his fur. "It's okay, boy. We'll find him."

He only grew louder.

I have to get out of here. Get him out of here.

On her feet, Aspen tugged on Talon's lead and hurried toward the glass door she'd seen opposite the top of the stairs.

Do Svidaniya

Nevsky Prospekt, St. Petersburg
Age: 15 Years, 8 Months

Hues of blue, gray, and white smeared the city into a somber landscape. White covered the snow, and the gray clouds hovered deep, forbidding the sun from making its appearance. No sun. Never any sun. Russia was dark and dreary. His life was dark and dreary.

A snowplow lumbered along the street, clearing it again for vehicle passage. Across the way, he spotted a group from his school. Six or eight of them laughing, pushing, messing around. Then she stepped out of the crowd: Svitlana Kitko.

As if his feet had iced themselves to the ground, he watched her wave good-bye to the others and hurry toward the small park that stretched out in front of his building. Their building. She and her family had moved from Moscow. He had heard the colonel speak of Svitlana's father—a Ukrainian scientist. Her mother, full Russian. Pretty light brown curls bounced along the frame of her face, the rest crushed by a cap to ward off the cold. As she stepped onto the sidewalk, their eyes met.

The sun stabbed into the gloominess.

She waved. "*Privet*, Nikol."

His heart stuttered as she said hi. But his mind whirled—*she knows my name*. Of course she knew his name. Everyone did. It was why they walked on that side and he on this one. No, the greater surprise was that she had actually spoken to him. He'd heard the others, especially Matvei Ilyich, tell her to stay away from him, that he was as mean and violent as the colonel. They were right—she should stay away.

But there she was. Boots up to her calves. A thick white coat with a fur-trimmed hood. And that smile. That beautiful smile. He wanted to wave. To smile. Anything to let her know he thought she was the most beautiful girl in all Russia.

He gauged the distance, the angles. They were too close. The colonel could see them if he had come home early. Although he almost never did that, Nikol wouldn't take the risk.

Letting her go inside without acknowledging her presence was rude. He gave her a nod.

She turned from her path at his nod.

He could not let her know the effect she had on him.

"Kak dela?" Hands stuffed in her pockets, she smiled up at him. Her eyes were blue. So pretty. Like the blue of a summer sky. When it was warm.

How was he? Stinking miserable. *"Harosho."* Saying he was fine usually ended the conversation. That was what he needed. They were exposed. He could be seen. It would not go well.

"Fine?" She wrinkled her nose and looked around. "How can anyone on Nevsky Prospekt be fine?" Her laughter could be the flowers in a field on that summer day. He wanted summer. Very much. But it was winter. It was always winter in Russia.

"Then why did you move here?" He should not have asked that. "Never mind. It is not my concern."

"It is okay. My father got this amazing job," she said, sarcasm thick.

"Then you are sad to be here." He started walking. Toward the building. The closer they stood to it, the less likely the colonel could see them.

"I was." She scuffed her boots against the snow. "I had friends in Moscow. I wanted to attend university there."

"You still can."

She smiled up at him again. "Perhaps."

Warmth speared his chest.

"But I am not sad anymore."

"Really?" Everyone was sad, were they not? Really, when they got down to it, what was there to be happy about? He wanted to be happy. But it was just a ruse that got him in trouble.

"Yes."

Snow crunched as they moved toward the building, then along it, leading to the front door.

"Are you not going to ask me why I am happy?" On the first step into their foyer, she turned and faced him. Her cheeks were rosied from the bitter wind. Things awoke in his frozen heart as they stood eye to eye.

Swallowing, Nikol glanced around to make sure they were alone. "Okay." He met her gaze again. "Why are you happy?"

"Because, I met you." She planted her hands on his shoulders, bent forward, and kissed his cheek. With a flutter of a swirl, she turned and hurried into the building. "Do svidaniya!"

Heart pounding, he watched her take the stairs two at a time.

Bitter and strong, an icy wind blew against his sunshine. He flinched, sensing the presence. To his right, a shape loomed closer. His gut clenched as the clouds once again dropped on him and whispered, "Do svidaniya."

Sixteen

Thudding above pulled Cardinal off the wall.

"Sounds like the dog is giving her a good run for her money." Santos smiled.

Calm down, act natural. "Yeah." It did seem like Talon was running. "Sounds like it."

"I think they went on the rooftop. It's good up there. Fresh air. Not much wind, so it is too hot for me."

Having a suspicious nature kept him alive.

It also drove him crazy. And the craziest thought just hit him: *That's my wife up there.* Not in any other sense than on paper. But if he didn't show concern, Santos would question it.

"So, you came all this way to find her brother?"

"Yeah." Cardinal returned to his spot holding up the wall. "Will you tell me what you know?"

"Sure, sure." Santos went to the kitchen, where he pulled bottled waters from the fridge. He offered one to Cardinal. "It's hot."

"I'm good." His gaze swept the home. Two levels—well, three if you counted the rooftop terrace. Plaster painted peach, with tiny flowers scrawling along the upper portion of each wall. "You said it's been two weeks since he was here?"

"I am no good at keeping track of time, but yes, I believe so."

"Why did he stay here?" Cardinal noted the worn furniture, the rickety rocking chair, the pictures that hung crookedly on the wall. The handwoven rug that spread over the entire twenty-by-fifteen living area. Incongruently beautiful in a home with faded, cracking

143

plaster, older furniture. . .

"He was injured."

"But you're not a hospital."

"True, but the beds at Peltier are limited. Camille and I visited there often, to encourage the patients. He. . ." A noise above creaked, and Santos grew quiet. "I hope she is well."

"Yeah, the flight really took it out of her." He peeled off the wall. "I'll go check on her."

On the upper level, he found the rooms empty. He tensed. Then saw a shadow drift across the rooftop terrace steps. He pulled open the glass door and stepped into the late afternoon sun.

Talon lumbered over, nosed his hand, then licked it before returning to Aspen, who stood at a waist-high railing, hands on the plaster, staring out at the Red Sea twinkling in the distance.

"Everything okay?"

A breeze rustled her hair away from her face. Sweat dribbled down her temples—wait. Not sweat. Tears.

"Hey." Cardinal touched her elbow. "What's wrong?"

Her eyes, which he noticed were almost the same blue as the water, met his. "He was here, Dane." Another tear slipped free. "Why would he be *here*? Why didn't he come home?"

Teary depths pulled him in.

She chewed the inside of her lip. Facing the sea again, she went quiet, her chin trembling. "He was here. And recently."

"What'd you see?"

She sniffled through a laugh. "You'll think I'm crazy."

"Hey." He sat on the wall, wedging himself closer between her and the plaster. "I think a lot of things about you, but that is not one of them."

Aspen looked down at him for several heart-thumping minutes then drew in a steadying breath as she once again turned to the sea. "When we were kids, Austin always arranged his room a certain way. I know it sounds insane, but he had this logic to it." She sniffed and shook her head. "I'm his twin and it *never* made sense to me. He always— *always*—put the headboard where the footboard went. And a bookcase near his head." She hunched her shoulders through a laugh. "He was never one for education, but he had this idea that the information would seep into his brain."

"Now, *that* is crazy."

"Yeah." She smiled at him. "But that was Austin. He'd kill me for telling anyone, but that. . .that's how I know he's been here."

"I'm sure he's not the only one who did something like that with the bed."

"True, the real clincher—was Talon. He got a hit."

"Maybe it was a false positive."

She laughed. "It's not a pregnancy test. It's his nose. His partner. His best friend. Talon *knows* Austin. And he *knows* he was in there. He went frantic. The way he whined—" She slapped the wall. "He wouldn't stop whining or sniffing." She turned away, eyes squeezed tight. Her shoulders bounced. "It made me as crazy as whatever he smelled was making Talon crazy. It was like he could smell him but couldn't understand why Austin wasn't there."

She jerked to face him straight on. "Two years, Dane. He's been gone two years."

He slowly stood, knowing he would need to help her find her balance.

"Why would he do this to me? Why would he let me think he's dead? Why would he abandon Talon—"Tears choked her words. "If you could've heard him. . . He wouldn't stop."

Cardinal pulled her into his arms, slamming a lid on the stirrings that erupted when she balled his shirt in her fist and clung tight to him. His pulse went haywire, holding her, comforting her. Not just out of attraction. But out of anger that Austin had hurt her like this.

Her body shook beneath the weight of her pain and tears. "Why? Why would Austin do this? Leave me, be here?"Tears soaking through his shirt, she pressed her forehead against his pecs.

"I don't know." And he truly didn't. Arm around her shoulders bouncing beneath her tears, Cardinal steeled himself. At least, he tried. *I'll drag those answers out of Austin Courtland if it's the last thing I do.*

Somehow, though it shook her to think of it, Aspen stood in Dane's arms. Warm, strong, capable arms. His words rumbled through his chest and poured like steel into her soul, strengthening her courage, infusing her with strength not her own.

She had totally lost it, listening to Talon crying for Austin. Because that's what she'd been doing for two years, hadn't she? Crying for her brother, the one the Marines had written off, declared dead.

Dead men tell no tales.

Well, this dead man would. Because dead men don't live in Djibouti with a missionary.

She looked up at Dane and cringed. "Wow, your eyes are really turning black."

He smirked. "First lovers' quarrel."

The admonishment was on her tongue when she saw Santos peeking at them through the door window. Panic punched her onto her toes. She curled a hand around the back of Dane's neck and tiptoed up. She pressed her lips to his.

Hands on her hips, Dane nudged her back. "What—?"

He'll see or hear us! She kissed him again, this time leaning into it, her mind on the man staring at them. Had to make it believable, right? This was the way they covered their tracks or something.

Dane pushed her away again. "Aspen."

"Santos," she muttered.

Dane snorted a laugh then ate it as he looked to the side.

"He's watching." The heat flared through her face, clutching her in a humiliating grip. "At the door."

"It's okay," he said to Santos and waved him onto the terrace. "Talon got a little excited, and it proved upsetting for them both. She was overcome."

What was he doing? Dismissing her? Confusion and anger coiled around her mind like a vise. How dare he relegate her revelation about Austin to nothing more than a hysterical outburst. Because that's what he was saying, wasn't he?

"I understand," Santos said, smiling. "When my Camille died, the littlest thing would make me hysterical."

"Hysterical." Aspen gulped the fury. Nodded. Great. Fine. They were writing her off as an emotional woman. And Dane. . .

He turned to her. "No, not hysterical. Concerned."

Platitudes. *That* she didn't need. She pushed him aside. "*Don't* patronize me. I'm not an idiot." She snapped her fingers to call Talon and returned to the room, humiliation her only friend. Down the two steps to the upper level then into the room with the queen bed. Once inside with Talon, she clicked the lock. She shoved back her unruly curls, breathing a hard thing to do at the moment. He was making fun of her.

He pushed her away.

Her belly spasmed as she fought the tears. "He didn't want me."

That's ridiculous.

But it's true.

Arguing with herself only inflamed her shame. Made her feel even more stupid. This was insane. Absurd. This wasn't some romance novel where they played married then fell in love. This was real life. Capitalizing on a situation to get real answers.

But he didn't even seem to want the kiss. Or like it.

And that after they'd nearly kissed back at Lemonnier. Or was that her imagination?

On the terrace, he'd pushed her away. Like a petulant child. Like a silly girl with a crush on the high school senior.

"I don't have a crush!"

"It's good to hear."

Aspen spun, pulse thundering through her veins. "How did you get in? I locked it."

Shaking his head, Dane looked down and closed the door. He slid the bolt along the upper portion of the door then planted himself on a whicker chair in the corner. He sat, bent forward, elbows on his knees.

"What are you doing?" Now she *did* sound petulant. "Never mind." Aspen slumped on the bed and covered her face with her hands. Her head throbbed. So did her feet. And her back. And her pride.

Click.

She lifted her head and found him in front of her, sliding the pen back into his pocket. At this angle, his shoulders seemed broader. His chest bulkier. And his stubble just a shade darker. He had the ruffian thing going on real well.

Curse the man. Why did he have to be so gorgeous?

"Why did you kiss me?"

She tore her gaze from him and looked out the window behind him. "I—I saw Santos watching us. Why didn't you kiss me back?"

Amusement danced in his eyes, making her feel like she was fifteen and had just kissed Tom Stanton, the prom king. "Did you want me to?"

"No!" A stampede thumped through her chest at the lie.

Dane stifled a laugh.

"Isn't that what you people do when others watch?"

His eyebrow winged up. " 'You people'?"

Aspen groaned. "Don't do this to me. I feel stupid enough as it is."

Dane took her hands in his and tugged her to her feet.

She resisted, at war with the way her heart beat like a bass drum at his touch and her determination to be angry with him.

On her feet, she swallowed and mustered a nonchalant stance.

Until his finger tilted her chin up and he frowned. "First, this isn't the movies. We don't have to kiss every time someone sees us alone together."

She tried to look away, but he redirected her gaze with a slight nudge of her chin.

"And let's be absolutely clear about one thing—our. . .*situation* is part of a mission. It's not a carte blanche for me to take advantage of you. I have no interest in crossing that line."

Aspen blinked and stepped out of his reach, still stinging from the words, *"No interest. . ."*

"Of course not." Had she been wrong at Lemonnier when they'd almost kissed? The shock of his words wore off about the time he said something about sleeping on the floor.

Sleep in the desert for all I care.

Why on earth was she so angry?

Because the wound was so familiar. Reminded her of growing up in the shadow of her twin brother. High school quarterback. Voted most popular, most handsome, most annoying—okay, that was her vote, but it counted. Homecoming king—both his junior and senior year, somehow. She was the one with the As, the scholarships to Ivy League colleges. But it was his dismissal of her as being nothing but a brain that drove her to prove him wrong. To join the Air Force instead. Good thing someone paid attention and landed her in the JAG offices, or she'd have been boots-on-ground deployed and possibly killed.

For that reason, despite the cutting words from Dane, she took the words in stride. Well, as much as she could. Why did she ever think she could come here, play spy, and find Austin? Everything in her was crumbling, falling apart. If they hadn't discovered that Austin had lived here, she'd have packed up and gone home already.

Since that wasn't an option, she'd settle for finding her brother. But tonight showed her she was way out of her league, both in the romance department and the military department. She just prayed she didn't get herself killed.

Seventeen ★ ★ ★ ★

Darkness sneaked into the room, circled the bed that held Aspen, and circled around the wooden legs till it wrapped him in its black tendrils. Sleep evaded him. As it had so many times over far too many years. Arm stretched behind his head and one draped over the yellow Lab, Cardinal focused on the wood floor digging into his shoulder blades. A good, painful reminder of where he'd come from. Where he belonged—in the hard clutches of pain.

Eyes closed to the darkness, he still felt it surround his soul. Longed for a pew and some stained-glass windows. Flickering candles. Peace...

He'd done the right thing with Aspen. Though that look in her blue eyes haunted him even now, it was right. It was better. They'd focus on the mission, track Austin down, and then they'd go their separate ways. He'd never see her again.

He turned onto his side, his back to the bed. Talon shifted behind him with a loud sigh. *You and me both, buddy.*

The wood pressed against his shoulder. He stuffed the pillow beneath his head. Then lifted his head, folded the pillow in half, and jammed his head back down. As he relaxed, the pillow hissed and slid out.

Cardinal grunted, flattened the pillow, and dropped onto his back again. A pew with its too-thin-cushion would be more comfortable!

You'd still have to live with yourself.

He had no problem doing that. He'd done it all his life. His hard life. Which is why he belonged on the hard floor. He spent his life avoiding things that made him soft.

She had soft lips.

Augh! Dane thrust himself off the floor and reached for the door. Behind him, he heard the bed creak and pushed himself out the door, down the hall and stairs to the bathroom. He gripped the stand-alone sink. Arms behind his head, he stood facing the wall, eyes closed.

"Stand straight," the voice boomed. *"Never cower—even when you face punishment."*

He shoved a mental rod down his spine till he stood as tall as the man wielding the punishment. Braced.

Crack!

He flinched as leather met flesh. Scalded his back. The tip of the belt buckle caught him just below his shoulder the next time. Bit off a chunk. Fire tore down his spine. His knee buckled beneath the agony. His palm caught the wall.

But he jerked upright, knowing if he didn't, that one wouldn't count.

Cardinal shook his head to dislodge the stinging memory. Fifteen whips. He'd bled that day with each strike that had mirrored a year of his life.

"It'll make you stronger."

If only it had.

Maybe it was him. He was the failure. Where had he gone wrong? He'd disciplined himself. Had a healthy body. Kept his emotions in check. Even now, he drew into himself, hauled together all those elements that threatened his calm, his focus. He tied them in a virtual ball and lobbed it into the sea beyond the house. He had to.

"You cannot be broken if you don't let it."

He trained his mind on his pulse and coerced it into a slower pattern merely by breathing slower, more intentionally.

But like a needle ripping over a record, his mind jumped tracks.

Aspen.

No. Austin. Finding her brother. Putting the pieces together.

There were no pieces. He was stuck here, on a dead-end—

No.

"Master yourself or you will be mastered."

Frustration smothered him in the small box-of-a-bathroom. Cardinal removed himself to the terrace. Warm, balmy air lured him into the darkness. He removed his shirt, spread his legs shoulder-width apart, bent his knees, and glided through his tai-chi moves. Though he wished for a support bar to pull himself up and do something more strenuous, for tonight he'd settle on this. Bring his mind and body into submission through controlled exercises.

I hurt her.

He hung his head, tried to shrink from the thought. Stretched his neck. Straightened. Changed positions. Yes, he hurt her. She was innocent and a bit on the naive side. Easily pliable for those who went that route. He wouldn't. Neither would he go the other route. Allowing, encouraging, and fostering feelings he could not return.

She was emotionally compromised in this mission. If she did not create a fissure between her affection for her brother and the bald truth that Austin had lied to her, she would end up crushed. As such, he could not encourage any romantic notions. The appearance of a marriage between them served one purpose and one purpose only—to provide a cover while they were there. To hide his real identity. To protect her by having him with her at all times.

Burnett was right to arrange it.

Though Cardinal would use it to end the tepid relationship between him and the American government. They had dragged him along far enough. Once he returned their asset to them, it was time for them to give him the promised head on the silver platter.

His eyes popped open. Cardinal blinked, unmoving as he assessed his surroundings. Where was. . . ? Oh. Rooftop terrace. He'd dropped into one of the chairs, propped his head against the wall, and had fallen asleep. But what. . .

Voices skidded on the blue hues of dawn. Whispers. Fast.

Easing his legs onto the roof, he controlled his body in an extreme fashion. He scooted onto the edge of the chair, concealed and listening.

Santos could be heard. But somehow, the other voice proved too quiet to discern.

"I didn't tell them anything." Santos sounded frustrated.

A pause. At least thirty to forty-five seconds long. Water lapped. Inside and behind him, Cardinal heard quiet movement—Aspen and Talon, no doubt.

"Why would they bring the Army? She's merely looking for her brother."

Something about this conversation bugged him. To hear Santos, who spoke just below a normal voice at dawn. . .

Cardinal stood and casually walked to the edge. Looked around, as if he'd stepped out here just now, and glanced down. Santos stood near the back corner that abutted an abandoned shop talking with another man. Shadows deep and long concealed the man.

"Good morning," Cardinal called as he raised a hand.

Santos's gasp could probably be heard at Lemonnier. For show: "Ah, Mr. Markoski. You are up early."

"Guess jet lag is getting the best of me."

"Indeed. Are you hungry?"

"Starving." The shadows hadn't changed, and nobody flitted away in haste.

"I will put breakfast on right away." Santos vanished into the home.

Alone with the early morning, the lightening sky, and the stranger in the shadows, Cardinal perched on the hand-wide half wall, his gaze directed at the sea. Waiting for a sight of whoever found it necessary to be scampering around in the predawn hours to talk with a missionary.

The sun rose, and with it the shadows faded.

Laughter billowed from the house. Aspen's laugh. Talon's bark.

But strangest of all—nobody stood in the shadow.

Hustling back toward the house with Talon's lead firmly in her left hand, Aspen rounded a corner. A shape slipped past her. Aspen's heart rammed into her throat. She sucked in a breath. "Oh."

Talon tensed. Locked on to the stranger. Growled.

The other person gasped—a light, feminine one.

"Talon, out!" Aspen knew the tension she felt radiated down the lead and back up again between them both. "Heel! Sit!"

Surprisingly, he obeyed, returning to her side and sitting.

The slight figure darted around them, head ducked.

"Good boy, good boy," Aspen said, her heart still thundering from the encounter as she rubbed his head.

But. . .a woman? Out here at this hour?

Aspen glanced down the road. Rubble half-giants cowered beneath the rising sun. Scattered trees. Older cars. Dead cars. Men in trucks. But no woman.

After her fallout with Dane last night and then this creepy encounter this morning, she was ready to get answers and get back home. Talon looked up at her, those brown eyes asking if she was over the fright yet.

"C'mon, boy." She hurried back inside and found Santos in the kitchen. His smile wavered as he glanced toward the front then back to her. "You are both early risers."

"Both?" Her eyes betrayed her and drifted to the small hall.

"Yes, he just went in to shower." Santos nodded toward her. "Your hair is wet."

"Yeah, I showered before I took Talon for a walk."

"A walk." Nerves bounced in his face. "You should take someone with you next time. It's not so safe as one might expect. Especially not for a pretty woman like you." He turned back to the stove.

"Eggs?" she asked, trying to shift the awkwardness from the room.

"Yes. A local woman brings them to me from her chickens."

"Oh." She sat on the small sofa near the kitchen. "I think I bumped into her in the courtyard."

Clank! Thunk!

She looked over at him.

"Dropped the spoon," he said with a chuckle. He washed it then resumed cooking. "I hope this breakfast does not disappoint. Dane said you both had a long day planned, so I hope it holds you over."

"I'm sure it will." Why was he so jittery? She made her way back to the kitchen. "Can I help? Set the table maybe?"

"Oh, yes. I'm afraid we do not have much, but it is enough for the three of us."

After getting direction on where things were stored, Aspen set the table with mismatched plates, two forks, and a spoon. "How long have you been here in Djibouti?"

"Seven years." Santos worked a big cast-iron skillet, teeming with eggs, on the tiny stove.

"That's a long time for mission work." And not many dishes. Not even enough for a couple to sit down and eat with knives and forks.

"When you believe in what you're doing, time holds no boundaries."

Interesting philosophy. It'd be even more interesting if the man believed what he'd said. At least, she didn't think he did. There was no resolution in those words. "My parents sent me on a mission trip when

I was a senior. I went to Nepal. I fell in love with it, but I am so over eating half-cooked meat." She shuddered at the memory. "Okay, just need glasses." Hands on her hips, she turned—and froze.

Dane entered. "Smells wonderful." He'd shaved. Hair wet, it made his skin seem darker and his appearance more rugged.

Crazy thought.

"Glasses are in the cabinet there." Santos nodded to a narrow cupboard that hung a little crookedly and whose door sat off-center.

"Great." Aspen shifted her attention toward setting the table, toward feeling useful instead of like a decoration.

"We'll need to eat quickly. We're behind schedule."

We are? The thought lodged at the back of her throat, forbidden from escaping lest she undermine whatever Dane was up to. As far as she knew, there was no schedule other than to work the area, talking to locals and trying to find a scent Talon could track. With his million-receptor nose, he could track a scent that was weeks old. A fact she still grappled to believe.

"I was talking with Mr. Santos about his mission work." Aspen tucked herself in at the table, her back to the wall.

"Yeah?" Dane joined her, extending a hand toward Talon.

Aspen snapped a flat palm at him and shook her head. Unless he wanted to lose it, he'd better remember Talon wasn't a pet.

Dane gave a subtle nod and kept the conversation going. "What denomination are you? I didn't notice crucifixes in the rooms."

"None," Santos said quickly as he served them. "I mean— nondenominational. The focus here is to share God's love. Not religious mandates."

Aspen frowned. Was there as much venom in his words as butter on the eggs he heaped onto her plate? She eyed Dane over the table.

He dug into the eggs and let out a moan. "Wonderful. Thank you."

"It is a pleasure to cook for someone besides myself," Santos said as he started cleaning up. "Oh, I will be going out to a village later today. Some are coming down with sickness. I want to see what I can do."

"No problem. We'll be gone all day." He stuffed down the last of the eggs then took a sip of water and nodded to her. "Ready?"

Aspen ate a few bites, but the heavy butter and protein meal weighted her stomach. "Yeah."

"You did not finish," Santos objected.

"I'm sorry. I've always eaten like a mouse."

"Here in Djibouti, you will regret that. Drink like an elephant and eat like one. The heat will fry you if you don't."

"Thanks for the warning." Dane stood and held out a hand to her.

Right. Hold his hand. Because he wasn't interested.

Two could play at that game.

Aspen picked up Talon's lead and linked up. "Ready, boy?" Talon stood, tongue out and panting, as he flicked his tail. Keeping the lead slack so there was no tension like they'd shared earlier, she led him past Dane. "Bye, Mr. Santos."

The man nodded with a distant look.

Out in the sun, Dane slipped on a ball cap and started walking. Fast. Aspen had to double-time it to keep up. Down one street. Up another. Past a cluster of women walking with children.

Aspen smiled at a small child, maybe three or four years old, who stared back at her with wide, expressive eyes. So did the mothers. No doubt her fair skin and platinum hair stood out here. Though she expected Dane to try to talk to them, he didn't.

"Aren't we supposed to be talking to people?"

He kept walking. "Quiet."

Petulant now? Disappointment saturated her mood. She kept up, sweat trickling down her back and temples. It wasn't even noon and Djibouti felt like a sauna. Though Talon kept pace, even he seemed to be struggling in the heat.

About to protest his careless regard for them, she bit her tongue as he stepped into a building. She skidded and followed him in.

Darkness blanketed her. From behind, a hand clamped over her mouth.

Eighteen

Djibouti City, Djibouti

Eluding the National Army was one thing. Deceiving guerillas tough, but they'd managed. Escaping a tracking dog...

Hands on the table, Neil glanced at Lina in the old warehouse they'd taken shelter from the heat in. They'd survived two days without tipping off anyone. It'd been good. Reassuring. But the information—*augh!* What good did it do to have proof when he had nobody to show it to?

Lina folded her arms. She'd been impatient with him the last twenty-four hours. He couldn't blame her though. Not exactly ideal circumstances. "What are we going to do?"

"We go on."

Her blue eyes widened against her beautiful olive skin. "Go on?" She took a step forward, her hand on her stomach. "But they'll find us. I ran *right* into her. What if—?"

"No ifs. They won't. We won't let them."

"This isn't a small army we're talking about, Neil. The Americans are the best, the most highly trained." Her long black hair hung over her shoulders. "If we don't get out of here now, we'll never make it."

"Do you think I'm so weak I can't make this work?"

She came to him and held his arm. "No, I just don't want to lose you. Or die trying to get this information to the right people. It's not worth it."

He thrust his hands up, tossing off her grip. "Don't you get it? That's just it!" He paced the abandoned warehouse. Dust bobbed on thin beams of light that poked through the slots and holes in the walls. So numerous, it reminded him of one of those orbs that cast constellations on ceilings. "If we don't finish this, if we don't make good—we're dead. Whether we're here or somewhere else, they will find us."

"Maybe they won't."

He fisted both hands and thumped them against his forehead. "How can you be so brilliant and so stupid at the same time?"

She drew back, her face awash with his crushing words.

He hated the way she looked at him, with that complete look of trust, believing he could do anything, including taking on world powers and dark, dangerous undergrounds. He'd stepped into a trap of a situation and had been fighting and on the run since. But how. . . *how* did they keep finding him? He hadn't been tagged, the way some operatives were. He'd been too new. His mentor told him to avoid it at all costs. Best advice he'd been given.

"Wait. . .make good?"

Neil wanted to curse himself.

"Make good on what?"

"Nothing. Let's just. . ."

That dog. . .that incredible, stupid dog. As long as they were in town, he'd be found. That had to be how they kept spotting him. Tracking him. Okay, that explained the Americans, but what about the other authorities? It didn't make sense.

What if he could eliminate the threat? Killing the dog nauseated him. But it was either the Lab or him.

"I need to put something into play." His mind whirred with the idea. "We'll hole up in one of the abandoned buildings. I think. . .I think I know how to get that handler off my scent."

It seemed there was only one way out: death.

But it wouldn't be his death. Or Lina's.

It'd be theirs. Starting with that dog.

A low rumble erupted into a snapping bark.

Cardinal's gut clinched. Talon had gone primal on Watterboy, who had a hand clamped around Aspen's mouth. Hackles raised, the dog lowered his front end—he'd pounce any second.

"Release her—the dog!" Cardinal shouted.

The danger must've registered because Watterboy released her and stepped back.

"Talon, out! Out!" Short of breath and a little pale, Aspen straightened her T-shirt as she let Talon sniff her hand. She met Cardinal's gaze and gave a short nod. "Thanks."

"That was some kind of muffed up. . . ," a lanky soldier said, his M4 propped over his chest, one hand on the butt. "That dog was going to take a chunk out of your—"

"Hey," Candyman slapped the guy in the gut, "watch your language."

"No harm intended." Watterboy shot an apologetic look at Aspen. "I was afraid you'd cry out. We didn't need that kind of attention."

Something twisted sideways in Cardinal when Watterboy manhandled Aspen into submission in the darkened building. The soldier whispered something to her, she nodded, then he released her. Also dressed in camo and a flak vest, Timbrel went to her friend.

But Cardinal saw the disquiet clouding Aspen's face. Saw the confusion that still clung to her. "Give her room," he said, feeling a surge of protectiveness. "Let her get her bearings." He touched her arm. "You okay?"

She swallowed and gave him a quick nod. "Surprised me, that's all."

"I couldn't warn you. When I spotted the signal, we were in the open. You did good." Cardinal turned to the captain. "What've you got?"

He waved a hand as he and five others headed to the rear and climbed a flight of stairs. "Burnett contacted and said things are still a go. But he said to be on our guard."

"About?" Cardinal hustled up the stairs pocked with bullet holes and peeling plaster. He rounded the rail, glancing down to the floor below. Hogan filled Aspen in on mundane things.

"Your missionary, Courtland, and this." Palms spread and arms stretched over the table that took up one side of a large open room, Watterboy stared up through his brow.

A political map of the area bore Xs and a few circles. In his quick purview, Cardinal knew things were heating up. What worried him was the squiggly line separating Djibouti from Somalia. It'd been marked up with numbers and a series of hyphenated digits. Lat-long indicators.

"What's happening here?" He looked at Watterboy.

"That's what we're trying to figure out. There's been a buildup of fighters in recent months. DIA intercepted a phone conversation. . ." Droning on about the intelligence reports, Watterboy planted his hands on his belt. "But right now, Burnett wants us out here." He pressed his fingertip to a barren area about two klicks out.

"What's there?" Her voice had lost its quiver as Aspen came and stood beside him.

"It's a village. On familiar terms with your dear missionary friend."

"Why are we going there?" Aspen asked.

"Because," Watterboy said as he tugged out some photos from a manila envelope that sat beneath the map and spread them out, "UAV snapped these about two nights ago."

Leaning forward, Cardinal sorted through the photos from the unmanned aerial vehicle. Arranged them in an order that seemed to portray the layout of the village. A truck. Two men. A dozen villages. "Armed." That wasn't good. Not unusual in these parts where you negotiated a cup of goat's milk with an AK-47 on your back.

"DIA is working to ID the two men. The truck is driven by Somalis. We believe they're the same pirates who hijacked a shipping barge last week."

Cardinal met Watterboy's gaze. "And what was on that barge?"

"Weapons. Hundreds of them."

"Why would anyone be shipping weapons?"

"That's what we're going to find out." Watterboy grinned, his hazel eyes gleaming. "Right after we destroy the weapons."

"How's the honeymoon?" Candyman needed to be punched.

Aspen shifted. "So, we're headed to the village?"

"Roger," Watterboy said. "We're going to rendezvous with a medical detachment from Lemonnier and go in under the ruse of a welfare visit. They'll have a couple of nurses and doctors pass out goodies and deliver much-needed meds. Our contact there is Souleiman Hamadou, a Somali sultan—or at least he thinks he is. Most of the village sultans are overruled by the Djiboutian government, but out in the desert—"

"Out of sight, out of mind?" Having spent a little time there before things went south, Cardinal held a haunting awareness of the poverty that gripped the land.

"Pretty much." Watterboy shifted around, grabbed two bags, and tossed them over the table. "Suit up. We bug out in fifteen."

ACUs and body armor waited in the kit bag. "Weapons?"

Candyman shot another grin at him. "Right here." He pointed to a long box.

"Here, you can have some privacy in this room," Timbrel said to Aspen, and they headed off.

Waiting till he heard a door shut or their voices faded enough, he turned to Watterboy. "What aren't you telling me?"

The seasoned combat veteran betrayed nothing with his face or body language.

Muscles tightening, Cardinal eased closer. "Let me be painfully clear with you gentlemen. Nobody cares more about this mission than me."

"Aspen might disagree."

"If she knew what I did, no, she wouldn't." Lips tight, he glared at them. "If I so much as get a whiff that you're going to stiff me—"

"This isn't about stiffing you." Watterboy tucked his helmet on. "And the clock is ticking. We pull out with or without you. This is a favor, briefing you. Take it or leave it."

Cardinal ripped off his shirt, stuffed it in the bag, and lifted out the brown T-shirt. Threading his arms through it, he vowed to make sure he never let his guard down from now on.

A whistle carried through the battered room. "Those're some scars."

Ignoring Candyman, Cardinal slipped on the ACU jacket and body-armor vest. He strapped himself up with the knee and elbow guards.

"You do that like you know them."

Were they complete idiots? Or hadn't they read his files? No. . . they were just needling him. They knew very well he spent months in Afghanistan with Courtland. He may not have been career, his stint in the line of combat—officially—might have been short, but he was no stranger to playing this role. And part of that role meant knowing how.

Shirt tucked, he ran a hand through his hair and pivoted to ODA452, who were so tense, so alert to his every move, it was a wonder someone didn't accidentally shoot him. "Weapons."

"For your leg holster." Watterboy handed over a Glock. Then he passed an M4A1 and a mic/earpiece.

Tucking the piece in, he heard Talon returning.

Aspen came around the corner, adjusted her vest as she muttered something to Timbrel. The ring sparked on a beam of light.

"Take off the ring," Cardinal said. "You'll be a hot target with that."

"And without it, you'll be a hot target for every unsuspecting male." Timbrel glared at Candyman.

"Hey, I'm not unsuspecting."

Aspen tugged off the ring, slipped it into a pocket, and then her gaze lingered. . .on him. Traveled down his frame then back to his face. "You have weapons."

"So will you."

"Only a Glock," she said as she turned to Watterboy. "I can't handle anything bigger when I have Talon on lead, and I assume that's part of why we're going—so Talon can track. But you do know, he's not trained for explosives or weapons."

"That'd be Beo." Timbrel winked.

"Understood. No worries. Burnett wants you on-site, you're on-site." She had found her courage. And her groove.

And he liked it. "We should go."

At times, Dane stood like an impenetrable fortress. That was 98 percent of the time. The other 2 percent, she saw. . .something. Not quite vulnerability. The thought made her want to laugh. That man, vulnerable? Not in a million years. Scared? Of what? She had this feeling he could take care of himself—and anyone else who messed with him. And that whole thing when he'd intercepted the situation before Talon took a chunk out of Watters's arm or throat—brilliant. It made her heart swell because he'd been attuned to her, to Talon. Few had ever gotten to that place. It'd taken her months to get there with Talon as his handler.

"Let's do it." Watters pointed to two men. "Java, Pops, stay here with coms and maintain contact with base. Watch that feed from Aerial Two. We've got air support ready just in case."

Heart in her throat, Aspen realized this could be her first real op. And her last.

She fell into step behind Timbrel, the captain, and Candyman as they scurried down the stairs. Rock and dust dribbled around them as they moved. Behind her, she heard Cardinal and the other two members of the team—Rocket and Scrip—bringing up the rear. They buttonhooked out of the stairwell and hurried to a rear room.

Two beat-up Jeeps waited.

The doors flung open. Aspen held out her arm and showed her palm to Talon. "Talon, hup! Hup!" He leapt into the back, then she guided him over the seat into the rear.

"Hey."

The voice, so deep and masculine, drew her around. Cardinal stood close.

"Listen," he said, craning down, "don't trust your eyes out there."

She frowned. "Don't. . .what?"

"Trust your instincts"—he nodded to the rear—"and that trained warrior. Understood?"

Okay. Sure. That sounded good, but. . . "Why?"

"Because eyes are deceiving."

"Let's move!" Watters's bark carried across the makeshift garage.

They left through the rear of the building and jounced onto a side road that pushed through two buildings in a narrow alley. *Just breathe. Things are fine.* Even if she was sitting in a Jeep in Djibouti with a team of trained warriors and a man who was, legally, her husband.

Dane leaned forward, a hand clutching the seat. "How many in this village?"

"At least fifty, sixty skinnies," Watterboy called over his shoulder. The open window made the keffiyeh around his neck flap like crazy.

They talked up numbers and locals and warlords and terrorists.

Aspen's ears were going numb, and her back, thanks to the Kevlar vest, felt like a warming plate for hamburgers. With each jolt on the axles from the pothole-riddled roads, Aspen felt the heat rubbing her shoulder raw where the vest met flesh.

With the heat at 105, she would have to closely monitor Talon. She glanced back to him and found him panting. Thankfully, Timbrel had known to bring water for Talon. The others seemed oblivious to the needs of the working dog. They wanted him to work yet didn't know how to properly prep for the op. She dug a bottle of water out of the kit bag and reached over the seat. She uncapped it and drizzled some into his mouth. He smiled at her, his eyes nearly squeezed shut in thanks, then returned to panting.

Easing back into the seat, she tossed the empty bottle in the bag and sat back. Dane was still talking, laughing. He had the beginnings of laugh lines around his eyes. She'd noticed that the first time they met. It'd made her like him, like his smile. It was that, somehow, that told her she didn't have to fear him, even though there were times so unnerving she wanted to run away.

He'd been all business this morning and, well, even last night, when she'd made a fool out of herself. He hadn't exactly laughed at her, but it was close. *"Not interested."*

Why?

That was a stupid question. Aspen pushed her gaze out the window, watching the heartbreaking poverty as it slid by. And wasn't that just the way the world worked? People were starving here, dying of diseases easily cured in America, and the world just slid right on by. She'd known there were places like this, but being here, seeing it, experiencing it firsthand. . .she really had no clue how bad things could be for a people.

Was Austin out there somewhere? Walking among them? Did anyone know him? He'd stand out. Granted, there was a hefty French population, since this had been one of their territories, but Caucasians were still the minority here. As were Christians.

Laughter drew her attention back.

Dane slapped Candyman's shoulder. Something akin to jealousy squirmed through her stomach. She wasn't jealous of Candyman. That'd be crazy. But that he got Dane to laugh. . .a real laugh, a nice laugh, with his slightly chiseled jaw and that dark dusting of stubble. . .

"But this man? Is fine. *With a capital* F.*"*

Aspen tucked her chin as Brittain's words slipped through the hot Djibouti sun and straight into her heart. Yeah, her friend had been right. He was fine, though the word Aspen would've chosen started with an *h*—*hunky*—or a *g*—*gorgeous.*

"I'm not interested. . ." His words resounded like a gong against her pining.

Aspen pushed straight in the seat and shoved off the silliness. The Jeep jounced as it turned onto a strip of dirt that had ruts instead of lane markers. Nausea swirled as she saw the conditions—homes built with

164

corrugated boxes, lean-tos draped with fabric and wobbly steel. That had to be hot during the day. But it'd provide shelter at night.

Beside her came a small whoosh, drawing her attention to the side.

Blue eyes made her stomach squirm. A grim expression stole through his normally stoic face. "This is one experience that never fades, no matter how long you're gone or how many times you see it."

Humanitarian, too? Aspen eyed him. With the headgear and camos, his features seemed amplified, stronger. And natural. "How long were you in the Army?"

"Not long enough." He winked. "And too long on the other hand."

The Jeep slowed and pulled to the side of the road.

Aspen peered through the front windshield as another vehicle bounded ahead. Only when she saw the uniforms did she remember Watterboy had said they were going in as a welfare mission—and that vehicle must have the medical staff.

A few more minutes delivered them into a village of four, maybe five huts, but dozens of people. Skin darkened by the sun and glistening with sweat, they were vibrant in their multicolored garb. Beyond the front bumper a cluster of Djiboutians stood with a handful of soldiers. "National Army?" But the vast majority of the soldiers were white.

Dane leaned forward. Said something to Watters she couldn't hear, then climbed out of the truck. "Stay," he said in a sharp tone.

"Bravo, Nightingale One this is Alpha One," Watters spoke into his coms. "Contact with French Army. Unknown intentions. Hold position." With that, Watters stepped into the heat. His body still protected by the armored door, he rested his hand on his leg-holstered Glock.

Talon shifted up, his head appearing over the seat as he panted almost in her ear. "What's wrong?"

"They're French." The snarl in Candyman's words made her hesitate. "That's bad. . .why?"

"Don't you find the fact they're here when we show up a mighty big coincidence?" He huffed. "This stinks. Get ready to fight."

Nineteen

If it smelled like a trap and looked like a trap. . .

Fingers itching for the weapon holstered at his leg, Cardinal took in the scene. Though twenty or more villagers huddled in the background, it was the fear on their faces that warned him. Cardinal stood in front of the Jeep, praying he shielded Aspen from view. He wanted her presence made known when he deemed it safe. He scanned the foreign nationals. Next to the captain stood a man with no rank. Interesting.

"Hello." Watters said, as he came to the front. "Is there a problem here, Captain?" He seemed as tense as Cardinal felt. Scanning, checking, assessing—just like a good Special Forces soldier.

"No problem," came the slick-accented reply. "We are visiting the villages."

"Fancy that." Watters brought his gaze to the captain. "So are we." He waved to the secondary vehicle. Doors opened. Dirt crunched beneath boots. "Our doctors are here on a welfare check and visit."

"The generosity of the Americans is astounding." The captain shifted to the man on his right. *"As tu obtenu ce que tu voulais?"*

Mentally, Cardinal went on alert. Physically, he kept his posture detached, curious. Hand on his weapon, the other on his hip, he waited for the response from the one who stood a few inches shorter.

Only a quick nod served as the man's reply.

"Il semble que tes craintes n'étaient pas fondées. Ils sont aussi aveugles qu'ils sont stupides. Très bien. Je vous laisse à votre mission de miséricorde, les Américains."

Blind as we are stupid? And what unfounded fears are they hiding? But he had to play it cool. Play it off. With a quick look to Watters, who shrugged, Cardinal cocked his head. "Come again?" he asked.

The captain held his gaze for a few seconds longer than was necessary. "Forgive me."

Cardinal would if the request had been sincere.

"I forget myself." The captain didn't lie well. "We were just leaving. Enjoy your day, and stay hydrated." With that he waved to the men, who hustled toward a truck. The French soldiers climbed into the back.

At least, he heard them doing that. But Cardinal honed in on the captain's little minion, who ducked his head and looked into the Jeep.

Adrenaline buzzed through Cardinal's veins.

Barking erupted. The Jeep rocked. Inside, he heard Aspen giving commands to Talon, who whimpered, turned a circle, barked once more, then obeyed the command, but tension rippled through the Lab's coat.

Aspen turned back to Cardinal, and their gazes locked. He went to the door and crouched. "What happened?"

"I have no idea. That soldier looked in here, and Talon just came unglued." She swallowed, her cheeks flushed by the heat. "What did they say? Talon must've smelled or noticed something—were they aggressive?"

The rattle of a diesel clapped out conversation. Cardinal watched as the French made their hasty exit. Just like the French, though—quick to leave. "No, but that's the problem."

"We clear?" Watters called.

Looking over the top of the Jeep, Cardinal hesitated. The French wouldn't have hung around if they had rigged something. Wouldn't have let their faces be seen when an IED along the road would've taken out the Americans in a cleaner, hands-off situation. But something large and unsettling wafted on the hot winds. "Let's get this done and get out of here."

"So, it's safe?"

"It's never safe." The French were talking about something, and the stiff-necked response of the minion bothered him. And the words the captain spoke—something was off. But they had a job to do, and they'd better get under way.

He stalked to the rear of the Jeep and reached for the handle.

"No!" Aspen leapt out of the vehicle. "Please, don't open that. Talon might take it as an aggressive move." She brushed a curl from her face. "Sorry. I just don't want him to make strange or attack you."

Cardinal sniffed. "Neither do I." He stepped back and lifted his hands. "He's all yours."

"Nightingale, you have the all clear. ODA452, circle up."

Cardinal strode toward the much-shorter villager, the man who must be the sultan by the way the others deferred and hung back—and ironically, the way the bodies of the villagers were angled toward him. "You are Sultan Souleiman?"

Wire-rimmed glasses framed a weathered, sun-darkened face. He stood a little straighter with the acknowledgment. "I am. You are Mr. Dane?"

"It is an honor." Cardinal inclined his head to offer his submission to the man's position within the community. When he looked up, the sultan's eyes were wide and focused on something behind Cardinal. He glanced back.

Aspen. With Talon, who darted back and forth on the sixteen-foot lead, sniffing. Hauling in big, hard breaths through his nose. What had he hit on? He traced the path from the children—who squealed and jumped back but then burst into laughter when Talon nosed their legs—back toward Cardinal.

He shot a questioning look to Aspen, who shrugged.

A slew of Arabic flew from the sultan.

And that's when it hit Cardinal.

He needed to bridge this gap now. "Sultan Souleiman, this is Lieutenant Courtland. The dog is a working dog named Talon." Again, Cardinal inclined his head. "I hope his presence will not be offensive to you."

"They are not clean." He seemed aghast that they'd brought this animal into his village.

"Please, Sultan, do not be concerned. The dog will stay with his handler. Nobody should touch him. He's trained to protect the woman with his lead." *As am I.* Cardinal pointed to the village, away from Aspen. "Ready?"

With one last concerned glance to Aspen, or more specifically, Talon, Sultan Souleiman shifted around and headed toward a hut. It did not surprise Cardinal that the sultan of this village wasn't even old enough to be his own father. With the median age of twenty-two, most males had a life expectancy of only sixty or sixty-five. And of the entire population in Djibouti, only 3 percent were of that age. Daunting and haunting to know you wouldn't live long.

"Stay close," Cardinal said to Aspen. As the words sailed out of his mouth, he stiffened, praying she didn't take them wrong.

"She's not a dog that obeys your commands," Timbrel said.

"You're right. She's a smart woman who wants to stay alive." He glanced back, so proud of her unwavering resolve and grit-determination. "Ready?"

Aspen gave a nod. "I think he has a hit, but on what, I have no idea."

"Think it's your brother?"

"Out here?" The question wasn't one of information but one of confirmation. She'd thought the same thing and wanted him to confirm it.

"Keep your eyes out. You never know."

"Roger."

Already, the gaggle of children had crowded in around Aspen and Talon. She'd have her hands full keeping them away. Maybe he should offer. . .

"Talon, heel! Sit! Stay!"

The Lab trotted to her side, sat, and squinted up at her as if to say, "Yeah, okay, it's hot out here and I can smell something, but you're cute so I'll sit."

Cardinal felt a smirk tug up the side of his face. She'd read his mind. In that case, time to divert the sultan's attention. "It's so good of you to talk with me, Sultan." He pointed to a shady spot beneath the only two trees he'd seen for miles. No doubt the reason the nomadic villagers had set down stakes here. "Perhaps we could sit here and talk?"

The sultan lifted his chin a little higher. "Good, good."

As they walked, the sultan spoke of the poverty, of the search for jobs, of battling the refugees, and the effect not having rain had on the villagers. For a second, Cardinal worried about leaving Aspen alone. But when he glanced back and spotted the Lab with her—and Timbrel behind them—his fears were allayed. Talon would maul anyone who tried to hurt Aspen, and Timbrel would finish them off.

"He's dehydrated."

"I'll grab the water." Timbrel jogged off.

Whimpering, Talon panted and paced, his tail flicking, but Aspen kept a tight lead on him to keep him in the shade and from wearing himself out. "Talon, heel. Sit. Stay."

He complied, his belly jiggling in and out rapidly beneath the frenetic panting. She glanced back to the vehicles. Timbrel and Candyman were digging through a bag, searching. He must've made some comment because Timbrel shoved him. He grabbed the edge of the vehicle to catch himself. She was sure a smile hid beneath that gnarly beard.

Whimpering tugged her attention back to her partner. She smoothed a hand over his coat. "Easy, boy."

Talon had all the earmarks of dehydration or heat exhaustion. Jibril's sister, Khaterah, had warned her to watch for it.

Still whimpering, Talon lowered himself to the ground and lay on his side. His panting was ramping up. She checked his gums and cringed. Losing pigmentation. "C'mon," she called to Timbrel.

"Here, here." Timmy dropped the bottles.

Once she uncapped the bottle, Aspen doused Talon with the water, coaxing the liquid into his dense fur. Dogs only sweat through their bellies and the pads of their feet, which was why in this heat, she had avoided using the protective paw covers, though with the raw pad of his right foot, she feared they might have to use them.

They tugged out a collapsible waterproof nylon bowl and filled it so Talon could lap up the water. "It's okay, Talon. You're going to be fine." He fed off her emotions, so she worked to stay calm and confident—two things she wasn't feeling right now. As he drank, she doused him again. "It's too hot."

"I'd turn down the heat, but it seems the man upstairs likes it hot here." Candyman stood over them, his headgear, keffiyeh, and vest making him look forbidding. When he spoke she wasn't sure whether to laugh or what. She'd seen him in Afghanistan and the guy had been as cool and at ease as if he were back home at a barbecue—just like today.

Aspen poured another bottle over Talon and noted, with pleasure, that his panting had grown a little more regular and had slowed. "I knew you'd reset, buddy." She rubbed the spot between his eyes, and he slumped back, totally relaxed.

"Here they come," Candyman said.

Aspen swiped the sweat from her forehead as she looked toward the huts.

A group emerged with the sultan explaining something to Dane. The two had talked for more than thirty minutes beneath the shade of these trees. With one leg drawn close and the other hooked, Dane had seemed so at home. Was there anywhere he didn't manage to fit in? Fresh waves of respect and admiration sluiced through her. And, of course, the younger, unmarried women—at least she hoped they were unmarried, or maybe it would be better if they were married—trailed Dane like lovesick puppies.

His gaze slid across the open area and rammed right into hers. She felt it. All the way in the pit of her belly. She looked away and focused back on Talon, who stood on all fours now, as if to say, "Okay, I'm done with this heat stuff. Let's get outta Dodge."

Then he lifted his head and drew in a couple of big sniffs. More whimpering ensued. Talon trailed back and forth between the trees. Sniffing, whimpering, trotting. Blood blotted the sand.

She winced.

"Aspen, his paws."

"Get the protective booties."

Shouts and a loud bang exploded from somewhere.

Talon yelped and tore off.

Aspen held the lead, but it ripped out of her hands. "Talon, heel! Heel!"

He slowed, turned a circle, then scampered under the Jeep.

Disappointment and concern flooded Aspen. She trudged over to the truck, her head pounding from the stress of tending Talon and the unrelenting heat. Sweat streamed down her face and back as she went to her knees.

A soft touch on her arm. "You okay?" Dane asked.

"Yeah." Who was she kidding? "No. I don't know." Did she sound as psychotic as she felt? She gave a soft snort and wiped her forehead again. "Talon's been on edge for the last thirty minutes, whimpering. He got dehydrated, but I think it's under control. But now he's whimpering again, then that noise—" She stopped short. "What was it?"

"A couple of kids horsing around crashed into one of the metal walls."

"Oh." And the poor dog had lost his courage. So did she, knowing Talon still wasn't ready. It broke her heart. Tugged at her. Like that mother standing with the sultan beneath the shade tree now, with an infant strapped to her breast with a scarf-like sling, and another in another sling dangling against her hip. She held tiny little fingers of an older child. Three children. All skin and bones. All looking hungry, sad. Just like Talon.

Just like me.

Dane's hand rested on her shoulder. "Aspen?"

The tears were coming. She could feel them. Pushed them back. "It's all. . .wrong." Her eyes burned.

"Hey." Dane's hand slid to her neck, and he nudged her chin up with his thumb. "Aspen."

She shook her head, refusing to meet his gaze.

"Hey." He waited for her this time, but as soon as she looked into the eyes of iron, the squirming tangled up her stomach again. "It's good— good that you're feeling this way. It means it's changing you, that you won't forget. The worst thing we can do is walk out of here and forget."

She loved that he didn't want to forget, that the world around them impacted him. But more than those concerns plied at her. "It's not just that—Talon's not ready. If he can't even tolerate loud noises, how on earth can he find Austin? And the heat is getting to him, and he's injured his paw, so he has to rest for days if not a week, and—"

"Whoa."

She looked up at him and once again shook her head. "Why did I think I could do this? He was Austin's partner. His superior. They were inseparable. What am I doing out here?"

"Getting answers." Dane lowered his head and peered into her eyes. "Let's get him out from under there and get back to Lemonnier. We'll debrief."

Yanked out of her emotional collapse, she widened her eyes. "What'd you find out?"

He smirked. "A few things." He patted her shoulder. "C'mon. Let's get Talon and move out."

On her knees, she peered under the vehicle.

Talon sat beneath the Jeep, head up—as much as he could manage. He scooched forward on his belly and paws then dropped something at her feet.

Aspen gasped.

Twenty

Camp Lemonnier, Combined Joint Task Force—Horn of Africa
Republic of Djibouti, Africa

Y ou'll need to work her. Find out what she found. What it means."

Breathe. In. Out. "I will *not* work her." Pinching the bridge of his nose—and grateful it didn't hurt as bad as it did a week ago—Cardinal clamped down on his frustration.

"Cardinal, we don't have time. Understand this: General Payne went ballistic when he found out you were there."

"And how did he find that out?" Showered, he stuffed his arms in a clean shirt.

"No idea, but he's yelling and threatening to have you hauled back here and thrown in prison for the rest of your life."

"My job is to figure this out and find Courtland." Cardinal stuffed his feet in his boots as he talked. "Your job is to keep the hounds off my back." He huffed. "Don't worry. I'll find out what she knows, but I won't work her. I'll *ask* her."

Burnett laughed, and the slurping of a soda filled the line. "What's the difference?"

"Night and day."

Burnett cursed. "For the love of Pete." He muttered something. "Look, Payne's storming down the hall, obviously planning to be a pain in my backside." He grunted. "Listen, Cardinal—get Courtland and get back here before the dragon breathes fire down your neck."

"Understood."

Now to find Aspen. *Talk* to her. Give her the chance to be straight with him. So he could keep his conscience clear.

Feeling as if he'd been through a sauna after his shower, Cardinal made his way past the containerized living units, heat wafting off the cement. At least they'd been accommodated in the portable buildings rather than a tent—that, he knew, was for Talon to stay cool in the AC-regulated environment. When they'd arrived back at Lemonnier, Aspen and Timbrel went with the med staff to get Talon hydrated and cleaned up. They'd agreed to meet at the cantina after showers and a change of clothes.

The central path that snaked around "downtown" Lemonnier was known as Broadway and led Cardinal toward the cantina, theater, PX—and Aspen. At least, he hoped it did. She wasn't in her building. As he made his way through downtown, he spotted a group playing basketball down the road a bit. Candyman with his thick beard and thick build stuck out. And so did Timbrel, though she stood at least a head shorter. She had more spunk than most women—especially to play a game with men nearly twice her size.

Cardinal slipped into the cantina, scanning the area. No go. He stepped back into the heat and made his way to the gym.

Bag in hand, Watterboy strode toward him.

"Have you seen Aspen?"

"Saw her heading to the chapel on my way in." He shouldered past another soldier but called over his shoulder, "Hey. Briefing with Burnett in twenty."

"Thanks." Cardinal jogged toward the chapel, which looked more like something that belonged on the plains of America than in Eastern Africa.

Stepping inside stripped him of any preconceived notions as music rushed into him, drawing him deeper into its sanctuary. The door closed, and his eyes slowly adjusted to the Spartan interior. Certainly no St. Mary's Cathedral. With wood paneling, fluorescent bulbs on the sloped ceilings, and black vinyl chairs serving as pews, the chapel was functional at best.

Sitting at the black upright piano, Aspen had her back to him. Immersed in the music filling the air. Peaceful. The tune coiled around his chest and drew him to the front.

As he came up beside her, she jumped and lifted her fingers. Silence dropped like a bomb and felt just as destructive. Somehow, her playing soothed the savage atmosphere.

"Please," he said as he eased onto the bench with her. "Don't stop. It's beautiful."

"I'm a *closet* pianist. I don't play in front of others." Her embarrassment glowed through her cheeks and shy smile.

"Where'd you learn?"

"My mother was a concert pianist, and though I inherited her skill, I did not inherit her desire and ability to perform in front of others." She shrugged and flexed her hand. "It's easier on the knuckles than boxing."

Cardinal ran a hand along his face. "And jawbones."

Aspen laughed. "Blocking helps that."

"So, it's my fault?"

She wrinkled her nose. "You just need more practice."

The challenge sat in the quiet building like a warm blanket. Finally Aspen plunked a few keys, the higher notes tinkling through the cozy chapel. Then a heavy sigh. Her countenance was depressed, her song now somber.

"What's going on?"

Chewing her lower lip, she again dropped her hands into her lap and stared up at the framed print above the piano. "I came in here to try to think through it all—why would he leave me, be alive and never tell me? Let me think he's dead?" She bunched her shoulders. "I don't get it."

Considering he had something to do with all that, he had to tread lightly. "There are those who make sacrifices for their country most people will never understand."

She considered him, her pale eyes piercing. "Are you saying he's making a sacrifice?"

Whoa. Too close there. "What I'm saying is, unless you can talk to him, don't try to understand. Just go with your facts. Let them talk to you."

Aspen looked down at her hands. "They don't make sense, like they're speaking a different language."

He'd have to nudge her. "You found something at the village."

She whipped her face back to his. "How. . . ?"

"There's not much I miss."

Guilt crowded her soft, innocent features. She was so easy to read, so easy to. . . Cardinal fisted his hand. He would *not* work her. This had to be natural. But his curiosity was killing him. "If you hid it from us, I assume you had a reason. A good one. At the same time, you've separated yourself since finding it." He cocked his head and arched his eyebrow. "Those facts are talking to me."

Her expression shifted, but was it one of being caught with her hand in the proverbial cookie jar or one of genuine curiosity? "What are they saying?"

"That you don't trust me."

She opened her mouth to speak and drew back. "I—"

"Let me finish." He noticed her hand had moved to the pocket, probably where she hid the item. "Second, your seclusion and pensive disposition tell me whatever you found probably has personal meaning or evokes a memory. And somehow, it has pushed you into self-preservation mode."

Her gaze darted over the white and black keys, her mind seemingly somewhere else.

"And last. . .you don't trust anyone with what you're thinking, what you're considering, which is why you're here in the chapel." He lowered his voice because it just seemed appropriate. "Seeking the counsel of the divine."

Just rip her open and read her heart like a book! How on earth had he figured all that out?

A nervous tickle pushed out an equally nervous laugh. "Remind me never to ask you to evaluate me again." It was hard, sitting here next to him. Smelling the freshness of him after a shower. He hadn't shaved again, and a thin layer of dark stubble shadowed his mouth and jaw. His black hair dropped into his face, still a bit damp. Hard to think. Hard to hold her ground.

"So, I'm right?" Something shadowed his eyes.

It almost looked like disappointment. Why did that thought corkscrew through her chest, the thought of letting him down? She couldn't hurt him. Didn't want to lose the little connection they'd established, even though he'd shoved her away not two days ago.

Dane stood and walked away.

Was he leaving? She twisted around and pushed to her feet. "Dane. Wait."

He hesitated then planted himself on the first row of black chairs.

She didn't want him leaving mad. "Please." Panic clutched at her— she didn't want him to leave at all. "It wasn't my intention to hide this from you."

Okay, yeah, she was trying to hide the token. But only because she didn't know what it meant. And she hated that everything that had happened since arriving in Djibouti left her with that thought—she didn't know. She was sick of not knowing why her brother did this. Why he let her believe he was dead.

She brushed the curls from her face. "Okay. Look, I'm sorry. That's not true. I just. . ." She took the piece from her pocket and held it out to him.

Eyes on her, he took it. Turned it over. "A flattened penny?" Questions danced in his eyes. "I'm sorry, I. . ." He shrugged.

Taking it back, she lowered herself onto the vinyl padded seat next to him, rubbing her thumb along the smoothed surface. "After our parents' funeral, Austin and I went back to our grandparents' house." The memory made her ache. "The house was filling with church members bringing casseroles, telling us all these stories about Mom and Dad, how wonderful they were, how they were in a better place, that we shouldn't be sad."

An unbidden tear strolled down her cheek. She brushed it aside. "It was hard. . .so hard to sit there, thank them for coming, listen to them go on and on." More tears. The rawness felt new, fresh, not as if it'd been eight years.

"I always had a little more patience than Austin, but that day. . ." She tightened her lips as a tear rolled over them and bounced off her chin. "I just. Couldn't. Take. It." With the back of her hand, she dried the tears. "I went out back on the porch. Heard the train coming."

She blinked and looked at Dane through her tear-blurred vision. "Austin came out, grabbed my hand, and led me to the tracks. When we were kids visiting there, we'd put pennies on the track and wait for the train to flatten them." She held up the penny. "That's what we did that day. And we agreed to keep them with us—always." Aspen tugged a chain from beneath her shirt and revealed a second penny, equally flattened and smoothed.

His face remained impassive. As if he wasn't catching on, but she knew better than that. Dane didn't miss a thing—he even said so. In fact, he saw more than she could ever hope to notice.

"Austin's here, Dane. He's *here*." The tears and hurt squeezed past her will to hold them back. "Why? *Why* is he here? Why did he let them lie to us, let me believe he was dead?"

Dane's arms came around her and drew her close.

Clinging to him, Aspen cried, relishing the strength in his arms wrapped around her. His chest was firm and toned, yet comfortably soft. His heart boomed against her ear, regular, steady. Constant.

Dane. A veritable pillar of strength this whole time.

Clenching his shirt in her fist, she let the shudders smooth out her angst. But an epiphany stilled her. "He wants me to find him." Elation nudged her head off his chest but was quickly tempered with confusion.

"What are you thinking? Tell me." A smile seemed parked on his face, ready to flash.

She flicked her gaze to him and felt a giddy sensation thinking she might actually be on the right track, that Dane already knew what she was going to say. That he agreed with her. But the thought. . .it proved excruciating to voice. Her throat constricted. She hated feeling this way, feeling weak, betrayed. "Why. . . ?"

"Go on. Finish that thought."

"Why would he want me to find him when he's been hiding?"

"What answers haunt that question?"

She swallowed. "I'm not sure I want to go there."

"Explore every option."

Aspen gave a mental nod. "Either he's in danger and can't let me know he needs help."

"A bit far-fetched, considering his occupation."

"True, but not *completely* implausible."

"Agreed." Dane brushed the curls from her face. "Go on."

"Or he's. . ." Adrenaline squirted through her. "It's a trap."

"Let me guess," Dane said with a grin. "He got the brawn, you got the brains."

179

"That black eye says I have some brawn, too." Her heart spun in crazy circles as his hand slid along her cheek then down, cupping her neck.

"I deserved it." Steel eyes seemed molten as they traced her face.

Aspen's mind cartwheeled as it caught up with what was happening as his face came closer, his dark lashes fringing eyes that dropped to her mouth.

Oh man. They shouldn't be doing this. But she'd felt connected to him since they set boot here in Africa. She had to admit she'd wanted this. For a while. A long while.

"Hey!"

Aspen jolted at the shout from behind.

On his feet in a flash, Dane erupted in a storm. Brows tightly knit, fury rippled through his arms held to the side.

"You sorry son of a—"

"Timbrel!" Aspen shoved upward, planting herself between Dane and Timbrel, her hand on Dane's chest. His pulse hammered under her palm. Fists balled, jaw tight, he was ready to fight.

Candyman walked behind Timbrel, who trembled as she spoke, "I told you, *told* you to stay away from her or I would hurt you."

"Excuse me," Aspen snapped. "You don't speak for me."

"I do when you get played."

Candyman stood there, not speaking. Watching. As if. . .as if he knew something—they both knew something she didn't.

"What do you mean?"

Another man stepped from the back, only then noticeable.

Timbrel thumbed over her shoulder to the brawny man in ACUs. "This is Will Rankin."

Aspen's mind ricocheted off the name. "You're. . .you were Austin's fire buddy."

Twenty-One

Djibouti City, Djibouti

What do you mean, you left it in the dirt for her to find?"

With a glowering look, he climbed into the truck. "I know what I'm doing. You take care of your responsibility, Admiral, and I'll take care of mine."

"What's wrong with you, leading her straight to you?"

He smirked. "How else do you kill a mouse than lure it out of its hole?"

"But she's with Burnett's pawn."

"Don't worry."

"Do you realize who he is?"

Seething, he stared across the room at the woman with raven hair and sky-blue eyes. "I know exactly who he is." He let himself smile. "And how to take care of him."

Camp Lemonnier, Combined Joint Task Force—Horn of Africa
Republic of Djibouti, Africa

Still reeling from the near collision of good sense and passion—*what got into him?*—Cardinal wasn't sure what this was about. And secretly, he was glad he'd been saved from caving to his carnal desires, to compromising himself, Aspen, and the mission with weakness.

Cardinal shifted everything in him to the man Aspen had just

181

named as her brother's partner. "Lieutenant." He nodded to Rankin.

The man skirted a look to Timbrel.

She crossed her arms, defiance granitelike on what could be a pretty face without all that attitude. "He doesn't know you."

Cardinal inclined his head and cocked it. "Is he supposed to?" Why did it make his heart thump a million different ways that Aspen had hold of his forearm.

Timbrel frowned. "You said you were on Austin's team."

Ah. "Actually, no. I said I was with him in Kariz-e Sefid." He looked at Rankin. "You weren't there that day, were you?"

The man shrugged. "No, I was sick. Heat exhaustion or food poisoning. Docs weren't sure."

Cardinal returned his gaze to Timbrel. "Your point is. . . ?"

"He doesn't know you, and you claimed to be friends with Austin."

Aspen turned to Rankin. "Hi, I'm Aspen." She stuck out her hand and the L-T shook it, a blank expression glued to his face. "Do you know who I am?"

"Well, no, ma'am."

She smiled. "I'm Austin's twin sister, Aspen."

"He had a twin?"

With a rueful look to Timbrel, Aspen nodded.

Rankin's face reddened. "Well, Austin didn't talk much, so I'm not surprised I didn't know about you."

The man was covering his tracks—badly. Which worked well for Cardinal. Really well. He offered his hand. "We're sorry to have wasted your time, Lieutenant."

"Look," Rankin said, his deadpanned mask falling away, "I'm real sorry about Austin, but he was a good friend to me. A combat buddy, so I just—if I can help, I want to." He pointed to Cardinal's hand. "You two married?"

Cardinal slipped an arm around Aspen's waist. "Newlyweds."

The guy grinned. "Guess that's why we caught y'all lip-locked."

"Actually, we hadn't. . .he. . ." Embarrassment made Aspen all the more appealing. Even if their lips hadn't made contact yet, the accusation was enough to make her jittery.

"Guess so." Cardinal would not let Rankin think anything contrary about their cover story. It also served as a really good reminder to not slip up like that again. *Never work the women. No matter what you feel.*

The words left a hot streak down the back of his neck and into his shoulder, tightening like a noose.

They said their good-byes to the lieutenant and waited for the door to close. And that's when Cardinal turned on Timbrel. "If you have a problem with me—"

"Oh, I do."

"Then take it up with Burnett, but get off my back. And keep this between us. This op is top secret—you drag in everyone you think it takes to prove whatever whim you have against me, and we'll end up with no answers or dead." He pointed to Aspen. "We're trying to find her brother. Get with us or get off the team."

Eyes narrowed, Timbrel seemed to feed off his anger. "Don't you dare make yourself into a Boy Scout. I've seen the way you watch her, the way you ogle her." She waved a hand at Aspen. "I knew she'd fall for you with all your charm and good looks. You've been working her from day one, and I warned her."

Candyman gently rested a hand on Timbrel's arm.

"Get off me!" She flung her arm up, free of the touch. "Stay away from her. She's not a plaything."

"Enough!" Aspen snapped. "Timbrel, I get that you don't like him, that you don't like men in general, but that gives you no right to act like this. I am a grown woman. I can take care of myself."

"You're naive."

The words sliced through Aspen's anger, leaving a gaping wound that showed clearly on her face. "I may be less experienced than you when it comes to. . .relationships, but I think I know my own mind. I know when I like someone and he likes me."

Timbrel's nostrils flared. "He's got one thing on his mind—like all men. And when he's done here with this mission, he's done with you." Her lips flattened as she nailed Aspen with a piercing look. "Don't say I didn't warn you. I won't pick up the pieces when he proves me right." She stomped out of the building.

Candyman started after her. "Tim—"

"Bug off!" she shouted as she punched the door. As soon as she stepped into the blinding sun, she vanished.

Pulse ratcheting down, Cardinal hung his head. He'd lost it—really lost it with Hogan. "I'm sorry."

As he turned so did Aspen, and her hand came to rest on his side. Her fingers danced off then back on. "No, it's not your fault." Rubbing her forehead, she looked back to the door. "I'm tired of her attitude about men, especially when she tries to destroy something special in my life. I mean, I understand she's trying to protect me, but. . ." She smiled up at him. "There's nothing to protect me from. I feel safe with you."

Cardinal's breathing shallowed out.

Another smile, this one slow and coy. Aspen tugged his shirt and gave him a smirk. "I trust you."

The words detonated like a nuclear blast against his conscience. "Don't."

She almost laughed as her brows slid in and out in question. "What?"

God, help me! He was doing it—using her, manipulating her. Like he vowed not to do. She'd fallen for every play he'd dealt. Trust him? That would be the biggest mistake of her life. "Don't trust me."

This time, the smile lost its flirtation and became nervous. "What do you mean? Of course I trust you." She reached toward his face.

He grabbed her hand. Hated to do this. It had to be done. "Don't. Trust. Me." *Leave. Walk out. Sever this thing that's growing between you and her.* "Don't ever trust me." *Just tell her everything and get it over with.* It was a sarcastic thought, but it slingshot back at him. *Tell her.*

Cardinal stepped back. Stared at her. Studied her. Memorized her confusion. Thinly veiled fear speared his heart. She *didn't* trust him.

"I. . .I don't understand."

Of course she didn't. Couldn't. Because she only knew a small piece of the truth. "I have things to take care of."

"Dane."

As he walked away, he let his eyes slide shut briefly. It wasn't even his name, or even his identity. Dane was the man she married. Not Cardinal. Not the real man behind the religious moniker. She didn't know *him*. That was good—it meant she was safe from that man.

The truth wounded him. Strange, he thought as he pushed open the door, that he even cared. He shouldn't. It took only one small step to become the man he hated. To blur the ethical and moral lines between doing a job and abusing it.

Embroiled in the heat and dust that was distinctly Djibouti, he let the brilliance blind him. If only it could sear the image of Aspen Courtland's hurt from his mind.

But no, he wanted to remember that. To memorize it. So he'd never forget. And never make the mistake again.

"Girl, just come back."

Aspen cradled her head in her hand as she Skyped with Brittain, who was on the other side of the world. "I can't." She fought the urge to cry. There'd been enough tears lately, and she was through being weak. "Austin is here. I am not going home till I find him and figure out what's going on."

"Is that a ring on your finger?"

Aspen straightened, feeling the heat in her face. "Yeah." She slid it off. "It's part of our cover while we're here. In fact, we're supposed to be staying with some missionary in the city, not here on the base. But Talon's still recovering from a cut on his paw and the heat."

"What are you going to do about Mr. Don't Trust Me?"

Aspen groaned. "I have no idea." She raised her hands. "What does that mean?"

"Hello?" Brittain laughed. "It means don't trust him."

Rolling her eyes, Aspen sighed. "But why would he tell me that? It makes no sense—and it defies what I feel. When he said it, I just couldn't move. It wouldn't. . .process, especially after he almost kissed me."

"What?"

Shoot. "Um. . .never mind about that."

"Oh no." Brittain's face drew closer on the screen. "No, you can't do that to me, girl. You need to spill. Now."

"Look, it's. . .an unusual situation."

"Uh-huh."

No, she wasn't going to lie about this, wouldn't downplay what she felt. "I like him." She looked at the flat surface that held her friend's visage. "He's strong—internally and externally. He has helped *me* stay strong when I just wanted to puddle up. And even though he said not to trust him, there aren't many people I'd trust the way I trust him."

"Uh-oh."

"I know what you're going to say, so don't say it."

"All right. I won't. But you need to hear it anyway—I can smell what's happening from all the way over here. You're falling for him, hard. Be careful, Aspen. If this guy is warning you not to trust him"— she let out an "are you dumb" laugh—"then you probably need to be listening to the man. Ya know?"

Fingers digging in the curls at the back of her head, Aspen nodded. "I know, but. . ."

"Look, girl. The only time you've got a bigger *butt* than me is when you're trying to rationalize."

Aspen laughed. "Normally I'd agree. But this isn't rationalizing. I. . . it feels different."

"What does?"

"What I feel for him"—she knew Brittain would jump on that, so she leapt ahead—"*and* the motivation behind what he said."

"You have such a good heart. Always have."

Aspen cringed. She knew what would come next. "But. . ."

Silence stretched between them, and she watched her friend, who stared back unmoving. "Aspen?"

"Yeah?"

"Someone's at your door."

Lying on her bunk with the laptop, she glanced over her shoulder. Through the small filmy square window, she saw a shadowy form.

Two solid raps hit the metal door—and banged against her heart as she rolled off the bunk. "Hang on, I'll be right back."

"No!" Brittain said with a laugh. "What if it's him? I'll go so you two can talk."

After a quick good-bye, Aspen hurried and opened the door.

A man wearing ACUs saluted. "Aspen Courtland?"

"Yes?"

"Here, ma'am. This just arrived for you." He handed her a cream envelope.

Three-by-four inches, the envelope was small and only had her name written in all block lettering. "Weird." When she looked up, he'd already started away. "Thanks," she called after him.

Back in her room, she dropped onto the gray mattress and criss-crossed her legs. Opening the envelope, she wondered who'd written it. She plucked a single sheet of paper out. Opened it.

Did you find the coin?
Boys' orphanage, tomorrow, Djibouti City

Cardinal sat in the outdoor restaurant, the remains of his dinner in front of him. The weight of the band on his left ring finger anchored his mind to it. Elbow on the table, he stared down, rubbing his knuckles along his lip.

"I trust you."

Three deadly words.

At least, they had been for his mom.

"Do you trust me, Eliana?"

"Of course I do, but. . ."

"There is no but. Only yes or no." The colonel held her face in his large, powerful hands. *"You said you loved me."*

"I do! I swear it!"

"Then trust me!"

Swiping a hand over his stubbly mouth and chin, Cardinal sat back. Pushed his gaze to the walkway, where seamen, airmen, and soldiers made their way to and from dinner.

"You've always been a great lover."

Crack!

Nikol jerked.

A thousand tiny splinters snaked through the large pane of glass from the bullet.

"And," the colonel hissed, *"a horrible liar."*

Crack! *The fractured glass rushed down like a mighty waterfall.*

"No more." With a great thrust, he shoved her backward.

Then the angel flew.

"Hey!" A clatter erupted.

Cardinal blinked. Someone stood in front of his table. Only as his mind emerged from the past and his brain aligned with his surroundings did he manage to respond. "No need to yell. I'm right here."

"When I have to call your name three times—"

He squinted up at the woman. "Maybe I was waiting for you to talk nicely."

Timbrel dropped into the chair, and next to her, Candyman joined them. "Listen, I might have been wrong about Rankin—"

"Might have been?" He couldn't believe how easy it was to annoy her. And keeping her unbalanced would make her do more stupid things. It'd keep the *balance* of power in his hands.

"But I'm not wrong about you." She leveled a gaze at him. "If you pull a stunt like that again, I'm going to Burnett and having him yank your sorry butt stateside."

Cardinal lifted his bottled water and sipped. "According to him, I'm married to Aspen and under orders to make it look authentic."

Anger exploded across her face.

"Wait," he said, an authoritative tone in his word. "First—you came in before we kissed. It didn't happen, thanks to you." It ticked him off how she seemed to gloat under that revelation. Ah, let her have this one. It worked better for him. "But if it had, it would've been real. I like her. She's a good woman. I'm not going to play her." His heart careened at the admission. "This isn't my first op. I know how to work the angles without messing with the heart." At least, he hoped he did. "Besides, it won't happen again."

"Why not?" Timbrel scowled. "You jumping ship on her that fast?"

"No." Man, she gave him no credit. "Thanks to your accusations, she doesn't trust me. And I don't want her to. Not here, not while her mind is wrapped around finding her brother. Her emotions are high, her adrenaline higher. What she's feeling can't be trusted."

Candyman grinned through his thick, mangy beard. "You're not sure she likes you for you or for the hero role you're in."

"Exactly."

"Markoski! Candyman!"

The shout from down the path drew their attention, Candyman coming out of his chair even before the sound of his name finished.

At the command building, Watterboy waved them down. "Move! Aspen's MIA!"

What do you mean, she's MIA?"

"Checked the base, the kennel, her temporary bunk, mess—everything." Captain Dean Watters stood, hands on hips, as he relayed the information. "She didn't sign out of the base, but she's not here."

Lance Burnett flung the Dr Pepper can in the trash can across his office. It hit the wall and clattered into the metal bin. "How in Sam Hill does a person go missing on a military base?" He stabbed his fingers through his hair and clenched his fist. "Look, you know what? I don't care *how* she got lost." Glaring into the webcam, he made his foul mood known. "Just get her *un*lost. I don't need any more gray hair than I already have."

"Yessir," Watters said, his grim expression betraying his displeasure.

Whether that was for Lance's anger or Courtland's MIA status, Lance couldn't decipher. "You take that irritation, Captain, and you aim it at finding this young woman. She might be former Air Force, but she's not seen combat. Out there in a city that is ninety-something percent Muslim is *not* a recipe for Granny's homemade pudding. Got it?"

"Yessir."

"The last thing I need is for some beautiful former JAG assistant to go missing, end up in the hands of terrorists, and have that all over the news. Because the Good Lord knows that it will soon come out that her brother went missing, too. And how will *that* look?"

Via live video feed, Lance again surveyed those gathered. "And where in Sam Hill is my man?"

189

"He said he had a few ideas."

The pot of hot water that sat beneath Lance's backside—the one Payne and the others would use to scald him right down to private—began to boil. "Ideas? About what? I want him on this feed right now. VanAllen!"

"Sir." Candyman straightened.

"Drag his sorry carcass back in there. Now. I want words with that no-good—"

Light ballooned against a wall in the small conference room at Lemonnier. A dark shadow slid across it, then the explosion of light winked out.

"As you wish," VanAllen said with a smirk and motioned to someone.

Cardinal stepped into view and handed something to Candyman. "Send that to the general." He peered into the monitor. "General, I need you to get Hastings and Smith on this as we talk. Have them work the images. They'll know what to look for."

It took one call and the others were on their way. Lance would love to reach through the feed and strangle that cocky operative if he could. But he was too doggone valuable. "Well? What'd you find?"

He stretched to the credenza beside his desk and used it to pull himself to the small fridge then tugged out another maroon and white can. When he rolled back to the monitor, he found Cardinal, hands planted on the table, towering over the webcam. Lips tight, nostrils flared, he looked ticked.

Lance set the can aside, bracing himself. "That bad, eh?"

"Candyman's sending the key feed clips to you." Cardinal looked around the room. "The rest can crowd up and see on this monitor. Aspen retrieved Talon from the kennel at 2215 last night."

"That's normal," Timbrel added. "Handlers prefer to keep their dogs with them, and she has an air-conditioned CLU."

"Yes, but the kennel has a controlled environment as well," Cardinal countered.

"Getting her dog at ten fifteen at night is normal?" Lance wasn't buying it.

"I find it curious considering Talon was injured and dehydrated when she left him in the vet's care. I know she's protective and vigilant of the dog, but I also know she wanted him to get better. The only thing that would've made her compromise his recovery time and process would be something related to her brother."

Tolerance was being stretched in the way Lance viewed Cardinal. Though he hated the man's rogue methods, more times than not, Cardinal got his man. Or woman in this case.

"So?"

"Ran security tapes." Cardinal flicked a hand toward the monitor. "Traced Aspen into the kennel and out. She went to her CLU and came out with a pack." Cardinal mumbled something to VanAllen about the next image. "MP at the checkpoint said no woman and dog left through the gate. Inside the wire there are rows of cement barricades. There's no way she could've scaled that, not with the dog, and especially not with his paw injured."

"If you'd like to give me a tour of the base, you're wasting your time. I've been there. Get on with this."

Cardinal stared at him. Then pointed to Candyman. "So, I ran a few hunches. Tried a few tricks."

"Am I supposed to be impressed?" Why wouldn't the man just tell them what he found? Get on with it, so they could begin the search. If he knew where she was, wouldn't he. . . ? "You have no idea where she is, do you?"

"I searched the egress logs. Cross-referenced that with destinations and capacity."

"Capacity." Watters nodded. "She hitched a ride."

"In doing these and searching the security logs, I came across this." Again, Cardinal pointed to Candyman.

The image hogged over the screen. The motor pool. Jeeps. MRAPS. A medical team could be seen piling into a Land Rover.

"That looks routine." Lance lifted his Dr Pepper.

"Except that it's happening at four thirty in the morning. And the medical staff returned with us from their weekly rounds to the villages."

He squinted at the image. Not the best quality, but that was to be expected with the security cameras.

"Look at the airman, second left. When the person turns and says something—"

A dog trotted out from behind a container and hopped into the back of the SUV.

Lance sighed. "And why didn't the guards at the gate notice him leaving?"

"Sir, we had coms get into the computer Aspen had here. She had a Skype call last night with one"—Candyman read from his computer—"Brittain Larabie."

"On it," one of ODA452 said as keys started clicking.

"She's her best friend," Timbrel said.

"She's also the reporter who interviewed me," Cardinal added. "Get her on the horn."

"Yep," the ODA452 team member said, diverting his efforts to a phone. A few seconds later, he handed the device to Cardinal.

"Miss Larabie, Dane Markoski here. . .yeah. . .good, listen, we've got a situation here. Aspen is missing. . .calm down. We'll find her, but I can't do that without your help. Last night you Skyped with her. Did she mention anything that raised concern for you?"

Riveted to the monitor trying to gauge the conversation happening, Lance watched Cardinal. What was Larabie saying? Why had Cardinal gone silent? "Markoski?" Lance popped the top on the soda can, his mouth nearly watering at the *tsssssssssk* that erupted from the depressurization of the can.

"But she said nothing about leaving or. . . ?" Cardinal nodded. "Okay, good. That helps. What time did your call end?" More nodding. "Thank you. It's very helpful. . .yes, of course. As soon as we can."

"Well?"

"Anyone here go to Aspen's CLU last night around eight?" When everyone responded to the negative, Cardinal sighed. "According to Larabie, while they were Skyping last night, someone knocked on Aspen's door."

"Who was it?"

"Larabie doesn't know because they ended it so Aspen could answer the door. I'm going to dig around and see if I can figure out who went to her and why. That might give us some indication of what provoked her to grab her dog and run."

"Got it," Lieutenant Hastings said. "I scrambled through the various video feeds. I found one that's really shady, but give our analysts a few hours—"

"Aspen's already out there. We don't have hours."

"Give us some time and we can have this guy's history. But he's about five eleven, brown hair, wearing ACUs. He has something in hand—looks like an envelope. We lose him when he steps under the CLU's walkway."

"Time stamp?"

"Twenty-oh-eight."

Finally. A break. "That's our guy. Find him." Cardinal fisted his hand. Something was going on here. A woman with a dog didn't just walk off a base. Or ride off in a Land Rover. There were too many security protocols. So, how'd she bypass them? Why did the man in the motor pool help her?

No sense. It made no sense at all.

"Hey."Timbrel dropped her booted foot to the floor and sat forward. "Whoever that was, he had to have something pretty important in that envelope. Aspen doesn't have adventure in her blood like some, so her leaving means something."

"Agreed. But what?"

Timbrel shrugged. "I'm not going to do your job for you."

"Markoski, that SUV you said she might've climbed into?" Lieutenant Hastings spoke up from the Pentagon. "I cross-checked gate logs. It went out with supplies for Peltier General at 0630."

"Who signed out?"

"Uhh. . .no name—oh wait, here we go. Lieutenant Will Rankin."

The idiot. He had no idea what he'd just done.

"Let's go."Timbrel punched to her feet.

"Hold up," Cardinal said. "We know where the truck was headed, but—"

"Talon got a hit there, so it makes sense she'd go there again. Maybe she thinks she can track down Austin. Since that SUV left at six thirty, that means she's been on her own for over six hours. We don't have time to—"

"That's right." Cardinal tempered his frustration with Timbrel's charge-first, think-later method. "We don't have time to rush out there with unknowns that cost us time. And if we all went out there as U.S. military, everyone would clam up."

"Then we break up into teams." Timbrel stuffed her hands on her hips. "I'll go with you."

"No way."

"Why not?" Timbrel had gone into confrontational mode.

"I need to go into town as a husband worried about his wife's disappearance. That will get me local sympathy and awareness—people will start talking. If I can suggest a reward, then that will spread like wildfire. They'll bring me word. It'll go faster. I'll book a room at the Sheraton. Brie," he said, talking to the Pentagon again. "Once I'm there, relay the phone so it will come to my sat phone."

"Roger that."

"Markoski," General Burnett spoke up, roughing a hand through his tightly cropped hair. "I have to get clearance on this change."

"Then get it." The general was trying to stall. Though he probably had a great reason, Cardinal didn't have time for them to work out all their theories and probabilities. Aspen was out there, with her dog, but utterly alone. She didn't know the language, probably didn't know customs. Forget that she was beautiful. "But cut me loose to do this, my way."

Burnett's rugged face glowered. "Now, listen—"

"You and I both know if we all go out there, if all these uniforms show up, we'll never find her." He leaned in. "I work better on my own, and I can do it faster. Let me find her and bring her back. Things are screwed up, and we need to move swiftly. I can do that better alone."

"What are you afraid of?" Timbrel challenged. "Afraid you ran her off with your sweet-talking and charm?"

Wrong button to push. Cardinal swung around. "If you want to play the blame game, fine. My interest is getting Aspen back—alive. What you aren't thinking about is that someone seems to have lured her off the base, alone, in the middle of the night. And I don't know where you come from, Hogan, but in most cities I grew up in, that was a death sentence. Now, do you want your friend and handler back alive, or do you want to bring her home in a casket?"

Timbrel swallowed, and in doing that, signaled her retreat.

"Burnett—"

"Sorry, son. I have to put my boot down. Payne's being the royal pain I warned you about, and if he found out—and no, I'm not hinting you should do anything rogue. If he found out, they'd rip these stars off my shoulders." He wagged a finger at Cardinal. "This is a direct order: Do not go out there alone. Things are hot. Something's off, and we need to figure it out before we go guns blazing after her, not to mention we need to get some things in place before it's too late."

Cardinal frowned. "It's already too late."

"Are you forgetting who's in charge here?"

Cardinal's heart pounded. It'd been a long time since he'd directly disobeyed an order. "I'll get back to you on that." He cut the live-feed transmission, stood, and saw the others coming to their feet, clearly ready to stop him. "I need twenty-four hours to find her. That's it."

No one moved. Good sign.

"Let's send two teams," Watterboy said. "I'll return to the base in the city, across from the missionary's home. Candyman and Timbrel can go to the hotel as well, posing as tourists—"

"No," Cardinal said. "Watterboy, you and Timbrel get a room at the hotel as well. Candyman's too noticeable with that beard and thick chest."

Candyman frowned, holding his hands up as if inspecting himself. "Yeah, guess this body is on America's Most Wanted list."

"Good plan change." Timbrel narrowed her eyes at Candyman. "His ego wouldn't fit in the hotel room anyway."

"Agreed." Cardinal focused. Trained his mind to quiet. "Candyman, make sure your team is ready to jump if we get a lead or eyes on target."

Candyman nodded. "Roger. But for the record, I'm not too happy with the captain here shacking up with my girl."

If only there was time to joke. "Listen, I won't kid you—Aspen out there is not good. It was foolish for her to go off on her own."

"Assuming she's on her own," Watterboy added.

"We have to assume that she wanted her brother back, and her one weakness pushed her to make a stupid move." Cardinal gave a nod. "If she's not alone, then once we find her, it could be a fight to the death to get her back."

The door banged open. Rocket burst in, his face flushed. "A team just got ambushed. Admiral Kuhn is locking down Lemonnier under McLellan's orders. Nobody in, nobody out."

Lance cursed. "Okay." He sat up, took a swig of his sugary addiction, and then focused on Cardinal, who stood waiting, glaring. "McLellan is the personal assistant to Colonel Hendricks."

Cardinal stilled. "Payne's Hendricks?"

"Yeah." Adrenaline spiraled through his system like a gusher. "So listen up—nobody tells anyone we know this." Another swig. Another. There was a lot of work to do. Even more to hide. Because if Payne had sent Hendricks' man to usher Aspen out of there. . .

Lord God—what does this mean?

Cardinal scowled at the man with an extra jowl. "Burnett, if this means what I think it means—"

"We don't know what it means, so I'm going to start digging. You get out there and find that girl."

God have mercy on her. Because if this trail was leading where he thought it might, Aspen Courtland could already be dead.

Twenty-Three

Boys' Orphanage, Djibouti

Sitting in the shade of the building, the warmed cement and plaster against her back, Aspen smoothed a hand along Talon's ribs. Lying on his side did little to ease the heat discomfort. But at least they had shade and water, thanks to the generosity of the orphanage director. She'd never been a good liar or pretender, so she'd just gone with a narrow version of the truth: she was waiting here to meet someone. That had been good enough for the director, who said he'd gladly welcome visitors, especially those who would give something to the children, whether laughter or treats.

A guilty knot tied in Aspen's stomach. She had nothing for the children. Muslims viewed dogs as unclean, so most of the adults were appalled that Aspen had brought Talon. The children, however, could not be dissuaded.

In fact, there had been peals of delight and laughter throughout the morning as she demonstrated some of Talon's simpler skills.

Back at Lemonnier she'd spotted Rankin gearing up, and intentionally plying on his guilt over Austin's death/disappearance, she convinced him to give her a lift into the city. She'd said she was going to the orphanage and let him assume what he wanted. He agreed to pick her back up on their return route. Two more hours.

Aspen blew the curls off her forehead. With an exhausted groan, Talon stretched then went limp as he drifted off to sleep. Though Aspen would love nothing more than to catch a few Zs, she couldn't risk missing whoever had sent the note.

A shadow slid out and touched her, drawing her gaze to the doorway. "You want eat?" Director Siddiqi asked.

Talon pulled off the ground, ears and attention perked. He let out a whimper, and his tail thumped twice. Peculiar. Had he understood the word *eat*, or was it something more? But here, Aspen knew the orphanage struggled to feed the dozens of boys. She'd seen the kitchen and the grill donated by the servicemen and women at Lemonnier. In a world where your next meal wasn't guaranteed, she wouldn't dare take from the mouths of children.

"No, thank you." She'd brought her pack with Talon's food and hers, knowing that anything could incapacitate Talon, and that meant he wouldn't be at the top of his game to track.

"You friend not come?"

She swatted away a fly and the discouragement that lingered over the contact not showing up. "Not yet." She squinted over the empty play yard, eyeing the cars that sped by. Surely whoever had gone through the trouble of getting her off the base wouldn't just leave her here. "Soon, though."

He smiled and nodded. "Soon." Director Siddiqi turned and let the building swallow him.

Had the note instructed her to meet somewhere less safe, less open and public, she wouldn't have risked everything—including Dane's anger and disapproval. She'd had several hours to attach a meaning to what he'd said: *"Don't trust me."* Though part of her railed at those instructions, a deeper part of her couldn't let go of one thought: her trust terrified Dane. Aspen shook her head as she pulled out a few treats.

Talon's ears and head perked up, and he cast those soulful eyes at her as he pushed himself into an attentive "sit" position.

"Focus," she gave the command that instructed him to look into her eyes, a confidence builder, the dog trainer had said.

His gaze bounced from the treat to her eyes almost instantly.

"Yes! Good boy." She gave him the treat and smoothed a hand over the top of his head. Now how was it he could do one-on-one moments so well, but add noise and he was a puddle of panic? Like with the children. Oh man, she'd gotten so worried. He'd started shrinking and looking for a place to hide as the children shrieked and squealed, running around the playground.

"We should've stayed in Texas." She rustled his fur, gave him another treat, then leaned against his thick shoulder. "And I shouldn't have rushed you back into working, but I am glad you're here." It almost felt like she had a piece of Austin with her. And a very good friend. "I wouldn't want to be here without you, Talon."

At his name, he flicked his gaze to hers and swiped his tongue along her cheek.

Aspen laughed and turned away to avoid a slobber-fest. As he nudged her hand, she noticed his nose wasn't quite the shiny black it should be. She pushed to her feet. "C'mon, boy. Let's get some water."

She led him into the building and made her way to the kitchen. There, she filled a water bottle, dropped in two tablets, tightened the lid back on, then shook it. Using his collapsible bowl, she dumped in the contents and let Talon lap it up.

Voices skated through the hall outside the kitchen. Stern, quick words. Probably one of the teen boys getting chewed out again. She'd seen it a few times, only because the boys were pushing their boundaries as expected. Lord knows, Austin did it enough back home. Mom and Dad were at their wit's end, then Austin up and asked them to sign for an early entry into the Marines. Dad was relieved, Mom terrified— *"There's a war going on. They'll ship out."*

Ironically, it wasn't Austin who died a few months later. It was Mom and Dad.

Talon consumed the water in what felt like two heartbeats. She opted not to give him more because they might be stuck here for a while. Especially if the mystery guest didn't show.

Call of nature came. She stood, dried out the bowl, then folded it and stuffed it back on her pack. Since she couldn't very well tie Talon off to a tree—there weren't any—she led him down the hall to the bathroom. A cozy little closet of a thing that stunk to high heaven. Aspen made quick work of relieving herself then used her own sanitizer to clean her hands as she made her way out of the bathroom.

Shouts stopped her. They were still arguing? Gran would've said to take a switch to his backside. Nowadays, if you did that, someone would call it abuse.

But then. . .something about the argument piqued her curiosity.

She ambled down the hall, back toward the kitchen.

"This has nothing to do with you, Nazir."

"But this my orphanage. Bad things happen here, they close doors. Where boys go?"

Bad things happen? What bad things? What was the director talking about? Was this man threatening him?

"Not my problem, old man. She has the dog with her?"

In the space of two heartbeats, Aspen's world upended. *He's asking about me! And Talon!* She took a step back.

Talon whimpered.

Aspen flinched and tensed. He must be reading her body language, smelling her fear. She lowered her hand and rubbed his ears, trying to reassure him—and her. This couldn't be what she thought it was.

"Yes." The answer had been so quiet. . .so resigned. . .

"Good." A laugh sounded. "Say, anyone here know how to make dog stew?"

Hand over her mouth, Aspen backstepped. Talon stayed with her. She spun and hurried down the hall. Out the door.

"There! Stop her!"

"If you go out there," Candyman stated, sounding perturbed, "and they kill you? Don't blame me, man."

"If they kill me, I doubt I'll be able to blame anyone." Cardinal grinned. Waited for the point to sink in.

"Hey, this isn't a joke. You're talking about exposing yourself, possibly getting peppered full of holes."

"I'd prefer to skip the peppered full of holes, but yes, I will be exposed." In more ways than one. Going after Aspen compromised every Cardinal rule that existed. But he'd already lost one Courtland. He wasn't about to lose another.

Timbrel fumed. "I should be going with you."

"What you should be doing," he said as he slid a black skull cap over his head, "is going over every log and surveillance video with Candyman. Find out who gave her that envelope. Find out what it said. Find out where Rankin went and why."

Watters entered the room and locked it behind himself. The way he lingered there, staring at the knob, then the floor, set off a dozen alarms in Cardinal's mind.

"What's on your mind?" Cardinal asked.

They shared a long look, one that told him Watters was surprised he'd been read that easily, but then the next, more lingering message became one of camaraderie. "It makes no sense."

"What's that?" Cardinal stilled, watching the captain. A man he'd grown to trust. A man whose instincts were crazy accurate.

Watters hiked up a leg and slumped against the table around which the rest of ODA452 had gathered. "Base is locked down due to a supposed ambush, right?"

Cardinal gave a slow nod as he continued gearing up.

"We can't find out who got ambushed." Watters held up a finger. "There's one team out right now—Rankin's team. On a supply run through the city. There's been no activity that Burnett or his people can find. No radio chatter for help, backup, nothin'."

Very interesting. "That non-chatter chats a lot, doesn't it?" He smirked.

"Something's going on."

"It's some kind of messed-up insanity. Wasn't this supposed to be an easy mission—get in here, find the man who'd been lost?" Candyman sat on the end of the table, his boots on a chair. "And now, we got ambushes with no personnel, a missing dog handler, and a spook about to go rogue."

"Spook?" Timbrel straightened and looked at Candyman. Then Cardinal.

"He's referencing your insinuation that I'm not who I say I am." Cardinal lifted the water bottle and took a nice long guzzle.

"I swear, Markoski, if you hurt her. . ."

"Hurt her?" Cardinal laughed. "Timbrel, I wouldn't be willing to get my head blown off if I wanted her hurt."

"I didn't say what you *wanted*." She jutted her jaw. "I know your type. And she's too sweet to get it."

"Okay." Candyman hopped off the table. "Let's get this show on the road."

"Agreed. Keep your eyes and ears open. See what you can figure out." Cardinal huffed.

"Don't worry. I intend to find answers." Watters had a rare type of steel running through his veins.

"Time to play decoy with the dummy." Candyman grinned, and how he didn't end up with a mouthful of facial hair, Cardinal didn't know. And right now, he didn't care. His only concern was Aspen.

"Ready?" Watters's eyes seemed to sparkle with the thrill of what they were about to do.

With a nod, Cardinal looked to the others. Adrenaline thrummed through his blood. Creating a diversion so he could slip through the barriers was risky. They didn't want anyone getting hurt, but they also had to make this significant enough to draw eyes off the perimeter fence on the southeastern side. He'd bolt to the water and swim his way to safety. Grab some dry duds from a street vendor then check in at the hotel. That should be high-profile enough to attract some attention. Get his name on radars. He just prayed—and if he could find a chapel he would pray, honestly and truly—he could get a location on Aspen before someone put lead between his eyes.

They left the room a few at a time, going in different directions. Two here, two that way, one on his way to the cinema. Nothing that attracted attention...that is, unless someone looked close. Bulk could be deceptive, but anyone who did a double-take would figure out he had a second layer of clothes on. They ducked behind the first row of stacked CLUs then scurried to the fence.

Squatting at the perimeter behind one of the cement dividers, Cardinal adjusted the flak vest. Choked back the memory of Aspen's frightened blue eyes when he'd told her not to trust him. A stupid move. Showing his hand. But the thought of her trusting him when he was nothing she believed him to be...

He shouldn't care. Shouldn't be concerned with what happened to her at the end of this mission. But he was. In fact, he couldn't get away from the thoughts of the moment she discovered he was not Dane Markoski. Watters crouched beside him with the wire cutters, setting up a rerouter for the electrical current so it wouldn't attract the attention of the MPs.

"If you find her, get word back to us."

Cardinal nodded.

"Hey."

The hesitation, the softer tone, pulled Cardinal's attention to the captain.

"Candyman told me…about you and Aspen." Watters held his gaze strong, firm. "I don't care if you have a thing going on, but don't let it get in the way. Because I'll come after you for compromising me and my team, and our target."

He'd never had someone be direct with him like that, in such a friendly but threatening way. Well, he'd had those who were going to cut his heart out if he double-crossed them. That was evil. This was… justified.

"I have one goal, Captain," he said, meeting the guy's intensity, "to get her and her brother back, even if I have to die to do it."

"Good to know." Watters smirked. "I think her friend would prefer it that way—with you dead."

"Good thing my fate's not in her hands."

Something flashed through the captain's face. "Whose is it in?"

Cardinal felt like this was one of those defining moments. One of those—admit you're weak and then you get killed moments—and he wasn't sure he wanted to face it. "I'd like to hope God's got it."

"He will if you let Him."

Cardinal gave a slow shake of his head. "Not sure it's quite that simple."

"Sure it is." Watters patted his shoulder. "We humans are the ones who make it difficult and complicated. Surrender is the only way."

Crack!

The first indication of their plan igniting—literally—pounded through his chest. He and Watters gave nods of affirmation that said *this is it.*

Boooom!

Just a little longer…

Sirens wailed.

Watters cut a hole in under fifteen seconds. "Go!"

Cardinal folded himself through the fence. Once he made it through clear, Watters should bolt back. Double-checking the base conditions and Watters, Cardinal turned. The spot Watters had occupied sat empty. As Cardinal whipped back around, he caught the hulking form of the captain in his periphery, skimming along the barriers back toward the CLUs.

On my own.

He eyed the guard hut and saw two guards pointing toward the explosion Timbrel and Candyman had created with a vehicle. He bolted across the road and over the field.

A crack of gunfire pierced the hot day.

Dirt spit up at him.

His pulse amped up. They'd spotted him. Ten seconds to the water. He pumped it hard, pushing to safety. Feet beating a quick path.

A blazing heat whipped across his ear. He sprinted, darting left. Then right, doing his best to make it impossible for them to get a bead on him.

Five seconds. He freed the first buckle of the vest.

Four.

Water erupted in several distinct spots.

Three.

He ripped an arm free of the vest.

Dove for the water.

Like a lead fist, a tremendous weight pounded into his back.

Twenty-Four

Djibouti City, Djibouti

N eil! Neil, hurry!"

He bolted out of the bathroom in the run-down apartment they'd rented with cash. "What?"

Lina stood at the window, peering through a razor-thin slit in the triple-layered cloth he'd nailed over the hole. "Look!"

At her side, he angled his head to see through the skinny space. The street bustled with the normal gaggle of women carrying infants and toddlers in slings, guiding other children down the streets as men hurried here and there. "I don't see anything. What?"

She extended her arm and pointed up the street. "Past the bank. Watch the shadows." Lina smelled fresh, even though the shower was anything but. Not for the first time did he consider her beauty, both inside and out. "Not me, out there."

He grinned and slipped an arm around her waist as he once again checked the ground from their second-story apartment. "I'm still not—"

Something moved, this time north of the bank. He leaned forward a little and shifted toward the window.

Lina held his shoulders as she peered over his left. "Is it. . . ?"

He spied blond curls and yellow fur running beneath the balcony of a two-story shop. "Crap!"

How had she found them? This was unbelievable!

A distant pop froze him.

She slipped into an alley.

205

His heart stalled. "Someone's chasing her."

"Doesn't that work better for us?"

"Yes, but what if they miss?" He grabbed a ball cap and started for the door. "Lock it. Don't let anyone in and don't go anywhere till I get back."

"What are you going to do?"

Neil hesitated. He knew. Knew beyond a shadow of a doubt but couldn't tell her. She wouldn't understand.

Aspen slid around the corner, hauling Talon with her.

Plaster from the arches spit at her. She ducked but kept moving. Talon had kept up with her, but he was limping. They needed a break. Needed rest. Had to find a place. A safe place.

Scanning doors and alleys, she didn't stop. Couldn't afford to. Her legs felt like pudding, heavy yet jiggly. Her heart pounded so hard, she struggled to breathe. And Talon, God bless him, continued without complaint.

Not that she could just let him keep going. The dog's heart was one of the most loyal, going and loving and doing whatever it was to make her happy, but he would let her run him straight into the ground. She had a responsibility to find a place to give him rest.

God, help me!

Feet pounded behind her. The men's shouts as unrelenting as their pace. Didn't they need to breathe? And who was it exactly? She didn't know the people chasing her. How did they know her? How had they known about the coin?

Why had she thought this was a good idea?

Because you always want to rescue people.

Plaster leapt at her.

She yelped, shielded her face, and banked right.

Two feet in, darkness dropped on her. About the time her mind registered the dead end, a form emerged from the shadows. "Back!" she snapped.

"Here," the man said in a hushed whisper. "Hide in here." He pointed to the side.

Aspen stopped. "You're helping me?"

With a nod, he lifted a panel and waved her into the spot. "Hurry!"

As he bent forward and waved, his dark hair dipped into the light.

Talon did his high-pitched whimper thing.

Aspen didn't have time to lose. She scuttled into the narrow space and tugged Talon in with her. "Talon, heel! Sit! Stay!" She said the commands rapid-fire.

Two large pieces of two-by-fours strung together dropped over the space, sealing them in.

Aspen sucked in a breath and placed a hand on the wood. "Wait!"

Thunk!

Though she thought it impossibly dark, Aspen could see through the slivers of light that the man had sat down in front of the wood. What was he doing? His head was down. He looked...asleep?

Feet pounded nearby.

"You got her?"

Head against the wall, Aspen closed her eyes and held her breath. *God...this would be a great time for Talon to be completely happy hiding.*

"Nothing—hey, you!"

The man flinched. "Hey, was—"

"Drunken fool. What are you doing back here?"

"I'm not drunk," the man, the hero who'd stepped into the line of fire to help her, stood tall.

"Then what are you doing back here?"

Her lungs were on fire from the exertion of slowing her breathing from a dead run to a quiet rhythm not detectable through the wood. Talon wasn't panting hard—or at all. Maybe he sensed the danger. When he was on alert, his jaw snapped shut. Was he doing that now? She traced her fingers along the top of his broad skull.

"Getting away from my boss for a nap."

"Did you see a girl run past here with a dog?"

"I didn't see anything—I was asleep. Besides, why would she run past here? It's a dead end." Her hero shifted away from the wood, toward the other side of the alley.

"Forget him," another man shouted. "We can't lose her."

"Can I help if you have lousy aim?"

The voices faded and with them, Aspen's alarm. Her muscles ached. She opened her mouth and expelled the fiery breath, slowly bringing her heartbeat to a normal rate. Quiet descended over the next several minutes, even though somewhere not too far, she heard the two men still shouting.

"Stay here till nightfall," the hero said.

"My dog needs water. He's dehydrated."

"You'll have to wait. If I bring water back, they might see."

And with that, he was gone.

Aspen nodded, not trusting herself to speak—to fall apart.

Time ticked by with the weight of an anvil, each second pummeling her courage. Wait until night? Panic thumped against her silent consent of his order. She couldn't wait till dark. Then she'd have no way to get back to Lemonnier. In fact, if she didn't find a way back soon, she'd be alone. All night.

Indecision rooted her to the hiding spot.

Letting herself slide down, Aspen wedged herself in the tiny space. Her knees grazed the plaster. This must be some kind of stoop. A steel door pressed against her spine, but the lock wouldn't budge. Trapped.

Then it registered—Talon's rapid breathing. His lethargy.

She couldn't look at his gums, but she'd bet the heat was getting to him again. *You are the most irresponsible handler ever. Austin would string you up.*

But Austin was gone. Or here. Or. . .whatever.

Had the coin simply been a coincidence? She thumped her head against the wall. Leaping without looking to help others. Good intentions—she always had good intentions, but they most often got her into a ton of trouble.

God, I need serious help. And I have no idea what to pray for. Just. . .get us out safely.

Quiet coiled around her as the city slowed and the traffic, both foot and vehicular, dulled from the roar it'd been when she was running for her life.

An urgency clutched her by the throat. *"Go, now."* She tried to quell the thought, not give in to panic. But then realized—it's not panic.

Just urgency.

That still, small voice. *"Go."*

Aspen pressed her hand against the wood. It budged, but barely. She straightened in the space and pressed both palms against the wood. When she gained an inch on the left side, she dug her fingers in and pulled it aside. A heavy crate sat in front of it. She hiked her leg over it then hopped out. "Talon, come."

Slow moving, he appeared, just his head.

Aspen sat on the crate, realizing this was what the hero had done, then wrapped her arms around Talon's chest and hindquarters. With a small grunt, she heaved him over the crate and set him down. He plopped his rear on the ground, panting, and turned those soulful brown eyes to her, as if to ask, "Do we have to?"

"Come on, boy. We need to find water."

She stood, noticing the aching burn in her thighs from her flight earlier. Her legs trembled, but she'd have to shove mental steel down them to hoof it back to the orphanage in order to get the ride back to Lemonnier.

"Hey."

Aspen spun around, fully expecting Talon to lunge at this person. "Talon—" But she froze. Tail wagging, Talon let out that pathetic whimper again.

"I told you to stay hidden till dark."

"My dog needs water, and I have to get back. . .home."

"You don't live here." His brown eyes seemed to enjoy knowing that.

"I didn't say I did."

"Look." He came closer, glancing over his shoulder then back to her. "You need to get out of here."

"That's what I intend to do."

"No, I mean out of Djibouti. Now." He stood closer and reached a hand toward Talon. "Hey there, buddy."

Talon whimpered more, wagged his tail so hard she thought he might break in two, then rubbed against the man's hand.

"Heel!"

"He's okay." The man looked at her. "Seriously—get out. There's some bad stuff going down. Those men who were after you—"

The man tripped. Only he hadn't been moving. But he pitched forward and rolled to the ground.

"Go! Run!" he grunted as he collapsed. Something dark spread over his chest.

"You're shot!"

"Go, now! Talon—seek, seek, seek!"

Talon tore off, Aspen hauled behind him.

★ ★ Twenty-Five ★ ★

Where? Where?" Cardinal shouted into the phone as he drove the tiny import away from the Sheraton, barreling through traffic like a drunk.

"Last known reporting of shots fired is on Avenue Georges Clemenceau. A woman called the police and reported two men chasing a woman and dog through the alleys," Lieutenant Brie Hastings said. "You're about a mile from the address provided. Take the next right—Rue de Paris, north for about a half mile, then left on Rue de Bender."

"Thanks, Brie. Do we have a satellite monitoring the area?"

"Officially, no."

Then unofficially—yes. "Good. Get on it, find her. That area's pretty heavy with sidewalk vendors and market shops. I need an extra set of eyes."

"Okay, but you are so going to owe me."

Why couldn't Brie just let it go? He wasn't interested. Never would be. She knew his profile, knew his history. Knew he didn't date.

No, but you try to kiss cute blonds in chapels.

The pang of conscience clunked him over the head.

Cardinal concentrated on weaving through the tangle of pedestrians and traffic. If he didn't exert more restraint, he'd draw attention to himself. He'd been at the hotel not twenty minutes when he got the call that police were flooding the scene of an incident. By now, he'd be too late. Unless. . .somehow. . .by some miracle. . .Aspen had escaped.

He'd questioned God's existence, His power, since his mother's death, but he could not deny the strange draw he had to cathedrals.

All the same, putting his life in the hands of some greater power defied good sense. *Make your own destiny. Master your own life.*

He swung into the painted area of the street that divided the two lanes and stuffed the gear in PARK. "Going to foot."

"Satellite's coming online. . .now."

Running would draw attention. Walking would be too slow.

Cardinal would love to crawl out of his skin, break into wings like his moniker implied, and soar over this place. *C'mon, Aspen. Where are you?*

Large parasol umbrellas arched over wares. Tip to tip, the material shielded both the products and their sellers from the unrelenting heat. Even with the sun going down, there was almost no reprieve in the summer heat. It'd topped 113 today. And Aspen was out there with Talon, on foot, running for her life.

Something in his gut clinched. A dose of guilt sprinkled over his thoughts. Pushing her away, telling her not to trust him—had those words contributed to her willingness to fling herself into the arms of deadly danger?

"Okay, I've got a line on you."

"I need your eyes on the market, not on me."

"No duh, Sherlock, but I have to know where you are to tell you where to go, and right now, I have someplace *very* hot in mind."

"I'm already there." He wouldn't play into her irritation. He had enough of his own as he scanned the long stretch of street. Vegetables, fruit, rugs, clothes, sandals. . .

Barking slowed him. "A dog. I hear a dog barking."

"Hmm, might want to hurry before they turn it into dinner."

"Muslim, smart aleck. They consider them unclean."

"You spoiled all my—wait."

Cardinal slowed, turning a circle. "What d'you see?"

"Head toward that three-story apartment complex."

As he came around, Cardinal saw a building with three rows of windows. Another with balconies lining the front. Another that seemed abandoned. "Brie, which one?"

"The one with the dishes on top."

Cardinal sprinted in that direction.

"Yeah, I see two people with a dog. In an alley. Tell me that's not curious."

"Thanks." He stuffed the phone in his pocket and sprinted toward the buildings.

He hurdled over a mound of oriental rugs. The seller shouted at him with a raised fist. But Cardinal's eyes were locked on the building. On searching for any sign of Aspen.

Movement caught his attention at the top of another building. A man. . .up there. . .waiting. . .

Sniper!

"No!" Cardinal pumped his arms harder, faster. His feet felt like they'd tangle over each other. So heavy, so tired. But he couldn't stop. Wouldn't. Not till he had Aspen safe again.

He whipped around a porta potty. The door flashed open. Nailed him in the cheek. He grunted, spun around, and picked up where he'd left off.

Across the street. He saw the opening to the alley. Saw the laundry strung from balcony to balcony. The clothes draped the alley in darkness. No way to see if Aspen was there. Or still there. *Or alive.*

Oh man. He didn't need that thought.

Chest burning, legs rubbery, Cardinal pushed. Hard. Harder.

A car burst from the left.

Cardinal dove over it. Banged his knee. Cursed but didn't stop, despite the numbing pain. Couldn't slow. Couldn't stop. Aspen.

Weakness gripped him. Slowed him. His mind screamed not to slow. His body warred for supremacy.

A scream from the alley punched through his chest, ripped his heart out and bungeed it back to its owner.

"As—" Her name caught in his dried throat. He nearly choked on the gust of air and his parched esophagus.

Overhead the clothes danced like soulless ghouls hovering over the city.

Cardinal propelled himself the last dozen feet, the material flapping above. A fourth building behind the one with the satellites shielded the location from sun.

A blur exploded from that direction. Rammed into him. Knocked him backward, into the plaster wall of the satellite building. He clamped his arms around whatever barreled into him.

A scream blasted his ears. Another scream. Barking and tiny

punches against his leg warned him of the dog. His mind reengaged as the curls bounced in his face. The fist drove forward. He narrowly avoided another jolt with her fist. "Aspen!"

The writhing, flailing frame of Aspen Courtland slowed. Terrified eyes stared up at him. "Dane?" Her confusion bled into sheer panic. She fisted his shirt. "Dane!" She glanced back. "They shot him!"

He guided her out of the sniper's line of sight, his mind roaring at the sight of blood on her face and shoulder. "You're bleeding."

As if the words slowly brought reality into a violent collision with her nightmare, Aspen looked down at her clothes. "No. . ." She shook her head and swallowed. "It's not my blood. It's his. They shot him. He was right there helping me, and they shot him."

"Who?"

She bunched her shoulders, as if warding off the pain, the trauma. She swiveled around and pointed. Aspen jerked. Looked to the left, the right. "He. . ." She covered her mouth with her hand then lowered it, her eyes glossing. "He. . .he was right there. He collapsed." She slumped back against him, and he could tell she was about to lose it. "He was *right* there. Dead. He was *dead*!"

"Hey, it's okay."

She jerked to him. "No. It's not okay. They shot him. I saw it. Now he's gone. But I saw it, Dane. I did!"

"Hey." He tightened his hold very gently, just enough to give her some grounding, some reassurance. "Let's get out of here, get you and Talon to safety. We'll sort it out there. We have sat imaging, so we can scour to see what happened."

Her vacant expression warned him of the shock taking over.

"Aspen?"

Pools of pale blue looked up at him. Her chin trembled.

Cardinal wrapped his arm around her and tugged her close. "Just. . . hold on. I'll get us out of here." He couldn't let her fall apart till they were no longer in the open. He cupped her face, searching for recognition that she was with him. "Okay, Angel?"

He held her face. Did he know he held her heart?

Calling her Angel—the nickname her parents and grandparents

had given her as a little girl—it righted her universe. Enabled her to muster the minuscule drops of courage left after seeing that man shot right in front of her.

Aspen lifted her jaw. She would not be a teary, whiny basket case in his arms. She swallowed, coiled Talon's lead around her wrist once more, then gave Dane a nod.

Dane wrapped his hand around hers. "Okay, hold on. Don't let go. We're going to the safe house."

"Got it." And she did. She got it that Dane was there to help. That even though he said not to trust him, his actions demanded it of her time and again. And honestly, she had no problem giving it. No problem letting him shoulder the burden of this disaster. It was nice not having to carry the world on her back.

He stalked through the alleys at a pretty fast clip, eyes alert, tension radiating off his strong build. The moments before he showed up were like being on a Tilt-a-Whirl at a fair, where the lights, the images, the people all blurred into one frenetic mural of chaos. Then Dane stepped in, caught her, and made everything right again.

Darkness had descended by the time they made it out of the shops and tangle of street vendors into the dusty, abandoned section of Djibouti City. A million questions peppered her mind, but she stowed them. The night, the danger, the men—they all prompted her to follow his lead. If he wasn't talking, she wouldn't talk. If he walked fast, she walked fast. If he slowed, as he had now, then she slowed.

"Just a little more," he said, sounding as tired as she felt.

As they strolled up the street, she spotted Santos's home. Would Dane lead them there?

Almost as soon as the thought flickered through her exhausted mind, he crossed the street, slipping behind a row of crumbling buildings. "You don't trust him."

"I don't trust anyone."

The retort was so quick, so sharp, she wasn't sure if that included her. She prayed it didn't. But she was too exhausted to fight the sadness that encompassed her. What was keeping him locked up, his heart smothered?

She stumbled, her feet tripping over each other. She grunted—everything hurt. Her eyes burned, her feet ached, her back throbbed, her mind screamed. . .yet her soul was quiet.

I don't understand, Lord. She should be a cracked nut by now. But she wasn't. Why?

A verse from Psalm 23 drifted into her mind: *"Yea, though I walk through the valley of the shadow of death, I will fear no evil."* She had nothing to fear. Yet she had everything to fear—the man, whoever he was, warning her to get out before she got hurt. Austin—where was he? They were in this place, and it seemed everything was going wrong. Yet she had peace. The same peace that carried her into the dilapidated safe house.

Holding her hand, Dane shifted, bolted the door with all four dead bolts. Her shoes crunched over the dirt and debris. Talon padded along beside her, head down, shoulders drooping. In the middle of the building, a room had been walled in to prevent light from seeping out and giving away their position.

Dane gave a quick rap then eased into the room.

Two men dressed in ACUs stood with M4s aimed at the door—at them. Aspen remembered them from Candyman's team, which made her wonder where he and Timbrel were.

Inside, Dane engaged the locks as he said, "Evening, gentlemen."

Rocket let out a whistle. "You scared us. Nobody said you were coming."

"Sorry. Didn't tell anyone. Going to use the back rooms. You got motion detectors out there, right?"

Rocket nodded.

"Shoot to kill anyone else who shows up." Dane started for the back then stopped. "How'd you get off base?"

Rocket shrugged with a cheeky grin that Aspen didn't quite understand. "After that little diversion, word came down it was a false alarm."

"Huh. Well, glad you're here. She needs to rest and eat."

"Scrip here can get something cooked up." Rocket nodded to his partner.

"No," Aspen said, her objection much weaker than she'd intended, "it's okay."

"Bring her whatever you can." Dane strode toward the back with her in tow.

215

She peered up at him. Why had he countered her?

"You need the nourishment to rest well."

Only as he turned did she realize they were still holding hands. He hadn't let go. He hadn't surrendered his position of control. And he was still asking her to trust him. Did he realize that?

In the back he led them into the rear room. A bunk bed, a table, and chairs hunkered in one corner against a peeling and cracked wall. A makeshift shower stood in the other with a curtain pinned to the walls that stood at right angles.

"Here." Dane guided her onto the lower bunk and squatted in front of her, once again cupping her face. "Rest. I'll be here. So will Talon."

"Talon. . .he needs water."

"I'll see to it. Just rest." With that, he slipped out and returned in what felt like seconds later with a bowl of water. He set it in front of Talon, who splashed it around as he inhaled the liquid.

Dane smoothed a hand along her cheek again. "Aspen, rest."

Mutely, she obeyed. Curled on the gray mattress with the thin sheet wrapped around her shoulders, Aspen stared at the ground. At nothing in particular. Just something for her gaze to rest on. The replay of those terrifying seconds in the alley replayed over and over. She shuddered, her mind taking every element down to the microsecond. Talon had never hit or alerted to the danger. Strange.

She must've drifted off to sleep because when her eyes opened next, Dane was gone. Aspen drew herself off the mattress and sat propped against the wall, her knees pulled against her chest. She tugged the sheet around her. Not that she was cold. She wasn't. Couldn't be—not in one-hundred-plus-degree weather. But there a chill coiled around her bones. From the stress. The anxiety. The man calling Talon by name.

"You okay?"

She turned, feeling numb and out of touch with reality. Dane eased into a chair in front of a computer, the side door ajar. She pushed the curls from her face and drew in a long breath, her mind hung up on the man in the alley. "I think I knew him."

Dane sat back, expectation hovering in his handsome features. "Yeah?"

She shook her head and shrugged at the same time. "I don't know. It's ludicrous to think someone I might know or have met is here in

Djibouti, the armpit of the world."

"But. . ."

"There was just. . . something." She sighed. "I can't explain it." As she extended her legs so they draped over the edge of the mattress, Talon pushed himself upright and cast those soulful brown orbs her way. His gaze darted to the mattress then to her as if begging for permission. Like he needed to. "Hup," she said and held her palm out over the mattress.

He leapt up and slumped against her side. She wrapped her arms around him, finding familiar strength and warmth in his pure devotion and loyalty.

"So, he felt familiar? Or something?"

"Yeah." Aspen dug her fingers into Talon's fur and bent to kiss his head. "Even Talon never made strange with him."

"Is that unusual?"

"Think about when you first met him."

Dane nodded. "Noted."

"A total stranger, and Talon doesn't warn the guy off with a throaty growl?"

"Do you think it could've been Austin?"

"No. He didn't look anything like my brother."

"You're sure?"

She laughed. "Trust me, I know my brother."

"Disguised, maybe?"

Searching her memory banks, she scoured the mental notes of the man. "No," she said slowly. "He didn't look anything like my brother. Black hair—"

"Could be dye."

"Brown eyes—Austin had blue like mine."

"Contacts."

Aspen wrinkled her nose. "Wrong nose. Austin's was aquiline. This guy's nose was hooked."

"Broken nose?"

"No, it was wide and hooked—what is this? I told you I didn't know this guy."

"I know, but sometimes it's those things that feel familiar, that we can't quite finger, that are the biggest connectors. Can you think of anything else that seemed similar or familiar?"

She sought more differences, but it stopped there. "No." And thank goodness. She couldn't grapple with the thought that the man could have been Austin and now he was shot and killed, right in front of her eyes. A shudder wiggled through her spine.

Dane stood and came to the bed. He perched on the edge next to her, making her stomach squirm. "But you said he felt familiar."

She nodded as she traced his profile and frowned when his jaw muscle popped. "What are you thinking?"

His steel eyes rammed into hers, sending a silent, intense signal of warning. "I have to go back to the alley."

"No!" She shoved off the wall and scooted to the edge of the bunk bed. "Are you crazy? Someone was out there *sniping* at us, and you just want to walk back into the middle of that?"

"Not want, have to." He remained undeterred. "Two things need to be ascertained—whether the man is dead and who he is. Why he knew what he knew."

"Maybe he knew Santos. There are a thousand explanations. But you don't have to go." Her heart pounded at the thought of him out there, exposed and getting shot at. "Please."

He hesitated, watching her. A war seemed to erupt within him, dancing in his blue eyes. It was something deep, something. . .dark. "I *have* to do this."

Somehow Aspen knew that this moment was a new one for Dane. In all the times they'd been working on finding Austin, he had rarely taken the time to explain what he was doing or justify it.

He was opening up to her. Something told her to give him the room to do it. To give him another reason to trust her. She almost smiled as that word—*trust*—sneaked into their relationship again. "Okay."

Dane's eyebrows danced for a second. "That was easy."

She laughed. "I'm never easy."

"I knew there'd be a catch."

"Just help me understand what is going on in that mind of yours. You never smile."

"I just did."

"No, that wasn't a smile. It's a smirk. Now, what's the look that's haunting you?"

He drew back, surprise etched into his face.

Spurred by that reaction, she knew she'd somehow hit on something. Maybe even something close to home, close to his heart. "Please."

"Okay."

Her heart rapid-fired.

"When I get back."

★ ★ Twenty-Six ★ ★

Special Operations Safe House, Djibouti

Weren't we supposed to find something here?" Candyman glanced around, eyes shielded by his sunglasses and the bill of the baseball cap he wore low over his brow. The sun glinted off his thick, sandy blond beard. "Like a body?"

"Should've brought the dog." Watters walked to the end of the alley where the building abutted another.

"That dog don't go nowhere without his girl," Candyman countered. "And I don't like going nowhere without my girl."

"What girl?" Watterboy turned from his surveying and scowled at his buddy.

"Timbrel."

"Dude, you've got a long, hard road if you think she's going to be your girl."

"I got time. And hard roads—they're the best kind."

"You're begging for trouble."

"Nah, see, it's like this—the biggest trouble yields the best reward."

"That's some messed-up thinking." Watterboy patted his shoulder, a big grin ripping through his dark beard.

Ignoring their banter and honing his skills, Cardinal stood at the intersecting paths, examining, studying, thinking. They were both right—Talon would've been an asset in tracking down the man. Or the body. Considering the disruption of the molding cardboard, the stench wafting up from a freshly exposed patch of wet earth—no doubt caused

220

by the overturned cardboard—whoever went down, whoever terrified Aspen when he got shot, that person was still alive.

"Thinking we should bug out. Keep our heads and body parts where they belong."

Cardinal looked at Candyman. "What?"

"He doesn't want to get shot and lose his chance to win the woman whose head is as thick and stubborn as his." Watterboy started out of the alley.

Candyman grinned wide through that scraggly beard. "See? I knew you understood."

"Give me a minute." Cardinal stalked down the alley, searching the dirt, the cardboard. A rat scurried from one box to another, surprisingly nimble for its fat body. But it wasn't the rodent or the smell that drew him in. It was the trail of blood. Smeared up and over the seven-foot cement block wall that barred the exit.

Who are you?

Cardinal breathed out in frustration. He knew the answer. Didn't want to admit he did, but the gnawing in his gut told him he couldn't ignore this any longer.

Austin. Somehow and for some reason, the only man Cardinal had ever brought under his wing to train and mentor had turned on him.

Which meant when Austin cornered Aspen—the man *knew* she was his sister.

Yet he didn't tell her.

It was rare to have an agent go rogue and in such a super-expensive way like this. He couldn't be Austin. Not with the cost of plastic surgeons and experts it would take to create an entirely new identity. It meant Austin wasn't working alone—he had a handler.

A new handler.

Who was Cardinal's competition? Who had ripped his agent right out of his fingers?

You're really reaching with this one, Cardinal. This was all speculation. Trying to put the pieces together that were dangling in front of his nose. Options. . .options. What other options were there?

Austin wanted out.

No. He had thrived and excelled. Said he loved getting to take care of things that were otherwise undoable due to laws and such. Cardinal tried to remind him they weren't necessarily breaking laws. Just bending them. Really far.

Options. . .Austin. . .found. . .something. Or someone.

Okay, that made some sense. One of Austin's last communiqués mentioned meeting someone. Cardinal had taken it to mean a contact.

What if it was another agent? What if someone turned him, made him a double agent?

Cardinal ran a hand along the back of his neck. That thought had a ring of truth to it. Somehow.

"Hey, Spook."

Cardinal dragged his attention back to the two soldiers.

"We should get moving. Dark's coming." Watterboy thumbed over his shoulder. "And we have an audience."

Cardinal's gaze shifted to the narrow space between the two buildings. A small crowd had assembled at the corner of the northernmost building. He nodded and started back. The ride was made in relative quiet, affording him the time to sort out his thoughts. Anything was plausible at this point. Until they had some more facts. . .

"What're you thinking?"

Cardinal met the ironclad gaze of Watters just as Candyman slowed and turned into the alley behind the safe house. "Too much."

"You do remember we're on your side, right?"

"This isn't 'my' side—it's a mission." He flung open the door, agitated with the questions, the ones that had no answers, just more mystery. Inside, Rocket and Scrip pushed from their seats. Both lobbed questions at him.

Cardinal gritted his teeth and kept walking. Down the hall.

Growling announced Talon's presence seconds before the yellow Lab and Aspen stepped into view at the other end. The sight of her, those blond curls framing that beautiful face, slowed him. *I'm failing her.* The sidewinder of a thought spiraled through his chest and rammed into his heart.

Cardinal lowered his head and banked right. Flung back the door to the stairs. Climbed them three at a time, moving quicker with each advance until he jogged toward the door. Pushed through it. Agitation kept him moving, his mind warring that he had to corral his buzzing nerves.

Sticky, warm air coiled its arms around him. He paced. His nerves vibrated. Nothing was going right. Everything was wrong. The mission. Austin. Burnett. Payne. Aspen—especially Aspen. This wasn't supposed to happen. This—the way things had changed between them—was the reason he had Cardinal rules. Cardinal Rule #1—*Never work women.* He had others—never stay somewhere longer than you have to, always have an exit strategy, never engage the heart.

The door groaned and creaked behind him.

"Hey, you okay?" Aspen's sultry voice was as warm as the air. Her shoes crunched over the rooftop as she came closer, trailed by the soft padding of Talon's paws.

Just give her the facts. Get the game plan established. Move on it. That should be enough to keep his mind active and his heart inactive.

He pivoted and dropped against the half wall that served as a barrier against the two-story fall. Arms folded should send the message he wanted: he was closed to her. Had to be. "No body."

Aspen frowned. "I guess that's good."

"Good? No, it's not good. It means someone wants that person dead. And if that person tries to contact you again, it puts your life in jeopardy."

"*Our* lives."

He shoved off the wall and turned around. Had he really done that? Funneled down the danger to include only her? Is that where his mind had gone? Not good. Anger tingled through his chest, down into his arms. To avoid fisting his hands, he gripped the ledge. Stared out over the darkening sky.

A devastating realization spread through him. Aspen. He was worried about her. Austin he could sort out. The mission he could handle. Aspen. . .if anything happened to her. . .

And the angel flew.

No! He snapped his eyes closed against the image, against the face becoming Aspen's. *Oh merciful God! Help me. I can't go there. . . . I can't fall for her.*

"Dane?" Aspen came to his side and touched his oblique. "What's going on?"

"Nothing," he ground out. His mind reared, ordering him to pull away from her.

But he couldn't. Didn't want to. Her warm touch soothed the beast within. Made the sun shine in a storm-ridden life. Just as someone else in his life once had. "My mother."

Aspen gave him a quizzical look.

Worms. A can of worms. But. . . "She died when I was fifteen." He slumped against the wall and forced himself to straighten. Look at her. "There are very few amazing women in this world. When she died, the world was one less a beautiful, amazing woman." Torment smothered him. *Don't do this. Don't go there. Not with Aspen.* "I always wondered if I could've saved her, stopped her death." He looked at her. Knowing he was defeated having opened that cauldron of history. "I don't want to have that regret with you, Aspen."

No sweeter words could've moved her heart more. And yet anchored her life more firmly in his hands. He cared about her. A lot. That's what all this "don't trust me" stuff was about.

"Dane, you're not God."

The fight seemed to have drained out of him. "Trust me, I'm completely aware of that."

"But you're trying to be Him, trying to control the outcome." Emboldened by his openness, she reached out to brush away the hair from his face.

He caught her hand and held it in midair. "Please, Aspen." He shook his head. "I'm not. . .I can't do this." He lowered his gaze then tugged her hand to his face and kissed her palm.

Butterflies swarmed her stomach. "Then you shouldn't do things like that." She smiled as she inched closer to him. "Tell me about your mom."

The shift in his demeanor was swift and large. "No."

"Why do you think you could've saved her, stopped her death?"

"She was murdered." His breathing grew heavier, his eyes clouded. "Murdered right in front of me."

"Oh Dane, I'm so sorry." Less than a foot remained between them, but the romance dimmed beneath his words.

"I just stood there, watching, like I was disembodied." His words whispered his agony. "But I wasn't. I was there. *Right there.*" His brows rippled. "Why didn't I stop him?"

"You were only fifteen."

"But she was my life, the only good thing besides my sister."

Waves of grief and awe crashed through Aspen—first that he'd paralleled what he felt for her with what he felt for his mother, murdered. And he'd just told her he had a sister, too. "Is your sister still alive?"

Dane blinked. His grief washed away. "What?"

Oh no. She saw it. The vulnerable side of him blinked out, like darkness when a light is turned off, and in its place returned the formidable fortress that was Dane Markoski. Aspen cupped his face. The move surprised them both.

"Dane, don't shut me out." She leaned closer, just inches from him. "Please—I see what you feel for me. It's a reflection of my feelings for you. It's not wrong or bad."

"No, but I am." He stood, and she saw the move for what it was—his attempt to place distance between them.

"You're what? Bad?"

Though he stood at least a foot taller than her, he sagged beneath whatever weighted him. "That's an oversimplification. I'm just. . ."

"What?"

He cast a sidelong glance in her direction, the moon and city lights, sparse though they were, reflecting off his face and eyes. "This is upsetting you." He turned and stalked the three feet to the other ledge. More distance.

"No." She snorted off a laugh as she trailed him. "You are upsetting me by consistently pushing me away when I can see as plain as day you are attracted to me. Whatever it is, Dane, whatever is haunting you, you need to get out from under its power."

"I wish it were that simple."

Aspen didn't yield. "Why isn't it?"

He traced her cheek, tingling and shooting darts of heat down her neck and into her stomach. "You are sweet but nai—"

"Naive." She smiled up at him. "Yeah. It's not the first time that's been said about me. And it's not a bad thing, I'll have you know. Just because I believe in you, believe in the man you are—"

"You don't know who I am." Razor sharp, his words sliced through her heart.

Fear and uncertainty swooped in, striking at the essence of what she believed was happening—clearing the air, deepening their relationship. She wanted that. Wanted him to break free from whatever stopped him from accepting her.

"See? You aren't even sure. Is that what you want?" His words weren't as confident this time. Hurt glowed like a halo around them. "Doubts, fears—about me, being afraid of me?"

What was he saying? Why did he look at her with that loathing expression?

"So, you're not Dane Markoski, technically and legally my husband?" Man, she wanted to smack him, smack some sense into him. Or the cantankerous side out of him.

After a long, lingering look, he turned away. "Right now, he's the only person I want to be."

"How is it you can face untold terrors and dangers in the field, on missions, but when it comes to what you feel for me, you run scared?"

"I'm not scared."

Aspen nearly laughed. He sounded just like Austin in high school, when he gave his litany of reasons why he couldn't ask Amanda Blair to the homecoming dance.

"Baloney!" Aspen slapped the curl from her face that kept batting her cheek. "Fear is driving your campaign of misery. Fear is stopping you from what you feel for me. When will you man up and face whatever is eating you alive? If this isn't who you are, then *be* who you are. Show that man to me!"

Fire spewed from his eyes. "Be careful what you ask for."

"Why?" She stepped closer, furious. "Are you afraid I might actually like him better?"

Everything in him seemed to swell. His shoulders bunched. His fists balled as he curled in on himself, his chin tucked. "You will never see that man." He took a breath, and the fire gushed out of him. The difference reminded her of a balloon, deflated of helium. Shriveled. Used. Empty.

Though something in her wanted to quit, to walk away from this insane argument with him, she had a larger sense of dread that if she did, Dane would be lost to her forever.

Fight for him. The words boomed through her. So, he said she'd never see that man, huh? "Why? I'm not good enough?"

"Once you see that man, you'll beat the fastest path out of my life."

Oh no, no he wouldn't get away with that. Wouldn't blame her for walking away. "Give me more credit than that. I might be stupid and naive in your book, but at least I have a heart and give people a chance, believe in them—in you, Dane." How many times would she have to say it before he believed and accepted it?

"Then your belief is misplaced."

"No." Breathing through the pounding of her heart hurt. "No, it's not. Your fear is crippling you, Dane. Robbing you, stealing joy from your life. You sit in cathedrals longing for something you think you can never have because you're too afraid to reach for it."

Dane jerked toward her, scowling. But silent.

"That's the same thing happening right here, right now. I know that. I feel it deep"—she touched her fingers together and pressed them to her abdomen—"in the core of my being."

"Can't you see?" He took a step toward her but held himself tense. "You're angry. *I* made you angry. Do you think it ends there?"

"Dane, people fight. They argue. Get mad at each other. It's normal."

"No." He returned to the wall and stepped around her. "Not like—" He clamped his mouth shut. Lips in a thin line, he lowered his head.

There. There it was, whatever was haunting him, turning him into this stubborn, thickheaded oaf who wouldn't release whatever insanity held his mind and heart captive in a painful prison.

"Like what? Like you?"

He wouldn't look at her. Wouldn't talk. Wouldn't move.

Aspen went to him. "Dane. . . ?"

"The c"—he drew in a long breath—"the man who killed my mother."

Was that who Dane feared? Why? What did his mom's murderer have to do with him? The dots wouldn't connect. "Talk to me, please. I want to help." She touched his side, felt the deep rise and fall of his breathing. "I'm not going anywhere, Dane. I'm here. I love you." The words rang in her ears, startling. Exhilarating.

Locked on to her, Dane's eyes searched her face. "Don't say that. Please. . .don't. I don't want to hurt you."

She couldn't help the smile. His words warred with the longing, the aching resonating through his handsome face. "Well, I *do* love you, and you *will* hurt me. It's what people do, but it doesn't mean we shouldn't try."

"You are so beautiful, so pure. . ." His hand slid to the back of her neck as he captured her mouth with his, pulling her deeper beneath the swell of his strength and passion. It felt as if she tumbled into a hot tub, the warmth bubbling around her as his arms encircled her. Crushed her against his chest.

Abandoned Building, Djibouti

Neil Crane cursed. God forgive his Christian upbringing, but he did. That whopper of a kiss severely complicated things.

"You ready?"

He turned to Lina. "You kidding? That"—he pointed toward the building where Cardinal and the American team had holed up—"screws up everything."

"It changes nothing." She turned and lifted a phone from the windowsill. Eyes on him, she pressed a button then placed the phone to her ear.

"Who are you calling?" He drew his own phone out, surreptitiously hitting the record button.

With a rueful smile, she walked away from him. Out of the room. "Privet. . . *On v lyubvi.*"

Neil turned from the window. Russian? She was speaking Russian? Since when? He moved carefully, quietly, closer. He watched the screen as his phone received the words and translated them for him.

HELLO. HE'S IN LOVE.

Thank God for gadgets.

". . .da. . .*nyet!* Nyet, *on slishkom khorosho.* . . Khorosho. *Prekrasno.* Da, *segodnya vecherom.* . ."

YES. NO! NO, HE'S TOO GOOD. . . OKAY. VERY WELL. YES, TONIGHT.

She stood by a wall, her head in her hand as she listened. "*Poka.*"

BYE.

Neil pocketed the phone and drew the Ruger from its holster. He eased into the room, aiming at her head.

Twenty-Seven

Special Operations Safe House, Djibouti

His universe tilted a degree. Cardinal felt the implosion of everything he'd carefully constructed to keep him safe, to stop him from perpetuating a curse. And Aspen Courtland had dismantled every trap, every barrier, every reason.

The way she fit in his arms amazed him. The kiss had been long enough to sear his conscience. Long enough to tell him he wanted more, so much more. Long enough to scare the living daylights out of him, too.

Perfect. She was perfect. Being with her was perfect.

A perfect formula for disaster.

Cardinal closed his eyes against the thought, swallowed and inhaled the sweet scent of her hair. Lavender. Maybe some vanilla. He hated that he knew those smells because they would forever be ingrained in his mind as belonging to her. He'd never be able to forget her. Forget what had just transpired.

"I love you."

She had no idea *who* she loved. She didn't even know his real name. The question burning against his conscience was, did he love her?

He'd do anything for her. Maybe that was the terror of it all—he'd kill for her. Kill anyone and anything, including his feelings for her, if he felt that would keep her safest. Because suddenly this woman, who was sweet and sensitive yet had an iron will, seemed like a glass rose in his large, clumsy hands.

Aspen drew back and looked up at him again.

Cardinal couldn't help himself. Or rather—he *did* help himself—to another kiss. So sweet. So willing. He liked the way she stiffened at first under the touch of their lips then relaxed into it. Her hands on his back, fingers pressing into him, deepening the kiss burned the last of his resolve.

Something bumped against his leg. Pushed between them—no, pushed them *apart*.

Giggling, Aspen drew back and looked down. "I think he's jealous." When she met Cardinal's gaze again, she wore a shy smile.

Talon plopped between them, panting as he peered up at them.

Cardinal eased against the half wall, hauling in his reeling thoughts, and petted the Lab. "I think it's me who should be jealous." Smart dog. Wedging in, planting himself solidly in a position as if to say, "Back off. She's mine." As he reached toward the dog, a low rumble carried through Talon's chest. His tail flicked.

"Hey. Sorry. That's normal—he's not a pet, and sometimes—"

Talon's bark severed her words.

Aspen ruffled his head and rubbed his ears. "It's okay, boy. I can handle having two handsome guys in my life."

In her life...

Didn't she realize that couldn't happen? Man, he'd never felt the urge to backpedal faster than he did right now. Fear. No, it was bigger, stronger. He could feel it. Aspen was right. He was afraid of this. Letting go of his strict Cardinal rules was like jumping off a cliff. Free fall. Straight to his death. Maybe even hers.

And the angel flew.

"Aspen, listen." Cardinal raked his hand through his hair, groping for some tendril of sanity. Some way to lower the boom. "I...I can't—"

Again, Talon's growl leapt into the night. Cardinal glanced at the dog, who pushed onto all fours and walked to the other side, sniffing the air. He barked. Whimpered. Sat down. Looked at her then scooted closer to the wall.

"That's...weird." Aspen turned toward the dog.

Cardinal stood, using the distraction to turn the conversation away from his weakness. "What?"

"That's...I think that's a hit." She looked at him with a frown. "But on what?"

The door flung open. Candyman leapt out. "Hey." He slowed for a second, his gaze taking in the scene. No doubt the entirely too observant grunt knew what was going on. "Downstairs. Burnett's on the line. We're moving." And just as quick the guy disappeared the way he'd come.

Downstairs, Cardinal, Aspen, and Talon gathered with the others. A full ensemble.

"Circle up." Watterboy motioned them around a laptop that sat on the table. "Go ahead, General. We're all present."

"Where's the happy couple?"

Cardinal arched his eyebrow as he planted a hand on the table and leaned in. "You're not funny."

Burnett roared, his broad shoulders bouncing. "Yeah, I keep telling my doctor that." He pounded a fist on the table. "Lousy, no-good—he put me on a diet! Said my blood pressure is too high." He wagged a finger at the camera. "That's your fault, you know. I'm not drinking no crappy Diet Dr Pepper, so get me some answers I can cram into this leak that's pouring dung into my lap."

"What leak?"

"Payne!"

Cardinal digested the news. "What do you have?"

"Show him," Burnett said as he stabbed a thick finger at the webcam.

Watterboy flattened a map between Cardinal's hand and the laptop's keyboard. "Here and here."

"What am I looking at?"

"Caravans."

Cardinal peered through his brow at the live-feed video. Was that word supposed to mean something? "There are caravans all over the place. I see them every day."

"Not like this."

"Why?"

"In and out," Watterboy said. "Same route. Twice a week."

"Where are they going?"

"Sliding right past our base to the docks."

"Cargo?"

"That's what you need to find out." Burnett popped the top on a DP can and took a slurp.

"It's muffed up," Candyman said, chomping into an apple. Juice dribbled down his beard.

"You're disgusting," Timbrel said, her lip curled.

"Hey, hazards of the beard." Candyman winked as he used his sleeve to clean up.

Cardinal waited for someone to elaborate. He hated being the last one in on the information.

"At first look," Watterboy said, "we thought maybe weapons."

"No way." Candyman pitched the apple into a metal bin. "Pardon me, General," he said as he leaned in, keyed in something, and drew up images. His thick, tanned finger jabbed toward the screen. "Check it. Those aren't weapons' crates, and though there is a butt-load of illegal weapons traipsing across this desert, that's not a known weapons' cache."

"Where was that image taken and when?"

"A half-dozen kilometers outside Omo National Park."

Pushing up, Cardinal frowned. "Sudan?" It made no sense. Clearly Burnett and Hastings had been busy, tracking the caravan from one place to the next. "Aren't there gold mines out there?"

"Yeah, but dude, c'mon." Candyman grinned. "They aren't smuggling gold. No reason to. Everyone knows that's what's there and that it's being mined. Besides—" Candyman traced a path on the map from Sudan, past the base and to another point. "FOB Kendall is funneling whatever it is through their little camp then giving them clear passage to the docks."

Cardinal stared at the information, at the maps, at the images. "What else is in that region? Minerals, I mean."

Watterboy shrugged. "Got me."

Though the man feigned ignorance, Cardinal had a gut instinct that he could wager a pretty accurate guess. "Gold mines." He rubbed his jaw, thinking. Actually, *not* liking what he was thinking.

"What is it?" Aspen stepped closer. "What's wrong?"

"There are gold mines there, just like Candyman said." He sighed. "Some uranium is also recovered as a by-product with copper, or as a by-product from the treatment of other ores, such as the gold-bearing ores of South Africa."

"Uranium?" Aspen scrunched her nose.

Candyman whistled. "Yeah, aka, yellowcake."

Curses flitted on the hot air and from the laptop.

"Hey, get me back on!" the general growled. At his command and a few clicks, Burnett's round face glared at them again. "Cardinal, if you really think that's what's happening out there, then we have to find that—"

"Should be easy. The uranium decay puts off radiation."

"Think I need you to tell me that, VanAllen?"

Contrite and smirking, Candyman lowered his head. "No, sir."

"Then shut up."

"General," Cardinal said, wanting to laugh, "your blood pressure."

"Get off my back. I know what I'm doing. And you bunch of girls are the ones blowing my pressure through the roof. Now, get down there and find those crates. I want this solved."

"Sir?" Cardinal eased into view again. "Think Payne is connected to this? Think that's why he wanted me out of here and the rest of us locked up on base so we couldn't catch wind of his little operation?"

"That's exactly what I'm thinking. But we don't have time for guesses. I need proof!"

Cardinal looked to Watters. "Where are the crates now?"

"Port of Djibouti."

"We need to move or we'll lose them."

"Gear up!"

Abandoned Apartment, Djibouti

Lina turned, her eyes widening as she lowered the phone.

"Hands up." He stared down the sights of his Ruger, shoving his mind away from the feelings that had strangled his good sense, stopped him from figuring this out sooner. "Where I can see them." He nodded as she turned, arms held out. His head pounded—why had he ever trusted her? "You've been working me."

She swallowed. Guilt. Nerves.

"Who are you?"

"It doesn't matter who I am. What matters is that we have the same goal."

Neil laughed. "I don't think so."

"You want Cardinal captured. So do we—I."

233

"No." He cocked his head. "Let's go with your first try—*we*. Who's we?"

"I cannot tell you that."

"Then let me put another hole in that pretty head of yours."

"Don't be stupid. You kill me, you don't get Cardinal."

"Hey, doll, if I don't kill you, then I *don't* get him—because you're going to take him right out from under me, isn't that right?"

She had a will of iron. "You will get your answers." She lifted her jaw. "Then I get mine."

"That sounds mighty tidy. Too tidy."

"We're out of time." She wasn't the Lina he'd been willing to spill his guts for two hours ago. The soft, innocent facade had evaporated with her seething anger. "We do this or we don't. What's it going to be, cowboy?" She tossed a look over her shoulder. "They're leaving."

Neil rose from the chair and walked to the window. He tugged back the dingy sheet and peered along the sliver between the material and the chipped plaster wall. Darkness inside and out made it easier to see without losing time for compensating as vision adjusted to the new light setting.

He was right. "They know." Then he'd been right not to trust Cardinal.

But he'd been wrong to trust the woman beside him. He'd been sucked into the old romance trap. Bought it. And the island in Arkansas.

Gah! Had he really been that stupid?

As he watched their vehicle lumber onto the road and speed off toward the docks, he heard something. To his right.

Tones.

Neil mastered his body. Forced himself not to betray what he'd detected—she was using a phone. Why couldn't he see the light from the display? Had she killed it somehow? What was she sending through that device?

What if. . .what if *she* was behind everything?

They're heading toward the port. Fury wormed through him. He'd been right! They had known. Cardinal. Burnett—they had to know. Why else would they make a run to the docks in the middle of the night? A dead weight plunked into his gut.

Cardinal had told him once: trust nobody. Not even yourself. And Neil had failed. He'd trusted himself, trusted his instincts. Believed that this demure woman was innocent. That she really cared about him and was in danger. Classic damsel-in-distress game. But...how? Why? Why would she target him? *I'm nobody.*

Yeah, a nobody with an arsenal of information and secrets.

Safe House, Djibouti

Cardinal. What did that mean? General Burnett had used it while talking to Dane. Was it some type of code?

Aspen shrugged off the questions, her mind still racing at the idea of going into a dockyard and sneaking around crates that potentially held yellowcake. She didn't know enough about the mineral to know if she'd end up with radiation poisoning, so she trusted that Dane wouldn't lead her into a situation that could potentially hurt her or the others.

Sitting between her feet, Talon panted and seemed to sense the thrumming adrenaline in the vehicle. Leaning into her touch, he whimpered. At least—she thought he did. With the high engine noise and the road chatter, sounds collided. He'd really been off lately. On the rooftop, in action. He'd been through a lot, and she wasn't sure he was weathering the storms very well.

Next to her, Timbrel bumped her knee against Aspen's. "You okay?"

Aspen nodded as her gaze made its way to Dane, who sat with his forearms on his legs. Decked out in an Interceptor vest and a weapon across his legs, he stared at a map using his small shoulder lamp. Intense. Direct. Strong. Being in his arms, that kiss. . .and just as swift, that regret.

Something bigger than herself compelled her to stand her ground and not let him slink away from their mutual attraction. She'd never been like that, confrontational. In fact, that type of behavior was Class-A Timbrel. Maybe her friend had rubbed off on her some.

"Go easy, Aspen," Timbrel said in her ear, soft but firm. "He's not who you think he is."

Aspen glanced at her friend, surprised. "What does that mean?" Her attention swung back to Dane.

Watterboy said something that pushed Dane upright, and he adjusted the weapon on the strap and stretched his neck. His gaze struck hers. The granite expression softened, a flicker of a smile wavering on his lips. But she must've had confusion still on her face because his brow knotted, then his gaze slid to Timbrel. The momentary softening vanished as the granite slammed back into place.

The vehicle lurched to a stop. "All quiet," Watterboy called.

Unloaded, they grouped up in the night-darkened alley behind a building that squatted in the dirt like a fat spider. Despite being a good seventy yards from the docks, port noises drifted loud and clear to their position.

Aspen lifted a ball from her pocket and let Talon nose it. It'd be his reward once they got back to the safe house and now served as an initiative to do a good, quick job.

With a Glock strapped to her thigh, Aspen had firepower, and with Talon at her side, she had dog power. But the power she found the greatest comfort in was her heavenly Father. He'd been her rock and fortress through every storm. Though she didn't have the answers she wanted, the comfort of His presence remained true and steadfast. More than any human ever had.

Aspen would be a liar, though, if she didn't admit to having an increased measure of comfort in the presence of someone else, too—Dane. She found herself looking to him even now as the team prepped to sneak onto the barge with the purported yellowcake.

Watterboy gave the signal that launched the mission.

The precision and stealth of the half-dozen men—Watterboy, Candyman, Scrip, Rocket, and two others whose names she couldn't remember—amazed her. She'd been in the Air Force, but sitting behind a desk at the JAG offices didn't compare to this in-your-face tactical stuff. She prayed for strength, prayed she could do her position as Talon's handler justice and make the guys proud. Make Dane proud.

She scurried along the wall, sandwiched between Timbrel and Candyman, keeping Talon at her side. Though the preferred method for a CTT dog was to be off-lead or on a long lead, until they got on the boat they had to stay close and quiet.

The team slowed at a juncture, and she watched as they gave silent signals. Two bolted away from the building, their boots thumping quietly—but it felt much louder at this hour with the emptied docks and port—as they beat a path to a smaller structure. A shack that probably served as an office of sorts. Or something.

The lineup shortened as each member made tracks to the other side until it was her turn. She reached down and touched Talon's head. "Go," she said in a hushed but firm voice.

Aspen rushed from the protection of one building, across the alley, to the next. Only as she and Talon stepped up with the others did she release the pent-up breath. Muttering praise to Talon, she checked the others, checked for Dane.

His strong back was to her. He faced front with Watterboy and Candyman, assuming a stance to cover as the other two hustled the last dozen feet to the ship. With all the swishing of tactical pants and thumping of boots, she marveled that they hadn't drawn attention. Then again, those not looking for trouble rarely found it.

From this position, if she peered out. . .just a little. . .she could see the barge that jutted beyond the lip of the harbor. Its red-and-white hull shone clearly. Water rippled and lapped, glittering. She glanced up at the moon, full in its brilliance, unfettered by clouds. Which meant the team could be seen just as clearly.

From her protective cover with Timbrel and Rocket, Aspen waited as the others did a close-up assessment of the barge. Candyman shifted and gave hand signals.

"Move," Rocket said as he darted toward the barge.

Aspen and Timbrel jogged toward the team, Talon working with grace and without hesitation. It gave her hope that he'd be okay.

Watterboy and Candyman leapt from the dock onto the deck of the self-propelled barge. A dark form moved out from a shadow. Watterboy wheeled around and aimed his weapon. A small muted spark exploded in the darkness. The form wilted, and Candyman dropped in behind to catch the man and lower him to the steel.

On the dock, next to a barrel that gave flimsy cover, Scrip knelt, eyes out as he scanned the dock down the barrel of his M4.

"Candyman wants the dog," Rocket said, hand on Aspen's shoulder. "Go."

Aspen's gaze bounced to the deck where Candyman stood, motioning her up. Stomach in her throat, she moved forward with Talon. Even as she made the climb, there was resistance on the lead. "Talon, seek, seek!"

He surged forward, but as his paw hit the metal plank up to the barge, he turned back.

"Talon, hup!" Aspen continued forward, keeping her fear smothered and her authority focused. If she let him know his actions distressed her, it'd only add to his confusion, his momentary panic. He needed her to lead, to express certainty about their mission.

As they jumped across, Candyman hooked her arm and tugged her aside, into the shadows. "That way." He pointed down a narrow steel catwalk that stretched over an open area filled with containers. Did he want her to cross it? Alone—she'd be completely exposed with the bow to her left and the stern with the wheelhouse to her right. Though she didn't *see* danger, this hot, humid night screamed it.

Great. Heights and danger. Didn't they know she wasn't a combat veteran?

Yeah, but you have a combat *tracking team dog.*

"Go!" Candyman prompted, his teeth gritted through the word.

Right. Okay. Talon was trained to protect her and the others by scouting ahead for danger, so she needed to let him do that. But they'd been through so much. He'd come a long way in their relatively short time together. Letting him go ahead of her, knowing there could be insurgents, Aspen knew how this could end.

She pushed that thought from her mind as she stepped onto the catwalk. It bounced a little beneath her feet. Talon's nails scratched on the steel as they hurried over it. Not much separated her and a twenty-foot fall to the well floor. And nothing protected her from being seen. Bent, she crouch-scurried toward safety.

"Hey!"

Aspen froze as a shape loomed ahead of her.

★ ★ Twenty-Eight ★ ★

Two shapes stood on the catwalk. One was Aspen. The other was trouble.

Cardinal threw himself around, bringing his weapon to bear. He aimed—but in that split second, he knew if he shot the guy they'd alert everyone within a couple of miles to their presence. Would Aspen know to catch the guy? If he didn't shoot, the guy would make a lot more noise.

Cardinal applied pressure to the trigger. Felt the kick of the weapon. Kept his eyes trained on the target, who jerked back—the impact of the bullet.

Like lightning, someone darted behind the guy. Caught him. Lowered him to the rail. Watterboy motioned Aspen and Talon onward. The breath that had lodged in the back of Cardinal's throat finally processed as he trailed Aspen hurrying to cover.

Squatting at the lip of the deck, she looked down and hesitated. In that move, he saw the dilemma—Talon. The jump was too high for him. She eyed the canisters. That'd be a big jump, but worse, it'd be loud. They'd wake the neighborhood. Or at least the men shacked up in the cramped living quarters below deck.

Talon jumped. Right over Cardinal's head and onto the first canister.

A metal thwunk resonated through the well.

Cardinal tensed, listening, alert. He flinched when he saw Aspen moving down the rungs of the wall-mounted ladder. Two more thwunks sounded by the time Aspen touched down.

Weapon pointed up, Cardinal's gaze traced the wheelhouse, waiting for a light. For a shout. For a sign that Talon's adventure had been heard.

He sensed something at his side and glanced there. Aspen stood next to him, coiling the lead around her arm, her expression tense, a mixture of relief and fear. She gave him a half smile that told him she felt safer with him, a smile that extended thanks for saving her from the guy on the catwalk.

"Phil? That you?" came a wary, groggy voice.

"Yeah." The voice came from Candyman. "Just tripped. Go back to bed."

"Bed? What the heck are you talking about?" Light flooded out from a side door and delivered a man into the middle of the team.

Cardinal grabbed Aspen and spun around, pinning her between himself and the crates stacked twenty feet up. From his location, he peered to the side, watching that door well.

Candyman slid up along the wall, hidden, as the man in overalls stepped into the open.

A scraggly, unkempt beard and hair framed a sea-bronzed face. Clearly the codger had seen years on the open waters. He looked around, scratching his head. "What are you tal—?"

An arm snaked around the back of the guy.

Old eyes bulged in fright. The man gripped the arm that encircled his neck.

A hand thrust a needle into the man's carotid. Old Man of the Sea went limp, and Candyman dragged him out of sight between two of the fifteen-foot-tall canisters.

"Frank?"

Candyman widened his eyes and held out his hands, as if to say, "Seriously?" then jumped back against the wall again. Seconds later, the last guy joined Frank. Someone took out the light, and they were back in motion.

Cardinal keyed his mic. "Intel has about a dozen more men. Let's *not* wake them."

Candyman nodded.

"You okay?" Cardinal asked Aspen, who seemed to wilt now that the immediate threat had been eliminated.

She gave a nod.

Lowering his gun, he bobbed his head toward Talon, who trotted toward them. "We'll find the crates. Keep him on guard."

Aspen nodded again, smoothing a hand along Talon's head.

About forty canisters sat in the well. Roughly a dozen of them could hold a small import with ease. But the smaller crates numbered close to thirty and resembled the images Burnett had shared with the team. If they had to search all of them, it'd be a long night. But that's why they had the radiation device.

Cardinal joined Rocket and Watterboy who walked the crates, waving the device over them. They rose to about shoulder height on the outside and at least twice that in the middle. Stacked carefully, the crates in the middle had the best chance of being their gold mine.

He watched, waited, all the while keeping tabs on Aspen and Talon. As the minutes ticked away, so did his patience. Those crates had been buried well within the center of this cluster. Intentionally.

Cardinal wouldn't surrender. Not yet. Not ever.

He climbed atop the crates and started shifting them. He motioned to Candyman to give him the device. Reader in hand, he wanded the wooden crates.

The thing squawked a positive reading. He grinned and tossed the reader back. Tapping the blade of his Ka-Bar knife between the lid and the rest, he worked it in then wedged it against the wood and lifted. A loud crack echoed through the well as he lifted the top.

Candyman climbed up next to him, his shoulder lamp hitting the packaging. "Vaults. Yellow vaults. That supposed to be a clue?"

His sarcasm only served to grate on Cardinal's nerves. Cardinal snapped the lock with a multitool and flipped the lid.

Candyman cursed. Several times really fast.

Couldn't have said it better. Cardinal slapped the lid closed, praying the radiation levels of the decaying uranium weren't strong enough to contaminate him. "Check the others," he said as he sheathed his knife. Knuckles against his lips, he watched as the others opened the other crates.

He eased back on another crate and drew out the camera and opened the live-feed connection to Burnett. Toeing the lid, he opened the vault and filmed the contents, then let the lens scrape over the rest, just enough to show Burnett that this shipment had to be intercepted before it got to wherever it was going.

This barge couldn't deliver its contents. Most barges were hired. So maybe the owner didn't realize what he carried. Or maybe he was being paid off—just like Admiral Kuhn? The shifting of the plot elements in this nightmare felt like tectonic plates colliding beneath the earth. There were bound to be seismic-scale responses.

Who was behind this? Where would the contents end up? Did that really matter when something like this being under the cover of darkness meant it wasn't on the up-and-up? That meant treaties or laws or embargoes were being violated.

What if this stuff was headed to Iran?

As if led to that thought via the divine, Cardinal's gaze fell on the canister across from him. More precisely, the markings on said canister. He climbed off the crates, squinting. Tried to aim the shoulder lamp at the stenciled marks as he moved.

"Whaddya got?" Candyman asked, his voice quiet and quick.

In a terrifying shift, the past surged over his barriers and rammed into the present. Heart backfiring, Cardinal traced the stenciled lettering.

Беларусь

Talon straightened, his keen eyes locked on one man. He rose and padded over to Dane, nosing the man's thigh. Talon had done that a thousand times to Aspen over the past year as she struggled with her brother's disappearance.

Sitting at Dane's feet, Talon gazed up at him perceptively. Whimpered. Inched closer.

Dane didn't move, his attention glued to the rusting red canister that loomed over him. Hand on painted letters that had once been white, he stared. As if he could see straight through it.

"Dane?" Aspen whispered to him as she joined him.

No response. What was wrong? She peeked around at his face.

Haunted. Stricken.

Something rumbled in the pit of her belly. Aspen touched his back. "Dane?"

Jaw tightened, he snapped out of it. Lowered his gaze to the side but did not look at her. "We need to clear out."

And that was it. He morphed back into the super soldier or whatever he was. "Cardinal." The word burst from her lips before she had time to consider what it might do. What it might mean.

Dane flinched. Started to look at her. But froze. He turned—away from her. "Candyman, get a picture." He tapped the canister. "Let's move out."

They were headed to the ladder when he strode past her.

She caught his arm. Held tight.

Though meaning flashed through his face, he seemed to harness it. Anger shifted and slid through his expression. His gaze went down. Then bounced to hers. "Can you get Talon topside or do you need help?"

Topside. Right. How *would* she get Talon out of there? Aspen felt disembodied from the events. Something happened back there. She wanted to know what it was. *"He's not who you think he is."* When she'd used that term—*Cardinal*—he'd responded. But it wasn't the response she'd expected, though she wasn't sure what she expected. Or why she'd even spoken the word. It'd made him angry.

Her gaze went to the hall where the ship's workers had come from. Would that work?

"No." Dane glared at her. "Too dangerous." He shifted to the ladder as he scooped Talon's lead from her hands. "Candyman, catch."

Dane took Talon's lead and tossed one end up. He clipped the other to Talon's vest. He pointed Aspen to the ladder. "Climb with him."

She started up the rungs, one arm hooked around Talon, who clamped his mouth shut, unsettled with the lifting method. " 'S okay, boy." Up...up...up.

Paws on deck, Talon sat. Huffed through a closed snout, letting his objection be known.

Aspen took his head and reassured him as she led him toward the catwalk, glancing back as Dane reached the top. He might have avoided the conversation for now, but he had some questions to answer. It wouldn't change her feelings. She'd known for a long time he hid things. He was a master at it, in fact.

He hooked a leg over the top and pushed to—he pitched forward.

Aspen sucked in a breath.

Sparks flew off the hull.

"Taking fire! Taking fire!" Candyman barreled into her and slammed her temple into the ship. "Down!"

Pain ricocheted through Aspen's head and down her neck, jarring. She yelped and reached for it. Hearing hollowed. Vision blurred. All from using her noggin to break her fall. Warmth slid down her face.

Spine to her, Candyman shoved her backward, using his boots to push them to cover. Talon whimpered and dug his snout beneath her arm. Poor guy. No doubt this was too familiar.

M4s pounded the night with their report. *Tsings* and cracks rattled the barge.

Aspen wiped the blood from her cheek and watched as Dane rolled to the side, to cover.

"Move!" Candyman shouted as he fired off several rounds. Suppressive fire.

Dane lunged toward them. Sidled up and plastered himself to the steel that protected them. She felt stupid. Out of her element. The mortal danger reminded her of what was important—living.

"Now!" Candyman hauled her up as he once again fired. He hookthrusted her across the catwalk.

Dane was with them. Holding his side.

"You ok—?"

"Go!" He pushed her forward.

"Coming out," Candyman shouted as he keyed his mic. "Cover!"

Had the others made it out? Where was Timbrel? They reached the far side. A few more steps and they'd bound over the three-foot drop into the water and onto the dock. In reach. Talon jogged with them.

Aspen aimed for the jump that would put her on the dock. Her foot slipped. Heat seared down her leg. She cried out. Stumbled. Kept moving.

Deft hands carried her up. Over the drop.

Panic hammered erratically through her. Mind buzzing. Ears ringing. Leg burning. Vision blurring. Only as her feet left the deck of the ship did she feel the rush of adrenaline that carried her over the drop.

Her right knee buckled as she landed.

Again, a hand kept her moving. Threw her toward the barrels that lined the dock. She crashed into them. Gulping air. Choking on fear.

Someone landed on her.

Talon's yelp forced her mind from the fraying panic. "Talon!"

Another whimper. Behind. She twisted—and cried out.

"Stop moving," Dane hissed in her ear.

She stilled, realizing his hand had clamped onto her arm. She glanced down and saw moonlight glinting off something dark on her arm. "Blood?"

Their eyes snagged together.

Ping!

Dane ducked and pushed himself into her. "Candyman—get us out of here!"

"If you'd stop flirting and start shooting, we might get out of here," Candyman shouted back.

"You sound jealous."

Aspen glanced from one man to the next, aware they were both fully engaged in what they were doing. Dane—stopping her from bleeding. Candyman—stopping them from getting killed.

Wouldn't it be better if they all worked on that last one?

"I'm fine." Aspen dragged herself free and reached for the gun holstered at her thigh. Only. . .it wasn't there.

"Looking for this? You dropped it when they tagged your arm in that jump." Dane held up her Glock. "Can you walk?"

"My arm was shot, not my leg."

He arched an eyebrow.

"What?"

He nodded down. She looked and blanched. Where had that come from? A tear, not a hole. She must've sliced it on something. "It's just a cut."

"Okay, they're coming in for us."

"Where are the targets?"

"One in Blue Two." Candyman pointed to the northeastern side of the dock. "Who knows where else. I can't peg them."

A vehicle ripped around the corner. Tires squalled.

Even from here she saw the bullets pinging off the hull. Thank God for armor plating!

It whipped around. Rammed into reverse and roared toward them.

Tires screeched again as they skidded to a stop five feet to the left.

"C'mon, c'mon," Rocket shouted from inside.

Dane pulled Aspen up, propping his arm around her waist and shoulders. "Ready?"

Teeth clamped as fire tore through her leg, she nodded. They rushed forward.

Candyman used his weapon for cover fire and his broad shoulders and back to shield them. Talon leapt into the vehicle. Aspen jumped in after him.

"Go, go, go!" Candyman shouted, banging the hull.

"Wait." Aspen glanced back, knowing Dane hadn't climbed in. She saw him throw himself at her.

The vehicle lurched forward.

Dane landed with a thud. Right behind him came Candyman, crawling over both of them to get out of the way as the rear doors flapped closed. Rocket secured them.

Aspen laughed and extricated herself from Dane, pulling herself onto a seat. Relief swirled fierce and potent. That was close. She tried to shift her legs, but Dane—

"Dane?" She reached for him. "Why isn't he moving?"

Candyman cursed again. Grabbed Dane. Flipped him over.

Blood trailed down his temple. Gushed over his neck.

Twenty-Nine

Neil Crane stuffed a wadded-up T-shirt against his chest, biting through the pain. "*What* was that?" Glowering at Lina, he waited for an answer.

Hatred spewed from her eyes. "I told you—leave Cardinal alone."

"No, you said I couldn't kill him." He flung the rag across the room and yanked off his soiled shirt to see his wound.

"And you just might've. If he's dead, then—"

"Then what?" he hollered. "Are you going to shoot me? Kill me?"

"I should."

Which meant she wouldn't. But he didn't care. He was too ticked off. Coupled with this Russian woman. Someone he thought he knew. Thought he loved. But didn't know the first thing about. When she ripped off the mask of innocence, he couldn't have been more shocked at the demon beneath.

Now he was totally screwed. Back to where he was eight months ago. Nobody to trust. No answers. Just a barge full of trouble.

He stomped to the back room and cranked the knob on the rusting sink. Water poured out of it, brown, then slowly cleared. He lapped water against the wound, hissing.

Soft, gentle hands touched his side.

He flinched and looked at her.

"I need to sew it up."

Why? Why wasn't he surprised she knew how to do that? "Why would you?"

Her blue eyes lingered on his, soft then razor sharp. "Because you're

247

more useful alive than dead."

Neil grunted. "Thanks. Good to know."

"Come sit down."

Neil muttered a curse and gripped the edge of the sink. This was totally messed up. If he had *any* options, he'd ditch her. Vanish. Just disappear into the vast sea of people who populated this crazy planet and become a real nobody.

"Stop brooding."

"You've gotten sassy since you ditched the whole innocent-damsel-in-distress routine." He turned and stalked into what used to be a family room of the abandoned apartment.

"And you've gotten grumpy."

"Nah, I've always been that way."

"That's true." She pushed him into the chair and went to her knees, a small bowl and supplies set up on a towel on the floor. He grunted—cold. Her fingers had always been cold.

"You'd better hope Cardinal is not dead."

"Actually, I'm hoping he is."

She pinched her lips together as she cleaned the wound then used scissorlike tongs to reach into it.

Neil pulled his head up and clenched his eyes shut as pain burst through his abdomen. Fresh warmth oozed down his side. She dabbed. Probed. He thought he might vomit. A groan wormed through his chest.

"Sorry."

Clunk.

"There."

He glanced down and saw the fragment. They'd nailed him on their way out. But he'd landed a few of his own in them.

"What. . . ?" Lina's voice was whisper-quiet.

He looked at her, surprised at the sudden rush of innocence that flooded her expression and mentally pushed him back a foot or two.

"What if he didn't betray you?"

Neil watched her. Tried to read her. She looked. . .stricken. Could he believe her?

No.

But there was something different here. Something. . .weird. The change in her had been too drastic. Cardinal had taught him to pay attention to little things like that. Follow them to their logical conclusion or end. "If he didn't, then who did?"

She dropped her gaze. "Would it matter? Your vendetta has been against Cardinal. If he didn't shoot you, then. . ."

Why would she even bring this up? He'd already shot the guy. Killed him, if the fates were on his side. "I guess it doesn't matter now, huh?"

"You're stupid." She snatched up the supplies and pushed to her feet. "You deserve what's coming."

Pentagon, Arlington County, Virginia

"What part of 'stealth' don't you sorry excuses for soldiers understand?" Lance Burnett's pulse pounded against his temple warning him to calm down. Like he would. He banged a fist against his desk, glaring at the bearded face in the monitor.

"Sir, with all due respect—"

"Don't even go there."

"Sir, Cardinal's down."

Lance felt as if someone had dumped ice down his back. "How in Sam Hill did that happen?" He grabbed for his Dr Pepper and hit the top. The drink toppled over. He cursed as he leapt up to salvage the disaster. "What happened down there, VanAllen?"

"Unknown, sir. We encountered some unfriendlies while in the hold but neutralized them and continued. On our way out, we came under fire. Several were hit, Cardinal went down."

"Down? How down?"

"Unconscious, sir. Dr. Helverson came over from Lemonnier."

"Good." About time something went right. "Well, what'd you find down there?"

"Exactly what we expected to find, sir."

"God have mercy." He mopped his brow then used the napkin to mop up the spilled soda. Things were out of control. Someone was down there picking off his men. Uranium oxide sitting in the port.

"We could go down there," Lieutenant Hastings offered.

Lance chewed the idea. "VanAllen."

"Sir."

"Keep me posted."

"Yessir."

Ending the call, he leaned back in his chair. "What'd he send?"

Hastings handed the digital reader to him. "Video footage of the lockers. More than fifty of them. All marked dangerous. You'll see he opened one of them. Radiation readings are high."

"We'll need to force that ship not to leave port."

"Already done," Smith said from the chair beside Hastings. "Seems there's a problem with their permits."

Lance grunted. Man, he felt like crud. He reached for his DP, more carefully this time. "How soon can we be down there?" There were too many variables involved for him to manhandle this from another continent. And he had this twitching feeling that if he could dig deep enough or reach far enough, his fingers would coil around the neck of one General Payne.

Hastings smirked. "Flight leaves in an hour."

Lance laughed. "Got my suitcase packed?"

"On its way up from the front desk as we speak. Your wife says she'll miss you."

He laughed again. "More like she's partying now that she got rid of me for a while." He sighed and ran a hand over his face. He felt old. Old and out of shape. Maybe he should've listened to the doctors.

Well, too late for that. And now he had a brewing international disaster. Cardinal was done—that went beyond bad to the hellfire and damnation bad. That man simply could not die. Because with him went a bevy of information and contacts and resources. Not to mention that Lance's obligation to the man, long overdue, had yet to be paid. If the Grim Reaper came for Cardinal, he'd come for Lance. Sooner rather than later.

"Where's Payne?"

Smith lifted his chin. "Officially? Taking personal time with his family."

"Unofficially?"

"Security cameras at Lemonnier have a man who looks just like Payne." Hastings tapped another picture into view. "That's a mighty deep pocket, reaching all the way to the Dark Continent."

"Let's empty that pocket. Give Payne a little pain of his own."

Special Operations Safe House, Djibouti

Arms wrapped around her waist, Aspen stood as the doctor emerged from the room where he'd worked on Dane. "How is he?"

The doctor hesitated, glancing at Candyman.

What? Was it bad news, and he didn't think she could handle it?

Candyman gave the doctor a nod as Timbrel came to her side.

"He was hit twice—head and neck. And he lost a lot of blood." Dr. Helverson accepted a bottled water from Rocket, uncapped it, and guzzled. "He needs to rest, but the bullet did not nick his carotid, thank goodness. If it had, we'd be planning a burial."

"Two hits?"

Aspen closed her eyes and turned away.

"What about the head?"

Candyman's questions drew her back round.

"Just a graze. Head wounds are messy because they bleed a lot." His eyes seemed to bore into her. "How's your head?"

Her fingers went to the knot almost on their own will. "A headache, but I'm okay."

"Dizziness? Blurry vision?"

"No."

"Let's hope it stays that way," Helverson said as he started for the door. "If she becomes disoriented or she doesn't make sense when she talks or her speech slurs, call me. She could have brain swelling."

"I think she already does," Timbrel said. "She likes that guy in there."

Aspen couldn't resist the smile but shook her head at her friend. "At least I can admit when I like a guy." She rolled her gaze toward Candyman.

Timbrel stiffened.

"Night, folks." Helverson glanced at his watch. "Make that, morning."

"I'm going to go in with him." Aspen clicked her tongue at Talon who lumbered out of his sleep and onto his feet to follow.

As she slipped into the next room, which was barren of furnitu or decoration save a chair, a sink, and the table upon which Dane was stretched, she allowed Talon in. He curled up in a corner, apparently exhausted from the excitement an hour ago.

Feeling drawn like a flower to the sun, she went to Dane. A blanket draped over his legs and waist, his upper torso bare. Two white bandages glared against his olive skin, one on his neck, one just above his temple.

In the chair, Watterboy sat up and gave a sleepy "hey" then pulled to his feet. "Doc says he's going to make it."

At the table, Aspen took in the man she'd fallen in love with. So incredibly familiar, as if she'd known him all her life. Yet a stranger. A very handsome, rugged, brooding one. But handsome all the same.

"Thank God," Aspen said. "Hey, if you want a break, I'll stay with him now."

A small divot of his hair had been shaved near the graze at his temple. A shame. She'd liked the way the strands near his temple always dropped into his eyes. She brushed the hair back. He probably wouldn't let her do this if he was awake. He'd tell her she didn't know him, tell her not to trust him.

"He's a good man."

Her heart zigzagged. She'd almost forgotten Watterboy was in the room still. "Yeah, he is." But she sensed that the team leader was trying to tell her something else, something *more*.

She looked at the man with the dark hair, still garbed in his tactical gear, blood on his shoulder and chest from hauling Dane into the space that became the surgical bay. Candyman had radioed en route for a doc, and thankfully, Helverson had been at the hospital, just minutes away.

Watterboy was a stark contrast to Candyman, who was all play and games. The man before her took his job seriously and himself even more. What was his hidden message?

"Do you. . .*know* him? I mean—really know him, Captain?"

"You care about him?"

Aspen couldn't hide the blush if she wanted to and let her focus to Dane, still unconscious. Sedated. A beautiful face. She swiped a thumb over his cheek and rested her hand on his shoulder. Did she love him? "Yeah."

It went way beyond that. Seeing him with all that blood, him being dead, leaving her alone—it terrified her. More than anything she'd experienced losing her parents. Losing Austin. They all seemed like the end of her world. But then Dane came, and she felt like the world was a good place to be again.

Watterboy's expression softened. "That look on your face. . ."

Aspen's cheeks heated even more as she met the man's hazel eyes. "You must think me silly."

"Hardly." He gave a quick shake of his head. "But. . .just remember what you're feeling now."

Remember? "When? What do you mean?"

"I should grab some rack time." Watterboy left the room without another word.

Confusion settled on her like a weight. Ominous words. She turned back to Dane, contemplating Watterboy's words. It left her unsettled, much like Timbrel's warning had. She studied Dane. The pads of her fingers tickled at the stubble on his jaw and chin. Such chiseled features. Everything about him was chiseled. With his chest bared, she couldn't help but notice, though she tried to keep her eyes on his face. His heart had even seemed chiseled—right out of granite—when she'd first met him. But little by little, that mask crumbled.

She brushed her fingers through his hair and bent down, planting a kiss on his left temple. "Father, bring him back to me. We'll figure it out. Whatever it is." She planted one more kiss, resolving to brave the coming storm. And there was definitely one coming. It made her stomach quaver. She'd been through a lot in her life, but nothing like this. And never had she felt the accompanying peace that quieted her panic. Gave her strength.

"I love you," she whispered against his ear. When she eased back, her heart jackhammered as a steel gaze bored into her. "Oh. Hi."

A smile wobbled on his lips, then his eye fluttered closed.

"Dane?"

Nothing but the quiet rise and fall of his toned chest.

Would he remember waking up to her whispered confessions of love? She moved to the side and dragged the chair Watterboy had occupied.

Without lifting his head, Talon peeked at her with one eye.

"You're a good boy."

His tail thumped twice, and he returned to chasing squirrels through the dream fields, just as Dane had returned to the drug-induced dreamland.

The side door creaked open. Candyman entered. He'd changed out of his combat duds into jeans. A circular tattoo of some sort dipped below the cuff of the black T-shirt that stretched tightly around his bicep. She'd not noticed with all the gear he wore how barrel-chested he was. His blond hair hung damp. She wasn't sure, but it looked like his beard might be wet, too.

"Watterboy isn't here."

"Yeah." He thumbed over his shoulder. "Headed to the showers." One hand rested over his other, which was balled into a fist. He looked tense. No, not tense. Uncomfortable.

Maybe he was nervous about losing Dane. No, he'd heard Helverson reassure them. . . "You okay?"

"Yeah." His gaze sparked. "Actually. . .can I talk to you?"

She hesitated. Wasn't that what they were doing?

"About Timbrel."

Smothering her smile, she nodded. "Sure."

"Good." He stuffed his hands in his jean pockets. "See, I'm crazy about her."

Aspen nodded again, not trusting herself to talk.

"But she's. . ." He held his hands out, waving them, clearly searching for the right word. "Unapproachable."

His shoulders slumped. Poor guy. "Yeah. I mean, I see it in her eyes that she digs me, ya know? But. . .just when things start to happen, or seem like they're going to happen—bam!" He pounded his fist into his hand.

Talon jumped.

"Sorry." Candyman held his hands out in a placating manner. "Sorry," he said to Aspen. "I just thought you might know. . .what am I doing wrong? How can I get her to give me the time of day?"

On her feet, Aspen smiled. "Stop wearing a watch."

Candyman shot her a blank stare. "Come again?"

"Look." She hated the truth she'd have to put into her words. She could do no less for the man who'd protected her, Talon, and Dane in that firefight. "Timbrel's. . .unique. She's been through a lot."

"Like what?"

Aspen shook her head. "Sorry, that's not my tale to tell. If you want to win her, it's going to take time. A *long* time. And honestly," she said with a heavy sigh, "I'm not even sure if it will ever work."

"Look, I get it. She's been wounded. Probably used and/or abused. I've seen it in the field and off the field." He scratched his beard. "But I can't figure out how to convince her that I want to give this a shot. I mean a real one, know what I mean?"

"No." She crossed her arms over her chest. "What do you mean, Sergeant?" Something protective and challenging rose up within her. "You just met her."

"Actually, no—remember in Afghanistan with the other handler, Ghost?"

Whoa, the guy had a killer smile. It really made her want to see Dane's even more. And suddenly, instead of this combat-hardened Special Forces soldier, she saw a nervous cowboy.

"I took her picture." He grinned bigger. "I wear it in my helmet. Have ever since. She's what keeps me coming home."

"Candyman, you haven't even—"

He held up his hands. "I know. It don't make sense to someone like you." He scratched his beard again. "Well, for most people for that fact, but I knew when I first met her out there in the desert that she was for me. Seeing her here on this mission, spending time with her—it sealed my fate."

Aspen laughed. "Don't tell her that."

His frown dropped. "Why not?"

"Timbrel doesn't believe in fate."

"What does she believe in?"

"Why don't you find out?"

He studied her, eyes narrowed. "Seriously? Just like that."

"Don't beat around the bush with Timmy. She doesn't play games, you've figured that out."

"No kidding."

"But let me give you one warning."

"Yeah?"

"You'd better love big, tough war dogs."

He hesitated, glancing at Talon. "She has a war dog?"

"Ghost calls him the Hound of Hell."

"Oh man." The man's face fell. "Those dogs hate me."

Thirty

Clothes floated like ghouls around her. Rising. Falling. Twirling. An eerie sky embraced them as they rose once again then fluttered down. So beautiful. So terrifying. A sheet dropped with a bang.

She jolted. Looked around. Turned a circle. Like blank walls, two sheets stood perfect and straight. A dark, bloodied form drifted through them.

Her feet wouldn't move. Her heart stopped. She couldn't breathe. Run! Hurry!

The man came forward. Closer.

He looked kind. Reached a hand out, extended in friendship. In kindness.

Aspen saw her own arm stretched toward him.

A screech ripped through the air.

Lightning struck—struck the man.

Flames devoured the sheets.

She screamed. Tried to run. Her feet tangled. She dropped to the ground. Hand in front of her face, she watched the man, now singed and smoking, float toward her. His face. . .

No, it wasn't possible!

"No!" It couldn't be. "Austin!" she howled.

Aspen bolted upright. Drenched in sweat, she groped for light in the darkness. A dream. . . She hauled in a thick breath. One hand over her chest, she pressed the heel of her other hand to the bridge of her nose and stifled a sob.

A soft thump-thump-thump drew her gaze to the side.

Talon stared up at her with those gorgeous brown eyes. Tail wagging, he wanted to reassure her that everything was okay.

Aspen patted the cot, and that was enough for him. He leapt up next to her and stretched out. Arms around him, she buried her face in his fur. Where was Austin? What was wrong? What if. . .what if Dane had been right? What if that man *was* Austin?

Exhaustion pulled at her limbs. At her mind. Seeing Dane nearly die. Watching over him for four hours till Candyman relieved her. She wouldn't have left, but she could barely keep her eyes open.

She smoothed the dense fur of the Lab, his paws already kicking as he chased prey again through the field of dreams. He hadn't been himself lately. Could it be. . .that Talon knew what Dane suspected?

Crazy.

Only crazy in that it was entirely likely that if the man *was* Austin, Talon would know. Better than anyone else. The thought took root. The children's hospital—had Talon spotted that man? Is that why he took off then hid beneath the house, terrified by the bullets?

But Austin would never shoot at Talon. They were partners. That bond was thicker than blood.

That's what I thought—that the blood bond was thick. But if this was true, then Austin abandoned that bond.

The ramifications were heartrending.

No, there was no way Austin would do that. Not after what they went through with losing their parents. Their deaths had been brutal on Austin. He'd never knowingly do that to her.

Not even for some noble cause?

The question challenged her beliefs. Hadn't she done things she never thought she'd do—like climbing aboard a barge filled with radioactive material—in the name of national defense?

Was that the same?

She dug her fingers into Talon's fur and stroked it. So comforting, so warm, thinking. . .culling. . .formulating. . .remembering.

The man had Austin's build. Even—*oh my word!*—his walk! Austin was a toe-walker, using the balls of his feet to walk rather than hitting heel first.

She flopped onto her back, one arm under Talon's neck and the other propped over her head. Was it possible? Really possible that the man in the alley, the one who warned her and called Talon by name. . . was he Austin?

Possible.

But not probable. Aspen just couldn't let that be the truth. Austin loved her too much. They were twins. They'd often joked that when one got hurt, it was like hurting the other. They'd promised since they were kids to always—*always*—protect each other.

"Angel, they're gone now, but I will always be here. I'll do everything to protect you."

The words were sweet. They comforted—at the time. But even then, she'd wondered at those words. Austin was the rambunctious twin. The one who got in trouble. Her best friend had often called him the "evil twin" because of his sneaky side. How deft he was at—Aspen's pulse slowed as her thoughts powered down to that final word—*deception*.

Water rushed in, deluging the barge. "Aspen!"

She whirled, blue eyes wide with panic. "Talon, I can't find him."

"He'll be okay."

"No, I can't leave him. I'll never leave him."

Cardinal rushed to her, waters sloshing against his feet. He glanced down. Why was he barefoot? No time to figure it out. "Come!" He reached toward her. "Hurry!"

Her fingers thrust forward.

The ship canted right.

She wavered with a yelp.

"Aspen!"

Behind her, a wall of water dropped. Like a blanket.

Weird.

The spray blasted against her. Eyes wide, mouth open in a perfect O, *she stared at him. Clanking reverberated through the air. Vibrations wormed through his very bones. He knew what would happen. He tried to lurch forward.*

Feet wouldn't move. Legs hurt. Water swirled around him.

Then the angel flew.

She flew backward, straight through the water. Vanished.

Forever gone.

"No!" Cardinal lunged. Fire raked his neck and head. Booming thundered through his skull.

He raised his hand. . .or did he?

"Dane?"

Light seared his corneas. He moaned and looked away. Squinting and blinking at the same time, he stilled at the vision hovering over him. No, this couldn't be hell. There was an angel standing over him.

Man, that was crazy-corny. But it was true. With the light ringing her curls and her ivory-pale complexion and her white top. . . "Angel." His grin felt lopsided. So did his head. Sweet, swift relief staved off the panic as the dream rushed back to the front of his mind. Just like that squall that overtook her. Dropped like a blank—

No, not a blanket. A wall of glass. The dissonance of the dream alarmed him. His mind combining the past and present. Didn't like that his brain had shifted the "angel" in his dream to Aspen.

Fear. That was fear driving that. Worrying about her. That he couldn't protect her. That she'd be lost to him somehow.

But for now, she was here.

Groaning, he peeled himself off the table and sat with his legs dangling. He didn't care if he'd lost a limb. Aspen was alive. He couldn't take losing her. Not the way he'd lost his mom.

He caught her shoulder and pulled her into his arms. Held her tight. She was here. Aspen was okay. He tried to breathe without pain. But. . .there was so much. . .

The room spun. He closed his eyes and waited for the dizziness to pass. "How long have I been out?"

"It's lunchtime—eight or ten hours." She shrugged. "I don't know. I was. . .I don't know what time we got back." Aspen stood close, worry marring her beautiful face. "The doctor checked on you about ten minutes ago—you lost a lot of blood. He wanted you to rest." She smelled good. Looked good. Talked good.

He remembered. . . "You kissed me." He touched his temple. "Here." He smiled. A real one.

Aspen held the corner of her lip between her teeth as her gaze skidded to the floor.

He took her hand and drew her closer, noticing the red, angry scab on her forehead. "How's your head?"

"Apparently, my head's just as hard as yours."

"Good. Then we might just survive." He kissed her. Savored her warmth—*she's alive!* The docks. Seeing her getting shot. The blood. The dream. . . *Oh man. The dream.* His mind had tangled past and present. Twisted them up so tight, he'd been ready to slay a thousand demons to get her back.

Aspen curled into him. She was soft. Sweet. But then she pressed a hand to his chest and nudged him back. "You're awfully cheery— you even smiled. I think I need to call the doctor back in. That bullet might've grazed more than your hairline."

Cardinal tested his legs. Not quite solid, but they'd hold.

"Hey." Concern replaced Aspen's smile. "Should you be getting up yet? You're not even dressed." When that concern deepened, he knew she'd seen the scars on his back and shoulders.

Instinctively, he reached for his shirt. "Sorry."

Her cheeks rosied. "I just meant—"

"You said you loved me."

Her bright blue eyes came to his. She shifted, her arm around his waist, supporting him, though he didn't need it. "I told you I do."

He stared down at her. "I don't deserve you." But he wanted her. Wanted to never be separated from her. Even he knew that wasn't in his power. Just like the churches, just like the feeling that the universe righted as he sat on those pews, Aspen did the same thing for him. Why? How?

"That's sorta the point of love, isn't it? Something we can never earn but is freely given."

It felt like there was a chunk of cement in his chest as three words churned through his mind. He wanted to say them. But you didn't get to that point after a few weeks of running an op. But nearly dying sort of changes a man's mind. Yet. . . No matter how much the planets aligned or God—*are You there?*—set in motion. . .

She doesn't even know who I am. And in a way, without his career, without his identity as Cardinal, did *he* even know who he was anymore? "You need to know the truth. Everything."

She shifted. "When you're ready."

He let out a breathy snort of disbelief. "You may never speak to me again, but I want you to know the truth. All of it. You deserve that."

Clapping resounded through the room.

Aspen gasped.

Cardinal flung himself around. The room rebelled, spinning and twisting.

"Very moving," Neil Crane said as he produced a silenced weapon then dabbed a finger against his eye, as if drying a tear. "I almost cried. Really. And Cardinal, I'll take that wager."

Refusing to take his eyes off the man, Cardinal noted the door wasn't locked. Noted the man was entirely confident that he was in control. And that's what Cardinal needed to go along with. If the team was down—

The thought tightened the muscles in his shoulders. Fighting wouldn't do any good. Having been through surgery, losing blood, he would lose. Fast. And Aspen. . .

He moved his hand to her and tucked her behind him as he watched the man sidle up next to Talon, never showing them his back. He grinned at them then glanced at Talon, who sat up and panted, his tale thumping.

"Hello, boy." The man petted Talon then stood, wagging the gun at Cardinal. "I see you managed to get your shirt off."

"You shot me." It was a guess but one Cardinal didn't think was too outside the realm of possibilities.

"I couldn't let you undo what I'd orchestrated." He smiled as his gaze drifted to Cardinal's left. "Aspen, really? Falling in love with the world's most renown spy?"

"Talon, heel." Aspen moved forward a step, and Cardinal wanted to yank her back and whip out a weapon—but he didn't have one. And a sudden move could set off Crane.

Neil caught Talon's collar. "No, I think it's best he stay here."

"Who are you?" Aspen's voice wavered.

And in that hesitation and pitch of her voice Cardinal could tell she had accepted his theory. "His name is Neil Crane."

"Actually," Neil said as he shook his head and started forward, "that's the name you gave me, Cardinal." His gaze came back to him. "Tell her." He stabbed the weapon at him. And through gritted teeth demanded, "Tell her who I am!"

Thirty-One

Y ou did this to me!"

Had the world upended and dumped hell at her feet, Aspen could not have been more shocked. It was him. The voice. The mannerisms. All undeniably Austin. But the thought, the last two years of grieving whatever had happened to him, forbid her from fully embracing the thought.

"No!" Dane shifted, his expression dark. Angry. Frightening. "That is not my doing. You stepped out, you went your own way."

"No!" His voice scraped the walls with painful fury. His lips were tight. His mouth almost foaming.

Aspen shrunk at the rage and grief roiling through the man's reddening face. It was him. It was her brother. He still had the telltale temper. "Austin." She took a steadying breath.

The man's brown eyes bumped to hers.

A bubble of elation burst through her. A strangled cry. "Austin?" She took a step forward. "Is it really you?"

"Aspen." Dane's voice carried a measure of warning. "He's not—"

"Don't you dare!" Austin shuffled forward, waving the gun like a madman. "Don't you dare turn her against me. You've taken everything from me. *Everything!*"

Stumbling to mentally keep up, Aspen found herself moving away from Dane. Away from the security she'd felt two minutes ago. Away from the certainty. Dane? Dane had done this to Austin? But it didn't make sense. "Did he do something when he was with you in Kariz-e Sefid?"

Austin laughed. "With me?" He shook his head. "Oh, if only it'd been that. That's where he made sure Austin Courtland died. That's where he secured his latest pawn."

"You willingly joined DIA."

"Don't!" Austin snapped the weapon at Dane, who raised his hands in a gesture of peace. His soulful steel gaze hit hers. Telegraphed a message.

Aspen didn't know whether to hate Dane or trust him. To run *from* him or run *to* him. That was a fight for another hour. She focused back on her brother. "What. . .what happened to you, Austin?"

"Tell her," Austin said again.

"No, this is your story. Tell us. Tell both of us what happened."

"You *know* what happened."

"I know you vanished without a trace."

"Vanished because you betrayed me!"

"Enough!" Aspen turned to her brother. Her twin. Her mind tumbled through the questions, too many slamming her mind for her to even know where to start. And Dane—should she be mad at him? "Why. . .why don't you look like. . .like you used to?"

Austin grinned. "When Cardinal here betrayed me, I had to vanish—completely. A few surgeries and I became a new man."

"But your eyes are brown." Aspen couldn't wrap her mind around the transformation. He looked nothing like the brother she'd last seen at Amadore's.

"They'll be blue again eventually. The method wears off." He shrugged. "Keeps me hidden. And I need to stay hidden to bring Cardinal and his thugs down."

"You're wrong. This isn't my doing, but we can figure that out later," Dane said. "What are you doing here now? What do you want enough that you're willing to put your life on the line with that gun?"

Aspen heard the threat within the words. Dane knew how to take Austin down, even though Austin held a weapon and Dane didn't. Her nerves buzzed.

"No," Austin said with a half laugh as he moved to the side. "You don't get to dictate this. I'm here. I'm the one with the gun."

"Okay," Dane said. "Fine. You have the gun." Why did that sound like a challenge?

"Let's bring the testosterone down a level." Aspen had always mediated between Austin and their grandfather, both thickheaded mules. "Austin, if you want to talk, if you have questions, put the gun down and let's sort it out. I'd rather not get accidentally shot while you're ranting."

"He already shot me."

"Twice." Austin seethed. "I'd like to go for a third."

Dane huffed. "Then shoot me and get on with it!"

"No!" Aspen stepped between the two men, uncertain which one she would defend. Which man *deserved* being defended. Blood ties were stronger, right? "Austin, why are you here?"

"I want to know why he betrayed me."

Aspen stilled, a shudder of a blink swiveling her attention to Dane. What did that mean?

"Me?" Dane looked shocked. "How did *I* betray you? You're the one who abandoned the mission. Stopped responding. I spent two months down here looking for you."

"Looking for me?" Austin laughed. "Don't believe your own press, Cardinal. You aren't that good of a liar. You were down here working with them."

Silence drenched the room.

Dane drew up. "Working with whom?" His voice had lost its edge.

Austin pursed his lips. "Don't tell me you don't know!"

"Okay, I won't. Do you want me to tell you what I do know?"

Hesitation stretched between them. Aspen's heart thudded against the words. Did she want to know? Would Dane tell the truth? Could she handle the truth? *"You don't know me."* His words plunked in front of her like an anchor. *"Don't trust me."* Another anchor.

Austin finally said, "Let's hear it."

"Yes, I recruited you—in Afghanistan. I saw you were a stellar soldier. But I also saw the anger. That made you a prime candidate for covert operations because it drives you." Dane darted a look to Aspen, and she saw in his gaze the desperation. "I brought you in—but you came willingly."

"That's right. And then you had me killed." Austin arched an eyebrow. "Tell her about that."

"You're still alive."

"No. Killed me. MIA—that's the official report for a while, then the MIA is declared dead. Right, Cardinal?"

"You knew that when you signed. You can't claim ignorance or innocence. What is your point? Why are you so ticked at me?"

"Because—you told me something was happening in Sudan. You sent me there. But it was a trap."

"How?" Dane leaned forward, hands by his side. Very controlled. "How was it a trap?"

Austin's gaze bounced between them. "Don't listen to him, little sister. He's a master liar. He knows how to tell people what they want to hear to get his way. No doubt that's how you fell for him. He played your heartstrings like a prodigy."

Humiliation clotted Aspen's heart that had beat for Dane. Was it true? Had he worked her all this time?

"Aspen." Dane tucked his chin and met her gaze with those steely eyes. "I did not play you."

She could only look at him. Who should she believe? Her twin brother? Or the man she loved—thought she loved? Closing her eyes, she shook her head.

"Austin, you willingly joined. Nobody forced you. Remember, you agreed to become a spy for the American military. I sent you down here. There were rumblings about corruption. We couldn't get a finger on it."

"Oh, I got your finger—"

"Is it the yellowcake?"

Austin froze. "You do know!"

"Yes, we found it last night—you shot us trying to leave."

Austin frowned. "I...no...that was..." His voice trailed off. "Oh no."

"We found it last night. But I didn't know till then."

"How could you *not* know? The conspiracy goes all the way up!"

Even a master magician could not keep all the plates spinning forever.

Cardinal stilled at the words Austin Courtland, the man he'd remade into Neil Crane—precosmetic surgery—shouted. "What do you mean, all the way up?"

"Straight to the top." Austin glowered. "What? Feigning ignorance?" The weapon lowered toward Cardinal's leg.

Cement peppered his leg.

Lightning fast, Cardinal stepped forward. Sliced the bony part of his right hand against Austin's wrist and used his left hand to swipe the weapon. Flip it. Aim it back at Austin.

The man's grin turned greedy. He laughed.

This scenario was one Cardinal had faced a dozen times. The outcome the same—except this time, he wouldn't neutralize the threat the way he'd had to so many other times.

"Think you've won?" Austin sneered. "Think again—Talon, seek!"

The Lab looked at Austin as if the man had spoken Chinese.

"Talon," Aspen said, her voice calm. Way more calm than normal. "Heel."

With a flick of his tail, Talon moved to Aspen's side and sat on his haunches.

"When you left me, you left him," Aspen said. "He's not your dog anymore."

Finally! Something got through Austin's seek-and-destroy mentality. "Talon!" Austin nearly growled at the dog. "Seek, boy! Seek!"

Taking his eyes off Austin would be a mistake, but Cardinal wanted to see, to verify that the dog had not moved or even wanted to move. In his periphery, Cardinal noticed Aspen's arms dangling at her side in a loose manner. Her fingers rubbed Talon's ears.

Cardinal removed the magazine. Let it thunk against the ground. Ejected the chambered round. *Shink!* Released the slide. Dropped the frame and slide. His neck wound still burned. But what burned more was the way his world had just upended. "I'm not the enemy, Austin. I came to find you, find out what happened."

Anger whipping into fury, Austin launched at him like a tornado.

Mentally prepared for the impact, Cardinal tossed himself backward. Used the momentum to gain control. Flipped Austin onto his back. Rammed his fist into the man's face.

Though Austin worked to flip him, Cardinal maintained control. "Stand down!"

"Not on your life," Austin ground out, his face reddened as he struggled to push Cardinal.

Agitating him would only strengthen Austin's fight. "Let it go. Talk to Aspen."

"Don't use her!" Austin balled his fist and shot it into Cardinal's side. White-hot, blinding pain exploded. His vision blurred.

Hollowed vision.

Searing agony.

Thud!

Cardinal blinked and found himself staring up at Austin, arms pinned by the man's knees. Pounding agony in his leg eroded his thoughts. Another blink and he stared down the barrel of a weapon.

"Eye for an eye, Cardinal?" Staggered breathing. A greedy gleam in his eye, Austin was poised to fill Cardinal's brain with lead.

"Austin, *no!*" Aspen screamed.

Snarling and snapping vaulted through the room.

"He took *everything.*"

"No!" Aspen snapped. "You gave it up!"

Austin's nostrils flared and stared down at Cardinal. In that second he knew the belief that consumed Austin's thinking—killing Cardinal would solve everything.

"Even if you kill me," Cardinal said, "you won't find what you're looking for."

Shifting, Austin planted a knee against Cardinal's throat.

Cardinal worked to wedge his arm between his trachea and Austin's knee. He grunted and strained against the deprivation. Rocks bit into the back of his head, his shoulders, but that had nothing on the still-thundering throb in his neck.

"How's it feel, Cardinal? Master Spy."

"Austin!" Aspen shouted over the snapping and snarling.

"Not so tough. You took everything away from me—"

"Austin!"

"—now I'm taking it away from you."

"Austin, so help me, God—get off him and drop that weapon or I'll release Talon."

Scritching forced Cardinal to glance to his right.

Aspen stood, her feet planted as she held tight to the harness Talon strained against. The powerful jaws clamped and chomped the air. Begging for a taste of flesh.

Cardinal's heart backed into his throat. If Aspen released Talon. . . against her own brother. . .against Talon's former handler. . .

"Austin!" Aspen's scream went primal.

Booom!

A gust of hot, dirt- and debris-laden air barreled across the room. Slammed against Cardinal. He winced and jerked away.

Light and dark mingled. Dust cocooned the room.

Grit dug into his eyes and mouth. Cardinal coughed.

"Stand down! Stand down!"

"On the ground!"

"Drop the weapon!"

Blinking rapidly, Cardinal saw a half-dozen shapes emerge from the dirt cloud. ODA452 had blown the door and stormed in, all business. Candyman—the guy looked downright ticked, blood staining his beard. A big welt on his right cheekbone. No hat. No sunglasses. Whoever had undressed the guy also unleashed the monster within.

Watterboy's hands were bloodied. The others were there—Rocket, Scrip, Pops. . .all roughed up, clearly having fought their way out of a mess. Now, all that adrenaline. All that fury, trained 100 percent on Austin Courtland.

Timbrel hurried to Aspen's side.

Slowly, Austin raised his hand, gun still held firmly.

"Drop. The. Gun," Watterboy said, taking a bead on Austin.

Talon's bark continued. Shouts.

Two seconds later, Candyman shuffle-stepped forward fast. "Give me a reason, you sorry piece of dirt."

"Talon, out," Aspen said. "Talon, heel!"

Quiet dropped on the room, but the silence proved deafening with Austin's unwillingness to yield.

A flicker of movement.

Cardinal tensed. And in the split-second camera lens of his life, he knew it was about to end. Austin would force it to end.

The guy snapped the weapon toward him.

Candyman fired.

Then whipped back and to the side. Flopped. Groaned. Cried out.

"Don't kill him!" Cardinal hauled himself out of the fray as Candyman and Rocket dropped on the guy.

Watterboy helped Cardinal to his feet. "You okay?"

With a nod, he kept his eyes trained as the others subdued the man who'd been willing to end his life. He'd seen it—the same agonizing guilt. Cardinal felt it. Lived it. But he'd mastered it. Stopped it from mastering him. Controlling him. The way it had taken over for Austin.

"All right," Watterboy said with a huff. "Clean up. I'm going to call this in. Burnett won't—"

Thump. Thump. Clink.

A meaty scream announced, "*Frag!*"

Red-hot air blasted the room.

Thirty-Two

Blinded, Cardinal felt himself falling.

Or was that the world?

Spinning...everything...He swung a hand out. Hit something. His knee collided. Dirt...

White. Blinding white.

Ringing. Hollow hearing. A vacuum had swallowed him.

"Augh!" Though he knew air passed over his vocal chords, he heard nothing.

White succumbed to gray...

Holding his head, Cardinal waited out the disorientation. They'd been hit. Someone threw a flash-bang into the room. The overpressure of the concussion knocked out his vision. Sucked out his hearing.

Though he knew it'd only last three to five seconds, it felt like an eternity. No way to defend yourself. No way to fight back.

He didn't even know who to fight.

Was this Austin's doing? If it was, he'd kill that punk.

Shapes took form like pillowy giants. Cardinal felt the dirt beneath his hands and slowly straightened. Searching for bearings.

The door...where was it? He turned his head.

The room tilted. "Augh!" Warbling noises hammered.

Movement...the doorway! Light bled through it, piercing against his corneas, which were still traumatized from the concussive explosion.

Two or three shapes hurried out the door. Who?

"Cardinal!" Though it sounded like someone spoke his name under water, he knew it was someone close by.

He turned. Saw a large shape looming beside him. He shook his head—the room whipped around. He groped to steady himself. A hand caught his. His vision, still vibrating, brought the image into focus. "Watterboy."

"You okay?" The man wiggled a finger in his ear.

"Yeah." Coordination returned. Hearing, mostly. Vision clear.

"Everyone okay?" Watterboy asked, turning a circle.

As the affirmatives came in, Cardinal hesitated. "Nobody's hurt?" That didn't make any sense. He searched the team for injuries. Timbrel sat against the wall, pinching the bridge of her nose. Candyman knelt beside her and offered a rag for her nosebleed. Rocket and Scrip were still shaking off the effects.

Wait. Cardinal jerked. Nearly fell. "Aspen." She'd been right there with Timbrel. He whipped around. Ignoring the way the room canted to the left. "Aspen!"

His mind ricocheted back to what he saw.

He sprinted for the door. *"Aspen!"*

A curse sailed through the air behind him. Boots pounded. He burst into the inner room. Two of the four men they'd caught were down. Cardinal threw himself at the rear cavernous area that served as a garage. How long? How long had it been? Ten, fifteen seconds?

He sprinted into the garage. Gaping open. Sunlight shatteringly bright. He flinched. Popping! He ducked then realized it wasn't gunfire. Tires! He bolted out. Saw a black SUV stirring up dust.

Cardinal plunged through the bay. Bore down on the vehicle spitting rocks as he scrambled for traction on the dirt road. The rear end fishtailed. Caught purchase on the paved road. Squealed and tore off.

He pushed himself. Hard.

Couldn't stop. That was Aspen in there. Someone had taken her. He'd kill them. Cut out their hearts and feed them to the dogs.

A high-pitched whistle shot through the day.

Trailing smoke careened past him. Hot. Wicked fast.

Grenade?

He spun. Candyman, kneeling at the corner of the building, an M203 propped against his shoulder, pulled the trigger again.

Boom!

Cardinal jerked around. A building rained down dirt and fire.

271

The vehicle swerved. Banked right.

Boom! The building in front of Cardinal exploded.

Tires squalled. The shriek of death.

And they were gone.

Teeth grinding, Cardinal stared at the fires that mottled the poverty-stricken street. Breathing hard and struggling not to allow the demons of his past, of his ancestry, to awaken, he dug himself out of the chaos. Aspen was gone.

And he knew exactly who was responsible.

"Sorry, man. I wasn't fast enough," came the empty words of Candyman.

Cardinal pivoted around, stalked toward the man decked out in gear, patted his chest, deftly swiping his thumb over the flap. "Thanks. You tried." And with one expert move, he extracted the Glock from Candyman's chest holster.

"Hey! Stop!"

Confirming a round was in the chamber, Cardinal stormed back into the building.

Thirty-Three

FOB Kendall, Djibouti

Trailed by a security force and his two senior officers, General Lance Burnett strode into the command building of the temporary forward operating base covered in dust and heat. The wake he and the others left as they stormed ahead shone on the faces of those serving under the command of Admiral Kuhn. The hushed whispers haunted his steps.

Banking right, Lance caught sight of two armed sentries guarding the offices of the commanding officer. The two snapped to attention, fingertips pressed to their temples.

Burnett returned the salute. "At ease." He slowed and hesitated, staring at the door handles. He shifted his gaze to the left. "How is he?"

"Quiet, sir."

With a nod, Lance entered the office.

A gray steel desk anchored a spot in front of a window. Behind it, the chair swiveled around. Admiral Kuhn rose and saluted. "General Burnett."

Lance gave a stiff response, lowered his hand, then huffed. "At ease." He strolled to the window where cheap plastic blinds served as a flimsy barrier against the miserable Djibouti sun and its heat. He'd been baking since he stepped off the aircraft.

And he wasn't the only thing baking. "For cryin' out loud, Mack." He turned to him. "Well? What do you have to say?"

"Shouldn't I have a lawyer?"

"Do you need one?"

Kuhn pointed to the doors, to Hastings, and the security team. "You brought yours." He grunted then dropped back into his chair. "Ya know, I'm glad."

Lance frowned.

"I'm glad it's over." He removed the stars from his uniform and thrust them on the table. "Hendricks put my nose to the fire, threatened me with punitive action if I didn't look the other way, then he vanishes."

"Vanishes?" Lance couldn't digest the information fast enough. "Punitive—so, you're willing to testify?"

"Absolutely. The man yanked my career out of my hands."

"I think you did that, sir," Hastings spoke up. "You are the one who acted."

"Tell you what, Lieutenant," Kuhn said, "when you're out here baking your assets off and nobody gives a rip if you live or die except one man willing to make you dead—well, lines get a little fuzzy."

Lance planted himself in the chair and mopped his sweaty brow. "You said Hendricks vanished?"

"Yeah. Nobody knows where he is. Haven't seen in him. . .well, since your man showed up."

"Cardinal."

"That's the one. Payne flew down here, and they rode off into the sunset together." Kuhn shrugged. "The people here are oppressed enough. They don't need American power mongers making it worse."

"Yet you helped make it worse." Lance pushed to his feet and motioned the security forces toward Kuhn. "While I clean up your mess, it's your turn to ride off into the sunset."

"Don't even move."

Shedding the Neil Crane persona and returning to his original identity, his birth identity, felt incredibly freeing. Head pounding like a bass drum still, Austin focused on the two men who held him at gunpoint. They had good reason. Anger vibrated through him.

"That's my sister, you moron!"

"Yeah. Well, this is my M4." The man with a dark blond beard hefted it a little higher, nearly blotting out the beard.

Austin growled. "If she dies—"

"Stop him! Somebody—stop him!"

Austin peered over the shoulders of the two men.

A storm swept in named Cardinal. Eerily calm. Striding straight toward—*Me!*

One of the nearby men swore. Took a step back.

So did Austin—when he saw the weapon Cardinal held low.

Fury darkened the man's face. Something inside Austin curled up and died. He'd never seen that expression on Cardinal. In the mirror—yeah, a lot. On others. But not on Cardinal, the guy calm as a tranquility pool.

"He's got a gun!"

Boots thudded as two men raced up behind Cardinal.

Austin's feet seemed to have turned to cement. He couldn't move. Saw it coming. Saw the future in one heartbeat—Cardinal was going to stuff that Glock in Austin's mouth and make him eat a bullet.

He's blaming me for Aspen.

"I didn't do this." Austin stepped between the two men who had shifted from guarding him to protecting his life. Not that he'd put his life in their hands. He wouldn't. Wouldn't trust anyone on that level. Never again. He held up his hands.

"Where is she?" Cardinal demanded. Two men hooked Cardinal's arms, hauling him backward. He wrestled against them, seemingly possessing supernatural strength because he came forward several paces. "Tell me!"

With the tangling and wrangling of arms and legs, it looked like an octopus writhing before him.

The Glock slid across the room.

Grab it. Maybe he should.

A brunette lifted it from the ground and stuffed it at the small of her back.

Austin let himself draw in a breath, steadying his nerves. This man had mentored him. Taught him so much. Then betrayed him. "Even if I knew," Austin injected as much disdain into his voice as possible, "I wouldn't trust *you* with that information."

Though Cardinal tried to wrest himself from the two men, their restraint held. Cardinal again attempted to jerk free before slumping back, looking defeated, as he said, "The gun's gone. What can I do?"

Watterboy gave a nod.

"No!" Austin's shout mixed with another. Apparently someone else saw what Austin did—Cardinal's body language belied the fury roiling off the man. Loose, Cardinal would kill him.

Seconds took on supernatural length. Cardinal shot forward. His foot swept Austin off his feet. He landed with a thud. Cardinal was on top of him, pinning him with his knee. His fist rammed like a ball-peen hammer. Right into Austin's face.

Shouts and a series of pops erupted.

Lance hesitated, glancing back to Hastings, whose eyes had widened. He shoved himself through the building. Through one door. Another. He burst into the safe house, drenched in sweat after the quick ride out from FOB Kendall.

Two men wrestled a third beneath them. Legs and arms thrashed.

Another was laid out cold, blood snaking out his nose and down his neck.

Scrip dug through a sack on the floor.

Suddenly, the writhing mass of bodies stilled.

"Get off me," came a familiar voice.

"Not liking that idea," Candyman countered.

"What in Sam Hill is going on?" Lance demanded.

Candyman and Watterboy shifted toward Lance. Slowly eased off the third—Cardinal. The man pushed back on his legs and stayed on the floor. Lance never fully realized how big that guy's shoulders and fists were.

"Cardinal?" He hated that name.

The man pushed onto his haunches. Then stood.

Watterboy and Candyman stepped back, and Lance noticed they seemed to be guarding the body on the floor. Watterboy's gaze skidded to Lance, and he gave a nod. "General."

"What's going on?" He sounded like a broken record, but considering nobody had answered, he didn't care.

Cardinal swung toward him.

Instinct pushed Lance back a step. He bumped into someone.

Hastings muttered an apology as she shifted aside, her gaze locked on Cardinal. "Da—Markoski?"

Death lurked in that man's eyes as he stalked out of the room.

Lance took a step forward. "Hey—"

Cardinal held up a staying hand but didn't look back. "No." He hung his head. Took a breath then walked out.

Silence drenched the tension that seeped through every pore and crack in this crumbling former storefront. Hastings started after Dane.

"Leave him, Lieutenant." Lance had never seen that look on Cardinal before. And he had this feeling the guy just needed some time. "Watters—fill me in."

The man nodded, glanced to the man on the floor, then crossed the room. "We got hit not ten minutes ago. That guy showed up with a team, Russians. They put us in lockdown, while he came in here with Aspen and Markoski."

"Lockdown?"

Candyman muttered something as he paced.

"Yes, sir. They held us at gunpoint, but thanks to Scrip"—he nodded to the man on the floor, who now slumped against the wall—"we subdued the captors and blew out the door. When we got in here, he"—another indication, this time to the unconscious man—"had Aspen and Dane at gunpoint. Two minutes later, someone lobbed a flash-bang in here. By the time we were able to sort out what happened, Aspen was gone."

"Gone?"

Watters's expression tightened. "They took her. Markoski sprinted after them. Candyman went with him. Me and the team tried to hold the other guy down—we don't know who he is."

Lance strode over to the man and squatted in front of him. "Russian, huh? And nobody's ID'd him?"

"No, but Markoski came back in—"

"Took my Glock right out of my holster." Candyman grunted. Disgust shaded his features. "Did it so fast, I didn't know till I saw the gun in his hand."

"He came storming in here and was about to kill that guy."

"If Markoski says he's a threat, then he is. Hogtie the heck out of him." Lance straightened, his mind racing as Candyman and Rocket went to work zip-tying the man. "Pops, get on the horn. Notify the embassy that an American has been kidnapped. Leak her information to everyone."

He stormed out of the room, biting back curses. Hating that he didn't have a single Dr Pepper handy.

Hastings stood in the open area at the back, eyes on the upper level.

Lance took the cue and headed toward the stairs that lacked a banister or other support.

Behind him he heard steps. Over his shoulder he saw Hastings and Smith trailing him. "Stay with the team. Get a game plan. Wake that man up and find out who he is."

Hastings paused, her gaze tracing the upper level again. He'd have to be blind not to know she was smitten with Cardinal.

"Go on. Get it done, Lieutenant."

With a reluctant nod, she turned.

As he continued up, he wondered if the entire thing would collapse without a guardrail. Plaster dribbled. Three doors presented themselves. He pushed open the first door. His body swayed and swooped—straight toward the ten-foot drop. He grabbed the doorjamb and yanked himself back. His heart dropped with the gaping emptiness. Only half the room still existed. The other half, blown out with whatever relegated this building to abandonment. Hauling his stomach and courage back, he eased the door closed. Whispered a prayer of thanks to his maker.

As he made his way along the narrow ledge, he tried to avoid looking to the right, the drop to the lower level. The next door, he decided, sat too close to the previous one, so it most likely had its space missing, too. Lance tried the last door. Darkness spread its venom. He scanned the black void. Nothing.

As he turned away, a shape caught his eye.

He whipped back to it. Strained against the darkness to figure out what snagged his attention. There, in the corner. . . "Cardinal?"

Whispering wind was the only response.

Lance stepped in, embraced by the shadows as his eyes slowly adjusted. Sure enough. There sat Cardinal. In the corner, each shoulder blade pressed against an adjacent wall. Legs bent and pulled close, he rested his arms over his knees.

This wasn't the time for booming sarcasm. Nor for biting wit. What he'd seen down there, Cardinal completely unglued, required delicate and precise wording. An arrow to aim right at this man's steel-barricaded heart. Cardinal would like Lance to believe he didn't have a heart so he couldn't do any damage. But Lance held the firm belief that *every* person had a soft spot. The trick was finding it.

"I want you to know," Lance said, treading a thin line, "whatever's going on"—his mind ping-ponged over the facts, over the past, over his knowledge of this über-skilled operative he'd recruited right out from under the nose of the Russians, right out from under the man's father—"I've got your back."

"It is a nice sentiment but unrealistic and therefore false." Cardinal's sigh carried heavily through the dank room. "And if you knew the price of that statement, you'd backpedal so fast..."

There was entirely too much truth in that statement. Already, thanks to Payne, Cardinal's role within DIA hung in jeopardy. Lance's own position there could be compromised.

"I know what the price is," Lance said. "I also know you're probably the single best asset we've ever had."

"Again, nice sentiment, but it's not true."

"What's going on, Cardinal?" Ominous quiet rankled Lance. Something huge had shifted in the man before him. Left Lance with a bad taste in his mouth. He knew the whole marriage thing to Aspen would push the man, but he'd really thought it would make him work better, harder. Had he been wrong? "If this is about the marriage—"

"When you walk out of here, you'll never see me again."

★ ★ Thirty-Four ★ ★

Cardinal never thought this day would come. But that was foolhardy. Expecting to live this life—to actually have a life. To think his father would never find him. . .

"Cardinal—you can't."

"I can." He drew himself off the ground. "I should have done this a dozen years ago."

"Done what?" An edge had crept into Burnett's voice that marked him as angry.

"Vanished. Disappeared."

"You did that. Became Cardinal."

The man was trying to talk him out of it. "Good-bye, General."

"So, that's it? You walk out of here. What happens to Aspen? Someone took her."

"Then you should stop arguing with me and find her. You have the resources."

"You and I both know finding her is next to impossible without a lead."

Cardinal steadied his breathing. Was the general implying he didn't know where she was? That. . .surely he knew.

Wait. Of course he knew. Had to. "You're baiting me."

Darkness worked wonders to conceal facial expressions. The general hadn't had as much experience as he in detecting silent signals.

"She needs you, Cardinal."

"No." His heart ka-thumped through the next few beats. "She needs to be saved so she can live a long, happy, healthy life."

"Word has it, you and her hit it off."

He would *not* be goaded.

"Real well. In fact, someone suggested you made that marriage legitimate."

Guilt harangued him. He hadn't crossed ethical lines. Perhaps succumbed to weakness. Made a foolish error in judgment. Let his feelings get the better of him. "You're wasting breath and time, General."

Cardinal walked out of the room, across the lip, and down the stairs. He spotted Hastings.

"Dane."

He held up a hand, and apparently more of his foul mood showed in his body language because that slight signal was enough to stay her response.

"What's he doing?" someone—it sounded like Candyman—asked.

"Leaving." Burnett stomped down the steps.

"Hey!" Candyman shouted.

Cardinal kept walking. Reached the door.

Boots thudded behind him.

"Hey, you sorry piece of crap!"

The door squeaked closed. Cardinal let it. Let it shut on the guilt they wanted to heap on him. The weight that oppressed him.

Thap!

"You sorry son of a—"

Cardinal glanced back.

A fist collided with his jaw.

He stumbled back, but there was no fight left in him. Not after what happened. Not after feeling disembodied as he watched the demon of a man within him take over. The one that was so like his father he couldn't tell the difference between that man and the colonel.

Chin up, he swiped the blood from his lip. Eyed Candyman.

"She loved you!" Candyman's tension radiated a nuclear yield. "She gave you everything, trusted you. And this—*this!*—is how you repay that?"

Cardinal took the blow. Turned. Started walking.

"I see. It's only a game to you. You're a spook, so you screw people over and move on, is that it? All Aspen was to you was a warm body?"

The words twisted around his heart. He slowed. Hung his head.

"You're unbelievable. Walking away knowing full well she could be dead by nightfall."

"She won't be dead."

"That's right. Because she's already dead, thanks to you."

Cardinal stretched his neck. "If they wanted her dead, they wouldn't have kidnapped her. She won't die."

"That's right. She won't die," Candyman said, his nostrils flaring, "because some of us actually care about her. Some of us are willing to fight to the death for one of our own. Because some of us didn't play a beautiful, innocent woman's affections."

"I did not play her." *Can't go there. . .can't. . .open. . .that. . .*

Angel headstone. Glass shattering. Screaming. Flash. Bright light. The sickeningly hollow flap of her clothes as she fell to her death.

Cardinal flinched. Clenched his eyes. He raised a hand as if to ward off the jumbled thoughts. *What's happening to me?*

"Hey." Candyman's voice changed. "You okay, man?"

Cardinal met the ironclad gaze of the special operator. A man who'd been an ally. Cardinal glanced down the road where he'd seen that vehicle tear off with Aspen inside. He'd known then, hadn't he, what happened? Who took her? Even though he unleashed on Austin, he *knew*. The beating he'd given her brother was pent-up rage. He'd been found. He'd been cornered. Trapped. And they had bait.

"Look, whatever spooked you, I get it. But she needs you. And right now, you're the only one primed to do this." Candyman's left eyebrow dipped. "In fact, by that look on your face, I'm thinking you have a good guess about what happened."

Cardinal said nothing. Didn't want to give voice to the demons rising up from the past to consume him, his life, his soul.

"Who?" Candyman stood a couple inches shorter, but the man measured feet above the rest in courage. "Who did this?"

The second Cardinal's mind started to answer, he shut it down. He rerouted his thoughts to a solution. "Take the dog. Go to Russia." With that, he started walking.

"Dude, in case you missed the news flash, Russia's big. That's not helpful. And by the time we figure out where to go, she could be dead."

At the gate, Cardinal muttered, "She won't be dead."

Because he wants me to come for her. But he couldn't. Wouldn't go there, literally or mentally. Could *not* enter that psychological war zone again. He'd escaped it twenty years ago.

"Dude! Seriously?"

Cardinal turned. Eyed Candyman across the grounds. "If you want to find Aspen, find General Tselekova."

Burnett stepped into the open. Hands stuffed in his pant pockets, he frowned. A frown that said a lot. Said he knew what was happening.

Arms wide, Candyman shrugged. "Who the heck is that?"

"My father."

Thirty-Five

Warbling plucked at her hearing. A steady vibration wormed through her being, each microbounce jarring her further awake. Her head thundered. She swallowed, and her ears screamed in protest. She winced and curled in—at least tried. Only then did she realize she couldn't move her arms. She tugged but felt something holding her by the wrists.

She tried to open her eyes. . .but as she lifted from the fog of sleep, she felt her whole body rising. *What on earth?* Her eyes—she couldn't see. No. . .no, something covered her eyes. A dart of fear mingled with adrenaline as she remembered being in the safe house. Remembered her brother and Dane—Cardinal—going at it. The explosion. . .then. . .

Dizzying images. Being. . .

She grimaced as pain smacked her head.

Why couldn't she remember it clearly? Crazy wobbly. The world just seemed to be on fast-forward and reverse combined, images and memories shifting and colliding.

Being flung around.

She shook her head. If something was tied around her eyes, could she get it off? Aspen tried rubbing her head against whatever it was. Not the floor. Too soft. The swish of the fabric spoke of leather or vinyl. Her shoulder dug into something. Ached.

Again, she dragged her head over the material. Lifted and used her shoulder to— Light peeked in under the mask.

Aspen tensed and stilled.

Airplane. She knew that much instantly. How did she get on an airplane? And why?

Voices skidded into the cabin. Hurried footsteps.

Aspen dropped back, her stomach lurching at the sight of a man in black looming over her. He bent closer, a needle in his hand.

"No." Her voice faded out as she slumped back, feeling a strange warmth spiraling through her arm. Her muscles went limp. Again, her head swam in that thick ocean of confusion.

"Sir, I think you need to hear this."

Lance looked across the room where Hastings had been interrogating the previously unconscious man for information. Two hours. He'd been in country for two hours, and things had gone south in a handbasket. He hoisted himself off the chair and lumbered over to the room. It took every effort of mental energy not to just turn around and go home. He didn't have that luxury.

Neither did Cardinal, but he'd left. Curse that man! Handling him was like trying to contain a fire with your bare hands. He'd known that for years. But he'd been willing to put in the hours, the exhaustion, the aggravation. And it'd paid off. Until today.

As he crossed the room, Lance spotted Timbrel. She'd been working Candyman down for the last twenty minutes since Cardinal had beaten the path of least resistance out of here.

Lance entered the room.

Hastings stood beside the man handcuffed to a pipe that held no function other than being convenient for interrogations.

"My name," the man began, his face a little bloodied, "is Austin Courtland."

"Well crap." Lance wanted to curse. "You're an enemy of the state, Mr. Courtland."

"No, sir. I'm its patriot."

"Do tell, and while you're telling, explain why you no longer look like Austin Courtland. Ya know what? On second thought, I don't care."

"I went off the grid because I came upon the operation to hide the yellowcake. I couldn't ascertain who was involved and who wasn't, so I had to wait it out."

"And that took you eight months?"

"Yes, sir. But...the woman—"

"What woman?"

"My girlfriend—well, I thought she was. Discovered a couple of days ago that she's a Russian operative."

Lance muttered his mom's Catholic oaths. "Russian, so that's where you got those thugs that hit my men?"

Courtland stared hard. "Yes, sir."

"That is some seriously bad news, Courtland."

He gave a slow, contemplative nod. "And now, they have my sister."

Unswayed by the man's sudden surge of patriotism and familial duty, Lance shook his head. "Don't tell me what I already know. You left your mentor and handler in the lurch. You abandoned protocol. That tells me I can't trust you—"

"I saw Cardinal down here with Admiral Kuhn. I had to assume collusion."

"Assume." Lance grunted. "You know what assuming does, right, Courtland?"

The man gritted his teeth. "Let me help find her, General. I can do this."

Yeah, right. And Lance was a monkey's uncle. "Nothing doing." Like he would really put the lives of one of his best operatives and an innocent civilian woman on the line. "I can't trust you, and I have more experienced assets than you."

"The best bet you had walked out of here." Courtland jutted his jaw. "I'm the next bet."

"No, that dog is. And you're going back to Virginia like Kuhn." Lance pivoted and stalked out of the room. He'd managed to get Kuhn strung up on charges related to his obstruction of justice and collusion with the enemy to transport fissile material. He just had to make sure it stuck.

Man, he just didn't have time for anything. He just didn't care. Didn't want to stand in there and listen to that traitor spout off his puffed-up, vain-riddled reasons for dereliction of duty. An asset going rogue on shifty information told him the man couldn't be trusted. Told him the man was no longer fit for duty.

Demons had a way of sneaking up on you, especially ones from the past. If this was what was truly happening, then they were in deep kimchi.

Tselekova. Lance Burnett sat with his head in his hands. God have mercy on Aspen! But they had a chance—a prayer, if one liked to think along those lines, and right now he couldn't afford to offend—with the dog. If they could just rig a few favors, get over there with Talon, they might have a chance to get Aspen back. Cardinal gave them the name to go after. They had the dog. . .

"Talon, heel!" Hogan stood a few feet away. Her voice had been firm. Authoritative.

The yellow Lab hunkered and inched closer to the wall beneath the table. Head down, he trembled.

"It's no use," Hastings said.

"You're no use," Timbrel shot back, glowering.

"I could just kill that man," Candyman said, pacing and muttering. He'd been primed since Cardinal left an hour ago. In that time, they'd formulated a plan.

"What's with Kuhn?"

Lance checked his watch. "Should be en route, in protective custody, back to Virginia." Did he sound smug? That sorry excuse for an officer had put lives at risk—but worse, entire countries at the hands of brutal dictators. Lance couldn't wrap his mind around it. The very thing they were trained and seasoned to thwart and interrupt—corruption, crimes against humanity—Payne had perpetuated.

Lance dropped into the chair and focused on Hogan, a tough girl who approached animals with more consideration than she did people. Lance nearly grinned. He kinda liked this woman.

"Hogan." He motioned to the dog. "Do we have a prayer?"

She lowered herself to her knees. "I don't know. Clearly that percussion grenade affected him, but I am pretty sure he could detect Aspen's panic. Imagine being able to sense that but not being able to do anything about it, when he's trained to protect at all times?"

"Yeah." Candyman stomped closer. "I can relate to that *real well*."

"Why don't you come off your testosterone trip and help—"

Candyman pounded the pavement to Hastings. "You want to go there? Do you *really* want to go there?"

Lance sat up, knowing by the look in Candyman's face that things were about to get ugly. It wasn't personal—well, it was personal. Candyman had failed to protect an asset. The guy would go ballistic on anyone right now, Lance imagined.

Hogan darted between the two. "Hey." When Candyman tried to skirt her, she shoved him back. "Hey! Get a grip."

"I'll get a grip all right," he mumbled as he skulked away from the others, led off by Hogan like a dog on a lead. His eyes shot RPGs at Smith and Hastings, who took up sides with each other.

The two stood off to the side, and though Lance was no expert, he thought they acted a little cozy. A thought struck him. He stood. "Hogan."

Hand on Candyman's arm, she looked at Lance.

"What was the sitrep with Aspen and Cardinal?"

"He was a sleazy scumbag who deserv—"

"Hey!" Timbrel nudged Candyman's chest. "Stop." She looked back to Lance. "Well on their way to the altar if Aspen had any say about it."

Heat churned through Lance's gut. He came off the chair. "Oh man." He swiped a hand over his weary face. He angled toward Hogan again. "You're sure—the feelings were mutual?"

Candyman frowned, easing away from Hogan. "What's on your mind, General?"

"Trouble." He grinned. "A Russian storm named Nikol Tselekova."

Thirty-Six

Oppression.

Despite the late hour, the heat held its fist-hold oppression on the city, much the way this situation did on his heart and life. Cardinal sat on the beach, staring out over the night-darkened waters.

He had her. Cardinal *knew* that the colonel—wait. He's a general now. Cardinal smirked. Though the man had risen in rank, he would always sit at the lower rank in Cardinal's mind. Colonel. It'd been the only noun he'd been allowed to use in reference to the man. If he called him father, Cardinal got a beating.

But one didn't use a nice term such as that with a man like Colonel Vasily Tselekova.

I thought I escaped him.

There was no escape from a past like that. It shaped his life. More like *disfigured* his life. The same blood that drove his father to be a cruel, hard taskmaster pumped through Cardinal's veins. For the last two decades, he'd worked to master it. Master the anger. The rage.

He wanted nothing more than to become a better man than the colonel.

Tonight, he completely failed. The way he'd unleashed on Courtland.

Breathing hurt as the memories assailed him. How he felt the feeding frenzy off the pain and fear in the man's face. The bloody nose. The busted lip fed the demons chomping on the chains he'd wrapped them in.

Cardinal roughed a hand over his face and eyes. *I let him out. Let the beast out.* Failure. Weakness.

"You are weak, Nikol. I must do this. Can't you see? Weak men fail."

Cardinal tilted his head back and opened his mouth, searching for a clear breath. Not one stifled by the suffocating, brutal past that so often felt closer than his next breath. Head in his hands, Cardinal tried to block the barrage of memories. He allowed his mind to settle on one.

"Don't let them make you weak, Nikol. Show them who's in control. Show them who has the power. Make them obey you, or get rid of them." The colonel knelt in front of him. Held his shoulders. "You are my son. Destined for great, great things. Great power! Just like me." He shook Nikol. "You see this, yes?"

But Nikol's eyes drifted to the window. To the place where the angel flew.

"No!" The colonel jerked him. "She is where she belongs. You are where you belong—with me. Da?"

There was only one acceptable answer. "Da."

"I failed her, God." Completely. Utterly. Stood there while the colonel threw her to her death. *I could've stopped him.* But he hadn't.

Just like now.

No. It was different. There was no proof this was the colonel.

The devil was in the details—quite literally. He couldn't deny that this had the colonel written all over it. He'd taken Aspen. That's where she was. In Russia. It was the only plausible explanation with the presence of Austin's Russian girlfriend. The Russian lettering on the yellowcake crates. BELARUS.

Hand fisted and on his knee, he stared up at the stars. Let the fury build. Why? Why take Aspen? There were many more high-value targets there. Austin. Admiral Kuhn.

Why didn't he just take me?

Control. This was about control. About making Cardinal come crawling on his knees. Admit he'd been wrong. Made a mistake. Cower and show his weakness groveling over a woman.

No, he wouldn't grovel to that man. Never. He wouldn't give the colonel what he wanted. He wouldn't satisfy the sick need for control and power. That meant he couldn't go after Aspen. In his career, he'd made it a Cardinal rule to never, *ever* play into someone's hands. He'd walked and turned the tables. Turned the power.

God. . .I can't. . .go back there. I just can't.

Where were the stained-glass windows and peaceful flickering candles when he desperately needed them?

"I am here."

Warmth spread through his chest. "God. . . ?" What an idiot. *Do you think God cares about you? He has a universe to run.*

An image, searing and terrifying, of Aspen lying dead on a bed of springlike grass ripped through Cardinal's mind. He tensed, tucked his chin, waiting for the image to pass.

Blood. . .in her blond hair.

Lips dry, cracked.

He squeezed his eyes.

Her arm outstretched. To him.

"No," he ground out. The surreal tapestry spread out before him. Panned out. Not just the ground. The surroundings. Crosses. Stone houses. A wrought-iron fence. Headstones.

"The cemetery," he whispered. Fire wormed through his stomach and squirmed into his chest. No. . .no, he couldn't.

They aren't the same.

He pushed the thoughts back. Pushed the past into the great oblivion from which it'd escaped.

"And the angel flew," he heard himself say.

She had flown out that window. Terrifyingly eerie. Terrifyingly haunting. Watching her slide out of view. Frozen like marble to the spot in his bedroom. Staring at the hole in time and space that had held her not two seconds earlier. The thump—

Oh, God! Please. . .no. . .

He'd tried to forget. Tried to bury that memory. He'd stayed there. Right in his spot. Stared at the hole. Then the sharp glass glistening in the early morning light. And the colonel. . .

Cardinal tasted the bitter herb of vengeance. Yes, Colonel Tselekova took his mother from him. To make him stronger. So he wouldn't be weak. And it'd worked—just not in the way the colonel expected.

He'd failed his mother. And going after Aspen, having to face the colonel, the man who'd bred him through a mistress. . . "I can't. Don't ask this of me. Send someone." Anyone. *Just not me.*

"I do that all the time."

Cardinal jerked to his feet, stunned to find a smelly beggar squatting a few feet from him. Scraggly beard matched scraggly hair. "Talking to myself, ya know? Or maybe talking to God when no one's around. That way, I can ignore what I don't want to hear." A fisherman's jacket hung on bony shoulders. A jacket? In this heat?

The man smiled, the moonlight catching a hopscotch pattern of teeth.

"Don't worry, boy. I'm not going to hurt you." He reached for a makeshift spit where a fish sparkled under the moon's glow. "Say, can you hand me that plate?"

Cardinal frowned. "What pl—?"

A plate lay less than two feet from him.

Where did that come from?

"Couldja hurry?" The old man wagged his gnarly, dirty fingers. "It's burning."

Cardinal bent, retrieved the plate, and handed it to the homeless guy, then started to turn.

"You had dinner?" The man slid the fish from the spit and tugged the stick out. He patted himself down, each slap poofing a foul odor Cardinal's way.

"Not hungry." As if to defy him, his stomach growled. Loud.

The man cackled. "Sounds like your belly would disagree. C'mon." He waved Cardinal back to himself. "Pop a squat. I won't bite—and neither will this fella." Another cackle. "Say, you got a knife?"

With an annoyed yet amused snort, Cardinal tugged his butterfly knife out, worked it open, then handed it over. Why he sat down, he didn't know. Maybe it was the weariness. He just didn't care anymore. And he was too tired to fight. Didn't want to be alone with his thoughts. With the guilt.

The old man gave him a piece of wood on which half the fish waited.

"You look like you could take a load off your mind." The man chomped into the flesh.

Cardinal wondered for a second what it was like to chew with half your teeth missing.

"I knew this fella once, when I was younger." He waggled his eyebrows. "And had my looks about me still. He could talk a horse dead and never say a word." The man ate more fish, grinning as he did, and nodded toward Cardinal. "I'm thinking you're like that fella."

"Maybe he didn't have anything to say." The fish proved tasty.

Cardinal finished it off in just a couple of bites.

"Where you come from, Lone Stranger?"

Cardinal bunched his shoulders. "Everywhere, I guess."

The man laughed, lifted his leg, and slapped it. "If that ain't a sailor's answer, I don't know what is. I come from just beyond the horizon." His eyes snapped at him, keen and inquisitive. "So. Don't mean to pry—well, yes I do, I guess. I overheard you say you can't do it. Mind if I ask what that is?"

Cardinal looked out at the water.

"Eh, don't mind me. I get up in people's business and make 'em mad." He waved a hand around the beach. "It's why I'm out here." He laughed. "Can't help it if I care about people. You know? I mean, what else is there? People. . .and animals."

"Chaos. Corruption. Evil."

"You got the right of it there." The man clucked his tongue. Ate the last of his fish. "I seen a lot of that in my time." He shook his head.

Cardinal couldn't help but notice how the man suddenly seemed weighted. Man, he could relate.

"But you know, I seen good, too." The man nodded, his jaw jutted and lips pressed tight, almost as if he had no teeth at all now. "Sometimes, you have to look for it. Get out of where you are and look—really look for it."

Good? The only good in his life had been. . .Aspen.

"Sometimes," the man said, his voice bearing the burden of grief, "it gets taken from you."

Shooting a look to the old man, Cardinal tried to ignore the sudden electric dart through his gut.

"Sometimes, we got choices to make when that happens. And sometimes, we make a choice that hurts."

"The wrong choice," Cardinal said.

The man scowled, his bushy eyebrows pulling together like a snowdrift over blue eyes. "Son, jus''cause it hurts don't make it wrong." The man sniffled loudly then swiped a hand beneath his nose. "Takes a real man to fight that battle. Yes, sir."

Cardinal's stomach warmed. "Sometimes, a bigger battle is won by *not* fighting, not engaging the opponent."

"Yep, you're sure right." The man shrugged in a way that told

Cardinal there was more coming. Yet only the lapping of the nearby water whispered in the warm night.

The man had nearly stepped on Cardinal's toes—metaphorically. He wouldn't hand him a personal invitation.

"There was this man," the beggar spoke, leaning closer and spiraling his stench over the area. It was strong. Almost spicy. "He'd stolen something from his brother. Pretty much the entire inheritance. Right out from under his brother's nose."

The man swiped his thumb under his nose. "Decades went by, and he finally wanted to return home. Felt he was supposed to. So he starts heading home."

Something I won't do.

"He was so scared, he had his people go before him."

The man must've been rich to send people home with him.

"And he was still so scared, he sent his wife ahead of him. And the children." The man slapped his leg. "Ha! Can you imagine?"

"That's a coward."

Wise-beyond-their-years eyes came to him slowly. "Yeah, but he *went home.*"

The words sailed over the hot night and corkscrewed past Cardinal's every excuse, every defense, straight into his chest. Warmth spread. "I can't go home."

"That can't sounds a lot like won't, son." The man poked his shoulder. "Sometimes, we make a choice that hurts." He grinned his checkerboard grin. "But hurts heal when we face them. Leave them to fester, we have to chop off that limb or end up dying from the poison that infects our system."

Heady over the man's words, Cardinal felt a strange, alarming fear grip him. "Who are you?"

The man guffawed. "Shouldn't you have asked me that before you ate that fish?" He clapped a hand on Cardinal's shoulder. "Son, I think you know what you need to do." He grunted and strained as he pushed to his feet, wobbling.

Cardinal helped him, coming to his own feet as he did.

"Now, I'd better be gettin' back."

"You have a home?"

Laughing, the man patted his jacket as if looking for something.

"Nothin' like a fresh North African catfish to fill the belly."

Where were his manners? "Thanks." Cardinal touched his stomach. "I think I needed that more than I realized."

"Then finish it off."

"I did." Cardinal frowned when the man stared at him like he'd lost his mind then motioned with his arthritis-curled hand toward the wood. When Cardinal glanced at it, he was stumped to see several more bites. "Oh." But. . .he'd eaten it all.

He looked up.

The beach stretched and curled around the bay. Empty.

★ ★ Thirty-Seven ★ ★

Safe House, Djibouti

We need a game plan."

"No. Really, Sherlock?"

Austin skated a heated look to the only female left on the team. "Want to stow the sarcasm and actually contribute?"

"Hey." Candyman stepped up, his broad chest puffed. "Ease up there, chief."

"Let's all bring the tension down." Boots thudded across the open room as General Burnett joined them. "This entire thing stinks, but we've got to get a handle on it." He turned to Brie Hastings, an attractive late-twenties lieutenant who had as much spit and fire as Aspen. "What'd you find out about Hendricks and Payne?"

"Nothing yet, sir."

He wagged a meaty finger at her. "Keep working those channels—find Payne. He's the key. He went somewhere. I want to know where."

"Sorry," Austin said, his anger getting the best of him again, "but the bigger concern here is Aspen. We have to find her. She's not trained for this."

"She's stronger than you think," Timbrel Hogan said. Condemnation and accusation formed her venom-laced words. "She grew a lot after you abandoned her. Figured out where her priorities were." She smirked. "And she found a good man."

"Good?" Austin snapped. "He walked *out* on her and us!"

"Did he?" Hogan spat. "Or did he abandon dead weight, and right

296

now he's out there hunting down whatever idiot took her from him?"

Austin wanted to curse at her ignorance. "If you believe that, then you don't know the first thing about the man who played my sister."

Arms folded, Hogan glowered back. "I bet Aspen's thinking the same thing about her twin brother right now."

"All right, all right." The big guy sidestepped in front of Hogan, facing her. His voice softened and quieted as he spoke with her, his words shielded from others in the room. The salve of his approach seemed to soothe her, calm her down.

"Hogan," Burnett spoke up, "how's Talon?"

"A basket case," she said, once again nailing Austin with a glare. "His first handler pretty much screwed him up."

"Look—"

Burnett slapped his hand against the table, ending the argument. "Can you get him back together?"

Hogan hesitated. "I. . .I don't know. He's pretty shot."

"What about that vet you people use?"

"Khat?" Her voice pitched. "She's in Texas!"

"Do we have time to get her over here?"

Hastings shook her head. "I think we should have something pinned down in the next hour or two. And if we get word on Payne, we have to leave immediately. The jet's already on standby. We should be airborne within a couple of hours, at the latest."

Burnett muttered something about a can of soda then scratched the back of his head. He again focused on Hogan. "So get that vet on the webcam. Talk to her. Find out how to help him."

"Sir," Hogan said, Candyman hovering close by, "even if we talked to her—he's psychologically traumatized, out to lunch." Her gaze went to the Lab, still sitting beneath the table.

Austin's heart chugged with guilt. Talon had been one of the best and smartest working dogs out there. When the time came for him to disappear, he'd expected Talon, tough dog that he was, to be fine. It hurt—a lot—to think that his commitment to serving his country in a deeper way had traumatized the poor fella. And now, with Aspen getting snatched. . .

"Let me try." Austin's heart vaulted into his throat. *What are you doing?* Talon had already shown that he wouldn't respond to him.

Not anymore. He remembered him, that was clear. But letting Austin handle him?

"What?" Hogan raised her arms. "Haven't you done enough already?"

"No." No, he hadn't. "Not for Aspen." He saw it now. Going under deep cover like he had wasn't supposed to work this way. When you made that commitment, rules dictated no further contact with family members. For this reason and a plethora of other reasons. And staying here arguing like middle schoolers would land him in an institution, a room with a cozy jacket.

"Hey," Burnett's voice boomed as he scowled at them. "We'll need Talon when we figure out where General Tselekova is hiding, so do what you can. Use what you need. Just—get him operational." He pivoted and glanced at the other end of the table where Smith sat at a bank of computers. "How's it going on Tselekova?"

"Last known location was Moscow, officially. He got in some trouble, but nobody's sure what." Smith stretched his arms and yawned.

"Should we just head to Moscow?" Hastings suggested. "The flight time would give us extra hours to keep hunting. Once in country, we can go where necessary."

"Get that working," Burnett said.

She nodded and gave Austin a look.

"Timbrel, you got—"

"Khaterah, hey there!" Hogan pointed to a screen where a video feed showed a grainy image of a beautiful Middle Eastern woman.

"Timbrel?" She squinted into the screen. A man hovered over her shoulder. "What—is something wrong?"

"Yeah, there is." Hands planted on either side of the screen, Hogan sighed. "Things have been pretty exciting here, and Talon's not weathering it so great."

"Define exciting," the man said.

Highlighted with a glow from the monitor, Hogan's face amplified her hesitation. "Aspen was snatched. Markoski is missing."

A flood of questions and comments rushed through the camera.

"Hey, hey!" Hogan said as she held out her hands to stem the bevy of questions. "Khat, listen. We're short on time. But I need help with Talon. He's not responding. What can I do?"

"Okay," Khaterah said. "Are you able to give him his own safe place?"

"Yeah. . .no, maybe." Hogan nudged up the rim of her baseball cap. "We're about to get on a plane. I can crate him."

"Okay, have the crate. He'll need a safe place to go. But in flight, stay near him, and every time he looks at you, give him a reward—whatever you can find. Hot dogs, chicken strips, something that is more alluring than his panic. You remember the 'focus' command, yes?"

Hogan nodded.

"Every time he looks at you, give him praise and a treat. Then introduce noises but keep that focus command going. Rapid-fire it till he's looking at you every time the noise comes. We've got to build his confidence back up."

The conversation continued over the next fifteen minutes. Austin listened hard and fast, determined to right this wrong he'd done to his partner. His superior officer. At Talon's side, he smoothed a hand down the thick chest of the Lab, over the harness. Rubbed the soft ears that flopped down near his face.

"They said I was handsome, but I knew it was you the ladies loved," Austin whispered to Talon as he inched closer.

His jaw snapped shut, the panting demanded by the heat ignored. Wary brown eyes gave furtive glances in Austin's direction. Cheeks puffed with a stifled pant.

Too stressed.

Austin leaned away. "Good boy."

Talon let his pink tongue dangle as he panted again.

Hogan walked toward him with a bag of treats.

"Let me do it." Austin held out his hand.

She shot fiery arrows from her eyes.

Enough already. "He was my dog, my partner."

"And you abandoned him."

He hauled himself up to face off, and in his periphery he noticed her bulldog-champion coming closer. "I sacrificed my relationship with him and Aspen to serve my country, but that doesn't mean I don't love them both very much." He snapped his hand out for the treats. "Talon knows me. You've never handled him. You're a handler, right?"

She gave a slow nod, her brown eyes sparking with fury.

"Then you know these dogs are fiercely loyal. They won't work with just anyone."

"Including you."

Man, this chick knew where to hit. *Give a guy a break, okay?* "I want to help him remember what we had." He put his hand on the treat bag. "Please. Just let me try. I have to. No matter what you think of me, I love my sister. And I love Talon."

She didn't release the bag.

"You need to grab gear to head out. Besides, if you see anything questionable, you and your bulldog can take me down."

She darted a glance to the side. "You think *he's* big?" She smirked. "Wait till you meet Beo."

★ ★ Thirty-Eight ★ ★

Murmuring drew Aspen from a sleep fog. She lifted her head—and winced at the pain that spiked through her neck and skull. Pounding forced her to squint against the pain. She searched for an explanation to wherever she was. However she'd gotten there.

Her head hurt. Her back. Pretty much everything. She lifted heavy eyelids to look around but kept the moans and groans begging for release to herself.

That's right—the girl. The plane. But. . .this wasn't a plane. *Where am I? Where's Talon? Is he okay? He doesn't take stress well. Especially not the kind with chaos.*

Light winked at her as she peeked across the sun-drenched room. Light streamed from high windows down onto the pale gray, cracked surface. On the floor. In a warehouse? A wild guess but the most probable considering her limited range of motion and ability to see her surroundings. She blinked against the sunlight as she strained backward to see behind her.

Crates in assorted sizes towered over her, like guardians.

Or captors.

Her mind scrambled back to the attack when she was yanked from the safe house. Talon's deafening barks swirled in the jarring bubble of memories. Was he alive? Had they killed him?

And Dane. Her eyes shuttered closed remembering Austin's accusations. Remembering that Dane wasn't who he said. But he'd told her that himself, hadn't he? Warned her not to look to him for affection or attention. Told her he couldn't, wouldn't get involved.

301

Who are you?

She couldn't worry about him right now.

Escape. Maybe she could escape.

Okay, while many people would say she should do that, it presented a whole shipment of new problems—getting to the American embassy and convincing them of her identity. Before that, she had to *find* the embassy. She remembered Dane pointing it out when they went to the hospital. Good grief—that felt like a lifetime past.

After another check of her location to verify she was alone, Aspen pushed up on her shoulder then propped herself on her elbow—and a strange tug came at her right arm. Her mind registered the tightness around her wrists. Tied up. She huffed. Another problem to solve. But she'd do it. She hurried, knowing her time alone was probably short. They'd come back and beat the snot out of her. Or worse.

Then shut it and get moving!

She had a brother to smack senseless. A. . .guy to riddle full of questions, and a dog to lovingly coerce back to healthdom. If that was a word.

Skating a look around, she slowly hauled herself upright, expecting at any second to hear shouting or feel bullets riddling her body.

When nothing happened, she swung her legs around. Ankles tied. Okay, another problem. *Augh! Really, Lord? Can't make this easy, huh?*

She shrugged and hopped over her bound hands, bringing them to the front, beneath her knees. Fingers nimble, she worked the plastic cord. It wouldn't fray, but it was the type of binding that if she worked it enough. . .

Aspen grunted. Felt a fingernail snap. Below the quick. She hissed but hurried, scissoring her legs back and forth the bare half inch the binding allowed. They must've found this stuff lying around the warehouse. Her gaze again skimmed the building. The high windows. A high-level catwalk-type thing that ran along the perimeter. . .straight into an office.

Her breath caught. Shadows moved behind the blinds.

She dug harder at the binding. Slid out of view. Yeah! Scooting back, she worked the binding. Felt it give. Her heart raced.

Voices carried through the building. She couldn't make out their words. Just upset. And getting closer.

She scurried backward. Her ankles sprung apart.

Aspen swung around. Came up on a knee. Pushed to her feet. Darted between the rows of boxes that stood twenty and thirty feet tall on pallets. Reminded her of the cargo on the boat. As she sprinted down the long line that seemed to stretch for a mile, she remembered Dane fingering some lettering. Cyrillic, wasn't it?

She clung to the right, hoping to avoid being spotted by whoever cast the shadow in the office.

A shout shot up.

Aspen pushed harder.

The door—she could see the door! Freedom's call yanked her onward. Hands still bound, she couldn't run her fastest. But she pumped her legs hard. A whimper climbed up her throat. *God, help me!*

Shouts erupted back in the warehouse.

She plunged forward. Reached for the door. Hit it at full throttle.

The door flew open. Hit the wall. Snapped back. Thudded against her shoulder.

She yelped as it spun her around. Tripped her. She went to a knee. Pushed back up. Panting. Choking—air! She couldn't breathe. Couldn't stop. Couldn't slow. She had to go. Keep going.

To her left, a canal-like stretch of water.

Buildings lined the street to her right, sentries against her escape.

Aspen sprinted toward the buildings, praying she could get lost in the dizzying menagerie of structures. There were enough. She could find some place. Hide till danger passed.

Talon. He'd never ventured far from her thoughts. But what could she do? Nothing, unless she could escape.

She sprinted, tugging against the bindings on her wrist. It'd be so much easier. . .if they were free. . .

Something loomed in the horizon to the left. By the time her mind registered it, another three-story warehouse blocked her view. At the next street, she shot a look left.

Skidded to a stop.

Heart in her throat, she stared at the distant specter.

"No. . ." Panic swirled a toxic potion in her chest.

Spires leapt toward the sky above bulbous protrusions. Gold ones. Turquoise ones. Swirls of gold tracing the bubble up to the spire. Cathedral. "Russia." She spun. Searched the surroundings for landmarks. Signs. Anything to verify what had her heart misfiring—so much that it hurt.

Tires squalled behind her.

She whirled, her hair whipping into her face. Blurring her vision. Not for long. But enough to cost precious time.

A black vehicle lurched toward her. Rubber screeched against cement. Doors clunked open.

She sprinted to the left, willing back tears.

Feet thumped behind her. Several.

Weight rammed into her back with a meaty grunt. Pitched her forward. Cement rushed up at her. Fire lit through her palms as she slammed into the street.

Almost as quickly, she was hauled to her feet. Two men held her, their grips on her arms brutal.

More men stalked toward her. The first sneered, his nostrils flared. He eyed her from top to bottom—a look that made her feel undressed and undone. He smirked. Muttered something in a language she didn't know but guessed to be Russian. That was where she was, right? He bobbed his head toward the warehouse.

Aspen wrestled against them, knowing if she went back in there, in that building, she may never be seen again. She let her legs go limp, but they merely hoisted her up. She screamed. Thrashed.

Almost without warning, she flew through the air. Onto the ground.

The girl who'd been on the flight with her stood there, her face hard as marble. She stared at the man who'd raped Aspen with those stormy eyes. She said something to the man, her expression impassive. Unreadable.

The man matched her stonelike mask. He muttered something to her, and his lip curled.

The girl's chin lifted ever so slightly—just like Timbrel when someone said something that challenged her. Her eyes glinted. She replied to the man.

What Aspen wouldn't do for a personal translator.

The man's voice rose, and his words flew as he whirled around and stalked off. The second man with him shot Aspen a sidelong glance that almost seemed to carry an apology.

Her heart skipped a beat. She pulled her gaze from the man who wielded power without a lot of brute force, unlike the brute squad behind him.

The girl—who couldn't be any more than twenty-one or -two—merely uttered two words, her gaze still on the men who left. "Do it."

Aspen's gut churned. "Do what?" *Kill me?*

The grunts who'd held Aspen moved toward her. She withdrew, but one held her. The other pinned her leg to the ground. Drove his large fist straight into her calf. Pain blinded her.

Thirty-Nine

Safe House, Djibouti

Lid down and door locked, the bathroom became a haven. When he thought of what took place—or rather, what got deposited—in this room, the irony couldn't be any greater that he found it to be a place of quiet, a place to think.

Austin cranked the knob on the shower then sat on the lid of the toilet, waiting as the pipes filtered the junk and turned the water clear. From his pocket, he retrieved the phone. Ran his thumb over the screen, swiping away the sweat that mottled the display.

Calling her could unleash trouble.

Not calling her. . .well, he'd never know.

Everything in him wanted to believe he hadn't been played.

You're grasping.

Yeah, he knew he was. But still. . .he had to know. He'd never felt this way about anyone, till Lina showed up. Finding her, connecting with her, sharing the journey—

That's what he thought he'd been doing.

Was it all an act? A way for her to bleed him of information?

Austin stepped from the still-functional bathroom after a quick shower. He grabbed his gear and stuffed it in a duffel Rocket loaned him. Back in his old duds, Austin realized the clothes were rank. But at least he'd scrubbed down.

He crossed the open bay and spotted the others loading gear. They were trying to load up the steel crate. He smirked. Knowing Talon was in good hands with Scrip, Austin headed over to help. He tossed in his bag then waved the guys off. With a few deft moves, he collapsed the crate.

"Thanks," Rocket said.

"No worries." He motioned to the SUV. "Is this everything? We ready to go?"

"Just about. Waiting on the general. He's on the line with HQ." Rocket closed the rear hatch. As they headed back toward the main room, he glanced toward him. "Can I ask you a question?"

"Sure."

"Why'd you do it? Ya know—the spook thing? Digging deep and leaving your family?" The guy shrugged, his lanky build and squared shoulders a dichotomy. "Not sure I could do that."

"It wasn't easy, but I believed I could help my country. Help others." Austin shook his head. "I just felt it was right." Memories slipped and slid through his mind. "I went back to Austin twice. To check on Aspen." A raw burning began at the back of his throat. "The last time, I just. . .I saw her and Talon. . .and I knew I couldn't visit them again. It haunted me. But I felt I was doing the right thing."

"Do you regret it?"

"Sure." Austin hated admitting it. "Yeah. I do—hate what it did to Aspen, to Talon. But would I do it again?" He shrugged and pursed his lips. "I probably would. What I did, leaving, working for the country, it was important. I was one of the few willing to do it."

They stepped into the mini operations room.

Awareness lit through his mind. Energy—*bad* energy. Not that he was into all that mysticism. But whatever happened—

And Timbrel. She was as angry as a wet cat as she railed at Burnett, who held a hand over his forehead. "Where's Courtland?" she demanded.

"Right here." Austin moved forward. "What's going on?"

"Where is he? What'd you do with him?"

"Do with whom? What are you talking about?"

"Talon's missing!"

Forty

Weakness.

Power.

Disgraced.

Honored.

Shoved down.

Raised up.

Bent forward, elbows on his knees, Cardinal rubbed the knuckles of his fist. Polar opposites had served to define his existence, growing up under the authoritarian rule of the colonel. Terror had shaped Cardinal's performance. Terror that should he fail, no matter how large or how much, he would pay. And severely. Beatings were as commonplace as the smiles and love other children received.

"You never smile."

Cardinal sat back with a thump against the pew. Aspen's soft words played over in his mind, tormenting him. If he could get her back—alive—he'd smile for her every day of the year. She'd be the reason for those smiles.

Which was why he had to do this. Why he had to accept that the fisher/beggar man, whoever—or whatever—he was, had delivered a message.

Much like the one who had lured him into his current profession. Sitting in this very cathedral, agony the only warmth in life during the hard, bitter winter that defined his life. It'd been ten winters since his mother's burial. And that's all—a burial. Outside a small church. No service. The colonel had refused. To do anything, including acknowledge that she had been his mistress. That she had given birth to his son.

Thanks to the man on the beach, Cardinal realized his inaction regarding Aspen mirrored that of his father's. Refusing to dip his baton into the cauldron he'd stirred. Refusing to accept responsibility for the mistress he'd used and the son he'd fathered.

The only reason Aspen got snatched was because of Cardinal.

No.

Not Cardinal. That moniker belonged to the man sitting here now. A man who'd built his life with strategic moves, building block upon block. Creating a fortress between himself and the past. The pain. The shame. The very name. . .Nikol.

Just hearing the name internally whipped him. Made him feel like he lay on the stripped mattress in the dark, icy room. Punishment came in forms of deprivation. No heat in his room. No bedding. No dinner. Things mattered little to him when he could conjure up images of his mom. *Or Kalyna.*

His father could rape his mind, but he would never touch Kalyna. That thought seed had dug deep roots, enabled him to endure just about everything. Especially after their mother died. But then, he'd had to stop visiting Kalyna. Things got dangerous. For her. For him. It was the greatest coup he pulled on the colonel, hiding her existence. A great victory his mother took to her grave.

He'd lost her. . .lost Kalyna in the years, in the distance that grew between them. Both physical and emotional.

He peeked up through his brows at the colorful glass sparkling in the high walls and the brilliant frescoes stretching across the domes. . . straight to the one that held his heart. The angel.

Then the angel flew.

Angel. . .his mom. . .Aspen. . .

Cardinal blew out a breath and closed his eyes. "I'm here. . ." Was he really talking to God? He'd never cemented his stance on that existence of the deity. Sitting in cathedral after cathedral soothed his soul. Used the time to think. To sort out whatever problem or situation he'd found himself in. But he'd stopped, every time, short of acknowledging God.

"But You didn't do that to me, did You?"

Thoughts flitted from the moment Burnett put Aspen in his path, knowing full well that had Cardinal known she was a woman, the mission would've ended before it started. Then seeing Aspen for the first time. Sunlight filtering through her halolike curls. Then he'd crumbled beneath the fear, the frantic possibility of losing control and hurting Aspen. Her finding him at St. Mary's in Austin. Then Burnett "marrying" them. Then Aspen's declaration of love. Something Cardinal didn't deserve. And at the time shunned her and the thought, though everything in him wanted to seize it. Then to the beggar. Who fed him. Not just fish but courage. Purpose. Fuel to the fire that simmered in his gut.

Acknowledge God.

He avoided that—out of fear. Afraid of being vulnerable. Afraid of letting go. . . Because then, what did he have to fuel him? Drive him? Keep him focused?

He wasn't sitting here because he was trying to talk himself out of this. He knew what he had to do. That was just it. Confronting the colonel—*general now. . .*

He sloughed his palms together, wishing he could slough off the past. Wished the lethal and cunning precision he'd exerted in his profession could bleed into this situation. But the terror that suffocated his character as a teen surged to the front of his mind. That man. . . nobody held power over him the way the colonel did.

The kid inside him, the one who never had a childhood but a strict, militaristic, authoritarian upbringing, screamed to run. Flee Mother Russia before the general could do something.

"God. . .he. . .I can't. . ." Cardinal pushed back and pressed his spine against the wood of the pew. Weak. Weak. Weak. Thirty-three years old and still as petrified as at ten.

Pathetic.

Weak.

"You sit in cathedrals longing for something you think you can never have because you're too afraid to reach for it."

He hung his head. Aspen was right. But there'd been no condemnation in her voice. Only hurt—for him. *She believes in me.*

Like my mother.

His eyes traced the stained glass, the relics that held symbolic power. "Like You." Something inside him heated. "You believed in me, didn't You? Drew me here, to Yourself?"

The thought solidified. Gave him purpose. "God, I'm not going to let Aspen down." He swallowed the swell of panic. Felt the acid roiling through his gut. "I ask nothing for myself—save this one guilty pleasure: Help me save her."

Knowing he could save her, knowing he could thwart the colonel one last time. . . Facing Vasily Tselekova. Confronting him. Bringing all Cardinal was and knew to bear on this man. . . He nodded. Yes, he would die in peace.

Resolve hardened in his chest. He glanced to the cross over the altar. "Help me do this. Please. If she lives, I can die in peace. I am willing to do that. For her." Conviction, a familiar yet entirely new agony boomed through him with adrenaline. "Please."

And that's exactly what would happen.

Cardinal pushed up from the pew and strode out the side door. Greedy sunlight rushed into him, momentarily blinded him. A soft, wet nose nudged his hand. A smile threatened his stiff composure. He paused and knelt.

Talon stepped in closer and sat.

Arms wrapped around the Lab's chest, Cardinal ran a hand across the broad skull. "Thank you, boy. For your trust. For your cooperation." Incredible that he didn't feel odd talking to a dog. "She loves you, and I know you love her. We'll find her soon. Just. . ." His gaze drifted over the stone sentries peppering the grounds. "Give me a minute." He patted Talon then stood.

Squinting against the sun, he strode down the bricked main path. Turned right then strolled down the square stone path. Trees loomed overhead, wooden guardians of the granite coffins, sarcophagi, grave sites fenced in wrought iron. . .

Cardinal walked on, feeling the chill of that day. The terrible time of aloneness that engulfed him. Mother was in a better place, where she would be loved and treasured as she should have been on this earth. His father was a different, crueler man from that day forward.

Could it be possible. . .had the colonel loved her?

Or was he simply furious that he'd been pushed beyond the bounds of his self-control?

Cardinal turned down a narrow alley, noting the vines snaking around the iron and soapstone crosses, angels, and plain headstones. At the pauper's section, he wove a few more rows down then slowed.

Warmth flooded him as the past assaulted his mind.

Beneath his boots snow crunched loud and obnoxious. As if heralding his presence.

Nikol pressed himself against the bare-limbed tree, holding the bark as if it could save him from this nightmare. As if it gave him hope.

The earth, not too hard for burial, mounded to the left. Concealing the hole. Two men dressed in old trousers, jackets, and hats wielded shovels with such skill, Nikol knew they'd performed the soulless tasks of burial many times.

But he hadn't. And the thought of trespassing over the bodies of those who'd walked these places before him poked at his courage.

He should be ashamed! To stand here when she. . .

Something tickled his cheek. He scratched it, his fingers cold and hurting. Wet. Tears? The colonel will kill me! *He scrubbed his face—*

Thunk! Thunk-thunk.

Nikol stilled. Stepped out from behind the tree.

Laughter carried on the icy wind as more thunks and thuds joined the voices. Taunting.

He punched his way across the snow. No, they couldn't bury her yet! He hadn't said good-bye. *"Podozhdite."* Oh, please wait. *"Stop!"*

One glanced over his shoulder, surprise etched in his face when his gaze hit Nikol. The man straightened.

"Podozhdite. Pozhaluĭsta." Please, he begged again. *By the time he reached the mound, the sight on the other side of the large rectangle they'd dug, Nikol couldn't move. The box. . .so thin. So little to protect her. Heat and water ran down his cheeks. "Mama. . ." Seeing that coffin, that box. . .things became real. Hellish. He was alone. No strength, no hope to light his day, anxious to see her once more when his father felt "weak."*

She was gone. Gone! No no no no! He launched over the mound, sliding over the dirt. He dropped to his knees next to the flimsy coffin. He threw himself over the top. Sobbing. "Nyet, ne ostavlyaĭ menya." No, please, please don't leave me.

But, of course, she had. Not of her own choice. She died in her attempt to free him. Irony at its best—worst?—she ultimately freed herself. Completely.

"You are predictable."

The soft, feminine voice drew Cardinal up. Around. He stumbled back. Blinked. Heart careening at the image before him. Waves of amber hair. Wide mahogany eyes. *Mama?* No, no it was impossible.

She smirked as two men joined her. "Predictable," she said, her words thickened by her Russian accent. "Just as he predicted."

Cardinal glanced back to the headstone. To the name engraved: **Элиана Маркоски.** The Cyrllic lettering that spelled ELIANA MARKOSKI. Checked the dates. Yes, she died. *Shake it off.* This girl, this young girl, whoever she was. . .

Her gaze skidded from his to the headstone. Blue eyes seemed to absorb the information on the plain stone. Something blinked in her eyes. Flashed through her expression as she slowly dragged her attention back to him. Her mouth parted.

He flashed back more than nearly two decades. To the young girl in the woods, watching him. Calling after him. Cardinal hauled in a breath and let it out with her name. "Kalyna?"

Forty-One

33,000 Feet Over the Middle East

W here do we stand?" Lance closed the shade to the portal of the great blue beyond and turned his focus to the huddle around his leather chair. Thank God, Payne's lackeys had splurged on the Lear to get down to Djibouti lickety-split, or Lance would be hoofing it for twenty-four hours to St. Petersburg on a commercial liner.

"Not much. We know Tselekova fell out of grace with his superiors about two years ago." Lieutenant Hastings set a picture on the low table between the four chairs.

Members of ODA452 and Timbrel leaned in to get a glimpse of the man.

"What happened?" Watters asked.

"His ideas were—"

"Radical?" Austin offered.

"No." Brie locked gazes with the man. "Familiar. He wants to help return Russia to its former glory, and he believes it's acceptable to do it on the backs and lives of anyone. Since he was merely a general and not a politician or cabinet member or president..." She shrugged. "They sent him away to work some obscure job on a frozen base."

Ah, a lead? "Where?"

"Doesn't matter," Smith said. "He never showed up. Went completely off-grid."

"Why?"

"Because," Smith said, laying out more photos, "while politicians and superiors didn't like him, he had a fist hold over the throats and hearts of many under him. Promises of wealth and power were served up at every meeting. He's formed a quiet little insurrection."

Lance scooted to the edge of the chair, thumbing his bottom lip as he considered the information.

"Why does he want Aspen?" Austin knelt at the table. "Why her? What does she have to do with anything?"

"Yeah, why her? The hit was pretty deliberate."

"They didn't want her," Lance finally said. "They wanted him." He pointed to the image of Cardinal.

"Why? Why Cardinal? Because of the yellowcake?"

"I think that just tipped the hat." Lance eased back in the seat and wished for a Dr Pepper for the millionth time. This was bloody torture to be under this much stress and not have one single can of liquid genius. "Things heated up down here—first with you."

Austin's eyes widened. "Me?"

"When you found the yellowcake—what happened?"

"They hunted me down."

Lance nodded. "Thought so." He shook his head. "Then we sent Cardinal down here looking for you. Kuhn must've mentioned it to his sources. News travels fast when protecting an illegal—and international—operation. No doubt the heat alerted someone—or Tselekova himself. He sent his little minion to do the job."

"You seriously believe Lina is behind all this?"

"Absolutely."

"Whatever happened to 'innocent till proven guilty'?"

"You seriously think you'll be able to drag her into a U.S. court and fry her there?" Lance snorted. "Russia wouldn't let you get that close. Remember the spies discovered in 2010? If you'll remember, they went back to their homeland. Good ol'-fashioned spy swap."

"She just didn't seem the type—"

"Then she did her job well." Lance pointed to the table. "Go on, Hast—"

"Got it!" Smith shot up from the laptop on his lap. "Payne's wife just received communication."

Good news. Tell me good news, Smith.

"St. Petersburg."

"That's a big city, Lieutenant Smith."

He grinned. "Yes, sir. Another hour or so and I can get you within a mile of where the e-mail was sent from."

"Good. Relay that to the pilot. Divert to Pulkovo."

Smith leapt up and hurried to the front.

It took a lot of political capital to get the clearance necessary to enter Russian airspace—without getting shot down. His stomach churned and threatened to toss the modest airplane meal he'd eaten an hour ago back up the way it'd come.

The dog missing.

Aspen missing.

Cardinal MIA. Vanishing like this. . . *I ought to ring his ruddy neck!* This was *not* the time to go rogue. A lot of questions had been raised about Cardinal's loyalty and trustworthiness—all thanks to General Payne, who should be halfway to Langley and right into the arms of federal penitentiary guards.

Lance sipped a Dr Pepper and swallowed. He nudged the drink aside.

"You okay, sir?"

In the glass of the oval window, he saw Lieutenant Hastings's reflection. "No. Nothing is okay. The dog, Aspen—Cardinal! Even my Dr Pepper doesn't taste right."

"That's because it's a Perrier, sir."

Snickers sent a heated flush through his cheeks as he glanced at the bottle. Green bottle. He muttered an oath. Ran a hand over his face. "I think I need to retire." He glared at the others. "Don't you have work to do?"

"I thought you chipped your spies," Rocket said from his chair, where he sat with closed eyes.

"That's the movies, Rocket. If we can track them, so can anyone else."

Timbrel sucked in a hard breath. "Wait!"

"You okay?" Candyman asked.

"Better than that." She grinned—and wow, that girl was pretty when she smiled. She brushed bangs from her face. "I don't know why I didn't think of it before. I'm stupid. I mean—I'm a handler."

"Hogan!" Lance snapped. "Calm down and tell me—"

"Talon." She gulped air. "He's microchipped and has a tracking device. They tag all MWDs in case something happens and they get separated."

Lance snapped his fingers at Hastings. "Get on that. Get it tracked."

The air and space cleared as the others rushed to the table near the back where they went to work on getting them closer to stopping this nightmare.

As he pushed back in his chair, Lance eyed the men of ODA452. Two of them snored loudly, their heads cocked at odd angles against the seats and windows. Watterboy and Candyman were engaged with Timbrel, working to track Talon's chip. Weariness marked the faces of every last one. If he looked at his own, he was sure it'd show up there, too.

And after eight hours in flight, they were only halfway to Russia. He punched the seat as he sat down. Eight hours. *Eight!* Half a day. When Lance had given the pilot hay about the length of time, the man warned him that this was a good day. Sometimes, the flight took twenty hours.

Curses exploded from the back.

On his feet, Lance searched for the upset.

"Is it her? Can you verify it?"

Lance rushed to the back. "What's going on?"

"Sat imaging, sir. We piggybacked a satellite. I started checking locations connected to insurgents. After a few back-channel searches—"

"What'd you find?" Lance thought his head might explode.

"Aspen." Smith blinked. Looked at the screen. "At least. . .it looks like her. She appears to be running down a street. There's a black car. Four men." He dragged his finger along the screen. "Chasing her."

Austin swung around. Face red. Eyes enraged. He threw a punch.

Crack! Lance felt the world tumble.

"If she dies, you die!" Austin screamed.

Weapons snapped up. Hastings. Smith. ODA452. All aimed at Austin.

The man's chest heaved. "I swear—if she dies because of this, because of your agent—" He hauled in a breath, face tormented. "I swear I'll kill you."

"Why don't you stop wasting your energy on hate and venom, Mr. Courtland, and get to work helping us find your sister."

But the man's words. . .the rage. . .Lance could relate. And shared the fears that drove them. With eight hours—*hours!*—between them and Aspen. . .

Were they already too late?

BEAUTIFUL

"She's beautiful, isn't she?" He looked from the cherub to his mother's sweaty, glowing face.

"Yes, she is."

He heard something in his mother's voice and looked up. Red circled her eyes. "What? Why are you crying? She's beautiful and healthy!" But that wasn't the best. "And he doesn't know!"

Her brown eyes locked onto his. "But he will." Her chin trembled. "He always does." A sob punched its way out, and she clutched the newborn to her face, kissing her.

He watched them. His mother and new baby sister. Knew his mother was right. The colonel found out everything. He always did. Somehow. Someway. He just did. "We have to hide her."

"Give her up?" Panic clanked through his mother's words. "I can't! No, I can't."

Nikol stood, feeling every bit the eight-year-old he was. "We must. Just as we hid that you were pregnant."

"That's not the same, Nikol. He doesn't like me in his life, so it's easy to stay away. But you see what he's done with you."

"It's different." It hurt his heart to even think it. "I'm a boy. He won't want her."

Mother cried again. Slowly, she settled in the bed with his baby sister cuddled in her arms. Then she lifted her head. Lips slightly apart. Light settled in her eyes. She smiled.

"What?"

"There's a family. . .my brother knows a missionary family in Brno." She smiled through a still-wet face. "They're American."

"He'd never think to look there."

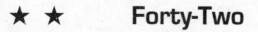

Forty-Two

Amazing the way a million things can happen in a microsecond. Cardinal noticed the blue eyes peering at him from over a headstone.

Kalyna's gleam, the thirst for him to hurt, that poured out of her eyes.

The way the weapon dipped.

Tiny explosion.

The report of her weapon registered a fraction too late.

Fire lit down his arm. Flung his arm back.

In the second it took him to recover, Cardinal lunged. Straight into one of the men who stepped into his path. Their collision barreled right into Kalyna. The second guy tripped trying to get out of the way.

As Cardinal went down, he saw a dark gray blur. Braced himself. *Crack!* Stars sprinkled across his vision, compliments of the gravestone he'd hit. He lifted but didn't release the guy. Flipped the man over. Cold-cocked him.

"Get up," Kalyna shouted. "I'll shoot if you try anything."

Cardinal fishtailed and scissored his legs, gauging where she stood, and ripped her feet out from under her. The gun flipped from her hand. She landed with a thud.

He dove for the weapon. Saw the second guy charging. Cardinal rolled, lifting the weapon and bringing it to bear. He fired, and the guy took one, center mass. Red bloomed over his blue shirt like a dark sun.

Cardinal came up. His mind registered Kalyna's movement, reaching for something. *Threat.* Quickly, he realigned. Fired again. This time winging Kalyna's firing arm.

The other man stopped, one hand clutching his chest, the other raised in surrender.

Cardinal pointed the gun at the man. *"Khod'by ot otelya."* Would the guy walk away as Cardinal ordered? Would he make this as easy as it could be?

The man shook his head. Muttered something about not being willing to die but then stumbled away. Down the path.

"Don't make any sudden moves," Cardinal said in Russian.

Kalyna shot him a look, holding her arm. Blood dribbled down it. "You shot my arm."

"I missed." Cardinal gave a slight nod to the man, telling him to keep going. As the distance grew, he shifted most of his attention to Kalyna.

"He has the girl," Kalyna said.

He would not, even though she was his sister, give her the benefit of seeing him squirm. "You delivered her to him." Disappointment churned through his veins. "How could you do this? Work for him?"

"Why not?" Defiant, she jutted her chin and raised her head. "You left me. My mother abandoned me."

"She gave you a life!" Cardinal growled. "Sacrificed *everything* for you."

"Sacrificed? A life? I was poor and the adopted child of a missionary family. Tell me, dear brother, do you know how shunned I was—raised by Christians, abandoned by my family?" She looked every bit like their mother. "He came to me, has given me *everything*."

Fury smothered him. "You foolish girl! *He* is the reason our mother lays there." Cardinal pointed to the grave. *"He killed her!"*

"You lie!"

"To you, never." His chest ached with the lies the colonel had fed her. Poisoned her with. And she'd bought right into them.

"I wanted nothing more than to know my family. You came to me, time and again. But never told me. Then—when I needed you most, you vanished. Never came back."

"I had to! He discovered you existed—that's why he killed Mama."

"No, it's not true. He's a good man."

"Only when compared to the devil!" He yanked up his shirt and bared his back to her. "Do these look like the marks a *good* man would give his son? To teach him to be *strong*?" He shoved down the shirt and looked back at her.

Fear quivered through her young, beautiful face. She could only be in her midtwenties. So impressionable. Had she really become what their father was? The spawn of the underworld? He could not believe it of her. She had always been sweet. Her nature gentle.

"She is my mother?" Kalyna looked to the grave marker.

"Yes." He held out his hands then motioned to her arm and took a step closer. "Once she discovered she carried his child again, she had to hide from the colonel. He'd beaten her bloody once before over an unwanted baby." He inched closer, slowly reaching for the lightweight jacket she wore.

She tensed, suspicious.

"Easy, just going to bind your arm." When she didn't object, he tore off a section of her jacket. Tore that into two strips. Tucked one in his pocket. Held the other as he lifted her arm. "She was so excited when you were born. I was so scared for her, for you. What I went through, I didn't want anyone else to endure." He wrapped, talking quietly, pleased with the way she hung on the words. Hungry, so very hungry for a connection. He understood. It was incredible to think this beautiful, vibrant girl was his *little* sister.

"She spent two months with you, making sure you grew strong and healthy before she could bring herself to release you to the Christians." He nodded to the cathedral over the hill. "This is where they met, where she delivered you to their safekeeping. It was the only place we thought the colonel would not think to look for you."

A sad smile shivered across her lips. "You were right."

He saw it. The uncertainty. The fear. Perhaps even the confirmation that what he'd told her gave credence to something she suspected. Time was short. The colonel had Aspen. "Where is he keeping her?"

Kalyna's expressive eyes came to his. "You care for this American?"

Cardinal felt his gaze start to dip but forced it to stay on her. "Very much."

"Do you love her?"

His heart thudded. "Yes, I think I do."

She gave him a weird look.

Feeling stupid, he shrugged. "It's never happened before. And it's happened fast this time. But yes. . .she means everything to me."

The sadness slid away. Tears pooling in her eyes blinked away. *"Vy prikhodili k nyeĭ, no ne dlya menya?"*

You would come for her but not for me? Dimples bounced in and out of her chin. Her accusation slashed his heart.

"No. It's not—"

"Tikho, Nikol!" She touched a finger to her lips, reinforcing her "quiet" command.

Not too far away, tires screeched.

She half smiled. "See? He always knows, yes?"

"Kalyna, come with me. Please. I could not find you."

"But you found her. When you love someone, you never give up."

"I did not give up!"

More squalling. This time closer.

"Kalyna, listen to me, *sestra*. . ."

"Sister." She nodded but fought tears and a grieved smile. "It is too late."

"Kalyna—I do love you. For your protection, I stopped coming. Sent money."

"Money?" Eyes blazed in outrage. "I wanted family! But you did not want me." She reached around to her back, her expression going hard. Her actions practiced. She produced another handgun. "If you want to live, you should run. Now."

"Kalyna, please!" His gaze darted to the black car barreling down the street. "Take me to her. Help me save her."

"If you got to her, he would kill her." Cold, hard eyes held his—no, that's what she wanted him to believe. Something in her expression betrayed her and filtered into her words. "Run, Nikol. Keep her alive until you can die trying to be heroic."

"I'm not running anymore."

"Sometimes. . .running does not have to be bad." A strange smile played over her lips. "Do svidaniya, Nikol." She aimed a gun at him.

Cardinal backpedaled. Saw the car screaming to a stop. "Please, Kalyna!"

She fired.

★ ★ Forty-Three ★ ★

Y ou're sure?" Lance stepped from the van and glanced at the old church. It sure fit Cardinal's MO, but the place sat eerily quiet. It'd been entirely too many hours in the plane. "Watters, Hastings, Hogan, VanAllen—check inside. Scrip, Smith, Rocket—check the cemetery. Courtland, you're with me."

"You mean, you don't trust me."

"There is that."

"I'm not your enemy here."

"Perhaps, but you're also not my ally. You broke protocol because you felt something was important enough to do that. Your sister is involved, and I'd wager my career you'd sacrifice every one of us if you thought it'd save her."

"So wouldn't you want that type of determination behind this hunt? It is my sister's life. And the man she loves." Austin pounded the back of the front seat. "This is stupid! Let me help!"

"Calm down. You're not winning points with that behavior. Decision's been made." Lance squinted toward the cathedral. "What's taking them so long?"

"It's a cathedral." Austin raised his eyebrows. "It's big."

This mission was so insane. So hopeless. If they couldn't find them in time...Being here, in Cardinal's homeland, his territory, added a level of uncertainty Lance had never experienced before. There was a reason he'd taken the DIA job—and staying put in Virginia was one of them. He was out of practice with field work. Like pitting an admin against an athlete. And with the lives of an innocent woman and a spy—a man he'd admired and respected since their first meeting. Right here.

"Mother of God. . ." Why hadn't he recognized it before?

"Yeah, pretty sure you'd find *her* in there." Austin smirked then stopped. Frowned as he leaned out of the van.

"Keep your jokes to yourself, Courtland."

Austin stepped from the van.

"What are you doing? Don't go any farther."

Courtland held out a hand. "Shh." He scanned the trees that hemmed the perimeter of the churchyard. He stilled, cocked his head. "You hear that?"

"Your mouth running is all I hear."

"Shh!" He tilted his head the other way. "Listen!" He pivoted. "Talon!" Cupping his hands around his mouth, he shouted the name once more.

Lance's pulse sped. Was the dog really here?

A commotion near the doors caught his attention. Watters emerged, holding the door as laughter filtered out with Candyman. . .who carried Hogan on his back. Hastings rolled her eyes. "Nothing," she called.

Austin bolted toward the trees.

"Stop him!"

He knew that bark! Austin sprinted, knowing he had seconds at best to find Talon before the others pummeled him into oblivion. Even now he heard them closing in from behind.

"Courtland!" one shouted.

He plunged into the trees. "Talon!" He skidded to a stop so he could hear. Breathing hard and his heart hammering, he couldn't hear. "Talon!"

Leaves crunched. Shouts.

He dove to the right and kept moving. "Talon, heel!"

"Courtland, don't make me shoot you."

"He's here," Austin shouted back. "Talon's here. I heard him."

"Check it out." Watters. Had to be Watters. He was the only one the others yielded to. "Five minutes, Courtland, and then your number's up."

Jogging in a wide circle, he slowly narrowed the field. Iron fences, stone crypts—man, this place was creepy to the nth degree. "Talon, where are you boy?"

Barking to the left.

Austin plunged through the forest, around shrubs. Over headstones. Around a mausoleum.

Snarling and snapping lunged at him. Talon strained against a lead.

Austin scrabbled backward. "Good boy. Good Talon." He held his hands out.

Hackles raised, Talon growled and snapped again.

"Easy, boy. What's wrong?" The lead wrapped around a headstone. Austin reached for it then saw the hand. His lunch climbed up his throat. The fingers moved. "Out," came a raspy voice.

Talon whimpered as he slumped back on his haunches.

Austin shifted to the right three paces.

Propped against a crumbling marker, Cardinal looked up at him, his face beaded with sweat and blood. He held his side.

"You look good," Austin said as he knelt.

A crooked smile. "It's the fresh air." He pushed to his feet, grimacing as he did.

"Markoski!" Hastings rushed toward them, the others converging on their location.

Austin shifted his attention to Talon. "Good boy, Talon." He offered a treat. Talon wolfed it down as Austin freed the lead.

Candyman helped Cardinal to his feet as Austin straightened.

"Here." Cardinal tugged something from his pocket. A bloody rag.

"Thanks, but—"

"Scent." He waved it. "He's a tracking dog, right?"

"Why didn't you go after her if you had Talon and that?"

"After they shot me, I scrambled back here to get Talon. That's when I heard your shouts. Thought they'd come back." Cardinal knelt beside Talon. "I thought they'd come back to finish me off."

"Let's see if this works."

"Oh, it works." Austin joined Cardinal next to Talon. "The bigger question is—will Talon?"

Forty-Four

An hour. Talon had been sniffing and tracking for an hour. Cardinal kept him hydrated, and Austin proved a great help as the team trailed in the van. Talon hopped up on sidewalks but mostly trotted down the road. Cars honked and drivers shared one-finger salutes, but Cardinal didn't care as he jogged beside Talon. Fresh spurts of warmth slid down his hip and side. He still couldn't believe Kalyna clipped him. It wasn't a full wound. A graze, but a deep one.

Was she just a bad shot? She didn't have the training he did. The colonel had drilled into him how to fire, how to nail a target from a football-field length.

She'd tipped her hand. Maybe intentionally. He wasn't sure he'd ever know. But Kalyna could've killed him. Should've. But she'd run him off. Told him to save Aspen. Running wasn't always a bad thing. Because running away then meant he could find Aspen and save her.

If he walked into the trap with Kalyna, the colonel would implant a bullet or two in Aspen's head. The man showed no qualms throwing his mom from a five-story building, so he'd show none when it came to killing a woman he'd never met.

The woman his son loved. Was that what this was about?

"Want me to take over?" Austin asked from the van.

Cardinal saved his breath for running and continued on.

Talon trotted up onto a sidewalk. Sniffed then paused. Snout in the air, Talon puffed his cheeks with his mouth closed. Processing the scent, no doubt.

"Think he lost it?"

"No way. His snout isn't broken."

"No, but his heart is," Timbrel countered.

"Quiet," Cardinal said as he gave the Lab room to search for his girl. "Give me the water bowl."

Austin produced the collapsible bowl and dumped a bottle of water in it.

Cardinal set the bowl in front of the dog. "Good boy."

"Cardinal, switch with Austin," Burnett said from the front passenger seat.

"No."

"It's not a question."

"I don't care what it is."

"You two can take turns. You're gushing blood all over St. Petersburg. Rest. Let him track him for a couple of miles."

Lapping the water, Talon seemed to inhale the cool liquid then jerked his head up. Cheeks puffed, black nose bouncing. He moved to the curb. Sniffed again.

It made sense. It was right. But yielding, knowing Aspen was out there with his psycho father, and with Kalyna. . .whichever side she was on. . .he just—

With a loud bark, Talon tore off around the corner.

"Got it!" Austin exploded from the van and beat a path after Talon. Cardinal gulped failure.

Hands grabbed him. "Get in, idiot!"

He fell back against the van. They hauled him up onto the bench seat as Watters floored it. Pain sluiced through his side and back as the van careened around other vehicles, even using the northbound lane for fifty yards.

"Watch it, watch it!" Burnett shouted.

"I'm good. I'm good," Watterboy responded as he navigated the tangled streets with the skill of a Russian familiar with the area.

But the only thing Cardinal cared about was Talon. He was the key. *Hang on, Aspen. I'm coming.* He would not—would *not!*—let the madman win this one. He wouldn't stand still while the colonel shoved the only person he loved into the afterlife.

The distance between the van and the dog-handler team lengthened.

"You're losing them," Cardinal said.

"No I'm not."

As they rounded a corner, Cardinal's pulse slowed to a painfully cruel rate. *Nevsky Prospekt.* No. He wouldn't have brought her here. There were too many people. Too many witnesses. His gaze locked on to the fifth-floor windows. The flat.

"Cardinal?"

That window. . .what had it looked like from the outside? Her falling. . .

The distance shortened. Slower at first then faster, until they caught up with them. The golden dog paced back and forth, sniffing. He leapt up the steps to the door. Then sat.

"I think he's got it."

Cardinal stepped out. Strode up the walk. Up to the door. Kicked it in.

Light reached across the floor. Its fingers traced the first step to the second level. Kalyna stretched over several steps at an odd angle.

"No!" Austin shouted as he darted toward the stairs. "Lina!"

Standing there, staring at his sister laid out, blood covering her chest and shirt, Cardinal realized he'd failed. One more time. The colonel *had* won.

"Lina, please talk to me." Austin lowered her to the floor, where her blood had puddled.

Cardinal drew in a short breath, blinked out of the dimension that had gouged out his thinking and ability to function. A dimension of the past.

"Make a hole." Scrip hurried to her side with a pack.

Candyman and Watters hurried up the steps, clearing as they went. Cardinal trailed them but climbed to the fifth floor. He kicked in the door.

A woman screamed.

Vision tunneled, hearing hollowed, he moved through the kitchen. The living room. Past the colonel's room.

"Nikol!"

"Mama, you are here?"

"Yes. It's a good surprise, yes?"

He wrapped his arms around her, savoring her touch.

Cardinal jerked to the hall. Strode down it. To the bedroom. *His bedroom.* He stood in front of the window. Lacy curtains draped the view.

Lace? The colonel would've hated that.

But that. . .that is where it happened. Where his father threw his mother to her death. He backed up a step then glanced at the window. No, another foot or two. Yes. This was better. He stood here. Where he'd done nothing as his mother was murdered. Right before his eyes.

If Kalyna was here, killed, then that meant the colonel knew. Knew Kalyna had warned him, tried to help him. That meant Aspen's time was short, if not already gone.

Cardinal threw a punch into the wall. Roared against the failures. The defeat. He dropped against the wall. Gripped his knees. *She's dead.* Aspen was as good as dead. There was no way she could still be alive. How would they find her now? She wasn't there. Talon didn't have a scent. In a smog-infected city. . .there was no hope.

He banged his head against the wall. Squeezed his eyes against the pain. Ran his hands over his head and gripped the nape of his neck. "Augh!" Rammed his elbows into the wall.

Tears warming his cheeks, he stared at the window. "I'm sorry," he muttered, something he'd never allowed himself to say before. "I am so sorry I didn't stop him."

He cried.

God, I did nothing to save my mother. Help me—help me!—*not make the same mistake now. Please, You sent me here. Now—show me!*

Something wet nudged his hand.

He glanced down and found Talon at his side. "Good boy."

Talon had found Kalyna and maybe saved her life. He'd done exactly what Cardinal had asked him to do—to find the owner of the rag. That was Kalyna. But he'd expected Kalyna to be with Aspen. She probably would've been if she hadn't gone up against one of the most ruthless, cruelest men in Russia.

"Hey, man. You okay?"

Cardinal shot a sidelong look to the man hovering in the doorway. "He will kill her if he hasn't already. Just to teach me a lesson."

"So, what? You're giving up?"

"Don't you get it?"

"Don't you?" Candyman snapped. "You're wasting breath. We could be searching!"

"How? How are we supposed to find her?"

"The girl." Candyman hooked a thumb over his shoulder. "She told us where Aspen is."

Cardinal came off the wall. "Kalyna? She's still alive?"

"So far."

Sirens wailed through the afternoon.

"We need to bug out."

"We have to take her. They'll kill her if she's found."

"Already loaded up. Let's move!"

Downstairs, Cardinal stepped out into the afternoon. Candyman climbed in the van.

Talon turned a few circles. Sniffed a tree.

"Talon, heel."

Instead, Talon tore off.

In the split second it took for Talon's movement to register, Cardinal *knew* the dog had hit on Aspen's scent.

Yes! Cardinal sprinted after him, ignoring the fire in his side. The renewed pain in his neck from the injury in Djibouti. Down the street. Straight toward Ligovksy Prospekt. The roundabout. Beneath trolley lines. He pushed himself.

Talon vanished when he banked left. What street was that? He knew this city. Walked it. Worked it. Prospekt Bakunina?

He careened onto the street. With one last push, Cardinal shoved himself onward. Wove around cars caught in traffic. His mind warred, knowing the others were most likely stranded in traffic, too. Which meant...

I'm alone.

Forty-Five

Y ou promised me!"

"You are lucky to be alive, General Payne."

Despite the crippling pain from her broken leg, Aspen focused on the two men arguing within earshot. Kept still so the chains anchoring her to the table didn't rattle as she tried to do a little recon on her surroundings and captors.

There was no chance to escape with the chain and broken leg, but she wouldn't have a prayer anyway with the horde of men working in the warehouse.

The men thought she was unconscious, and that served her well. The man she'd seen with the cruel soldier was American—clear English gave him away. They'd worked diligently for the last two hours, barely a word spoken as trucks were loaded with crates marked in the same fashion as the ones on the boat in Djibouti.

As more trucks left and the emptiness reigned in the dingy warehouse, the voices rose again. This time, angrier.

"I've sacrificed everything. Done everything you've asked, Tselekova. I gave him to you."

"Yes, and now our business is at an end, General." Tselekova flicked a wrist toward a man in uniform.

He aimed at the American.

Aspen clenched her eyes. But closing her eyes could not prevent her from hearing the primal scream and the gunfire that silenced it.

As her hearing and thundering heart cleared, Aspen heard the boots.

Right next to her.

"Get up," he said in a thickly accented voice.

Aspen stared up at him as she slowly rose to a sitting position, chains clanking.

Snarling and snapping echoed through the warehouse. *Talon?* She looked to the side, and her stomach heaved. Three Dobermans strained against chain leads. Eyes trained on her as they vied for permission to devour her.

Lord. . .

"You are dog handler, yes?" Tselekova stuffed a key into the lock and twisted it. The chains dropped to the floor, tugging the rest off her like a slithering snake till they piled in a mound at her feet.

The question all but forced her to look at the dogs again. The handler's bulging muscles and face warned he had little control left. The Dobermans jerked him forward. His feet slipped and slid over the cement.

Swallowing, Aspen skated a sidelong glance to Tselekova. Gave a slow nod.

He hooked a hand beneath her arm. Hauled her up off the crate that had been her prison for the last. . .well, she had no idea how long she'd been out. When she woke after they broke her leg, the pain had punched her back into oblivion.

He yanked her to the front.

Her weight fell on her right leg. She cried out.

"Your foolishness," he said, his breath salty and warm against her cheek, "in trying to escape, to thwart my plans, will now serve to bring about your end. . .quicker."

Was that a threat?

He smiled as the handler shouted, now straining with both hands to hold back the dogs.

Aspen swallowed.

"You love my Nikol."

Nikol. Was that Dane's real name? There was no use denying it. Another sidelong glance churned her stomach. How could the man look like an older version of Dane yet look nothing like him? "Yes."

"As I thought." The man's gaze fixed on something. "And it seems he loves you, too."

A truck lumbered out of the warehouse. Sunlight bled across the cement and delivered into the chaos Dane.

Aspen sucked in a breath. Relief flooded her.

Rabid snapping and barking.

He leveled a gun at Tselekova as he closed the gap. "Let her go."

"Where are your friends?" Tselekova's grip on her arm tightened. "And your sister, Nikol?"

"You already took care of her, *Father.*" Dane stopped. "Or am I still not allowed to call you that?"

"You never earned the right."

Dane smiled in disdain. "A son should not have to earn that right."

"I see you are already poisoned by this woman. You are weaker than you were before you left."

"No, Colonel, I am stronger than ever before." He nodded to Aspen. "Release her."

"If I release her, Anton will release them."

Both hands held the gun steady and sure. Aspen saw the pure determination in Dane's stance, his body language. The fear she'd seen before when he talked about the past, about the reasons he couldn't love her, were gone.

Dane held Tselekova's gaze. "I'm ready when you are."

Forty-Six

Calculated risks were always *risky*.

But the surreal confidence, peace, and laser-like focus on freeing Aspen from the colonel's clutches simmered in his gut. He spotted Aspen's nervous response.

"Do you know why I killed your sister?"

"I really don't care." Cardinal kept his breathing steady, his focus pure. Because he had the upper hand. Kalyna wasn't dead—she might die before the team got her some help. But for now, she was alive. The colonel didn't know that. But he did know that Cardinal *never* missed a shot. Because it was the colonel who taught him to shoot. Taught him to never miss lest he wanted raw, bloodied hands.

"You killed the one person who was on your side. Kalyna merely wanted your approval. Just like I did." Cardinal thrust his chin toward Aspen. "Release her. Without the dogs, and you walk out of here alive and intact."

"I believe you miscounted, Nikol."

"Dane!"

The sound of the shot hit him at the same time the bullet did. Winged him. He stumbled.

A flurry of insanity erupted. The colonel shoved Aspen forward. She screamed and dropped, holding her leg.

The colonel signaled the handler.

Free, the dogs vaulted.

On a knee, Cardinal took aim at the lead dog. The one headed straight for Aspen. Ignored the one that sailed over the air and cement

335

toward him. He aimed a few seconds ahead. Fired. Let the dog catch up with the bullet.

He swung around. Saw the meaty jowls widen as the dog pawed air. Cardinal fired.

Searing pain chomped into his hand at the same time a yelp erupted. The weight of the dog barreled into him and knocked him backward. The teeth came loose. The dog yelped again as he flipped onto all fours. He walked a wide circle around, away from Dane before collapsing on the ground, panting hard. Wounded.

Cardinal rolled, holding his bitten hand close. Two men sprinted after another—the colonel. Candyman threw himself into the back of the colonel. The two went sprawling over the cement.

A primal scream seared Cardinal's mind. The third dog! Aspen!

Forty-Seven

The first dog slid to his death at her knees. Aspen fought the tears, watching as Dane went down beneath the second dog. It'd all happened in seconds.

But her focus was on the third. Horror gripped her as the beast tore up ground toward her. No way Dane could recover in time. No way he could save her. Not this time.

The Doberman sprinted. Front paws nailed the ground simultaneously with back paws, launching it forward. One bound. Muscles rippling. Eyes locked. Canines exposed. A second bound. A third. He went airborne.

Aspen curled in, as she'd been taught to protect her vital organs and leave the meatier—ugh!—parts of her arms to fend off the attack. No doubt this dog wanted all the meat he could get. She loved dogs, but stopping these killers pulled the plug on her nice tactics.

Weight rammed into her side. She braced. Pressure clamped onto her arm. Pain exploded. She cried out. Fought. Kicked the dog. Punched with her other hand. The dog snarled and caught Aspen's shoulder. She screamed. Punched him.

"Aspen!" Dane's shout was loud but not close.

A blur flashed in front of her.

Thud!

A yelp clapped through the air. Turned to snapping and snarling. Barking.

Aspen looked over her bloodied shoulder. Heart in her throat, she watched. "Talon!"

He tackled the Doberman. They rolled and flipped. Snapping. Biting. Barking. Vicious and primal. Terrifying. Aspen scooted back against the corner of the crate, keeping her right arm close to avoid jarring the bites in her forearm and shoulder.

On its feet, the Doberman paced. Snapped.

Talon unleashed one of the mightiest barks she'd ever heard from him. Then another. Front paws spread, head lowered, hind quarters up, he took an attack position. Another demonesque bark. The Doberman paced, trying to come around and flank Talon, but her guy matched him, step for step. Only then did she see the blood around his neck.

Tears sprung to her eyes. He saved her! All those months training, working with him. She wasn't sure he had it in him anymore. But there he stood. Facing off.

The dog turned and trotted to its wounded compatriot and slumped down.

Talon growled one last warning to the two dog-thugs then turned to Aspen.

Wrapping her arms around him, she buried her face in his fur. Cried. Sobbed. "Good boy," she said, over and over. "Good boy."

Dane slid to his knees beside them. "Aspen! You okay?"

With a laugh-cry, she nodded. "Yeah. He saved me!" She assessed his injuries and knew they were not terrible. A few bites, but they weren't bleeding much. "I'm so proud of him."

Talon swiped his tongue along her cheek then plopped over her legs, as if to say, "All in a hard day's work."

Epilogue

A Breed Apart Ranch, Texas Hill Country
Four Months Later

How long will it take, Aspen?"

Pulling her gaze from where Talon bounded after the ball, Aspen peeked around one of her curls at her brother. "I don't know, Austin. I'm trying."

He looked down and gave a nod. But thick frustration betrayed him. "I'm sorry."

"You've said that about a thousand times." She rubbed her shoulder, the visible injuries gone but the invisible ones, the aches in her bone and mended muscles, still hurting. "Finding you has helped Talon heal."

She smiled as Talon trotted to the water trough, dropped his ball on the ground, then lapped some water. With winter approaching, he wasn't worn out by heat. And the PTSD symptoms were diminishing.

"I think fighting for you is why he healed." Austin stuffed his hands in his pockets.

She eyed him. Quite a concession.

Leaves crunched and rocks popped in the drive, luring Aspen's gaze to the car sliding into view. Her heart tripped. Dane! The sun glinted off the windshield, stopping her from seeing him, but she waved all the same as she started that way. "Come on. He's finally here."

Talon trotted to her side and followed her out of the training yard.

Timbrel stepped out onto the porch. " 'Bout time you decided to show up," she shouted as soon as the car door opened. "Food's cold."

Dane glanced up at the house but said nothing. In fact, he looked. . . not pleased.

"Hey you," Aspen said, her breathing a little heavy as she hoofed it up the slight hill to his sedan. "You okay?"

A smile tugged at one side of his mouth. "Yeah." He stepped around the door and reached for her hand, drawing her closer. He kissed her. Swept a thumb along her cheek.

"That's definitely the type of greeting a girl could get used to."

"Can we talk?" His gaze bounced to Timbrel then back.

"Sure." Aspen motioned beyond the house. "What's wrong?"

"Hey, Cardinal."

Dane's jaw muscle popped as his eyes went to Austin, who made his way up the hill to the house. He gave a curt nod.

Aspen touched his face. "Hey, what's eating you?"

"He's dead."

She blinked. Her mind hopscotching over those two words. "Who?"

"The colonel."

She widened her gaze and drew back. "I thought he was in prison, in the pink of health."

"He apparently had a sudden decline." His lips flattened. *Livid* was the word that came to mind.

"Dane, what are you saying?"

"Everything that I'm *not* saying." He leaned back against the car.

"You think someone killed him."

"I *know* someone killed him. I just don't know who or why." He scratched the stubble along his jaw. "A man like the colonel. . .people wanted him dead."

"I mean no disrespect, but in the months since St. Petersburg, you've told me many times you were afraid he'd get free."

"But now. . .now I get no resolution."

Aspen tilted her head. "What kind of resolution?"

He frowned. "What does that mean?"

"Nothing. Just that. . ." She touched his folded arms. "Dane, his power over you is gone. He's gone."

"No, Aspen. He's right here." He tapped his temple. "I hear his words constantly."

She smiled at him. Tiptoed up and kissed the spot he'd just touched.

" 'Therefore, if anyone is in Christ, the new creation has come: the old has gone, the new is here!'" She wrapped her arm around his neck and grinned as his arms snaked around her waist. "I really like the new."

"Do me a favor?"

Aspen craned her neck back a bit to look at him without her eyes crossing. "What's that?"

"Call me Nikol."

He'd insisted in the last few months that she *not* call him that. "That's one giant leap for Danekind."

"Nikol is the name my mother gave me. It was her father's name. I'd forgotten that, shut out the good parts with the bad. I don't want to forget her."

"She sounds like she was an amazing woman."

His steely eyes traced her face. Gauging. Watching. Searching. . .

"What?" she asked with a nervous laugh.

"One more favor."

"Too many and you're going to need to start a tab."

He kissed her. Aspen melted into his arms. Talon barked. Aspen giggled in the middle of the kiss. "He's jealous."

"So am I." Dane—Nikol looked at her.

"So, what's the last favor?"

He tugged something from his pocket. Handed it to her.

Aspen eased out of his arms and unfolded the paper. Right above *Nikol Tselekova* and the name *Aspen Elizabeth Courtland* were the words *Certificate of Marriage*.

Her heart beat in tune to a new, partially erratic rhythm. "I. . .I thought General Burnett annulled it." She eased back, staring at the paper in confusion. "Wiped the slate clean. And. . .your name. That's not the name you used in Djibouti."

"I asked him not to annul but merely to amend the document."

Rapid-fire drumming of her heart pulsed against her lungs. She raised her eyebrows. Though she knew what meaning *she* would attach to that statement, she wanted to know his. "Why?"

"Because I want you to marry me." He touched her lips with a finger as she started to respond. "If it takes two more years to convince you that I'm the man for you, then I have nothing better to do."

"You know, you're pretty thickheaded."

His face fell. "Is that a no?"

"That's an 'I told you six months ago I loved you.' Just one problem."

"Yeah?"

"I can't pronounce your last name."

He grinned. And she loved the way it pinched his eyes with joy. "Better start practicing." Nikol leaned in for another kiss.

"Aspen!"

She growled as she rolled her shoulder to look up at the house. "What?"

"They're waiting on you." Austin looked at a watch he wasn't wearing. "And. . .might want to come talk to Timbrel."

"Why?"

Austin shrugged. "She just seems edgy to me."

"She's always edgy. All right," Aspen said as she turned. She called Talon then joined hands with Nikol as they made their way up onto the wraparound porch. She reached for the door just as it flew open.

Timbrel stormed out. Brow knitted and lips pinched tight, she swung around. Her face blanched. "Oh."

"Timbrel," a voice called from inside as the sound of feet drew close. "Hold up."

"I gotta go." Timbrel hustled down the steps.

Aspen watched, concerned.

Candyman burst out. Dressed in jeans and a T-shirt, the guy seemed to have as much bulk as when he had his tac vest and gear on. "Where—?" He spotted her and hurried after Timbrel. "Wait."

In her brown Jeep, Timbrel backed out, tires spitting rocks at Candyman. As she rammed it into DRIVE, she glared over the half door at him. "I don't kiss beards. Period!"

"I—"

Scrambling tires muffled his response.

Candyman swung around and pounded a fist into the side of a blue truck and let out a growl that rivaled Talon's when he'd defeated the demon dogs.

"I don't know what he sees in her," Nikol said.

"Most men don't." Aspen eyed him then shrugged. "Don't take it personally. I already told him he's got his work cut out for him."

"I think he should quit while he's ahead."

"If he's got it that bad for her, I think he should fight for her with his dying breath." She nodded to the driveway where Candyman had climbed into his truck and tore down the drive after Timbrel. Yeah. . . this was going to be interesting.

April 9, 2003
Baghdad, Iraq

The ground rattled. Dust plumed and pushed aside the curtain, unveiling the specter of war that raged beyond. The bridge. . . The American Marines had already taken the bridge. The airport.

Boom! The concussion vibrated through the air and thumped against his chest. Wind gusted back the curtain again, once white. He traced the curtain. She had been so proud of that find in the market. White and filled with tiny holes. He teased her that she could purchase any old cloth and in a few years it would have its own holes. She swatted his shoulder with a playful smile.

A guttural scream choked the air. Pulled him around.

He stared at the striped curtain that hung, separating him from his mother who helped his wife, struggling to usher their firstborn into the world.

Another shriek spun him back to the door. To the east, to Mecca. *Please, Allah. . .protect her. I will live in peace. Always. Just. . .*

The familiar tat-tat-tat of automatic weapons sounded close. AK-47s. His heart ka-thumped. They were closing in. *Please, Allah!*

Pebbles thunked against the ledge, dribbled onto the floor.

Steady and tickling, a vibration wormed through the house. Like some evil dance to an unheard song, the walls jounced rapidly. The bowl of olives and dates rattled across the wood table. He saved them and set them back. She had loved those olives. Her favorite. He brought them home for her last night. Anything to let her know how special she was.

His gaze traced the simple dwelling. He had not done so well in providing for her. But some day. . .some day he would. If only—

Coming from Barbour Publishing in January 2014!

About the Author

Ronie Kendig grew up an Army brat and married a veteran. Her life is never dull in a homeschooling family with four children and three dogs. She has a degree in Psychology, speaks to various groups, is active in the American Christian Fiction Writers (ACFW), and mentors new writers. Ronie can be found at www.roniekendig.com, on Facebook (www.facebook.com/rapidfirefiction), Twitter (@roniekendig), and GoodReads.

SGT Kowtko & MWD Igor M064

My name is Sgt Andrew Kowtko. I am currently the Military Working Dog Trainer aboard MCAS Yuma, Arizona. I moved from MCB Camp LeJeune, II MEF, II MHG, 2d Law Enforcement Battalion where I served as a Military Working Dog Handler for four years. I have two combat deployments with II MEF—one to Operation Iraqi Freedom and one to Operation Enduring Freedom. I deployed as a Patrol Explosive Detector Dog Handler to both Operations.

Out of several bedtime stories, this one in particular comes to mind. We were deployed in support of (ISO) Operation Enduring Freedom (OEF); Military Working Dog (MWD) Igor M064—a Patrol Explosive Detector Dog (P/EDD)—and myself were supporting 3rd Battalion, 8th Marines, Kilo Company. We dug into an area untouched by Coalition troops since the beginning of the war. After setting up our Combat Outpost, we constantly patrolled the "Green Zone" for Taliban fighters fleeing the heavy fighting to our north in Sangin. We were located on the west side of the Helmand River adjacent to Forward Outpost Robinson. On a routine patrol, we were pushing into the city of Qaleh Ye Gaz looking for Taliban activity and to impede the enemy's free movement. While we were pushing around a compound, MWD Blade L612, along with handler Cpl Cory Bracy, showed a slight change of behavior on a possible improvised explosive device (IED). Upon our spotting the IED, a Taliban fighter detonated it by means of a command pull wire.

The blast threw me and the other handler back approximately 5 feet. Once we regained our senses, looking ourselves over making sure we had all limbs we walked in with, we immediately took contact from enemy fighters dug into compounds surrounding the IED. The small arms fire was extremely accurate with rounds impacting 1–2 feet around friendly positions. After about ten minutes, enemy guns were quickly silenced by our superior firepower. We utilized all means of firepower including tanks, mortars, and crew served weapons. We broke contact by pushing south. While crossing an open field, MWD Blade threw another change of behavior on an Afghan-built foot bridge; now, see, these can be extremely dangerous choke points to any patrol moving without the aid of a good dog team. Noticing wires protruding from the dirt, we quickly marked the location to push around. Within 30 feet, MWD Blade was sent to search a crossing into another field. MWD Blade showed a third change of behavior on a raised piece of dirt covered by poppy plants. Once again, we quickly marked the grid coordinates and kept pushing. We finished the patrol and returned to the COP.

If there had not been a Military Working Dog present on the patrol, multiple lives would have been lost. We train on a daily basis for the moment when we can save ourselves, other service members, and innocent civilians. Being an MWD handler, I have always sworn by utilizing MWDs on patrols in the relentless world of war. On that day, in the moments that we need MWDs the most, we proved ourselves to be true life-savers.

Sgt Andrew Kowtko enlisted in the Marine Corps in August 2007 and is currently stationed in Yuma, Arizona. He works as a Military Policeman, Patrol/Narcotics Detector Dog Handler. Sgt Kowtko has been awarded numerous decorations, including the Purple Heart.

Retired Military Working Dog Assistance Organization's goal is "To act and operate as a public benefit, educational, and charitable organization in (i) educating the public about the benefits to our Armed Forces of military working dogs, contractor working dogs and specialized search dogs; (ii) financially supporting active duty and retired military working dogs, contractor working dogs and specialized search dogs; (iii) preventing cruelty to retired military working dogs, contractor working dogs and specialized search dogs by helping financially with medical bills, transportation and any other necessary requirements for their health and well being; and (iv) facilitate the adoption of retired military, contractor, and specialized search dogs."

The Retired Military Working Dog Assistance Organization (RMWDAO) was founded in October of 2011 in Universal City, Texas. RMWDAO was formed after a push to get the military to reclassify Military Working Dogs from "excess equipment" to "canine service members" and to help get Military Working Dogs medical benefits after retirement. RMWDAO is a nonprofit organization that takes donations to help cover those medical costs after a MWD retires, so that tax dollars aren't used. RMWDAO is currently pending 501(c)(3) tax exempt status with the IRS.

Visit them online: http://www.rmwdao.org, and on Facebook: http://www.facebook.com/RMWDAO

PRAISE FOR *TALON* (A BREED APART BOOK 2)

"Action, intrigue, and romance the way only Ronie Kendig can write it—this is an author who knows her stuff. With characters you can't help but love—and a canine you can't help but fall for—*Talon* is an intense ride punched with high-octane drama that will have you bolting through the pages in a single, sleepless night. *Talon* is Kendig at the top of her game. Whatever you do, do not miss this one."

—Tosca Lee, *New York Times* bestselling author
of the Books of Mortals series

"*Talon* was a nonstop, heart-pounding adventure full of twists, turns, and romance. Every time I picked it up, I was transported to Talon and Aspen's world and felt every emotion that they experienced. It has a little bit of everything to capture the hearts of all readers!"

—Lisa Phillips, Founder/CEO of Retired Military
Working Dog Assistance Organization

"Now I know why they label Ronie's novels 'Rapid Fire Fiction'! With inimitable style, this book hooks you from page one and machine-guns you to a satisfying finish. Bravo, Ronie!"

—Creston Mapes, bestselling author of *Fear Has a Name*

"Ronie Kendig brings more than action and intrigue in her newest release, *Talon*. She reveals the soul of a man, a woman, and a dog—deep characterizations that bring each one to life. The story, the characters, and the plot twists engaged me from the beginning. *Talon* is another winner in a long list of excellent fiction by an exceptional writer."

—Miralee Ferrell, multi-publishe
award-winning author of historical roma